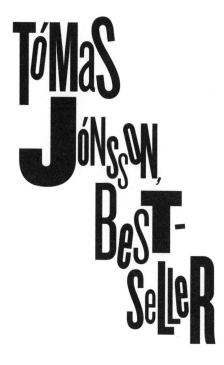

TÓMAS JÓNSSON, BEST-SELLER

by Guðbergur Bergsson

Translated from the Icelandic by Lytton Smith

OPEN LETTER
LITERARY TRANSLATIONS FROM THE UNIVERSITY OF ROCHESTER

Copyright © Guðberger Bergsson, 1966
Translation copyright © Lytton Smith, 2017
Title of the original Icelandic edition: *Tómas Jónsson: metsölubók*
Published by agreement with Forlagid Publishing, www.forlagid.is

First edition, 2017

Library of Congress Cataloging-in-Publication Data:

Names: Guðbergur Bergsson, 1932- author. | Smith, Lytton, 1982- translator.
Title: Tómas Jónsson : bestseller / Guðbergur Bergsson ;
translated by Lytton Smith.
Other titles: Tómas Jónsson : metsölubók. English
Description: Rochester : Open Letter, 2017.
Identifiers: LCCN 2017007197 (print) | LCCN 2017010114 (ebook) |
ISBN 9781940953601 (paperback) | ISBN 194095360X (paperback) |
ISBN 9781940953618 (e-book)
Subjects: LCSH: Iceland—Social conditions—20th century—Fiction. |
BISAC: FICTION / Literary. | HISTORY / Europe / Scandinavia. |
BIOGRAPHY & AUTOBIOGRAPHY / Literary.
Classification: LCC PT7511.G78 T6613 2017 (print) | LCC PT7511.G78 (ebook) |
DDC 839/.6934—dc23
LC record available at https://lccn.loc.gov/2017007197

*This project is supported in part by an award from
the National Endowment for the Arts*

ART WORKS.
arts.gov

This book has been translated with a financial support from:

Icelandic
LITERATURE
CENTER
MIÐSTÖÐ ÍSLENSKRA BÓKMENNTA

Printed on acid-free paper in the United States of America.

Text set in Garamond, a group of old-style serif typefaces
named after the punch-cutter Claude Garamont.

Design by N. J. Furl

Open Letter is the University of Rochester's nonprofit, literary translation press:
Lattimore Hall 411, Box 270082, Rochester, NY 14627

www.openletterbooks.org

TÓMAS JÓNSSON, BEST-SELLER

Biography

I am descended from the bravest, bluest-eyed Vikings. I am related to courtly poets and victorious kings. I am an Icelander. My name is Tómas Jónsson. I am old

no, no

first composition book

I think it would be easiest to begin this way, this First Book, and move without further delay right to the kernel of the matter, thus: during the first years of World War II, I took some lodgers into my apartment, Sveinn and Katrín, a married couple with five children: Stína, who died; Dóri, their son; an infant boy; and a small cat, Títa,   he naps soft and warm against me as I write and has come back, together with Anna and Magnús and Dóri   I think they're all grown up and moreover there's a new addition to the crowd, Hermann, I hear them call him,   cursed forever is the day they returned,   and the musician, who rented the small bedroom on the other side of the partition, i.e. this bedroom where I now live, after he moved into the other bedroom, which is much smaller. His rental terms and my own are identical. I consider the terms equitable, beyond reproach, they ensure that the property owner enjoys some privileges in his own home; the musician agreed to the rental stipulations, indeed, he got out of me a written document saying that he could practice his electric guitar every day between four and five o'clock, an amount equivalent to one meter square of space, for my bedroom is larger by a square foot, according to the floor plan. He accepted this because it wasn't legally practical to pay the same rent, and I made sure the rental agreement clearly stated: a state of complete silence in a bedroom, which is one square meter smaller than the other in the same apartment, must result in the party in question paying a higher amount. Theretofore the unusual, localized noise from the smaller room is accepted by the tenant in question, who is responsible for his sounds, and is obligated to pay the same rent in respect to the tenant who lives beside him. Two hours a day for guitar practice is, I therefore believe, according to my own opinion and the best of my knowledge, equivalent to one-meter square (1 m²). You old financial fox, I sometimes tell myself with a chuckle, you clearly ought to have a sideline in handling rental finances. I am inclined to believe the value of a property increases in such a manner, at least in the eyes of the one paying regular installments on a house. Selflessness and self-sacrifice is my philosophy, occupying and consuming every part of me. I strive to hone my discipline, to control the inevitable oscillations toward backsliding in my disposition, via a continual severity of externally applied arguments.   yes just call it a spiritual oppression   Finally I gave up on all such rental stipulations, once the apartment had stopped being a pigsty, a twisted den of debauchery; I lived alone a short while. It behooves a man to live totally alone by himself—O wonderful days of solitude—independent from everything save his own whims and eccentricities, which I compliment myself for having long vanquished and exiled. I became like the world around me. I lived all alone within my own four walls and I put things to the test hither and thither, fiddling and patching the things that had gone haywire while I rented out parts of the apartment. I forgot in the course of time that the gains from my prior renting had been eaten up, I got lost in myself, and incomprehensibly I started taking new renters, Anna and Magnús, on top of which I was remunerated with this blindness the doctors managed to keep at bay until now. I suffer from congenital blindness. (Blindness and baldness alike run in my family.) Clouds cover both my eyes, never drawing away from "the edge of the sun," shielding the light the whole day, until day wraps itself in civil twilight.   and yet I remain capable of distinguishing night from day; as peculiar as it may seem, I can tell red from white, and so I am writing this in red ink   In the past, I put my rental income in a special savings account book, and kept it safe there until I was given an envelope (brown) marked with an elegant signature—Sigurður at one point mentioned, in passing, that it resembled Copperplate—actually he was probably called Sigmundur, that teacher—I reckon I was about twelve years old. (For fun, in parentheses, I want to mention, so everyone knows, that I was one of the school children who received acknowledgment for my beautiful handwriting from the King of iceland and Denmark. Never since has anyone given me such recognition.) The middle of the envelope was labeled in red ink: Tómas Jónsson's Rental Income. Clear characters swam on blue waves. In every wave valley and under each wave crest was a little period. The far end of the signature rose, a rocky coast with a high lighthouse that shone over the sea. I considered it perfect, the lighthouse a symbol—my own symbol.

Sitting halfway up in bed, with the pillow behind my head, I became aware that something unusual was going on in the hallway. There came to my ears a sound like the rustle of low moans intertwining. I listened to the sounds in the dark, low but intense, and I kept mouse quiet.

sometimes a man's own integrity is insufficient and he knows he must throw the doors open, all other measures having proved fruitless

From out in the dark, from my own corridor in my own premises, I heard a stifled moan, at first low, then turning into a heavy moan or maybe a whisper from a half-open mouth, as if of a fist being forced into the base of a belly (I later verified this experimentally on myself). Because the lungful of air emerges unopposed through the throat and mouth, open about an inch, the gasp never becomes piercing or painful, but heavy, hungry, sensual. Or so I felt: lips nibbling kisses. Because I lived in darkness, there could be no doubt that the light had been turned on in the deep of night; I saw faint light in the keyhole and a strip of light from under the door. The apartment has no doorsill. Those disappeared with the arrival of the American military force. Clearly someone was wasting electricity late into the depth of night. After this incident, I set myself this rule: to take out the fuses from the board each evening. Before I went to bed I made sure to check that the lights everywhere were extinguished. The electricity bill was enough of a burden on me already, sparing as I was with light. And I dropped into the lease conditions some new clauses about light-times in the apartment (I was idiotic enough to include light and heat in the rent): on weekdays in all the shady months, lights must be turned off after 11:30 P.M.; moreover, the housework must stop by then and the apartment must be silent, with the exception of weekends, when the light-time is extended by one hour. And a clause about the use of lights around the major festivals: a) A week before the big festivals, christmas and Easter, the rules that apply on weekends will be observed (to allow for baking and the consumption of baked goods); b) On christmas eve, according to ancient traditions, the lights shall stay on, but the tenant shall replace their bulbs, ones with a smaller wattage. Instead of conventional bulbs, only 15-candle bulbs are allowed. In a chandelier with more than four arms, there must only be two bulbs. All wall sconces and standing lamps must be extinguished. Special provisions for light over the summer months: the homeowner reserves the right to remove all the fuses from the fuse box, other than the one labeled kitchen, and store them in his own room. Final clause: should a situation arise in which someone needs light after the lawfully-approved light time, he must have a flashlight available so he can go in and out of the house. Non-negotiable clause: The use of oil- or candlelight is strictly prohibited because of the risk of fire. Exemption from these regulatory clauses: If a student is in the apartment, he shall be authorized to have a night lamp on, provided the landlord is notified in advance of the bulb size and how long the student intends to read into the night.

Reykjavík, 13. January 1943.
Tómas Jónsson.

The musician fixed a little flashlight to his belt, attached to a key ring—cylindrical, finger-sized, with a convex magnifying glass on the tip, to amplify the light. He used the flashlight to get his key into the lock. The musician had a certain ingenuity; for example, he had marked his soap dish and toothbrush holster with a cap around the bristles of the toothbrush. Before he combed his hair, he spread his hand towel around his shoulders. These and other facets I noted in his character, and credited him for them. He never over-used brilliantine, as was common at the time. Instead, he used hair cream. He left his shoes in front of his door, making it easy to monitor whether he was in or out. This meant he never got the musk of shoe odor in the room; he put his socks inside his shoes. I sometimes sniffed the socks, but they never had an unpleasant fragrance. No one had a room key. No secrecy is needed in a house where each person respects the others' individual rights. I also wanted to be able to walk freely around the apartment, if necessary, at all times of the day.

The apartment is this sort of dwelling: from the main entrance you walk down into the basement, five steps of green, speckled linoleum. To the right, when you have come down, is my apartment's door. On the left-hand side another door down a short hallway leads to a shared laundry room for all the apartments in the building. Inside my own apartment you come first to a small vestibule. On the left is my bedroom door. The storage closet lies opposite. If you continue straight on through the vestibule and the open door with its window fitted with thin screens, you come into the hall. In the hall you find four doors: the kitchen and the musician's door on the right (the room still bears his name even though I have now comfortably moved in). From the far end of the hall extends a bathroom, and opposite the kitchen is the living room door. From the living room is the entrance to the couple's bedroom, the so-called inner room. (I commanded this room when I lived alone.)   the man felt fine about lying up against the big fat smudge on the wall Katrín's remnants it gave him pleasure to thrust his nose up against the stain smelling sniffing thinking how she had slept with Sveinn the smell of perfume unmistakable the patch on the wall on her side of the bed she must have had to lie with her ass squashed up against the wall her body steaming warmth

The bathroom features a bath. In the bathroom there's a chair bath, as I call it, i.e. the tub is shaped like a cistern with a pedestal for perching on once the water's drawn. I am opposed to long baths. Women have a compulsion for spreading a loose mat in the bottom as decoration, and feet catch on the mat above the slippery enamel, then you fall and there's almost no grip on the wet edges; one could likely drown. Jacuzzi tubs can be fatal, particularly for heavyset people. On the other hand, I could sit steadfastly on the perch of a chair bath and let the water flow over me from the shower without any danger. (Anna insisted on bringing a crocheted mat for the bottom, but I would throw it out onto the floor before stepping into the bathtub.) Because I've always been hydrophobic, I built myself a nose-cap, a kind of proboscis made from an old faucet to prevent water bubbling through my nose and into my lungs. I'd tightly fasten the nose-cap behind my ears using elastic, which worked wonderfully. Great time and ingenuity went into inventing and perfecting the cap so that it was fully functional. My inventions mostly came to me during the period when I lived entirely alone. I had nothing better to do in the long evening hours than think and ponder. I found it difficult to properly seal the device around my nostrils. No thanks to my over-abundance of nose hair, the water was still inclined to trickle down from my forehead, past the corners of my eyes, and into my nose through my nostrils. In truth, I should have been born during the Renaissance, when painters desired nothing more than to make portraits of hairy-nosed aristocrats. The newspapers, on the other hand, harp on about how we live in an Industrial Age of Innovation. How it is possible to expect significant artworks will be painted during an age when national industries dominate, or any other important ideas emerge when employment—think about that prefix, *em*—is the byline for this age? Initially, I was as gullible and empty as a fetus in its mother's belly; or did I suspect how things were embroiled? I have racked my brain on the matter, trying to emend the situation, without reaching a conclusion. I don't know there's ever been a safe conclusion found about anything. But I have described the exterior of the apartment, its embellishments, my tiny world that I assembled, for myself alone, from much-loved parts   take a nap, my sweet pussy   I have described the entire apartment except its colors.

The apartment is painted green save for the hallway (it was painted in a period when that color was believed to rest your eyes, and the house is therefore a green interior meadow), which is a light *muted* gray color. (The corridor was painted in the prevailing period of *muted* colors, "which no one could settle on," as the saying went.) Gold-bronze tiles covered the blue ceiling, but the doors and doorframes were white, since it cleaned easily with a cloth and mild soapy water. (Everything was painted in period colors, cleaned easily "with a soft cloth and mild soap and water.") The apartment is evidence for developments in taste when it comes to color between 1943 and 1950. The walls of the bathroom each has its own color and the ceiling is black (abstract). I had the doors and windows gold-bronzed; I do not really believe in the restful power of green. Immediately the uncomfortable suspicion snuck up on me that in the corridor a disgrace was taking place, something I, Tómas Jónsson, could not tolerate in my vicinity. The reasons for my inner suspicion remain unknown to me. Was I aware Katrín sold herself? To whom? A kept woman? Should we be protecting ourselves? So far, I have been rather naïve as to the possibility. Man is by nature suspicious, but I compensate against my tendencies in that direction. Believing people have the dignity to live according to true stories. But the shallow breathing bore unambiguous witness that the soul's moral strength was being smashed to pieces right under my nose by the coat hooks—and I was not raising a finger to help. Something held me back. It would have been sensible to rush out with the fruits of the night, to pour them over this fire (as was done at my childhood home with dogs in heat, when people could not sleep for the growls and barks. The bitch Mjóna slept in the garden dock plants under the wall, beneath the gable window, and my sister Björg kept a chamber pot on the table when spring arrived and the dogs had started to frisk about, as was their nature. From the table, she placed one foot on the windowsill and the other on the side of the bed, which made it possible for her to empty the pot, splattering a cascade of piss out the window and over the dogs. For a few nights, this alarm worked. The dogs had been spoken to. Then they started up again. Dogs are like that. Another time, mom adopted another, better plan, spreading cowshit on the bitch's ass to scare the dogs from her) but instead I scrutinized the paint and the shoes in the hallway. I spread the comforter over the alarm clock. Maybe I was most bothered about my shoe covers. I pressed the palm of my hand to the button on the back of the clock. I did all this blindly under the comforter, in the dark. I altered the regulator until I felt, more than I heard, a low crack. The clock would not ring. The button was no longer connected. All that . . .

(Part of the manuscript is missing here.)

. . . sat up in bad with the utmost care. In a pale sheen of streetlight somehow fumbling its way through a tear in the window shade, I could make out, using glasses and a magnifier, that it was only about four in the morning. Drowsiness and lethargy lay upon me. A body that had not received its fill of sleep and dreams. The deficit spoke for itself. I was exhausted from the drowsiness, clammy with sweat. The shallow breathing was still going, still as zealous. He must be slow, was my thought. Or maybe he has studied books, taught himself to last. I knew full well what was going on around the partition past the door. I groped about under the comforter and pillows, shamefully joining the team, and finishing first. I didn't need much preparation or time. I am like the animals in this respect. She glides from his arms wet and satisfied.
Because of the cold floor—
precisely because of the cold floor and because I am sensitive to changes in temperature, fearful of the cold of many weeks of cold and getting up and leaking piss you are warned—I walk around naked at night no sooner than I get under the comforter I realize my bladder is filling even if it's only a drop of pee I try to pee I must empty myself during the night I lift the lid from the seat and stand with feet a-straddle I hold the chain on the water tank and let a trickling sound trickle suggestively two short spurts of the constant urine-production standing on the cold and damp and chilled floor at night would damage my fragile health I've always been prone to colds not only during cold season mid-January to

March April but all year round   (Due to this sensitivity to cold I use a plastic chamber pot which I empty and rinse thoroughly under the cold water tap before the couple rises from their tepid bed. Enamel pots, once the custom, were piercingly cold. Until pots made of something other than iron were available, I started lining the outside of the chamber pot with old woolen singlets. I trained myself to grasp it, swing it up into bed, empty my bladder and shake myself dropless without losing any sleep. My method: I pulled the pot under the divan with a left-handed motion, bent my wrist and slid the pot under the bed fast asleep. But the cold contact of the pot with my body's night sweat earned me bouts of bronchitis or chronic blisters.

The advent of new plastic pots from Reykjalundur Rehabilitation Center was honestly a welcome delight, although it meant I had no choice but to dispose of a loyal friend for a new partner, which has in turn become the true friendship. I loved my chamber pot. I wrapped my erstwhile acquaintance in the *Morning News*, tied rocks to its ears, and drowned him in the sea by the harbor wall in the early hours of October 30, 1954. On the plastic chamber pot, I sewed a patch to its ears to streamline things for my penis. Plastic can be plenty cold to the touch, too, though no way near as much as enamel. The patch, which is really a small cushion, gets washed using a green alkali soap and dries on the oven during the day, while I'm out at work. This patch is made from sponge taken from old car seats, which Sveinn keeps in the storage closet. He can go ahead and call me a thief but I warrant he has larger concerns. The plastic pot is bright and more colorful than the clinically white enamel one. Far and wide in iceland, boys amuse themselves throwing their old night pots against fence poles and listening to the enamel explode away from the iron with an oddly piercing crack resounding long after the stone has smashed it. These splinters are dangerous to the eyes, though from the modern child's perspective plastic pots are no less an opportunity when they are set on fire and born aloft, a brand burning out the old year from up on a high pole.

—hauled myself back into bed, shivering with frostbite, because I was wearing practically nothing. While I was on my feet I did not honor my bodily health enough to buy it pajamas, even though no one survives without their body, as the ancient saying goes, and this sleep I reckon worth little, indeed it is tasteless to sit without underwear, since there're more emissions from the body during sleep than waking.

I continue where things fell off the thread broke I use to mark straight lines on the notebook's blank page I could barely make out the faint lines along the page's surface today I started foraging and came across a whole pile of old Snotru-brand composition books from the time when I tutored private students between six and seven in the evening until the incident with the washing machine while parents were trusting me with their children while I was healthy and before the time of oxygen cylinders beside the headboard and a mask hanging on a loop by my bedside and I realized that I was soon going to die so nothing better to do with my time than writing books scrawling in them insignificant things in this tome ass too much chit-chat when it broke for the time being after the mask's thread ripped on the nail I got from a catalogue and used to mark lines on the page I have never gotten comfortable with the distinction between voluntary and involuntary events now I have reached the time when I fidget with the book its lines having broken back her spine

It is an act of friendship when the puss, Títa, wets me

Due to the nature of my work, I wear a sleeveless undershirt and short underwear during the day.

yes: according to the terms of the lease it is Anna's duty to come three times per day at a minimum and change me though she does not come when needed most so it dries on me all by itself and what does Anna do then but turn her nose up and fuss over the strong odor in the room wanting my district administrative officer dead Títa you're the cat who found favor with the district administrative officer

The office is well heated—the state pays our heating costs. I travel there on foot. I can walk briskly in snowstorms, frost, any weather; nothing stings Tómas. Outdoor under the bare sky where it's often cold and snowy, in wet or dry weather. Nature is a stereotype, is boring, she never thinks up anything new. In strong wind, when I turn at a street corner, the cold wind breezes up my pants legs. I should wear bicycle clips on my legs. There's no warmth to be had except in thought. What thoughts? Petrarch thinks about Laura: Rime in vita di madonna Laura. My thoughts then were otherwise, which I nudriva 'l core in su 'l mio giovenile errore, quand'era in parte altr'uom da quel ch'i sono   yes yes che debb io far   che mi consigli elli   tempo e ben di morire   madonna Katrín e morta et ha seco l mio core e volendo seguire interromper conven quest anni rei nonono everything's forgotten and dead and vanished from the leaky scrawl of memory blind as a post and nowhere any warmth in thought she is aged bedridden and dead and scattered in the wind the field, the cut, and Rut picks up the ax a faint light seen occasionally and afterward one's hearing is turned off, sight too, so each lives exclusively within the body's meat I begin clutching the material for sustenance then I remember an oxygen mask sharpens one's thought   for example, I recall the old buses. I never went anywhere in a bus. Quite the opposite: I saved my money, it went in the envelope carefully marked *General Thrift*. And from this envelope can be heard the following subtext: Money saved out of contempt for buses, which foster strikes and increase chaos, mass hysteria and colds, the flu   in the office I would be too hot in long underwear   I keep the envelope in the bottom drawer. Sigurður wears long underwear. Often you can see his bulging underwear spill from his socks as he sits at his desk and draws his pants up by the crease. He is always the same as ever, knees in pants. Well, how would I react if a sudden announcement came on the radio saying people had been ordered to wear woolen underwear? For forty years I had worn long woolen underwear. I'd say shedding them seemed a step in the direction of culture. First, World War II divided households into two enemy camps—for or against woolen underwear, grandparents versus grandchildren—and mothers tried to make peace with normal undergarments. From this time a foreign influence has placed the nation's mental health in jeopardy. At the war's end a loud dispute erupted over nylon socks, chewing gum, Coca-Cola, and blush and lipstick, though occasionally Stalin hijacked these disputes from Hitler, and now and again people asked, Is Stalin worse than Hitler or Hitler better than Stalin? so as to achieve an intellectual variety in their discussions. What breaches our national unity now? Ten-year-olds no longer understand their parents' language and customs   en morale et langage sont des sciences particulieres mais universelles   they are not above considering teaching positions in the university accompanied by examination and study books in their pockets, those who prefer to continue in this heroic deed of noting everything down my whole biography continues just the same as anyone and anything and everything yes well at least   the other day someone approached me, talking and speaking about his understanding, his knowledge of some underwear, just come on the market, knit from so-called "nylon wool," which keeps the body at a constant temperature no matter whether the wearer is outside or inside, working hard or hardly, in winter or summer. These synthetics have great ventilation, he said.   Ólaf and Sigurður earnestly debate whether the icelandic landscape is more beautiful, magnificent and ever-changing than corresponding foreign landscapes we Icelanders cannot indefinitely survive the terrain we cannot eat the mountains we cannot drink the beautiful blue glaciers   Knit clothes require the right setting, like a manger on a hillock, a farmhouse with deathly blue women and children who have meadow-green mucus in their noses, men with itinerant, suspicious gazes. A reversion to this time would be like going back to doing it in your pants. We have to find a new material for our underwear . . .

Anna struck my paw I said I had not became bedridden while I thought about clothes you cannot shit yourself any more I shall remember Pearl Harbor always and forever what has become of my books burned sold destroyed lost and forgotten as if my life is only according to others' grace come you understand now your father when he said he would prefer to lie in the earth than in comfort and you pull back your head when this aged figure slowly drew a creased life insurance envelope from beneath his pillow handed it to his own son and yawned wearily like when he came home from the sea he took snuff to keep awake but gave up the ghost having previously carefully studied the price of a coffin, he wanted a black coffin no angels no flowers no gold bronze handles no grave with a stone before his short spell in his deathbed he was frugal because as his last days approached he solely ate water wished to die debtless in his sleep satisfied with the world he expired and expired on a fasting stomach you children failed to make him dependent upon you she said in the envelope there is enough for a sheet and pillowcases we have plenty of hay then Björg flung herself on the bed and cried she had forgotten to ask her father forgiveness but now it was too late for her to say that she had always loved him deep down behind her heart in the silence behind the wheedling but I turned on my heel hardened in my contempt for this which fed me living or dead and said I did not want to see them again the two could handle the funeral it would not be onerous for two robustly sprightly women though they busied themselves baking a funeral feast

The refectory has not been deprived of quarrels because we quarrel spiritedly and inspired by whatever the talk of the town is.
Here follows a short list of the main risks that beset the small population of the icelandic nation from 1939 up until the Marshall Plan:

a) Gymnastics softens the bellies of young men and makes them workshy; b) bicycle saddles destroy young virgins—"the priority being that every husband enjoys his wife on their wedding night; for girls, bicycles are no different than promiscuity"; c) the extension of school-going nourishes debility in people and hardens the mouths of adolescents (Enemy No. 1, Brynjólf Bjarnason, K. fl.); d) Contraceptives, "which are nothing but the assassination of fine upstanding citizens who are alive and fertile in the seed of those who desire nothing more than to see the creation of The One" in the fullness of time (Enemy No. 1, Katrín Thoroddsen, K. fl.); away with sheaths from the breast pockets of all men's jackets! A prophylactic-free land! All such new products in the stores amount to the end of the world, the plucking and eradication of the icelandic family. Merchants and shady dealers contribute to this I) with brilliantine, which renders Icelanders as bald as foreigners; II) burning people's stomachs with mustard and ketchup; III) increasing everyone's belching and wind by means of vegetables; IV) killing tourists in tents with canned poison in canned food; V) hollowing out the insides of people's heads via radio; VI) importing sexually transmitted diseases and sexual promiscuity with open foreign underwear, "which must be carefully boiled in a high strength alkali soap before wear;" VII) increasing appendicitis by importing overpriced raisins with pits in them; destroying women's brains with imports of high heels (2000000 blows daily to the spinal cord and cerebellum); all this that makes one's wife indifferent to housework and child-rearing.

And then came the nylon, which stuck to women's legs in the frost, blocked their pores, and "did not allow the normal bodily expulsions by which people void their innate germs." Women were not safe to be photographed in nylon underwear; they came out naked in the picture.

Against all these threats to the contemporary moment the nation found consolation in Q) the American army based at Keflavík Airport, "the largest and most advanced airport in the world and even further afield"; Z) iceland's geographical position, the most remarkable geographical location in the world, "the plan that will result for mankind in the upcoming war-game, the superpowers' child's play, the game of the atomic bomb (the first target of an atomic war: Keflavík;

W) the highest antenna in Europe at Lóran Station on Snaefellsnes (all nations, hidden or visible, admire the largest Lóran antenna in the world during peacetime).

I have been forced to take ignorant people into my property's square footage   but are there any laws against lawlessness   who makes laws dictating that apartments cannot stand empty and unoccupied in the struggle over housing   am I bound to be a sacrifice to the homeless and improvident, me who is almost blind, deaf, enfeebled   can I argue with myself   if you don't house Peter then Páll forces himself inside   according to the law no apartment can stand empty in this competition for apartments   I believe P no more than P but I do not house P and I defend myself therefore with him against P, then P comes with kids and his missus and demands an apartment and demands I let him fend off P   the nucleus of the problem from my standpoint is that both Peter and Páll live according to preferences that justify them taking possession of my floor area and in plain sight   my mistake from the start consists in being frugal, from deciding to own whyever I did so and Sveinn and Katrín gave notice and left the apartment standing empty for a while   the option was to welcome Magnús and Anna following their relationship with Katrín and Sveinn and Anna is a distant relative of mine, both on the side of the great Bergsætts, the chief family of this country, descended from the kings of Norway at the time of the Settlement, all the kings and queens and princes and princesses on the way to inherit a country a family with joint ownerships it is split into entrepreneurs and intellectuals   so it's reasonable that Magnús and Anna get to walk the floor here rather than some loose rabble from Skagaströnd who rip toilets out of houses and sell them   although the point always remains the same, snatching the apartment from him in due course once I am sufficiently senile, old and weakened from cohabitating this fragile-witted man cannot keep the entire apartment up by himself he must accept loans or donations break the tip of his hubris lose his healthy pride and now I force myself upon myself all by myself doodling on paper   I cannot think of anything that lets toxins into the blood through the nervous system but something that brings peace and quiet and balance and beauty ABOVE ALL BEAUTY while I pray to the reaper to come or else the messenger with the guide dog and bell collar   they reckon they can teach me to place all my faith in a dog and later care for my belongings with kind intentions they are planning to save those who will never be saved forever improvident who know nothing but foul language and create so much trouble that everything must revolve around the invalids or else the whole community will become invalids and then how will money be taken from Tómas Jónsson

You'll be one hundred percent safe, the dog won't lead you into any danger, they say; this dog is an expert in leading the blind in the streets. He could go with you in any direction, walking, in a coach, by ship, even in an airplane, and still find the way back home with you. It is about making blind people accept the same normality as if they were not blind. People are blind all over the world. You have no need to be ashamed of your blindness.

I could punch the friendliness of these voices right in the mouth

Remember, from now on your dog day is Wednesday. You're registered with the Blind Association, and we expect cooperation. The Blind Association doesn't leave any of its members up a creek. We have on our agenda a friendly relationship with all blind people, our desire to make the darkness tolerable.

Every Wednesday they bring me a treat from the Dog Bank, the loyal dog Trygg.

what do you do for recreational activities on your dog day.   I'm so awfully pleased with mine.   he's called Argos.   Everyone has a duty to be grateful to his therapy dog.   I take all my trips: in shops and on buses and public toilets. I am no longer left wanting when any human whims come. I do everything myself I can bake and cook and take out the garbage. sometimes I even forget I am blind from birth. I visit blind Jón his dog day is on Mondays and mine on Tuesdays. we do everything with the help of the dog and our dog days play their part. cooperation is everything. why don't you get together with blind Siggi you are on Wednesdays he on Thursdays this is ideal. The dogs and you can get betrothed!

He strolled, me in tow, around the area in front of my building from the trash cans to the gate and from there directly to the swing set and back to the trash cans I hung on to the leash for dear life afraid the dog would run after a cat or leave me out in the middle of the road

i know what you're afraid of but they do not run after cats. you know, we should all form a coalition a blind union and demand from the government one dog per person and three dogs as backup.

Were we tougher, we would demand guide dogs in the government. Blind Jón is embittered. He pauses, and all at once we're paired up, being led, six of us together, we start off like a ray of light from a christmas tree, singing hymns. We are organized into seven beams with dogs at the end closest to the burning tree, so no one runs into the candles. Don't pull the collar too much, let the dogs be in control, and sing, Tómas, you're not singing with us: In the dark shines the sun of life, sun of life. god give us a happy christmas. Hallelujah. Hallelujah. Now the blind hope the christmas elves bring them each a guide dog. But there the blind don't lead the blind; instead, they're equals among others.

Blind Jón makes an implausible Santa Claus. you'd recognize his voice immediately. you do not even have to close your eyes to recognize him as soon as he says: well, I got terrible weather up on Hólsfjalla but the dog coped. I heard that Jón and blind Inga who you talked

to earlier locked themselves in the toilets at the last blind ball.   we
called a meeting and agreed to censure people who disrupt the social
harmony.   tonight blind Bagga and blind Víkingur are making sure
no one locks themselves in the toilets.

Tómas.

He draws me into a monologue inside the craft studio, saying: Tómas,
as you know, we have gained a foreign import license from the necessary
parties regarding a new shipment of dogs arriving after the New Year.
So we have an opportunity to choose appropriately symbolic names for
them. And it popped into mind, because the union of shop stewards
has heard you're outstandingly accomplished in many fields—didn't you
teach final exams outside school?—whether such a learned man as you
might advise us. We were thinking of choosing dog names from famous
dogs from history, or names that refer to the dimming of the sight. We
already have, as you know, dogs with names like Trygg, Höðr, Oðin,
Heimdallr. These are extremely popular. Höður was blind. Oðin one-
eyed. Heimdallr had ears instead of eyes. I had to hold myself back
from christening dogs after famous dogs in the movies: Rin Tin Tin and
Lassie, although I know that this would prove amiable to most spon-
sors. Do you have any ideas for names? Argos is already taken. Cerberus
and Húi are famous dogs from mythology. Cerberus occurs in Dante;
Húi is a Chinese dog who saw tornados; Jama's messengers were two
dogs; Garmr fought with the Æsir—but all these were dogs marked by
death. You change the whole picture in certain ways, my dear Tómas.
Let's just forget all this and christen the dogs with some lovely icelandic
nicknames. He brought me back into the room, where we began playing
hide-and-blind-seek, and play-dancing to "Everyone's a Standing Statue"
and other games for the blind. But Anna never brings me to the dormi-
tory. I also flat out refuse to bristle brushes. Blind crafts are, and always
have been, abhorrent to me, and here's why: I developed an aversion
to the blind because of the peculiar gluey smell emanating from their
garments.

In the middle of the ring people play statues; one is the "hunter." Forest imps and water nymphs walk around them and sing.
Chorus:

> *These are statues standing here*
> *Standing in you there's an answer*
> *you are blind and this the cover*
> *which only has to touch her*

Imps and nymphs: Hi-hi-hi. Are you going to carry me?

Considering the diverse scientific discoveries of this nuclear century of which we Icelanders have become conscious, I have most been impressed by the construction of the ballpoint pen. A fire like no other lit within me when I bought my first biro, as ballpoint pens were commonly called. I always gave ink the evil eye. I could discover no ready advice as to how one might dip the pen-nib down in the neck of the inkwell without soiling oneself with the ink. Immediately from nine o'clock in the morning the average office worker has ink-blotches on his fingers. A great waste of time went into cleaning the nib with blotting paper, and no matter how carefully it was done, you inevitably got ink stains on your index and middle fingers. Ink stuck oddly to my delicate fingers. I was the most thoroughly ink-soaked employee in my department. And you know the ink-soaked people in each department by their hand gestures. My ink-soaked state was not due to carelessness, the usual cause, but by my hands' strange clamminess, which had plagued me since I was young, so much so that I avoided greeting people with a handshake, and still do to this day; I usually let a quick nod suffice. I believe this is directly related to the fact that I have cold saliva, and therefore have never dared kiss anyone. My mother would say: What's this, Tómas, your saliva is as cold as a dog's nose! I tested it out on Mom, Dad, Björggi, and everyone said: Stone me, his saliva is freezing. Of course, what caused the most excitement was the functionality and ergonomic qualities of the pen (although initially after the introduction of the pen, checks signed using a biro weren't accepted, based on the graphologists' opinion that written marks would fade with time. People at the bank asked in earnest: can I write in biro? And people replied: No, unfortunately, only ink signatures are valid). This invention directly affected my job, freed me from expense and worry. I set aside the use of a finger cap (which I will describe for you in my next article). I also set aside buying brushes. Because of the stupid ink I had been forced to shell out money for a nailbrush. Even so, the ink would never entirely disappear from my fingers, somehow instead sidling into the hard skin on my middle finger, resembling corns on protruding toe bones after a long work stint due to that damn pen nib.

I have experienced some sort of epiphany that persists through this whole article that has become my best essay the ideas sweep and stack into steam columns and I feel myself regularly being lifted I suspect very strongly that I still have a callus no it has vanished I could never be a famous writer because you need a pen-callus on your index finger there will be interviews with me . . . how did you get the callus . . . I'm always writing . . .

I made myself a finger cap   of course considered an expenditure, although on a small scale, the "general thrift" envelope never significantly raided   for hygiene reasons. For the same reasons as I had to procure a nailbrush. The bristles lasted poorly   I have a deep-seated aversion to blind crafts   inferior wire binding, the straw unevenly long and wanting to tear the fingernails by the cuticles, too easy to lose. One time my index fingers developed a chronic inflammation at the cuticles, which I blamed on the poor production quality of the brushes: the swelling did not subside until I boiled my fingers and out came a tiny fraction of hard straw.   for sure, brushes made by the blind are cheaper than other brushes but the cost must be tallied against the hundred drawbacks   With the new ballpoint pen, made of hardened rubber cased in the likeness of marble, I felt a joy comparable to Roland with his sword, Durandal. I struck the unbreakable pen on the table edge and fragments of his famous epic came to mind . . . L'epée cruist, ne fruisset ne ne brise. O biro, cum est bele e seintisme. I placed my money proudly on the glass table, hip height in front of the girl, where pens lay in three beautifully arranged ranks under the glass case, paid shillings, as it was called then, when she asked: Don't you want your name engraved on it; it's free; unfortunately, there's a waiting period. A week later, I was able to go around with the biro in my pocket, clearly marked on its side: Tómas Jónsson. And a rumor spread among the people: that a biro could write continually for ten thousand miles without running out of ink. Correspondingly, it could draw four ink circles around the earth's circumference, though it would run out during the fifth. With this advertising pitch the manufacturers successfully created excitement among the masses. You'd often see young men on the street with differently colored rows of pens in their jacket pockets. But I found the equation strange. It hadn't gone down well in the bank or in the office while Tryggvi was in charge. In geography, I'd learned that the Earth's circumference at the equator is 40 thousand kilometers, nearly matching the coast of Greenland. But the ingenious gimmick was pure advertising. Ads may be impertinent, whether for poetry, fish, or detergent: either they are pretty exaggerations or rhyming exaggerations. Anything that rhymes works better on the consumer. Typically today there's no rhyming but in advertising. Advertisers occupy the seat of the old icelandic poet-*skalds*; there are all kinds of asinine rhymes for products that fool the public without any difficulty, just as the singsong "andrarímur" did in past times. I would love to know who thought this all up, advertising a ballpoint pen with such imperial exaggeration and shamelessness.   In school I only ever wrote with a pen nib, then with a cartridge or fountain pen. I can manage a fountain pen better. The word itself evokes the sense of an eternal flow of water from its source, or in this case the ink that streams into the pen from the cartridge, hidden in the depths of the case. You find yourself in a sound mood for discovering poetic metaphors: because each element is made by the hand of a living man there is some degree of connection with Mother Earth.

I remember clearly when the slopes were still uninhabited land where houses now stand and grass on Hvolsvöllur is tall, succulent, and green where Guðrún is heading back down or Jónas, were he still alive, that great farmer who stood for innovation and thought about changing the wetness without landscaping and tussocks, an experimental dream of the land—who realized that the earth swelled in winter frost the way your legs swell from cold feet as you stand with the hens who look at you suspiciously in icelandic poetry they stop roosting lice from themselves down in their earth ridge in the sky a red cloud drags past and you think war is coming the world's end and the thought flies down and up Skeiðin past Hestfjall and over Vörðufell where the swans at sunset by the mountain lake maimed and knocked unconscious lambs with their wings and it continues into Hrepp where it meets Fall and you say September 14th I do not want to wait for the round-up at Hvolsvöllur but at Hvolsvöllur the grass hasn't died Hekla stands like a blue-white island rising from the sandy desert grass grows in luscious clusters you open the trunk and the house smell assaults your nose and you feel around the bottom and find loose-knit socks and spotted socks darned and then it reaches your senses and the smell of the house assaults you at Hvolsvöllur your senses you yell from behind the clothes hanging in the potato cellar over the milk cans at the outhouse over the wide-mouthed pissbog and in the Now a ballpoint pen rules   the chickens flock together for you to splash the fish bones from your clothes over their feathers they cut the fish spine apart with their beaks and suck out the gelatinous spinal cord, then hold the spine up for you a riddle about spines in the tail you say twelve and two or is there in the spine what I call marrow nonono he laughs with dirty fingers over his mouth full of rotted teeth lost you finally write when a letter comes from home god my god Tómas my Tómmas when will you stop being an inexhaustible burden for us you are now ten my good god will you endlessly lag behind other boys, you have no delight in sheep you have no satisfaction from fish, I get no profit from taking in laundry and your father earns nothing on the ocean I'm pregnant again will soon deliver hold out until christmas try you are

one of ten and I have been pregnant twelve times remember that and no
profit from laundry but I persist no harbor do you want to see me later
as kin as in a bog the yellow brush escapes from mom's hands and flies
back into the cloudy water she lies in the mud on her back intertwining
with the foreman (I can see him before me) wading in between the tubs
she screams don't let the damn old woman's bloody spittle mingle with
the fresh-washed fish haul her to the tub's side[1] they struggle with their

---

1. The washing-up tubs must have been in a row along from the fish supplies. The women would have been situated along the long side of a narrow
plank over the puddle which formed under their feet, so they gradually got wet,
wrapped with aprons and covered by arm-protectors made of oiled canvas. The
aprons would have been made of the same material. This protective clothing
was "treated" once a year, ideally in the spring, and spread on the ground to dry.
Ointment would fall from the folds, and hence it was necessary to look after it
well, otherwise it offered no protection. He must have been standing between
the chest and the saltfish station cutting the neck-blood from the fish with a
splitting knife, i.e. a knife with as long a blade as shaft, wrapped in string, with
lead bolts where blade and shaft met. Three planks would have formed the washing board, which rested on the edge of the tub on one side and, on the other
side, was nailed to a wood block underwater in the tub. After he had let the
blood from the napes, he dipped the fish in the water and laid them crosswise
across the board. That is called the soak, and it precedes the wash. She would
have reached across the tub for the wet fish and arranged them in front of her on
the board, four or five fish upside down at once, their napes toward her. First the
brush is brushed across the skin and then carefully under the fins with bristles
that are longer at the ends than in the middle of the brush. The bristles were yellow, hard but flexible so they didn't damage the fish; they were slightly crooked.
With one swipe, the fish is flipped and brushed with another swift gesture, the
bristles applied diagonally down the spine recess, and stroked crosswise if there is
any jaundice; if not, that was considered unnecessary. The washer wore woolen
mittens; he stroked them over the belly to get to the membrane, what's known as
plucking. In a single swipe the fish was folded and the brush went under the tail-
and back-fins; the fish was then cast back into the sink to float there, and one
needed considerable technique so as not to break it apart in the fall. Mom must
have slipped over herself at that moment in a slippery heap of newly-washed

burden they sling mom to the planks and flatten her oil-washed skirt yelling with turned-up sleeves do not open your thighs woman squeeze them together one person struggles with her deathly pale carries her in her flattened skirt hanging down to the ground and slings then she lies there

---

fish. The brush would have fallen from her hands into the grayish water full of liquid membranes which settled on the tub's bottom in the night and over time formed a thick putrefied layer. If the brush was new it would float upright thanks to the straw, otherwise it sank to the bottom or was half-submerged. If it sank, it was drilled up with sticks or staves. Washing fish was cold and hard work in the sheds, which were not warmed by anything but obscenities. The obscenities tended to rhyme roughly—what you might call dirty ditties. These verses would describe the terrible abandon of men and women, without parallel in the history of art, except perhaps in some of Rubens' paintings. And it is notable that both the primitive and the highly-educated court culture should have more in common than other kinds of mentality; both are un-bourgeois, basic, free. These dirty verses are extremely remarkable sources of human powerlessness. In them you find pain, the castration of the body that is bound its whole life to physical effort and sees no way out of the puzzle or toward liberty except in the abstract, in raging sexual intercourse, of which the body is incapable. Oil heating devices are part of this list of death, if they're not swiftly dealt with the support of public funding from Parliament throughout their life, this lone innovative and unique icelandic literary-sex literary tradition without compare.

second book

to put herself to bed as night comes she says there are embers alive in
the oven take these bloody pieces from the chamber pot and tear chips
from the tar paper where it flakes at the corner of the house and set
them on him and burn everything in a large firebox put pieces of wood
under it so it might combust all the more quickly then come back after
you burn it yes then she gropes for her glass of iodine milk and says in
the chamber pot was your brother or sister and drinks her iodine milk
my good god my Tómas try not to be a perpetual burden on us hold out
to christmas   it would be fun to know about all the people what's
become of them all of them I have known in my lifetime

how many people have died this very moment   how many are
being born while I say hey!   in x state in South America one-and-a-
half children are born every minute that passes   I have made myself
imagine the corn fields must resemble gold   I have never seen corn
except in pictures where it was, of course, still   other people need to
do a whole lot to prove as strange in old age as to have lived the varied
life of Oddný Sen   I remember her books about the Chinese Empire

the bridal couple in Amoy in the picture this bridal couple intended
to journey west they now live in Red China perhaps they have fled across
the Formosa channel

Snorri Sturluson's name is the lone icelandic name found in foreign
encyclopedias there it stood written out in Chinese characters   it must

be that Oddný knew the Chinese language must be she speaks Mandarin
or the Amoy dialect

as the Yellow Sea yellows from deposits of yellow sand out of the Yellow River   corn fields and rivers where an old man sleeps in a small
canoe and dreams tiny Chinese poems   beside the anchored boat
stand five stamps five dynasty pictures for the old man has been owned
by five emperors five periods

in the Ming period the mountains' pale blue peaks are darker and
rise up from the fog to where the clouds break   where is this written
in an icelandic poem

she has seen the Chinese Wall with her own eyes the one edifice on
earth distinguishable from the moon   a building raised by emperors
so no one steps foot in their region so they could live virtually undisturbed by barbarians the way I want to   until people recently arrived
from the borderlands said that barbarians no longer exist anywhere in
the world

but no one can build the wall higher than his thought reaches   the
emperors Tai Tsung and Tai Tsu lacked compassion   see here and
around the Great Wall   nothing is left but chaos   not since the
great conquest of Gibraltar has the world been safe   after *On the Origin
of Species* I am not explicitly created in the image of god   after the
publication of *Das Kapital* the proprietary rights to my apartment are
cast in doubt   undoubtedly I do not sleep the innocent sleep of a
child following the publication of *The Interpretation of Dreams*   even
dreams are not innocent anymore nothing is innocent   the damned
nineteenth century woke us up from innocence I do not know how
much travel improved Oddný but she recently gave a fascinating talk on
the radio about China's past and present as the girls out in the corridor
cursed the country perhaps at night she dreams of Amoy   she must
have traveled to China from Southampton sailing from there in one of
the greatest and largest ships to other countries and continents sites in
the geography book I learned from in elementary school   ignorant

people have taken to dwelling in my apartment I still have the first ball-point pen I ever had, even though it is rather beaten up. To me it is the symbol of a certain time, a better delegate for that era than many other larger and more instrumental objects.

Tómas Jónsson.

On Stationery up to the Present Time

I've been asked to say a few words here about the development of writing materials in the city's offices. I'm going to start this essay by briefly tracing the history of man's need for stationery.

a) connecting people

a) as tools for understanding

b) intermediaries

third composition book

It's great fun roving about and observing people, boats, and houses. Beyond seeing things in their own light, I see myself, my reactions in light of such things.

But I resemble the poet Jónas Hallgrímsson in one way: I sit still. Thanks be to the fact that I sit still, ever in one place (a bedside), and yet I travel constantly.

June 24, 1967
I must beg forgiveness from my conscience. All night she avenged herself on me with the most terrible dreams.

IV composition book

I see myself in my nation's streams,
she turns away and does not want
to see her image in me. I am feeble.

I am freshly nourished on oxygen and I managed to go urinate and defecate unaided without needing Anna's assistance to wipe myself that day which never reaches evening is not today I have resolved to live all of it the time is now half-five outside the weather is bright and ten degrees though August passes swiftly iceland is some kind of Hawaii

8-9-1967.

I sleep calmest and best when the weather is poor. I almost never use any of the protective weather gear that is in the cellar. Having it would be considered an advantage if I were fearful of the weather but I am very much the opposite, and consider this "advantage" to be an utter disadvantage in my tiny apartment. Ideally I would have some weather protection for when it is dry and windy and loose grit blows. The streets in this neighborhood are unpaved, at an early stage of their design, and there are foreign tourists. They got lost here, either drunk or insane, you would think the Town Organizing Committee had built some hocus-pocus, moving stone shacks into new streets (which in fact are old streets) or making construction rules in order to raise old houses instead of new ones. That is not so. The council, to which I have given my vote, seems to have totally forgotten this street, my "Tómasfield." I have always cast my vote according to this rule: If the majority cannot get things done, neither can the minority. I am in what's known as the first category of voters. In the second category are those who want to elect a minority and are activists and speak outside polling stations, from a distance, based on their belief, but under the cover of the polling stations their electoral convictions overcome them, and they cannot countenance this disastrous X-ing, their hands refusing to carry out the desired order which runs so contrary to the great trust the majority shows by kindly marking their cross. The second category chooses as the first category does and stabs their ballot into the box with a clear conscience: you *were* right to trust me; I will not betray those who put their faith in me. Generally, on election day this is labeled as undecided voting. On the other hand, the third category aims to rule in place of the first category, but chokes amid its party's slush. In the rain, these relatively narrow alleyways between the houses become almost impassable due to mud and puddles. Only rats, pigeons, and cats can cross these urban marshes, and folk like me in galoshes. You could call Reykjavík the Venice of the Arctic. That name better fits the city than her real name, Smoky Bay: smoke is hardly ever seen here except from factories and refuse dumps that emit the vapors of innumerable citizens; here the air is so limpid, so cold, that farts hang behind their owners, white plumes drifting into the cold winter day. All the loveliest animals teem here: people throw trash in bins, the rats eat so, so much trash, the cats swallow the rats, the pigeons peck at the cat shit and the children feast on their dove eggs under the steps. As the saying goes, you can observe the cycle in all its nakedness, its original image, from the window of a house. I wade daily in my overshoes across marsh canals. On the way to work I cross ten open canals going over a Ponte di Rialto of Frónkex cookie boxes. Pieces of timber sail like gondolas along the water of the canals. The rain pools into deep mud and slush; I take a rag with me to work, and stop on the steps to my office to wipe the dirt from my leather shoe covers.

do you remember the story of the rich shoe cover salesman, the time a fire broke out in the store and how his errand boy shot up to the fifteenth floor to where the shoe storage was in order to throw the stock down to the street to the salesman and risked his life for the company he wore pairs of shoe covers and another pair over each pair until he had the whole stock on his feet and to save them and himself in the face of the fiery tongues licking the window and igniting the paper bags he threw himself off the edge of the roof but because the material on the shoe covers was unbelievably elastic and the salesman only stocked first-rate brands the errand boy was hurled ever higher in the air nowadays he reconnects with the earth only every fifteen years and has gone grizzled gray do you remember this story about overshoes meant for toddlers and cats now I have told you it Títa you understand why you lift your head mewing into the sky just like everyone else you are waiting for some unbelievable miracle from above waiting for an errand boy in overshoes constantly on the alert remaining vigilant   tomorrow he will come down to earth for the last time   you long to become something more than what you are for example a bootied cat amid barefoot cats   and on the next arc the infamous over-shoed errand boy will jump past the sky's threshold helped by angels to whom he has promised shoe covers remember this story Títa   do not miss him tomorrow, but if he passes you, you can always live in hope the way the majority does that you will get to be a puss in boots with god   with hahahaha   yesterday it snowed. This morning, snow also. Dark over everything; storm winds and getting blown away. The window creaks though it is carefully latched on both hooks and the iron grate is shut. It is good to hunker indoors during rough weather. You feel a special ease and sense of security inside the walls of a house thinking about small birds. You fervidly wish for the weather to crash into the coming work day, thinking of your continual promised wish the electricity will fail (wretched men hanging from poles, creatures fixing the lines in dogweather) and the morning wakes you with a phone call. What are you saying—totally without power—the whole city. I just hope it's nothing serious. Now you are free to think of the right moment opening up: poor them on their poles and poor sailors at sea and poor pilots in Loftleiðir planes and poor farmers in turf huts and birds shelterless in this bluster. You throw a handful of cereal out into the snow for small birds. In such weather conditions, in the period between ten-thirty and eleven-thirty, before the struggle with the oil-fueled primus stoves begins, it's reckoned the population increases by 2.3%. Although the icy streets are treacherous I stagger along them with a loaded scrotum. I come across Björn opposite the entrance to the watchman's apartment. He is beating ice from a rope mat and driving nails into the filter holes on the drainpipe, which the mat normally covers and which has become blocked. Totally unnecessary for you to hustle out here, he says. Everything is dark as coal. Electricity has reached us, I say; it is too difficult to earn Björn's respect, he only respects himself. Unfortunately, it's rare for a power outage to last a full day, rare for offices to close because of a polio epidemic, dysentery, or vaccines. No dangerous epidemic infests this town except numbness. And it is bad to meet Björn alone. For some reason I think he must been gathering information on me, saving it up for a future time. He must have been a bystander somewhere when Lóa was raped. The door of the watchman's apartment is almost next to the store. All this may be my devilish imagination.

In any case, I managed to wake rested and refreshed after a deep sleep as the clock rang Sunday in. I was in no hurry to dress. I needed to wake, yawn, put in my teeth, release the piss from my penis, lie back under the covers, drink from my half-thermos, and lie still on my back, my hands at my sides on top of the comforter, which swells with air and feathers, take out my teeth, doze for five minutes, wake for another five, turn again to sleep, and wake in five minute intervals. I manage at least ten hours of sleep. The flesh prefers dormancy once it has begun to pale and die. After this night I took to springing up from a sound sleep in the middle of the night, frightened and scared. When a set rule has been once interrupted by exception, the exception stops becoming the rule. In such cases, a person is indeed liable to resort to great violence. By pure coincidence I learned from Bjössa that Lóa washes the floors early Sunday mornings while the city sleeps off the drunkenness from its body when no one is watching. I drew the clock under the covers. I scrutinized the dial. Four. I looked out the window. It had rained in the night. By nature I am very much an evening sleeper, an evening wolf. Such a nature must become rarer with each passing year in this nation. People shorten their days and lengthen their nights. Sleeping is not respected except for where there are sick people or the decrepit or those about to die. Before you die, you must be properly asleep. Preferable to die in your sleep. Hospitals usually turn off the lights at ten o'clock at night. I need my sleep dearly. But I would rather die than be frozen inside a retirement home. Once you get to my age, an orderly lifestyle is the surest defense against the force which fills graves. A long time ago I had to give up coffee with dinner. That was a great struggle. Almost impossible. Coffee in the evening, sitting in the comfort and privacy of a divan corner with the chair's seat clamped between my knees, the thermos within reach on the ground, morsels of letters on the back of the chair and the cup steady in the seat's depression, alone in your company, my puss, that was my life's true purpose, my diversion. I heard Katrín screaming in the corridor: I'm coming for your life next. And the kids screaming at her: I'll kill you you fucking snake, if you don't shut up. I only go out at night if I want to. Sveinn was at home, that rare event, and I heard him mewl from inside the bedroom: Use common decency and don't hit or lose your temper. I rose slowly to my feet, belched from the coffee and plucked the fuses from the board. Everything fell completely silent. I took out my teeth, exercised my jaw, undressed, and fell asleep. But you remember nothing of this. Feline instinct has little memory. Words spoken to cats in confidence are not used later in retaliation. The absence of coffee in the evenings. Life became empty and my environment impoverished in quality. So it ends. There comes a time you have to give up evening coffee and everything of quality in the world. I[1] had the hint of a suspicion, when I got up having slept badly, that I would wake up with a bad taste in my mouth following this night's tribulations, tired and bored and abused by evil dreams. I did everything as quietly as possible, with the utmost care. In the dark I plucked off my clothes. I would never dress in the dark, of course. Clothes put on that way are ill fitting. I'd go to seed before I let darkness clothe me. I justify my cowardice by saying in my head: I am sufficiently screened from the streetlights. Which of course is not true. Cowardice makes any act truthful. In fact, a tiny amount of light gropes its way past the ends of the curtains and through the slit in the middle. It is not particularly helpful given my weak sight. I hold to a constant rule: never get dressed before going to the bathroom and washing the sleep from my face. The rabble who rent from me sleep soundly at that time, having exhausted themselves first with quarrels and squabbles and then within their lairs, the couple engaging in an eternal wrangle with each other, and after wrestling heading to sleep. The corridor is deserted in the early morning. Anyone who rents past my little partition is awake at night and sleeps during the day. Early in the morning I am alone and proceed through along the hallway with my grooming tools. I can safely change out of my underwear. I can safely nose about in the refrigerator and cupboards to examine the negligence and junk inside. No one can know me in my sleep (except my dreams). I do not need to get to work until half past eight. Until that time, when it is time to prepare for my departure, I potter about in my room, tidying up around me. I am washed and brushed. I have cleaned the sleep from my face, my scrotum, and my hands with a washcloth. I brush the bad taste of sleep from my mouth with a toothbrush. I blow the sleep from my nose with a tissue. I wipe sleep from my eyes by closing them, rolling them five times in the sun's direction then counterclockwise the same number of times. I never feel comfortable until I have scraped off my stubble. The day begins as soon as the night's clamminess has left my flesh, the mind ready to start

---

1. Sic. T. J.

earning money. Dressed, I drink my morning coffee, of which I will also be robbed before long. Once in a retirement home, you get dishwater mix instead. I am prepared for the worst. I face it with the calm and tranquility of my early days. O yes. Inside the room I make my bed. A made bed makes the evening more manageable. I have opted for neatness. Difficult for one person to keep everything in order, unless he is by nature fastidious. I keep some hand soap on the radiator so that the air in the room is fragrant. It later gets used up in the laundry. It hardens when heated, and it is thrifty; it gives off a pleasant fragrance. On the other hand, the couple's hand-soap is gobbled away night and day in a waterlogged soap dish on the bathroom sink. In my room, things sit in their given places. Complete anarchy reigns in the other parts of the apartment. The kids buzz around their parents' heads, and objects buzz around the heads of both the kids and the parents. Blind, I could go to my closet, stretch out my hand, touch the key, turn it into a semicircle in the lock, open the door, and reach for the green pencil in a jacket's breast pocket; I could do other tricks like this. Orderliness has come in handy now that I am blind and decrepit. I leave the house as soon as my internal organizing and planning voice says: Tómas, everything is in its ideal place within your room. Even my thoughts sit in an organized series within my cerebral cortex.

My thought itinerary.
6:30: I wake up; I realize that I'm alive, I need to wash; I'm bursting to urinate; then shave, groom.
7: I start to clean up around me; subdivisions of thought: dust, chamber pot, tidying, etc.
7.30: Morning drink; subdivisions of thought: I am lucky there is bread in the oven; chew thoroughly; clean your teeth using your tongue, etc.
8: thoughts regarding getting myself to work.
8:30: pleased that I'm seated in my chair and starting to make money.
8:30 to 4:30: My money intake increases by the minute; withdrawal:

young Miss Gerður, her fingers, thighs, breasts, buttocks.
4:30 and after: my daily earnings today have reached the same as
yesterday.

10:30: I have added one day to the days of my life and shortened it
by one day, too; I now lack this or that many days filling the week
as age and remuneration touch; various thoughts about my bedtime,
fold trousers, arrange shoes, check whether I have set the chamber pot
exactly in place under the bed, the window, lock the door, turn the
key so that it is not possible to drill it out with another key from the
outside, etc.
11: and after: freedom of thought.
(I cannot control my thoughts and dreams during sleep.)

More because of my training than the faint glimmers of light, I get
safely and soundly into my shirt. I even did it up right. The best advice I
know for buttoning a shirt correctly in the dark it is to take the bottom
or top button first then move it over to the bottom or top buttonhole.
If you follow in order carefully then the buttons all ought to find their
way into the right buttonholes. I put on my socks and shoes. I was able
to perform this all with total accuracy in the dark. I have a pair of shoes
I reserve for Sunday use. Somehow, I cannot use my weekend shoes
as Sunday shoes, which wear better than the shoes adults use only on
weekends. In 1941, I took pains to use the word "boots," though I never
said shoe-boots, and then I started using the word "shoes." But somehow
I feel now that "Sunday shoes" as a phrase belongs to children: the shoes
of adolescents. Well. Saturday night I put my weekend shoes on the
floor in front of the divan, so that the polished toes point toward the
wardrobe, the heels beside the bed. On Sunday morning I tuck my feet
in the right shoes, wearing clean socks, of course. I hurry into my socks
without touching my bare feet to the ice-cold floor.
I sit there on the edge of the bed. I wait for them to leave. While I sit
still in the dark no memories come to mind. This may seem strange
and alien: inside I was empty.   I struck my shoulder   I discovered

I had a body the body is dressed on its exterior in skin under the skin there is flesh on the skin there is hair   I touch my body   I have a body   inside it: bones and entrails   But I could find no memories inside the body. I had never thought that my travels were entrusted with memories. I was told that as age increases and the flesh softens, drowsy memories awaken in the mind. That is not my experience.   for me, nostalgia awakens in the flesh   I do not know if this is my nature or a characteristic that I have acquired on the job. Anyway, I sit there void of memory, like a banker accused of embezzlement or fraud   their memories at some point eat the ice   For example, our CEO lost his memory after twenty million got lost somehow in the course of business and could not be found anywhere though people searched with beaming floodlights. Who is up to that awful responsibility of passing judgment on all the suggestions and speculations where an amnesiac is involved, asked young Miss Gerður. Would it not be more fitting to send him to a sick house and treat him with the appropriate remedies, rather than locking him away, forgotten, in some prison; as with similar conditions, he needs to be in that sort of place: if the director has committed a crime then the offense is no different from any other disease or disorder that needs to be cured through care and the continued confidence of his subordinates. So Tryggvi returned to his leather chair after a sabbatical year abroad and two weeks of rest at home while he got used to the change in climate (he had been sent to Switzerland, since it was customary to send amnesiac CEOs there and rejuvenate their blood. This transfusion was done in three phases, said Miss Gerður: 30% taken each time, and after the operation only 10% of their cerebral blood remains. But ten percent is probably sufficient to conceal the lost twenty million króna. And I do declare that whatever is innate in a man will not change, not in Switzerland and not here in iceland either . . .). What cured Tryggvi the most was being put back into his former employment, fully guaranteed, said Sigurður; the blood transfusion didn't do him any good: if you ran into him out and about this past fortnight, you'd find him always out wandering. No, friend, protested Miss Gerður, science is the twentieth century's only miracle. With new blood comes a new and unprecedented memory: the memory of the one who gave blood and of his spiritual need; the CEO in question remembers his womb-self and the future to come, so only natural they go crazy, believing themselves something they're not, these CEOs with the fraudnesia disease. Afterward, they become a man with the blood of twenty men in their veins, which is no easy task. After the procedure, they *are* and they become these unknown men, with their powers, of course, which can be in conflict; what's more, there's no blue blood in them at all.

I've never been forced to eat the ice to survive, as the saying goes. No chance, then, that I'll be able to commission a ghostwriter to write a bestseller in my name in time for the christmas market—I will have to write it myself—the way those others did, Schiaparelli the fashion queen, Rockefeller, and old Kalli, the lumpfish king. These are the labors of rich people in this country who do nothing for the arts, when they plead their existence, the publishers and the royalties there on the table to support writers, who do not need to focus on anything but spelling. Why are these wretches complaining, these ghost writers who are up to their knees in middling fish- and ship-owning men, bankers and notorious drunks? Do not complain about your brothers in America, ghostwriters. There's work enough to go around, no fear, if you're someone who knows how to write poetic phrases and rich imagery:

> *The storm was dying in the intense suction of the ocean, as fog hunkered over the surface, broad and vast, bright in the soothing evening calm, as if everything was covered with an oily film.*
>
> *It was early morning. Far and wide along the shore, breakers had washed loose kelp up onto the sand; it lay in huge tassels on the tide line. At the shore's very edge stood five children, stirring long sticks through the tufts of kelp, looking for lumpfish.*
>
> *The old man sat on a large basalt boulder up on the ridge, his huge, callus-covered fisherman's hands passive on his large knees. He*

had convinced himself. His face was marked with salt runes, with life's wisdom. Get up, whispered the springs, peeling off the lips of a generous man, you're calm now, satisfied, you great cannibal.

His attention was suddenly grabbed by the children crying out; they had found a rotting lumpfish. The old man got up, his withered limbs stiff, and inched his way slowly down the sharp rocks of the seaside cliff. In the past, he'd strolled along easily, young and adventurous when at sea and in foreign taverns with their drinking and the noise, among great men who took on all the challenges the world threw at them: as did he, Kalli, the lumpfish king.

Later the story continues with the writer in vigorous form, so when the reader puts the book away he is well satisfied, sitting in his chair after christmas dinner. The book is well worth its price, with its large doses of supple writing and exciting plot:

20% places and the names of people; 2% trials, peril at sea, and amazing rescues; 19% scenic descriptions scattered throughout the book's chapters; 3% poetic sex, which runs together with the poetry of the scenic descriptions (in bestsellers it's traditional to save sex for near the end of each chapter, so that the reader feels his brain has been mentally masturbated prior to reading the next section the next night. What's literature but mental masturbation for the emotions?); 7% reflections and conversations with intelligent animals the character has acquired as friends; 11% food and conditions on ships (comparisons of past and present); 15% forebodings and dreams (dream women, Kalli is far too healthy to get dream pussy at sea); 7% Kalli the lumpfish king himself, the creation of this character who is, of course, "driven by powerful contrasts" as the academics term it. A "lively final surge and conflict at the culmination." This is important stuff.

I, on the other hand, tortured myself on my bed. Self-torture is a healthy practice; through it, each and every one of us benefits, tormentor, slave and executioner.

I tremble if I laugh; I tremble if I cry; I tremble if I'm cold; I tremble if I'm hot; I tremble if I'm happy, terrified that she (joy) will disappear;

I tremble if I am terrified by lust. Conclusion: trembling is my natural reaction.

Put mildly, dreams are an abomination to me. I cannot feel sorry for myself. I know people who hang about at the kitchen table at night, pulling memories from the past and mewling and smacking their lips over past nights, infecting each other with highfalutin words and the plagues of memory, all bundled up in questions about the afterlife and stacking up problems for themselves about their burial: should it take place inconspicuously; should I get myself cremated; should I have myself buried; do I want a headstone; do I want a cross; do I want nothing at all; do I just want wood; do I want marigolds and stepmothers; would it be good to drown at sea; would it hurt to burn in flames; is it awful to suffocate; is it best to die of a heart attack in your sleep? These are people's real-life problems. But as I have said many times, my past, Tómas Jónsson's past, is as much hidden from me as is my future. I have no ill will in my conscience; everyone can be calm toward me. People's dreams represent pure agony to me. I want realism. I insist that people must think systematically, the way I do. To me, the old Snow White is much better than the new Snow White, the old Pinocchio more entertaining than the new Pinocchio, the descriptions fuller in the old Robin Hood than the new version. None of this new stuff matters to me. In my last will and testament, I wrote: I want a sloppily made, wave-washed stone on my grave; no flowers; a black coffin. And absolutely no graveside ceremony or hymns. And if someone wants to create a memorial fund, just give the money to any old charity.

why should I cause myself an inconvenience with contempt for the new-born or the unborn (who are in all likelihood going to get born)   both during World War II and after I often lay awake joyful at having been born in a country without military service glad to have been born at a time when the din of weapons was not customary amid a nation where people's sense of honor was so paltry that they did not defend themselves except perhaps when offended by a cousin or by never speaking to a sister the big nations should learn from us our delegates should tell them that at conferences and what would have become of me in the sagas   hunched & hands useless   I imagine mothers carrying their children outside the walls in the sun like badly repaired ceramics and struggling to buckle onto them wire arms and wire feet to take them to school   crying or with hairy faces like apes like the paupers in Turkey who ate edible seeds containing synthetic chemicals for controlling pests and Miss Gerður read to us about it from the newspapers terrified about the irresponsible mothers; if women were unexpectedly to start giving birth to cats instead of children like in a fairy tale that would not happen surprise anyone this adventurous century has made us immune to life's adventures could I hate something which was too much for me could I hate the mountains or the house blocking my view or the ocean isolating me

I am completely bound to the passing moment. I am the passing moment. I am time itself. I have no remarkable experiences. I have no spare moments from the past.

it seems that earlier in this work I regarded the ballpoint pen to be crucial, the end point of writing technology, an outdated opinion I can see through my typewriter and electric typewriter   and I am reluctant to admit that here in my small apartment that is different from all other apartments and the isolation of the ocean opinions become unique and much longer-lived than the thoughts they grow from   over time the electric typewriter will probably be wired up to people's brains   I must include these reflections in my sketch of thoughts about stationery, past and present   probably my thinking is less at risk of decaying probably I am unable to think in harmony straight for more than two, three minutes   I have grown so dulled   I was I was have reached this place I become   I who once put together seven columns of mathematical examples in my mind could compete with a calculator read Petrarch

at night could disrupt my thinking when the midday coffee caused me
to dream eccentric dreams and still connect my thought up again to
previous thoughts when I woke my Títa

    now I say cat and think about the unrelated topic of the blind men
in Brueghel's painting who in my mind are joined together by slender-
bellied guide dogs rather than sticks and I count up to a hundred and
two then I think about blind cows and count backward to one and end
the sentence as if I had always intended it   the cat lies in Tómas's bed
and see the experiment has succeeded tolerably my confidence restored
I passed the Stanford-Binet got a certificate in the ability to continue
where I left off

Sadness crept over me on the bed. Age, castration, and grief seized
me.   My god I was like a man out amid the lava powerless as when
rain falls and grass seed   I thought in my youth perfection was on the
way. Nothing will ever be accomplished, except what is inorganic and
dead: Death itself. Maybe I'm too fat to be able to remember anything
for more than a moment. The outer surface of my body is too far away
from my soul. Aristotle probably came to this same conclusion after he
grew older and fatter. My age keeps the century company, then the companionship breaks off. We diminish to the same degree as we expanded.
No one came to the president asking for vessels and equipment to explore
unknown western continents. He begged for the import of the electron
microscope. He looked into the microscope, where everything is terribly
large, multipart, and endless. Scientists are tasked with deriving a vaccine
from stupidity cells and vaccinating against knowledge that portion of
humanity which is of no benefit. Science covers all potential targets.
Maybe at Yale University in the United States they will succeed at eking
the wisdom material from Einstein's brain (his brain is kept deep-frozen
in the hope they will succeed; it is merely a matter of time) and inject it
into the brain of an unborn child; that would be a major milestone, for
a fetus to have Einstein's knowledge. The X-portion of the human race
that is not needed to develop or produce would be allowed to live in the

fields in perfect idyllic leisure, but the Y-portion would spend their lives in a laboratory, working to perfect the playground for the X-portion. A vaccine solution using knowledge hormones would give each Y-child a splendid advantage in reaching the multi-part desire Icelanders have to enter into the living life of Perfected People. (Miss Gerður said the Russians had managed to steal a piece of Einstein's brain and planned to get ahead of the Americans in producing a vaccine. DDR is a kind of DDT in German expansionism.) I wouldn't have minded antibiotics along with the multiplication table when I was three, Sigurður said. One could adopt this evolutionary course: the firstborn inherits the father's intelligence at his death—as he did in ancient times, taking ownership and custody of the family—and the world would quickly be transformed, said Ólaf. They smiled indulgently at Miss Gerður. Otherwise I don't see potential for breakthrough, says Ólaf. But I am sure: science will, as times move forward, nullify the smug irony of people like Ólaf and Sigurður. I am in favor of vaccine production being in private hands to allow competition for price and quality. Before my death arrives, they will have discovered eternity. Until that time, my only job is to survive. For what. Dear friend:

> *Life is worth more than all the wealth which is said to have been amassed during the many-storied past of the city of Ilion, so long as peace lasted, up until the sons of Achaia came there; it is worth more than all the treasures housed in the stone house of the bow-carrying god Phoebus Apollo on the dread rock Pytho. Oxen and fat sheep can be stolen, tripeds and bay horses may be taken, but a man's soul man does not return, nor gets handed back, once she has become a traded commodity.*

Was this apartment no longer my unambiguous property. Was I not master and lord. Why did I sit idle and let muttering barbarians hold me prisoner like a criminal conscience. I was captivated by the barbarians' mysterious muttering. I sat gravely still, a fossil on the bed

stand and be like stone

yet do harm to no one

and the muttering of the barbarians flowed over me. I was like Jónas, Guðrún's current husband in Hvolsvöllur:

> *Once upon a time, a rich farmer lived in the remote countryside. The farmer was unmarried and worked alone, ruddy-cheeked, of good physical health, short height, chubby, huge-lipped with red gums that grew over his teeth; blood constantly oozed from them. He was forty years old when he began to resent his celibacy. Reading poetry one evening raised in him nearly intolerable thoughts about womanly flesh. He engaged a housekeeper, Lýkafrón[1] by name: a doughy and fulsome young spinster from the nearest town, quiet, sweet-mouthed, mannerly, a worker. The woman took to all the farm chores well, though enjoyed the company of horses or being with the cows in the cowshed most of all. She refused to sleep in the farm, saying that her position was unfitting for a straw mattress and a bed, so she nested in the vacant bull stall. The farmer often poked into the circumstances and way of life of the woman in the cowshed. In the mornings, before he tended the sheep, the farmer snuck to the cowshed door and entered, going inside on several occasions without being found out. But early one Saturday morning, he stood by the cowshed door and heard verses being recited. Lýkafrón sang:*
> > *cows all alone merrily gnawed*
> > *tooth to belly ferrying grass*
> > *udders swinging as they chewed*
> > *in Jónas's well-tended pasture*
>
> *He cautiously opened the door and saw the woman standing behind a cow and washing her hair under its stream. Her locks were thick*

---

1. Lýkafrón is a man's name, and perhaps the author is suggesting that the farmer's housekeeper was a man under a spell, which explains her reluctance toward the farmer and her interest in manly farm work and how she was eager for her chastity's lock to be shattered, which would shuck the spell from her, but the author fails in his effort to make this evident in the story, whether from lack of ability of knowledge –T. J.

*and long and down to her waist. While Lýkafrón plaited her hair she
sang to the cows, a song known in Hvolsvöllur:*
 the cow is proud of its station
 pride sits in its heart
 never sick in herself[1]
 seen in my animals
*The farmer remained in the doorway no longer, song bursting from
his lips. Jónas:*
 my queen from dim lands
 do you drink in a cow's land
Lýkafrón answered in a duet:
 you have regarded my habits
 and I promise to marry you
*The farmer grasps the cowshed shovel and walks to the middle of the
stage:*
 Here you see a wretched rafter
Lýkafrón, playful, sweet-mouthed, bashful:
 Inapt confusion in the bull stall
The farmer, rejoicing:
 She gives me her chastity
*She (mimes; the cows light cigarettes [Verfremdungseffekt]; a banner
for emphasis) overwhelmed with emotion (a mask):*
 such breaking is life's course
*They embrace. And grateful for country life, they decide to wait until
their passion will be lawful.*
 Tómas Jónsson. A draft for the icelandic Opera.

---

1. The alliteration of the cows here is wrong:
 never sick in herself
All this rather flat writing indicates little knowledge of the work of icelandic
farmers in the countryside. Why would a farmer plan to loiter by the cowshed
door instead of looking after the sheep? –T. J.

All this happened in summertime (as you'll have noticed, the bull stall in the cowshed was vacant; the bull was of course out in its enclosure)[1] and every evening when the farmer returned home soaked to the crotch, having been haying in Þýfðastykk, Lýkafrón rolled up her sweater sleeves, knelt silently, and rinsed the farmer's socks with water from the pitcher. He sat over her the while, on the only chair in the house and peeled his calluses, which had become waterlogged and softened from exposure; he removed them from his heels and soles with the edge of the bread knife. The whole time he secretly made encouraging hand gestures for Lýkafrón's attention. Her arms were bright and untouched by sun or human hands.

exposed arms
but from there
all air and fluid, he thought, and immediately decided to be done mowing meadows or, in the autumn, to free her from the cowshed and bind her with lifelong icelandic promise- and faith-bonds. He felt most strongly that their interests and nature were of the same family, stemming from country roots and a love of the earth; they were both introverted and reticent. In the evenings they talked quietly about animal herding, wage exploitation, and "some" who put on airs with mowing machines, which tore up and wounded the grassroots. Before they asked god, in the name of Jesus, to give each other a restful night, the farmer said he intended to take on a winter laborer, a man who would free her from her more arduous outdoor work. After this, he wrote his diary, noticing that very day had been thirty years since he had first mowed Þýfðastykk.

Until this day, Þýfðastykk Day, Lýkafrón had never shown signs of any needs other than to demonstrate that her housekeeping was worthy of care and honor, but when he made his proposal of marriage, she welcomed the offer, and they were married in the Lutheran faith

---

1. What is this aforementioned enclosure doing here? I'm asking. Do icelandic farmers typically herd cattle in the summer? –T. J.

and vaccinated the first Sunday after the third lambing round-up, in a small rural church.

Rev. Páll from Staðastaður married them, expounding Titus's letter I: 10-13: "For there are many insubordinate, both idle talkers and deceivers, especially those of the circumcision, whose mouths must be stopped, who subvert whole households, teaching things which they ought not, for the sake of dishonest gain. One of them, a prophet of their own, said, 'Cretans are always liars, evil beasts, lazy gluttons.'" Rev. Páll had left them a winter laborer, and with these words he aimed to warn them. On the wedding night the farmer looked at his new stock, who was cheap to manage and whom he had gained without giving up any possessions (it would suffice to send Reverend Páll, for the next three years, the meat from lambs three-winters-old as a payment for the service performed), while she undressed and climbed into bed, eager to break the spell. The farmer had protested against Lýkafrón still sleeping in the bull stall, saying she could sleep in her knit cloak; it would be cold in this attic, and anyway, he himself always slept naked; knitted chafed tore at him in his sleep. He slept, however, with a rust brown sheepskin on his abdomen in order to soak up his pus. Lýkafrón cracked her fingers at such kindness and fell asleep. The farmer had a habit of reading poetry in bed at night before he prayed to god to set a wall of powerful angels over them, a defense against the devil's devices. He held to this faith. Lýkafrón was tired after the wedding preparation that had been added to her daily work. The excessive amount of food she had consumed during the day had given her wind, and when the farmer, after reading his poetry, made to treat her fittingly, to kiss her and reach out for her corner of the sheepskin, she snorted and sneezed due to the snuff which fell into her nose during the kiss; then she scampered over to the wall and turned her back onto him. He bit her then gently on the ear, the rural custom, and said:

Well, that's that, my lamb ewe.

The night passed like many other nights. They slept, woke, dressed, and yawned, content in the autumn dark.

Did you dream last night, my lamb? he asked every morning. And Lýkafrón said, content and satisfied with their fate, with waking to new work:

I dreamed that I slept like a stone, still in the bull stall.

The farmer found nothing wrong with this answer; he felt it demonstrated an unusual resourcefulness and spousal loyalty.

The winter laborer arrived on time. He would need a place to bed down, but it transpired Rev. Páll had omitted to send a bedroll with him, sending instead a hoof pick and five brass buttons. The merchant came at night; he was given skýr, and the farmer had an additional bowl with him. At once things flowed well between the farmer and the merchant, and the newcomer taught him to rub the udder fat on his lips, which were red and bleeding and cracked when he laughed, as farmers often do. When it was high time, the lack of beds was quickly addressed; there was no desire to drive the man out into the bull stall his very first night. All this was done with Lýkafrón's ready approval; she was not fazed by having all three of them in one lair.

At home, she said, we slept top-to-tail, the four brothers side by side, three sisters foot to foot. Everything worked out somehow, and we children had fun pinching each other's noses with our toes.

The farmer read his poems and prayed carefully and set his preparations on the nightstand, which was small and had a mail drawer; it had been inherited from the merchant at Bakka. But there was little in the way of sleep. Lýkafrón rowed up and down, her head collided with the others up by the headboard, and she was constantly stretching out her neck and peeking questioningly over the comforter at the foot end, where the winter laborer snored. The bed was one great throng, the continual kicking of feet, stifling heat under the covers. The farmer tried to halt Lýkafrón's movements by setting his

*arm across her stomach, but at the weight of the arm on her stomach
she flared up and only just about managed to sneak the chamber
pot from under the bed before she vomited. The farmer got up and
fetched her water, which she drank, groaning. During this upheaval
the winter laborer, who seemingly slept the sleep of winter, lying with
his head on a large pillow, sat halfway up in bed and mumbled. For
the rest of the night the woman's husband slept with a box, so if her
nausea returned, it was less of a distance to the pot, and yet he could
not sleep, though he was free from being disturbed by her. The farmer
moved up against the partition wall . . . Lýkafrón sighed until morning, but the farmer did not sleep; all night he had to ward his big
toe away from the winter laborer, who was trying to use it to scratch
his groin. The toe was large with uncut nails. Finally, the farmer
thought to grab the man's clothes and yank them up, tight between
his ass cheeks; the man smiled in his sleep. They didn't see any signs
of his restlessness in the morning, and none of them mentioned the
night's disturbance.*

*The winter laborer endured even as the workload grew; he was
brisk and fulfilled his obligation; and Lýkafrón seemed to flourish
and prosper. Her earlobes took on a golden redness; the farmer enjoyed
biting them in the evening, after she had turned her back to him,
and he said:*

Your ears are glowing, my ewelambeweylamby
And there we sat.

no this end is impossible the story abandons sense unfathomable its
characters all mixed up it is all over the place the author cannot deal
with the material or the style lacks concentration but maybe he will do
better next time be able to write something striking and memorable with
a satisfying ending for what is a poet other than a poetic stallion on a
racing track

yes, yes my next story will be a variation on Chekov the transitory
will take precedence a polemic on national affairs an outspoken satire

about citizens a story of a man who hid under his wife's bed every time her lover came to visit   I could tell a story about a colonial merchant who married a Danish woman and got his uncle to interpret for them the merchant did not know a single word of Danish but when they started kissing and more he said, I'll take over, but was not able to and so the uncle was the one who impregnated her for the merchant and nothing that truly mattered in the household was ever discussed without & Co   the nature of the family came into the picture by solely accumulating initial capital and collecting dividends without completing work   as a result the wholesaler dissolved and every shareholder immediately demanded reimbursement for the face value of their shares and a public scandal ensued with no end in sight until the merchant fled his wife and uncle, locked himself in a tower room where he shot himself with a sheep rifle that was not powerful enough so the shot sat there trapped in the merchant's brain without killing him his tongue and speech were mostly paralyzed so he only mewled or emitted similar sounds from the window he ended up emotionally unsound but shortly after a dog bit the Danish woman giving her rabies causing her to bark in the face of adversity and in this strange fashion they reconnected with one other after the crisis, neither of sound mind, he mewling inside the tower room, she barking at him through the keyhole, both arguing like cats and dogs until by and by their household fell to pieces the company went to seed in the region selling no textiles exactly the way Miss Gerður told me this story I remember it often having gone to this store not to buy things but to hear the fuss up the ladder and I would listen for the sounds not human beings running hard up and down the stairs but animal sounds the whole thing clearly audible from the back apartment though out on the street you would think they were both entirely normal two unflappable humans she prim and precise with a genuine silver fox fur on top of a gray close-fitting tunic and well-polished shoes with silver buckles across the tongue and he in a striped vest with a thick gold chain always wearing leather shoes that were not even dusty a far cry from a tragedy seeing the couple this way she even had a dog on a leash though slanderers said she had it to conceal the times she suddenly barked right in the middle of the street so people would think the dog had growled, one thing is for sure keeping dogs in town was prohibited but they had been exempted and people can be repugnant in their judgments about others nothing to do about it everyone considering them in the worst way especially where merchants are involved but this much is certain I saw her barking right in the middle of Austurstræti and she kicked the dog in the ass so it immediately began to bark and rage but when the three got distracted they all barked in a torrent and ended up in chaos and I could say that I felt pity for the couple she who came from overseas to have us louts on Austurstræti staring at her on these days of fine weather with the street full of people but they were hurried into the pharmacy and given injections and I think that they came out again superhuman and went about her day as if nothing had taken place yes this is a great icelandic tragedy

The hedonist bacteria had a good day in my flesh.

I leapt to my feet. I had to yank open the door. I had to talk to them with a commanding expression, authoritative. I must drive this disgrace out of my apartment with carefully chosen, rough words: Get this disgrace away from the apartment. Get out, electric-guitarist and prostitute! Yet I resorted to the same measures as the merchant, when he retreated under the woman's bed, taking more pleasure listening to caresses than embracing a woman himself. Originally, this was done out of kinship, said Miss Gerður. The acquaintance began through business letters. Don't you remember those erotic postcards. Well, the merchant received them. She worked for a Danish firm that produced them; put two and two together. Most romantic of all was that she wrote purely for fun on one card in the factory, on which was a young man smoking a cigar and a woman wearing a white shirt and holding a rose beside the smoke: Den som læser dette billedkort, han er min kærlighedssort; and she had no idea where the card would go, so it was all very exciting. And she did not imagine the postcard would be discovered by a local merchant on the lookout for an unmarried woman; he read it and became enamored. Miss Gerður smiled a distant smile, which seemed to stiffen her lips, what Sigurður calls a pepper smile. Reykjavík talked about nothing else in those days. Happy wishes rained over the fabric shop. As girls cast marigolds on the stairs, everyone was thrilled. Young girls in Reykjavík could be so romantic. I thought such things were imaginary, he said, out in the hall. Who pays attention to this peppery old woman, said Ólaf. When it stops bubbling down there, when their hot spring hardens, all that mud transfers from between their thighs up to their heads. I heard them laughing on the stairs. When I bent down to slip on my overshoes—I held onto a hook for support and lifted a foot to my knee, putting my finger into the overshoes so the heel did not crumple—she came over to me, half-bowing, gave a teasing surprised cry, and said: I'll be damned, well, there's a long woman's hair on your jacket sleeve. A blonde, for sure. She held the hair out to me and I looked at in in the daylight. It was clearly hers. This was not the first time a man had felt a barrette in his pocket, or she'd stolen over and sprayed perfume on the lapels of an overcoat (with no real difficulty: the cloakroom is opposite the employee's restroom). Perhaps a man has no ill intentions, is just wandering about perhaps, in the hallway, all by himself, calm and in his buttoned overcoat when she comes over and says grinning: No, she uses Evening in Paris—bonjour—Tabu, vive la France. And she strides out of the corridor and sits her butt down like a small eruption has taken place in her hot spring. I don't care for this desperate humor of hers, what Sigurður calls peppery play. I don't know what to say, where the weather blows, especially since I can't smell through my ferociously congested nose. At least she doesn't stoop to the last resort and sneak lipstick into my pocket. No, she dare not, not after she slipped toilet paper with a lipstick kiss into Sigurður's pocket, and he responded in kind, snuck a used condom into her jacket. At some point she is slugging around the coat hooks; someone comes past, she says, O!, and dives frantically into the bathroom. Maybe she is just smelling something, some change their pants in there. I envied Sigurður his sauciness. She complained to her supervisor, but since she did not want to mention any names or say what had happened—for reputation's sake, except for that she found it terribly frightening, and a woman cannot touch such a thing, a wet condom in her pocket, she was only looking for her glove—he got away with it (I actually had my part in all of this) and the case collapsed. She was sent home crying in a taxi, her fist closed around something—the condom?—and lay with a fever for two days. Einarína and Friðmey, the oldest girls on the bank floor, visited Miss Gerður immediately that evening. She had gotten an agonizing lumbago. You should just see the finery at her home, they said, all cushions and tapestries and a liquor cabinet that plays a song when the door is opened, and she serves a high-end cognac. She offered us vodka with juice; why don't you visit her, boys? She was lying there quietly with her lumbago for two days, but after that she returned limping to work, sat on an inflated rubber ring with a hot water bottle at her back, and was engulfed in a crying fit just before closing.

I was going to stagger to my feet. I was going to turn out the light. (How did they have any light, given the fuses were in my possession. They had gone behind my back, were putting spare fuses in after I'd fallen asleep at night. They are making fuses from nails instead of filament.) I had counted on either of them seeing a hint of light in my room and scramming without my intervention. I was about to cough a low, suffocating cough, like having congestion firmly seated in my lungs that I would need to hack to get rid of, and I was going to walk out with a bulging mouth full of sputum, to spit in the toilet, but it occurred to me that they knew I spit into my chamber pot. So I decided to drive them off with the alarm clock. Last warning: I whistled heedlessly, I scraped a chair across the floor.

Instead of taking direct action, I lay down in my bedclothes, which swelled around him the farmer pulled himself up in bed enjoying the intimacy and the winter cowshed laborer they used alternately he was absolutely still after animal herding the winter laborer tended the cows before he settled to sleep and threw old hay for the horses and stroked the wind-blown mare and locked the cowshed the farmer woke to a cold foot in his groin the cover had fallen off, and in the moonlight the foot resembled a corpse pale white and dead the moonlight shone on it as though it was dredged up from the earth when Jónas dug trenches in the cemetery and the dogs bore him into the air where merchants sleep he found the foot pawing there in the middle of the floor the next morning and the panicked farmer seized it deathly cold this foot with pins and needles he felt for the other and discovered a burning and sweaty foot under Lýkafrón's knitted cloak

Around this time, the bank opened a new branch. I expected to be appointed to the position of chief accountant. I do not know if I am the bank's oldest employee, but I definitely have the most experience. A totally inexperienced man got the post. His appointment caused me deep personal pain, humiliating me in my colleagues' eyes. I half-hoped someone would go to him and say: Don't get too comfortable in *your* new position. Having poor eyesight is not going to handicap him too long. But no one mentioned the appointment to him. Many of you fine employees are more qualified than I, he announced with all modesty, but his colleagues lacked humility and compassion: I do not understand why Tómas was passed over. A proud, dependable worker had been hurt, he sensed, he could feel the atmosphere around the card file, in the billing department, at the cashier stands, even on the stairs down to the refractory, he ought to step out of the way, not with a fist on the table or politely getting suspended with a month's notice and a golden handshake, and gradually his mysterious silence came to an end; he had a plan to isolate him, Tómas, Tómas, me, to conceal the responsibilities of the job, to entangle Tómas, to move me from one department to another, to bewilder me by replacing the accounting machine which he does not understand, to belittle him with friendly but impatient behavior: no, this is wrong, son, let me take the book, so no one needs to struggle and feel guilty or regret things. It'll all work out, my dear, as naturally as it does in nature, said Tryggvi (a cunning hare). Let this man understand that he, Tómas Jónsson, of such little character, has now become an appendix to the company. I believe that they should have been bold enough to call me to management and say: The Board agreed at their meeting recently to create a new post for you. Or, inversely: The Board was unanimous, we will abolish your job, which you have toiled over, due to efficiency measures; but, as a thank-you for your conscientious work we have decided to pay you thirteen complete months of salary plus a bonus, so you can keep your full pension, as required by law, for one year from the date of this notification. A heavy castrating frustration would weigh on this Tómas's breast, though he agreed to the solution without having to resort to defensive measures, to resign without provocation, or on account of his myopia. I endured at work undaunted. I sat at my table, though hardly using the stationery, when the message came: you are kindly asked to work the card file. So I roved between departments, and I discovered, as they did, that my flexibility had left me. The game was up. Step by step I was the audience to grumbling, corrections, complaints, complaints, innuendos: Tómas is not up to the job. How can a company move forward with antiquated personnel. Until I broke like a mirror. Facing my own termination it was the masses' opinion that I must have prepared myself thoroughly for old age. He cannot have nothing in his savings book. How could anyone have imagined that I had put money under various names during the permanent staff's summer vacation, while there were new people around, mainly students who came and went, temps. I worked the card file and so no suspicion came my way. Colleagues struck up surprised conversations at the lunch table over my sudden termination (I used my coffee time to talk about this). I must have been offered a better job; higher wages. I thoughtfully noticed the attention on their careless visages, the way people always look when someone gets a raise. We won't see you in the refectory, then; you'll go to eat at the best place in Reykjavík, at Hotel Borg. Termination does not mean that, that I'll change dining spots. I hid my new pay grade and my opinion, that I felt I was the best person to fall so spontaneously into the XII pay grade, etc.; by and by I got my revenge on Tryggvi. I didn't give him the pleasure of seeing his plot succeed, to see me mentally devastated. I have never heard Tryggvi mention anything conspiratorial, protested Miss Gerður. I can tell from the gnashing of teeth, I replied. There was a squabble about it, and the clique of my staff who ate with Guðrún, and who had the most powerful (if not the total) role in the bullying, finally managed to make me very thoroughly confused so much so that at one point I contradicted myself, and that was taken to mean I was wrong, even though nothing is easier than entangling the defense of a just cause, if the right techniques are used: you do not build your cause on concrete arguments or provide tangible examples. All arguments must be based on the concrete like a knitted cloak. I do not understand the concrete. I understand that usually the coarsest and most garrulous words are victorious. Jabbering away soothes their evil minds. They came to his defense through counter-arguments and launched an attack on the basis of lies: a person is too involved to understand his own dismissal, especially attacking him with insinuations of hostility. How could Tryggvi still employ you in the bank having heard all this. Tryggvi is so powerful that he can ignore the consequences of his actions, if he feels uncomfortable. But Tryggvi is an outstanding man, that is not in doubt. A very able man. Then the case was discussed in full from my perspective. Power erases any doubts about a complaint. For some reason a man who has worked the same job for thirty years suddenly feels things adversely affect him. Tómas, you have only yourself to blame for your dismissal; you boxed yourself into a corner. The loser is always to blame. I never accept injustice, I would rather lessen my years. They feel there's more gained from the daily humiliation of a person than in getting rid of him. I suspect, having once caught a man in a trap, as the law intends, the hunter alleviates the animal's torment not in the slightest, unless it sits tight in its anguish. Shortly after the midday news, after a half-signal, I was now irrelevant to their maneuvering; "the thing itself" was "a central issue of the case." I did not protest that they "looked at argument and counterargument from all sides" and examined the root cause "objectively without sentimentality," which led to their conclusion that "dismissal is a logical outcome within certain conditions," so "the case was remarkably remarkable for its insignificance." Initially I blamed the spontaneous, reflex nature of my decision, but as time passed and I began to consider, interpret, and make meaning out of the situation, I saw that with human dignity and honor, those rare phenomena, I had saved my colleagues from a loss of honor. And so my termination accrued considerable value. Of course, honesty and integrity are not vital; one might even feel happier without them. A normal person easily gets by engaging three appetites alone: I'm hungry; I'm cold; where can I get food and shelter. Had I listened to Sigurður's advice, I would for sure have been paid pension, but it was a worthless salary if it meant a year of the guilty awareness that others could humiliate me on account of the offer. In a tight spot, a man's hand is weak. Tryggvi was not given to praising his superiors (I struck that weapon from his hands): foremost against him I sent the highly-praised card file infantry, supported by an assault-gun crew from the deposits department, protected by an artillery of accountants. But faced with the complex electrical accounting machine, I shattered like a thermos. Here in my solitude I have demanded my brain reveal what my supervisors said. Everything is beautifully ordered, but where is the corpse. Does it lie dead in remainders beneath the accounting engine. No, the target made himself invisible. The cannons wept desperately, the repeating rifles falling silent from internal frustrations, the infantry spoke about their know-how; even the nursing bloc, Einarína and Friðmey, who visit people on their sickbeds to ascertain whether their patient is really sick (their intelligence is not perfect; I have heard an approved doctor's certificate is now required from the patient), were distracted by the blood transfusion bottles at hand: Tómas, you can count on us. And the military chief's exhortations died inside the internal speaker system, when it came out that he was taking money on the sly as compensation for the injustice of never having risen in status; the trust he enjoyed amid his department, though his lack of fitness for the job hindered him from higher office. Ólaf's opinion was that the Board had carefully seen to it that he never rose in rank, outright fearful of the skills he had developed. A rest from work and blood transfusions in Switzerland and resuming his job again, that was the only reprieve. Maybe he knows too much, suggests Miss Gerður carefully. Yes, Ólaf answers in an authoritative tone, he even knows their underwear sizes. Ólaf rises up on his elbows and adds: they barely dip him in the water; he sinks them all. Ólaf's epigram drew everyone's silence. He lifted a finger: A proposition, a way of demonstrating that the wolf will never escape the department—and Ólaf draws a quick circle in the air with his index finger and sucks hard on his pipe. Thereafter, he said abruptly: The main risk for the chief lies in the new branch. And I ask myself every time a new branch is opened: How can they pay off Tryggvi now; will he throw the aforementioned bomb—you can just imagine what the man has activities in store for them, having survived three blood transfusions and his drinking at work. Four, interrupts young Miss Gerður, four with this last. I can't speak to that, I didn't associate with him particularly in his little nest. I reckon they are on guard against him. In a position of power, he could easily use their tricks against them. You're really smart, Miss Gerður, says Ólaf. Don't be like that, Ólaf. I mean it, Miss Gerður. And the poor Miss worries at her gloves, which she holds in her lap while she eats. Why. She is afraid she'll find another condom, he says. I put the letter in a glove, not the pocket. If she hits Ólaf with her gloves he cries and turns his head away as it sinks down on his shoulders. god help her future husband if her beatings are a sign of friendliness. Why. But why. The treasurer suddenly casts large blue eyes from behind the cubicle glass. And the customers gather together to watch me at my broken machine, stuck rolling back and forth, spewing out cards. Why. I need to be working, I replied, refusing to touch the machine after the coffee break ended. The invisible man, as I called the man in the middle, came right away. Tómas Jónsson! His eyes spoke for him from head to toe. Do you want to forfeit your pension. Divide it among the lot of you. Without any particular scrutiny of my income I have been wanting to poison the atmosphere in the department before I say goodbye.   I enjoyed knowing what I was going to put into writing my icelandic materi- al   judging by their faces I was probably a marked man.   do you remember from the newspaper the unbelievable but true drawings of the aged baby boy who died of old age at seven years   after cleaning my desk, dusting the dust for the last time with my handkerchief and prop- ping up against the stapler the envelope with my pension documents inside, I took my leave. Give my regards to Lóa the cleaning lady who faultlessly emptied my letter basket.

From there, where I sit, I monitor Miss Gerður's slightest movement. My table is at the outer edge, to the right of her cheeks. I am content to watch Miss Gerður. Her countenance has a very set shape, almost harsh at the corners of her mouth, her nose straight and determined. She looks at people with sharp eyes, enunciates all her vowels, and her ears stick out of her thin hair. She must be endowed with great focus. (Of course, I only know her at work and at the refectory table.) One might consider her extremely cold, though her knick-knacks of friendship attest the contrary. On Monday morning, and not for erotic purposes, I stoop over as she counts notes, to see if I can make out her smell. But I never detect a scent other than a faint sour milk odor mixed with perfume. She stocks a high-end cognac, vodka, and juice for her guests, but she drinks soured milk. Her every movement is precise; no nervousness. No neurotic agitation like with the nurses; but they are widows. Away from Miss Gerður's supple, flexible, slender fingers I slip my eyes over my own fingers, bringing them together while she skillfully counts bills (she is usually in the counting department), measuring each bundle with a ruler. My fingers resemble wet icicles, my joints long since become stiff and senile. My hands move only at the wrist. At night, when I'm home and there's nothing special on the gramophone, Tómas plays with him- self creating bird and animal heads from shadows on the wall. He cre- ates majestic whooper swans, stately, swan-white swan heads with Miss Gerður's long and slender neck, when she was still new to the job. I open and close the long beak, my thumb and index finger, the soft lips Leda kissed. Miss Gerður longed to sing at our coffee gatherings the way moor whooper swans do in a still estuary, impressing with their singing and giving bystanders goose bumps; come autumn one manner of thinking would be to return home from the countryside my Tómmi, can't you just keep on until autumn christmas after they tried to assimilate you to the animals sheep you cannot assimilate with fish you cannot chickens not any of them you don't look at the clouds look at the grass don't stroke because then you will acquire the markings of a criminal but Miss Gerður's voice is that of an aggressive beetle, one he fears. Perhaps here we find the only evidence that Tómas was ever a young man. His play is truly ignorant. One eye in his head is almost milky white, the other powder blue like fishskin, his fishskin eye gaping into air. No one knows for sure whether his vision is gone. His face forever shines this strange apologetic blind smile, a mix of stiff and bitter. Not a smile but a grimace, his eyes fragile. Often Tómas Jónsson gathers shadows with his fingers shadows of light a whole garden of bellowing and twittering animals he moves with incredible facility to the keyhole then blows the troupe away with his lips. He keeps the animals in a keyhole cage, all except the elephants. The wardrobe is full of elephants. Some he keeps in medicine tins. Dóri invented playing cards for the blind. He took two decks, cut the hearts from the nine in one deck and glued them to the hearts on the nine in the other; but Tómas did not want to play with Dóri. He locks the closet carefully so the elephants won't wander around the apartment at night, and draws the screen over the window. I will not display myself to the world. He chirps in his den, decrepit and probably playing a whooper swan that knocked out a lamb with its wings, or howling like a coyote. He knows a coyote's scream.

I envy the animals I could probably become one and live in their company animals do not lie awake in the dark darkness until silence lulls them or mourns their sins for hours he watches animals animals are true to themselves which leads to a life perfected India is the widespread braying of elephants from Kipling's books he plays a haulage elephant with a nose-hand fastened to his head he swings it like a fast trunk that might pluck sewing needles from the ground animals in cages animals that jump across grasslands animals who watch endlessly from a lonely tree in savanna grass still in a picture and other animals who look at shadows and the garden trellis which is a chairback tree that looks at animals with its crown and animals and the tree hopping around each other on the grass

I look smiling at Miss Gerður. I wave fingers damp with hand lotion in her direction. I clasp my locked fingers around a large bundle of bank notes and stick them in my pockets, which I pat with a well-satisfied expression. She bobs up from counting, stretches her head down and so forms two double chins, screws up her face and looks at me with expressionless and empty ripped fishskin eyes through the glass in the cashier's cubicle. She strokes the tip of her tongue rapidly over her front teeth, purses her lips like she's sucking food scraps from between the teeth and her fingers go back to racing though bills. Her facial features express neither wonder nor joy unless over some amazing news in the newspapers or on Thursdays when her friend, who works as a detective, has gone carefully over the card file that weekend and indicated to the young miss, i.e. Gerður, "the goings-on in some homes over the weekend," then Gerður whispers to Friðmey and Einarína, who come storming along the corridor out of the mortgage department toward the bathroom: Listen up. And the corridor and the bathroom reverberate with whispers and the slosh of waters in the toilet. (Now it's forbidden for two or three girls to go to the bathroom together.) She spends her breaks in there, leaving the door open a little so no one can sneak up on them by surprise. While she speaks in a torrent, Einar and Friðmey alternately attend her, scraping dandruff from their hair with a fine-tined comb or giving life to their hair by pressing their fingertips to their scalps. Sigurður calls Tuesdays dandruff days. They seem to have developed a complete network in order to *know everything about everyone*, at the Health Clinic, in criminal court, with city doctors, and the police force. Everyone is repelled by these mysterious *sure women* who know all about all the city's major scandals and drug-use according to *certain files*—except for Sigurður's; he claims to be a political ambassador—the police liquor file and also various private individuals' additional files. I first entered into World War II in the file of Henna Ottós for alleged Nazism; now I am in the file of the U.S. ambassador for my alleged communism. I have the honor of being the most registered person in iceland: I am even in the marked file, bitten behind the left ear like a tagged sheep. His sense of decency is no more sensitive than Sigurður's is proud. Next to me, he is on file as one of the work-shiest people the company has employed since I started there. Miss Gerður is unflappable. You could even break wind in her presence. She has been trained to a certain refinement in her deportment and is said to be "neither shocked nor servile in manner." She is as dry and hard as reinforced concrete. She almost certainly knows she will not be the subject of harmless masculine teasing, at least not while she is note-counting. However flawed Miss Gerður is known to be—and she is certainly a very flawed person—she is still excellently qualified in her areas. As a wife, she would certainly stand in good stead running the apartment, keeping it hygienic and clean: she would brush dust from the baseboards daily, wash the kitchen down after every meal, open a window when she fries, go into all the corners with a floor cloth, clean the cobwebs from all the crannies, and wash her underwear nightly—but surely would neglect me, forgetting to tighten my oxygen mask at the right time. She has unlimited banking records for her note counting (both new and used notes), winning the medal in the Employees' Festival competition in 1942, and working to later possess the 1951 Cup. I took pleasure in closely scrutinizing her, back when it was a "dry finger" competition (contestants were forbidden from wetting their fingertips when counting). She also won many contests between banks even when she ended up in the first heat, counting new notes, which are cumbersome and stick together from the pressure; it didn't matter a bit. Behind the scenes, Útvegs Bank offered her tremendous money, but she said she would remain loyal to her old bank, proud thing. Now her work is obsolete following the introduction of the new banknotes, which get counted in the machine. Soon it will even be possible to count crumpled notes in the machine.

I remember how she competed before a packed hall. And I remember two departments sitting diagonally from her. As she entered the competition line at the table Ólaf was manning, the contestants with a timing clock and the crowd from our department shouted:

bills and mortgages teams

work together, one for all

now, now

And we got even more into the song:

the bank will soon be shut

after the shift Omega arrives

she strikes three

ready ready

We constantly barracked the Búnaðar Bank girl, who lost in her heat, pale and sweaty and apologizing for having started counting on the wrong fingers. All the tables in the serving-hall were densely populated; we cleared the calculators and typewriters and set them clattering.

Employee festivals got really lively after the liquor began to take effect. But we were all on guard, especially Sigurður. We, the middle-aged, sat by the radiator away from the draft. Some smoked cigars, others had cards or played with króna in each fist, or casually regarded the rotation of people on the counting floor. Then the women got their break and we struggled away and brayed laughing when Einar or Friðmey tried to haul us into the dance line by saying: Yes, but it'd be good for you to dance just once. We just laughed at this womanly fun. I would pass the time watching Miss Gerður. I wanted to be able to crawl inside her head for a moment, lurk inside her thoughts. We could only guess how her brain worked during her leisure time, the ways it plunged a chemise over itself at night. The ways people go around thinking: on the street, in the bank, scheduled to drive the last bus, having driven the same route his whole life. (If a bus driver should read this, I kindly beg him to start corresponding with me.) Maybe they fight against forgetting by calling up street names: Cape, Ace. How tantalizing it would be to have people's thoughts on tape. I would like to insert a little camera in Miss Gerður's nape. I would love to know what I would get from the picture. All that is remarkable in the world: movements across a street or through an open door. One has to get a lot from the smallest of things. I am utterly consumed by curiosity. Curiosity is my gasoline. Miss Gerður hastens over to the next person; perhaps she says: nothing to nab at the firm today. Her fingers squirming continually as though she's counting invisible banknotes. Maybe she's thinking, there and then: oh god I wish the employee festival was tomorrow so I could improve my former ranking; I am in the mood for counting   She perches one ass cheek on the desk's edge beside me, dangles a foot, her thickened thighs vibrating and jarring at her old, rusty, arthritic groin. I momentarily become a street urchin   her legs have no fat   I think, Tómas Jónsson this beauteous man. But I don't perhaps make time to attend to her, to discuss her lumbago; I might say: would it not be a good idea to exercise your back and thighs on skis. Some good advice for one's morning routine is to imagine you are snuggled in a twin sleeping bag up on some magnificent mountains, preferably around Landmannalaugar. Such tomfoolery is my sauce. Teasing is an evil habit. All of a sudden the Valkyrie has flown from my desk's edge to her seat. I hear papers click under her fingers, which have started to resemble a king plover's talons from all this eternal counting. She shuffles bundles and stretches a band quick around them. The whole time I was as a joker and mockingbird; a jolly companionship. Our Tómas is becoming a comic, I make people think about me. I watch her behavior and gestures which are nothing because Miss Gerður as a woman has been pasteurized. From now on, I will only write badly of her.

Jump down to the floor d'you want to or not I am not asking you to loiter here with me as though in a lair I will allow you to as if you are the best you degenerate cat you have probably become so feminine in habit that you are repelled by rats and eating rat

Aren't you going to drink your morning coffee Tómas
now Anna is at the door I act like I'm asleep

Tómas are you somewhat out of sorts are you somehow maybe sick
she asks I do not answer I am free to keep quiet and self-determine
whether I answer dimwitted questions

I want the mask, I say. I am short on oxygen.

I discover a rubber odor the mask over my mouth and nose hardened
rubber she screws the bottle and checks the dial after a short while I've
got enough oxygen to continue writing and draw breath and after this
gift I live on in all of my body

fifth composition book

my spirit has grown vigorous for some reason finds joy in these verses
which I sing aloud energized by the gift of oxygen
    I sit in an easy seat
    swing-rock with nimble feet
    my gaiety gets me to itch
    unspun wool will stretch
                  but I remain unable
remember how the verse begins
    to spin from fine thread
    the way delightful things feel
                      this or something like it
I bellow it as I remember it that's fine by me then rock music intones
inside my ears and carries to my ears the hoof-percussion of fast-footed
horses crescendoing in the silence and I fling myself awkwardly from
the chair nauseous from the oxygen sometimes I rush out and they hold
me down on the floor while life swells atop me abates ebbs I come to
equilibrium as a new percussion of hooves soothes Hvolsvöllur to stillness and Anna says did you scribble on yourself with a biro and stop
scraping away in the covers I do not want the burden on my conscience
of having to wash away whole novels from on the cover so I built a writing board   stop writing on the damask cover I am getting a plastic
duvet cover for you

my gaiety gets me to itch
unspun wool that stretches
now I'm going to take great care:
the sequence of waking expresses the presence of morning
a good sentence   or were the nightfields clearing home to turn back
to the day   still a better sentence a reciprocal sentence   I will
write ten influential sentences and ten reciprocal sentences   The
car splashed quietly along the wet street. The car stopped nearby here.
The day was coming to its senses after the night: first with a singular car
sound; an alarm clock rang; light came through the bathroom window; a
door slammed in an empty corridor or the front door. Silence. Then the
city's alarm clocks resounded, a choir behind double-paned bedrooms.
I sometimes paid attention to how the facade of the building opposite
awoke. The first lesson, how a building wakes in winter: Take a stance
by the window in your room. Let your arms hang. Relax your shoulder
muscles. Open your mouth, though not so much you drool, and stretch
your neck. While watching, a student could efficiently use the time to
urinate: place the chamber pot right in front of you. Look out between
the window hangings; the cold from the pane will wake you up. First, a
single light suddenly ignites. A luminous rectangle forms on the wall of
the house (someone waking before the clock does, dawdling to stand).
Open the window; light scurries up and down the wall, up and down
the stories crisscrossing with the noise of alarm clocks. One clock rings
the longest, one dim window (the window of the lazy man, planning to
doze five minutes more) the turd of society all the other windows look
down on contemptuously. A student's eyes must make darting movements to catch each light as soon as it lights. Two fire up simultaneously in opposite corners; the student has to use the chameleon method.
After the lights are on, the student can see before his very eyes the first
act in the day's play. Look at the stage: People appear briefly clothed
only in their underwear. Men, hungover from the weekend, swallow
aspirin and guzzle milk right from the bottle. They barely catch their
breath, open their mouths to warm their throats following the ice-cold

refrigerator milk. The door left open while they finish drinking from the bottle. They belch and slam it shut. By seven o'clock, a light is on in almost every window. Everyone knows this, man and child: people wash in their bathrooms; fetch themselves porridge cooked the night before, drilling the porridge out from under the skin inside the saucepan, using a wooden spoon which has been allowed to stand in the pot overnight; a wife willingly rises to her feet alongside the man, heats the coffee and examines herself between her breasts or her underarms while he gets himself clean; she will crawl back into bed after he leaves. She disappears from the kitchen while the man drinks coffee at the table (you can only see his mouth chewing below the kitchen valance), brushes her teeth in the bathroom. She comes back and bends over the man and it is almost guaranteed the light will go off for five minutes and after that you will only see an exhausted man, legs trembling after the flesh has exercised. At such times, the student should continue to study without instruction. I had never

From the shadow theater. Tómas Jónsson

before paid particular attention to the day arriving. I made little of it. Sly feelings of solitude attended me. Morning light tightened in my chest. I suppressed the restlessness in my neck; that much I remember. How long passed before I noticed my untenable position. I had sunk down in a heap in the bed. A snowman outside on the sidewalk had melted in the night, his head was broken across one shoulder; the coalcubes of his eyes had collapsed into elbow patches. My neck was stiff and sore, gray to the core from the cold, and the flesh on my thighs was curd-white and clammy. My body is close-cropped with hair except under my hands and around my genitals. Darker hair than on my head. My genitals are darker than my body. I noticed eyes scrutinizing me. Cats' eyes glow in the dark   and I and I   I was drenched with sweat, which I found out putting a hand under my undershirt. I could wipe the sweat off and make my navel overflow with the water. I have an innie now, but it used to be an outie. Mom called him the wick on the opening of a little cask or else beetleball, and my school friends were jealous that I had such a special navel, which sank into the sea and now—ten years later—rises again from the sea. My life story, my survival, could be traced via the movements of my belly button.

Note: Navel story. (parody)

I pushed myself up and got to the door beyond which there buzzed the same mutterings as before; only a little more tranquility and contentment—which is perfection—rested over everything. The muttering rumbled, whispered, and rumbled. Lying on both knees I saw the muttering. The immodesty totally evident to eyes through the keyhole. Muttering lying outside in in the hallway almost covered with coats and piled trousers heaped on hooks. Muttering standing hobbled by his pants. Their plan was to not stop until my coat breaks, falls to the floor, its loop worn out. Had I had my syringe at hand or an angelica stem I would have sprayed them through the keyhole with water or angelica seeds. Finally I woke from my hibernation, watching them move in uncanny fashion across the floor oneafteranother and plunging again under the heap of clothes, their buttocks quivering, one mutterer coming out from under the coat heap with hands over eyes and looking at the other, all laid up under my coat. And I . . .

. . . rise up against a chair back with stiff kneejoints; dizziness singing in my ears along with two telephone poles.

. . . take myself to the bed . . . let the alarm sound loud and cracking.

. . . sit for a while after the ringing ebbs out along with two telephone poles.

. . . open the door into the hall, which was shamefully dark.

. . . fumbled at the electric board, replaced the fuses in their housing. No evidence visible. The mumbling gone, they had never been there, though I saw them. Títa stared at me, the puss stood in the corner and wearing my overshoes. She picked me up and put me back to bed. I fell asleep and I woke to an alarm. I opened the door and peered into the hall ready to knock heads and slam doors. I had guessed correctly. My overcoat lay in a pile on the floor. The loop was worn through; now I could no longer continue to hang it. The loop was much darned (never

anything but poor table scraps) and no longer the color fasten together
wrestling with linen and tape or document clasps. Down the lapels and
on the overcoat's right side a film of mold adhered to the fabric and dust
from the floor thanks to the dirt in the streets. I brought it into to my
room. The overcoat had become a rag, more or less, but back when it
was new men envied me the way people once envied Jónas Hallgrímsson's blue coat. (I can't possibly do that: Jónas the great Romantic poet
stands forever in my mind's eye, more than a century back, stuck in a
snowdrift wearing his blue coat, the winter of 1841, and these verses of
Goethe, from Prometheus, came to his mind there: Hier sitz ich, forme
Menschen / Nach meinem Bilde, / Ein Geschlecht, das mir gleich sei,
/ Zu leiden, weinen, / Geniessen und zu freuen sich, / Und dein nicht
zu achten, / Wie ich. It was those thoughts the poet Jónas Hallgrímsson
used to free himself from a Reykjavík snowdrift.) I set the coat down on
the bed heedless of the duvet slip. I get my instrument kit—an old first-
aid box—with my shaving gear and walk down the hallway to the toilet
(sometimes I could sense Jónas waving a bottle and provoking the dead
city-life with its inner spirits either that or he lay flat and collapsed in
the snow, but the way he posed the blue color of his coat contrasts well
with the snow, with the poet dressed up for the snow and mountains)
but the door was locked from the inside. In all likelihood the mutterings
had moved inside. I put my eye to the keyhole and a white whirlpool of
flesh spun before me.

I find it impossible to understand how I dragged myself home unassisted
in the storm drenched and beaten by wind and rain   I have
lain here ever since not moving from my bed   I have not taken off
my clothes   Anna brings food in for me and puts the tray on the
chair   I sit embracing the cat and wait to let him have a go at the
rats   throw me in the trash and mill manure out of me in the waste
disposal station and take me over to the grasstender in our well-kept
garden when the landscaper, well the garden's owner now, says yes, the
frost has gone from earth and the time has come to see summer flowers

in beds the onions are coming up from under the sidewalk now it is time
to choose the right garden fertilizer

I returned to my room. I threw myself on the bed, defeated. Obviously
I was not man enough to openly oppose disgrace even in the confines
of my own home. Take my possessions away from me. Tan me with the
cane of self-esteem and I shall swish it with "when it comes down to it I
can get by without her" and "at least I make money from the lease" and
"if I do not rent to them I would be forced to rent to others." I think.
Lying prone on the bed. Lying pancake-flat without moving my legs or
joints in order to protect myself: the threshold, gold bronze baseboards,
the faucet tips, the cabinet doors, sensitive to ridicule because of my
outtie, when everyone use has a beautiful innie, each and every member
of the Homeowners' Association. I could not go to the meetings because
of the risk that someone would bend down and say: There's some sort of
pimple poking out your knitted vest. Perhaps it is just a button made of
bone on my trouser string, I would say. He would believe me, and soon
a rumor starts that I have a wart on my belly. People's curiosity would
increase, ending with a proposal for required swimming for the organization's members; no one is allowed to leave, or else he would lose his
favorable rental terms. And when I stood there naked (having given up
on finding an old-fashioned swimsuit, the sort that offers privacy above
the navel; swimming trunks nowadays only cover a man's genitals), the
belly button, Angler, would be exposed (I had named my navel Angler),
and they would burst out laughing and say: rent, and rent at high cost.
Look, we have ascended Stapafell Mountain. And they would take my
arm and let me poke inside their craters where most people are ticklish,
and laugh: perhaps you don't have much chance swimming; you'll probably sink to the bottom; god knows when you can drop that barrel and
learn to float. I barely took any notice as I lay there on my overcoat. I
felt I was too far gone now the tenants were showing the homeowner
their claws and acting so impudently. A man who goes to work in a stiff
white shirt daily, never arriving late. Going about in a worn overcoat.

His conscience frayed. I never allow myself the comfort of self-criticism, but instead will rush violently in on them in the restroom, where she is standing at the mirror shelf with an ashtray. It has Satyrs on it, crowned with laurels, riding horned asses and looking playfully at the white porcelain water glittering on the elephant bone skin of the nymphs who are at the far end of the forest pond, overflowing with cigarette butts and Sveinn's ashes. I will ask Katrín: Do you know the meaning of this? No, she says, surprised; a cheap ashtray, one I bought for next to nothing. It's German. No, you're looking at a biggish part of the god-world molded in porcelain. The tray is a bit obscene, she says, if you look at it closely. Tómas Jónsson the gentleman grins. In earlier centuries, Katrín, there was no clear distinction drawn between the world of gods and men, I tell you. The gods were even endowed with more human a nature than men themselves; all epic characters were heroes; it was the fashion of the time; the epidemic from Paris had passed their time. But it's remarkable, and how. Women in past centuries did not force their husbands to work in car-repair shops and suffocate in carbonic acid, which stifles them and incites them to mischief and manslaughter. Sveinn would not have done well back then; he prefers lying under cars, though not under me and my needs. What's the point of this ashtray. Okay, take it easy, artists are allowed to represent nudity in stories, photos, and paintings of gods; no one could be offended or blame god for their motives, perverse as they often were, so artists could deal in god-like emotions, taboo for men, such as lying naked by a forest pond and allowing someone to stare at you. She stares at Tómas with open mouth. Next time I take a shit, I'll keep the door open, Tómas, if that's what you want. I could maybe let a horse look at me at the lake by Þingvellir but I would be mad if I got naked down at the Reykjavík pond and let some genius like Hjörvar K. stand there painting a picture of me, although I have nothing against naked statues or pictures in the square. Would you yourself stand naked on a plinth. She is going to offer him coffee and discuss things further. I've never been able to put myself in a statue or painting's shoes, perhaps because of how cowardly and hypocritical I am. I'd hate being all stone;

I absolutely cannot have vaginas in front of my eyes. But I knew Sveinn had ordered her to sit on his pants facing him at the table on Saturday while they drank their evening coffee, having sent the youngest kids to bed, because I had seen her hurrying across the corridor as I was roaming about and I could not tolerate such incidents in the apartment, even if they kept it to themselves and pulled the shade down on the kitchen window.

she poured a rose-red bath salt from the canister into the tub's deep bottom and stirred the water with her hands as the salt grains dissolved the bathroom was locked from within but I heard water slosh with the slightest movement of her legs splashing over the rim to the floor singing she got out her hair wet and wrapped in a towel she let her bathrobe fall aside and the disabled old man look at her in the doorway her hanging breasts swinging easily she made a face and opened wide white eyes coughing head trembling hands that fiddled with the pencil he could see just a hand's width's distance without his glasses but sensed the bath salts felt for his glasses' case but she moved it from the chair bit her lip over the desk crept barefoot to him stood still as a grave at the edge of the divan which he touched and the comforter tautened and rushed into the air he twisted his mouth and turned up his nose as she let the robe fall to the floor and fell on her palms supporting against the wall a bridge over this disabled old man balanced on the divan and let her breasts hang over his writing board she moved her hands and rested herself against the sturdy resistant linoleum of the floor Títa puss are you there he fumbled around for her are you up on the chair she raked her nails over him and he cried out and struck out at the dangling breasts who the hell is this he made a sound pulled back and fell down onto the pillow cursing she slipped quietly away and kept screeching and hissing until she reached the kitchen covering her mouth writhing apart and together with laughter his forehead on the tablecloth kicking his feet in spasmodic fits almost rolling about the table laden with dirty coffee cups crying sighing in a fit I've never seen such a thing never such agitation from any animal he renders me witless and she gulps down cold coffee from a little pitcher and sucks at the grounds with Sveinn hiccupping he'll kill me for sure she thought and that struck her calm only occasionally shaking with laughter and went to the bathroom took her nose drop bottle filled it with water and sprayed it into his face from a distance so he yelled and cursed and she came rushing in what exactly is she up to anyway she brought the glasses' case over to the comforter at arm's length and scolded some imaginary kids how did you get in buzz off upstairs go home while he complained that the apartment gets left unlocked during the day threatened to drive them out the door and could easily make a scene so Sveinn herded him home before the old man fell asleep after the spraying thinking someone had splashed water on him some imaginary kids from the upper story while she erupts in laughter on the toilet seat and screws the nose dropper back on with shaking hands

When I venture back with the shaving kit, the house is awake. Moving about on bare feet which take me out of my room, the kids are at their morning activities, stacking chairs on the table like thrones or linking them together in a train

—We are arranged in a single line. We are standing close together. I end up in the middle of a row and am roughly handled by those behind me so I bump into the back of the guy in front of me and he says: Don't scratch me with that angler on your stomach. We are told to get out of our rows and circle around the pool, from which steam rises, the odor of sulfur mixed with chlorine. I sneeze and start to worry about our descent into the infernal basin. We only complete one lap, then some physical exercises to increase our flexibility, to make the blood flow and move; then there is a short speech from our swimming instructor about the need to have swimming pools for the citizens of a nation that floats in the ocean. We applaud his speech and line up at the pool's edge. He grasps our shoulders, pulls them back and draws his finger down our spines. You don't know what swimming is; you have such crooked spines. A green pool full of hot water will open your eyes and mouth wide, clench your toes on the concrete edge so you can kick off well. He walks backward with a whistle in his mouth, we bend our knees, and when the piercing whistle rings out and echoes in the moldy air, we stab ourselves forward and land flat on the water. Almost everyone's stomach hurts and we want to crawl back out to retch and spit out the bile. I drank a ton, and immediately became nauseated from the stench of sulfur. I am sent to stand in the shallow pool with two barrels on my back. I cling to the handles without the courage to let go the way the teacher urges me, preferring to just lie still and swing my hands uselessly in an arc; I bend at the loins and my toes, heavy as lead, sink to the bottom. I have to admire the others' skill, those who that very first day could retrieve a coin from the bottom. I just think that you have shamefully heavy lead-weights for toes, he says and comes to the edge of the brimful pool with a long pole, from which a loop hangs. I slip the loop over my head as he instructs me and am held out to dangle from the edge. The loop is fashioned into a swing and I hang there the whole swim session, to the amusement of the others. They swim around me, collecting the money the instructor scatters from his pockets. That first week I spent helpless in the swing. On the Monday of the second week, I could float by the edge. By the time the course was over my fingers had succeeded in grasp-ing a ring from the bottom of a shallow pool. I was awarded a swimming certificate: Able to Swim Independently. The others were all excellent swimmers, especially Herjólfur, who could fish one tiny coin after another from the deep end with his feet. Because he could swim so well he showed us considerable disrespect, especially the taunting he gave me. But on the last day, while we were covered with goose bumps in a cold shower, a stone fell out of his ring and bounced underneath the rail. Because he really didn't want to lose the stone, he bent down by the rail near the drain, his rear end on full display. I was seized by an involuntary response, grasping my chance to dart to the toilet, grab the toilet brush, which looked like a battle-ax, and drive the hard bristles against his sag-ging balls with immitigable pleasure, because he had wet testicles. Most youths got teased during the course. Sprayed with water, smacked on the ass with a wet towel by his neighbor, and other things, which the cheerful group came up with between them. My learning to swim may seem contrary to my character—hydrophobic—but the answer is that a person constantly breaks his own rules, approaching the incredible like the teachings in the book *The Argument Paradox* have proven. From within the couple's bedroom came the sound of Sveinn's morning hacking, the effects of the carbonic acid poisoning. The kids howled and fought for furniture with any weapon available: forks, spoons, knives, flowerpots. From the musician's room emanated neither sigh nor cough. It is no different than spending the whole day like a dirty sock, I thought as I prepared to shave. In a large mirror, between the nymphs and satyrs on the ashtray, I loomed large, made into a massive picture: an almost globular head with a freckled scalp and hairy ears: gray, obstinate tufts. The image turned carefully to the side: deep folds on the neck, slightly red (clear now) from friction against a stiff collar. A night-shadow beard, white and mad-spiked, peeks from the vein-split skin; a thick club nose with coarse nostrils and a greasy bridge; moss-eared; under the shoulder straps of his undershirt, by the bluish vein-marked chest, grow frostgray blotches; his abdomen swells out over thin curd-white feet which reveal the picture is sitting in a chair: the image steps onto the chair, lifts his torso and rakes white nails over the curd-white flesh of his clammy, cold belly; the image tries to perform some desperate hand movements but becomes increasingly thwarted in spite of his morning's exercise; it presses its face fast against the mirror to examine its mouth: the red uvula dripping drool; a throat covered with blue veins; the scabrous palate; the lappet under the tongue; the darkened teeth. The treads of the teeth marked by seventy-seven years cycling past. The image got goose bumps and sighed as it thought: I've become this sorrowful old picture. He plunked himself on the rim of the tub and sighed again. This man deserves rewards for his age and his decency. Here you sit. This is you. No, I was not allowed to think like that for long. The door was grabbed from outside, the knob yanked, twice. What, is the door locked, who's loitering on the toilet. I dove into my clothes, hesitated a moment, and doggedly resisted. I and I alone decide how long I will sit on the toilet, I thought. Now, because I have never made a habit of trampling on others and because I try my utmost to be obliging in my daily transactions, at least while in the office, I came to an agreement with myself: they must keep up their side of the bargain. The woman had discarded dirty kids' clothes in the tub and hung her lingerie, full of red bows, white lace and red string, on the shower (as she did when they took a bath together); his wet underwear lay in a heap under the chair. Because mess and chaos and a delta of water lay all over the floor, I rarely went into the bathroom on Sunday mornings. I was moved to tears at how they abused my affability.   I would put them out tomorrow   after the door was grabbed hard again, and having the strongest contempt for the little brats' laundry and the yellow milk shit I decided to get away quickly, before I vomited. Yet I proceeded carefully, pouring after-shave lotion up my nostrils and waiting for a minute to pass on the clock. I used embroidery scissors to trim the hair in my nose, sneezed, and washed my face with cold water. Oh, it's you, Tómas. I thought it was one of the kids, she said. Anna was waiting by the door, dandling an infant in corduroy bib overalls from her arm. Never mind, I replied. And there's dirty stuff in the tub, too. You might have not been able to take a bath . . . I washed myself earlier. She grabbed her intimates, stuffed them into the neckline of her dress and stroked her bosom with the palm of the hand. I went past her, headed straight into my room, opened the window, and ventilated the heavy air of its sleep. A fresh breeze flowed in and I pushed the door open a little. I needed something. I bore more of a grudge against Anna than Katrín. Anna always looked away when she talked to you. Sure, she'd answer, raven-haired and steaming, but she was smiling at something else: her son, Hermann; the door handle; her thumb, scratching nervously at her cuticles with the nail of her middle finger. Her every gesture revealed her rural character. When I do business with people, I make sure to look up or into their eyes while speaking. She knew, of course, that I had been born and grown up in the same area as her long before she entered the world, and that we were distant relatives. She had scarcely lived here for six months when her behavior and gestures altered, her answers changed, and Anna Þórðardóttir (actually Hansdóttir; she's illegitimate) stopped talking to me like a ghost or a deceased husband, through her nails, into thin air or her coffee cup, and instead stared at me with a provocative, defiant, aggressive expression. Since Katrín did not pay my words any heed, I started being formal with her. I was courageous, put her in her place and said: Madam, it seems to me that merely ignorant people adopt formal address. Aaah; she was surprised. I thought everyone was equal in modern iceland. She looked down, at her belly, where Stína hid, smiled a crafty grin, but slunk off to use speech the way a decent housekeeper should. Our fellow tenant Anna has never gotten familiar. Since the beginning, things were frosty, despite charming behavior from both parties. Anna is a devious personage. Shortly after moving in, she thought to offer me coffee. I looked at her and accepted politely. I always suspect a fish is sleeping under a rock. She was plying me with schemes, confusing everything with friendship and familiarity, a scam to get me to lower their rent. The artifice was too simplistic for me to step into the trap. In an affluent society, a wife loses her insidious nature, becomes tame, a dull but well-dressed house-pet, a degenerate lapdog; she is all surface, skin you stroke and fondle without any deeper pleasure. After relations she leaves you empty, seedless, emotionally untouched, and yawns in a loud way from the nest of her duvet, licks her lips and asks for a cigarette. Annakatrín. Annakatrín.

Now it happened that the sovereign king was dying, without having provided the state with an heir. He lay bedridden and thought about the future of the kingdom, which was occupied by a hostile army. Its bureaucracy lay in utter disorder, because originally the king did not want to have a lot to do with the victors, since they let him remain in his room at the palace, and brought him food and drink to have under the covers. He gained no other benefits. We, the defeated, attributed the king's sadness to his introspection, blindness and physical distress. The windows of his room were covered and he thought little of hygiene. His mind often wandered to former days, to their glories, if he was alone in his apartment with its ornaments and material pleasures, gold bronze edging and polished knobs, which he contemplated in solitude. How the once-sovereign king suffered. His negative thoughts tended toward his death, making off with his gray head like a stormy cloud breaking shadows over a beautiful summer landscape, destroying it, the rain and the winds blowing the leaves from trees. Nothing pained the king more sorely than never having sired an heir so valiant that he, the young king's son, could run this rabble off his hands and out of the state, having trained and hardened himself struggling with a hive-headed berserk dragon in an earth cave. Then a young maiden came in with a drink and a maggot-festered apple for the king to eat   no the apple is not poisoned, will not stick in the king's throat:

— Tell me, lowly maiden virgin, why wait on an addled king before he dies? said the king, looking at the girl's skirt, and continued:

— He asks a boon: his request is that you fulfill just one desire, that he may sire an heir who can banish his enemies and the Valkyries and the lunatic dragons of the sky.

The young girl was by nature rather simple, so her sympathy for the dying king began to stir.

— Oh, king. O, vanquished and defeated. Let your will become incarnate; I will ask my knight elegantly to grant me permission; the victors, who have settled in your palace.

And the girl went to meet the knight, who wore the magical Helm of Awe around the world, conferring power and wealth and elegant dress and a guitar.

— I do not understand why a king who has fallen from a throne needs an heir. The palace should be for the two of us alone. The cemetery is the right place for this aforementioned king.

The young woman grabbed him by the ears, and god had just then sown the pollen of sense between her eyes, so she said:

   – You magnificent knight, no matter how many heirs I nourish for you and let flower in the orchard of my womb, they would all be an ignoble family not legally entitled to inherit the state. But if I lay down with this elder, the lawful king, then at least one pollinated flower will earn us the state by fusing its pollen to my pear fruit. And once we are given the kingdom, it will never be taken from us.

The knight said:

   – Katrín, which means The Pure, do not pollute the flesh beneath your clothes.

On the oak table, ornamented with birch panels with painted common-forget-me-nots on the gold hinges lay The Holy Book. The girl opened it and said:

   – Knight, I am your shoe-drying-cloth. The holy book will justify my plan.

She read:

   – Then said the firstborn unto the younger: Our father is old and there is no man on the earth to come in to us, as is the custom on all places on earth. Come, let us make our father drink wine, and lie with him, that we may preserve the seed of our father. Then they made their father drink wine that night: and the firstborn went in and lay with her father; and he perceived not when she lay down, nor when she arose. And tomorrow the elder said to the younger, See. At night I lay with my father . . . And the elder bore a son and named him Moab; He is the father of the Moabites to this day.

The valiant knight said:

   – If you want Moabites for yourself, first you must wash him and brew wine for him, mixed with gin, whiskey, and schnapps, and lie with a man who is more like a corpse.

And immediately a two-headed dragon flew against the hall window and moved in a frenzy that trembled the windows in their lead frames. The knight grabbed his sword and prepared his armor while the girl bootlegged wine in a clay jar, stimulated the king with oxygen, and each of them fought their own dragon. And that is how they acquired legal control over the apartment state.

Annakatrín

I struggled against them but their over-weaning superiority on all sides quashed my resistance to nothing the water splashed in the distance when I grew cold I raised up shorn of my glasses and underwear tepid water pooled under my hands soap in my eyes and I cried and struggled when the water poured over my head from garments I gasped for breath I held myself stiff against the slippery rim shook my ass found a chair seat someone began to grab him dried him thoroughly sprinkled cool water over him while I replenish myself clean in my lair then sighs followed as I raised myself for a new game carried through the wind-stroked corridor in four arms in a gold chair go out don't hang about inside strong arms lifted under my neck and hot liquor flowed in through the sides of his mouth I bite the cup let me take this from you you are shivering badly I belched but held it down sleepy after a warm bath disappeared in the calm don't spit on the pillow greedy I thought about sleep are you dead even after your bath lay on your side do not spit you are not a man made of dough not out of cake batter your feet kick perpetually crazy you pinch me bruises let go no are you ready no I know when I am ready I found you you found nothing let me help you find you are ready for long coming find you sticky-palmed you have spit in my palm I can best find myself palm smudged over nose I took your breath take it away it is wet don't you feel he is drenched and obnoxious oh don't you feel you're ready you sleep the bottleneck set in your teeth I gulped at and fumbled in the sticky palms

The Princess sat at the troubadour's feet in the palace. She sang:
— *Ai eu coitada,*
como vivo em gram desejo
por meu amigo
que tarda e nom vejo;
muito me tarda
o meu amigo na Guarda[i]
She stretched out her white hand and clasped her palm against him;
they sang:
de parecer venceu quantas achou
hua moca que x' agora chegou[ii]
She added:
— *Place your fingers across the strings,* she said, *and see.*
He bent closer to her.

— *In the same way as lines form a network in the palm a family*
becomes a net in each knot of the fifteen palaces of the world,
which we have occupied; in every house we are connected by your
stringed instrument, as our offspring has learned to sing our glory.
In this manner the world celebrates its victories effortlessly with
the dulcet tones of song.

Toward morning they departed the palace for the next palace, startling
the king and queen there with accounts of red, bloodthirsty dragons
with steel claws, lying in wait on the mountains ready to spew venom
over well-tended flowerbeds, gardens, and hall towers.
— *With singing, we'll protect you from dragon venom,* they said;
with guitars. And that was the message throughout the winter
season: they built dance halls and siege towers so they could play
their two-part task: to keep the party going and defend palace

---

i.   I am ever more wretched / but what I desire / my cherished friend / he
comes late and later / pains in absence / my friend in Guarda

ii. in appearance everyone wins / honoring newly come girls *inhabitants, because if there is no joy there is no defense and the defenseless man is pitiful. Wine and delicacies were served at the tables, the beds shared the sweetest loving, so no one was afflicted with homesickness. Everything that could pamper them happened, they went on long hunting trips about the woods in search of unimaginable dragons that never appeared—but suspicions grew for the tenants forgotten in their hovels.*

– Burn their farms in the name of the king, said the domestic knight, shaking his blunt sword.

But the foreign knight appeased him and said:

– In our holy century, the thirteenth century, everything will happen in the name of the serfs; it is a sign of the times: for those and by those are all things.

And so they killed serfs in the name of serfs, and everyone was satisfied. Homecoming, tired, from distant forests or on erected poles where the dead dangled by their names, a sight for the sore eyes of others or a warning (they were allowed to choose between the two) the knights settled to eat, played stringed instruments, and the foreign knight taught them the electric guitar; the foreign singer taught them the tunes to all his songs.

aquest mundo x' est a melhor ren
das que Deus fez el i faz ben[iii]

Thus the years passed, and the days, in merrymaking and imaginary fears, which made the wine sweet on their lips and gave their drinking purpose.

I thought to myself: mine is mine and yours is yours. Neither my assets will be yours nor your assets mine. We deceive ourselves with a

---

iii. the state of joy exceeds the world / here the lord god's grace is given

These translations by Tómas Jónsson from the ancient Portuguese are largely absurd, but they are accurate and read well. They should really be worse.

T. J.

tremendous nonsense: that the two might be some times confused [here the manuscript is damaged]. Fixed assets, mine and yours. I am using the unscrupulous speech street urchins. Here, everything should be understood to be separate. She set her consenting hand on my prudence. She often drank coffee between five and six in the evening, standing upright at the threshold or leaning a shoulder on the doorpost, reaching out a varicose foot but silent and perhaps humming tauntingly as she raised the coffee cup screamed at her four children like a flounder

She always wore a large floral dress inside; other clothes to go visiting.

I remember how the man was utterly opposed to her dress, practically allergic to it. It sometimes happened, especially in winter, that they would meet by chance in the hallway early in the morning, as she tussled at coat hooks "herding the kids by their ass-ears," as she put it, off to school (the children were not particularly eager to learn). They got a lot of pleasure from the electric guitar (and also its square meter sounds; it was astonishing to me that the man Tómas could measure sound in meters); I played in a dance band at night while studying at the university. If he should pass in the corridor during this tussle, she made sure to swing her hip into him, as he made a detour in attempt to avoid conflict and sneak out. This little contact resulted in the appearance the next day of red patches on the lower part of his forehead between his eyes; they spread around his nose and eyes. These spots gave way to gray scabs, a kind of dandruff crust. He was always fiddling with his nose and rubbing the dandruff from his eyebrows with his fingertips, blowing it away so the dust didn't land on his jacket. He twitched and groped instinctively about his eyebrows. This chaffed skin plagued him typically for three to four weeks, then disappeared, but his forehead flushed in the cold. To me, the fighting was irrelevant, but when she asked Svanur, have you noticed this strange dandruff skin on my husband's nose, I did not know people could get nose dandruff, I could not help but tell her my opinion about both her and Sveinn. You should give your relative

complete respect—or me, she said, and rolled about laughing. I, produce dandruff—no, you are by far the genius of our family. My honesty
awakened in them a blind brutality, as often with "healthy workers," and
they refused to take me as a lodger the following winter. Laughable. The
first day in the refectory, I was quite surprised to see old Tómas Jónsson
there, sitting next to me at the table. I partially pitied the man, how cautiously he went to dinner with that skin on his forehead it was; primarily
because of the appearance of these fish-scales that his eyes seemed weary
of pleasure, marked by life, though food seemed to awaken pleasure in
him.

VI.

I lay my curse upon this day. I returned to my room, followed by Títa's eyes. I was tired from lack of sleep and my fingertips hurt. They didn't enjoy touching the cup and taking it out of the oven. I brought out the coffee thermos, wrapped in grease paper, which crackled awkwardly around my provisions: a rye-bread sandwich with paté, a sandwich of wheat and rye bread with cheese, two crumbly christmas cake slices, one of them usually an end slice. I do not know why the end piece almost invariably ends up being mine. I would say to the dinner matron: there is an odd coincidence, I think, the end piece always ends up in my food parcel. I sat facing the parcel of goods. In the mornings I have a rather small appetite and find it hard to choose between the unacceptable slices. Ideally I would have the christmas cake the next day, but that would leave out the rye-bread and cheese slices. I opened the sandwich; the cheese looked dry at the ends. I sniffed the paté and checked with my nail to see if there were pits in the raisin christmas cake. After this ritual, I set to work (I decided to attend first to the rye bread). Here, no one can pick and choose. I thought for a moment about my EEG; one cannot cough during the examination, the needle tip dances out a graph. After the EEG ended I managed to muster some courage and eat rye bread. First I nibbled the crust of the slice, saving the softer part for later bites with my teeth. I went about the wheat bread, which is more appetizing, the same way; the margarine softened the cheese. Every night I bring a coffee and a snack home from the cafeteria. I keep two floral cups in my closet. I drink from them alternately when I wish to give myself a treat. The clay is cracked on my everyday cup; coffee has cracked the glaze and stained it. But the bowl is unbroken. Originally, my Sunday cup was intended for guests. Sometimes it occurs to me to sell it but I have not come to that. One has difficulty making big decisions. Selling the cup would transform my attitude toward life. Giving oneself a treat is essential for good mental health. The doctor advised me to keep the cup for the time being. Who knows if someone will visit, he said. Don't offer visitors the thermos lid. No, but I could drink from the lid and offer the cup.

> *The problem still unsolved after visiting hours.*
> *I drank lukewarm coffee slosh sitting on the bed.*
> *I need to buy a new stopper for the thermos.*
> *The coffee barely stays warm overnight.*

where is Elizabeth do we think has she come down no stories about her and the Italian laying-hens she truly planned to kill the old hens and make a total improvement the old ones wanted nothing to do with laying any more despite artificial eggs and new stuffing in their boxes she got shells and the hens just laid eggs without shells various runts or double yolks it was natural she was tired of the whims I do not know any man in this country who has made friends with chickens

The dinner matron promised to give me a new stopper, taken from some thermos. Those kinds of bottles cannot be found any longer in this country. At least, not the narrow-nozzle type. She wrapped the cap in grease paper, then with plastic wrap to make it tight. Over time, the coffee has eaten up the cork, which has become little more than a brown froth. The warmth slips out somewhere, the cap dew-wet on the inside by morning thanks to condensation within the bottle. Well, the thermos has reached its time, its twenty-fifth year. It'll reach its silver wedding, we will, the thermos and I, god willing. Then I'll put cocoa mix in it. I bought this thermos downtown, the shop Nóra. One does peculiarly well in that store, poking around useful small stuff in boxes on the table. I remember I bought a newspaper quite by accident on one visit. Why did I buy that paper. Usually I studied the newspapers in the dining hall. The dinner matron does not wrap things between newspapers, but as she rations provisions into parcels, she has her biases. Because I bought the newspaper. I need to remember why   buying the thermos remains vivid for me. The girl had a paper or some dog piss in her hand. Something was written in bold typeface on the cover of the paper also a photograph of a cannon   the hard shall meet the rigid Hitler said at the beginning of the war. What drove me to purchase the paper what decided that on this very day I would buy a certain set of papers at a certain street corner for certain reasons. It remains strange. The power of forgetfulness is that it can absolutely put a man out of his mind. I do not understand.

I must have found the money in the gutter, which sometimes happened, but could not sort it into any of the envelopes, and so stood helpless with it stuck between my fingers. It wasn't until later I created the envelope marked Found Money. It occurred to me while I gulped down the tepid coffee thinking about it now it was almost unavoidable to delay any longer I needed to acquire a silver chain instead of a loop, which is not easy to repair. In the cloakroom I had noticed and examined chains on the coat collars of some of the younger workers   Tryggvi's overcoat has a chain too of silver inside the overcoat lapel the initials of the owner engraved in a decorative font   how are these chains attached I have to look for information   the younger men are a bit rough-looking for me Tryggvi I can ask without fear of objection   you should ask me not some mister nobody

Are you still there, drillcat. Don't lie hidden. Come burrow under the covers. Snuggle

no one can understand this cold spirit I present to younger folk think the contrary but it has been demonstrated many times it is inappropriate and unfortunately unhealthy to have too much contact with younger people more than what is moderate prudent employees do not follow such advice younger people no it is not right a man's spirit follows established rules even if they are unwritten I name none I publish no names of various things I know about others that shall be confidential have authority with youngsters guide them indirectly unlike some who ignore the new employees marvelously and then say ill-temperedly no work gets done by hand and rip down the classification system in the filing cabinets it is safe to keep on that rather popular man Tómas Jónsson— that's me—people address him constantly say he is steadfast this senior employee slowly and surely I find it bearable being called old it shows signs yes of confidence I am timid my work never drops from my hand most matters are important when each and everybody gives a solid day's work right through to evening a friendly reaction chokes

to spin from fine thread
many old ladies find my work delightful it is flawless reaches the bank director's ears he raises his hat greets me familiarly what's more he is going to respond partly as a treat for my ears and my mind an invitation to work less he trusts me to take care of dutiful rule-abiding people, I grasp his slender shoulders I say he lifts a glass to me at the launch ceremony he says we'll meet together at the opening of the new branch on the stroke of seven one night to come wearing formalwear and utterly impotent horses gallop from the meadow and prevent the chickens from laying under the young potato grass not the potatoes the hens are deranged the boy squeezes eggs from them with firm hands when they lie on the potatoes squeezes eggs from the creatures if the hen is hypnotized it falls into laying the winter descends upon Sólheimasandur a gaunt forsaken hen stands in the middle of the sand nerves shattered a white Italian hen on the sand's middle its belly flies a wreck over Landeyjasandur fishermen live destruction

It never entered my head: that I might purposely do someone some wrong or evil. How could I commit wrongdoing. My conscience was sleeping, unaware that it was Sunday morning. I sat on the bed in front of the covers, which I'd rolled up into a cylinder against the wall, drank my morning coffee, and picked at my lunch bag like a small bird, as I sometimes am wont to do, having dreamt of feathered rats. Autopsy: a decision to reappraise life, as Sigurður plans to in his miserable condition, a result of three weeks of drinking, but such a thing is quite unsuited to me; this: to stare endlessly at my navel. For my part I never indulge in such brooding, which indicates an insufficient character (I do not deny that it would be fun to see inside oneself via an annual X-ray and TB-exam, the curiosity being of the same kind as when you were a kid and put your index finger deep inside a chicken's ass to find the eggs and burst them: a scientific bent). He literally mewls for sympathy; such men always succeed in justifying themselves. Every healthy person, which I understand to be the majority of the population, should agree with me. I scarcely recognize this degraded but fully-grown adult man groveling with his dirty claws, caught in a frenzy of accusation like some religious youth, constantly confessing his sins; this damned I (capital) that is almost impossible to bear. That is how Sigurður is, screaming in agony when his hungover conscience gnaws at him (so says Ólaf). Sympathy does not thaw me. Most people wear the skin of wretchedness all too well. Or else he will finally arrive at his destination, be able to start a new life. He is a swamp. Who is not a swamp, when all is said and done (he lets himself tell *me*), you can see mud boil out the mud pool of the brain cells as you roll home at night to fuck (a word I do not want inside my mouth) the cat. Accord deep-sea fish due attention when they lose their way to the surface. The animals down there respect each other's lives, evidence of nature's ingenious design, some threading through the waterhole as the blind deep-sea fish swim out through the spout in full view. Even cats shake their heads at that language. Life's columns do not tally when the account is closed in duplicitous bookkeeping, I am going to crack him. (He will let me work on the bookkeeping, whether he likes it or not.) I have the strongest hatred for poetry. Of course not this: Nerine Galatea, thymo mihi dulcior Hyblae, candidior cycnis, hedera formosior alba; there a human being is not babbling his complexes out in the rain, footsteps sounding on a deserted street, rain falling on the window pane, the sun lowering to the blue mountainside, fleet-footed twilight dropping over the valley, or tourists taking photos of themselves and the sunset up on Vaðlaheið (where is classic serenity): The jeep and the sunset; the jeep, Jón and the sunset; the tent and the jeep; Gunna with the primus stove; light on the film. No, they can write overstuffed books, I will not read them, books that are made like the motion of the waves, rising and falling as chapters transition.

>   *She: Gísli.*
>   *The girl was strong.*
>   *He answered, tenderly stroking her cheek:*
>   *Unnur, even if I win the world . . .*
>   *No, Gísli. Forgetfulness will make you free and you will forget me, she interrupted, rising with the victorious pride of a woman who has given her all on a spring night. A spring night, the brief spring night their love passed into a still morning with broad-winged birds flying over a tranquil fjord. Hard realities replaced sweet tranquility in the girl's mind.*
>   *They stood on the farm slope, shy with one another, like children, both externally seeming disinterested as they faced their teacher.*
>   *Farewell, Unnur Ey, he said, and slipped awkwardly into the bag that held all his earthly possessions the old book a young hand had extended him in goodbye, an old, worn book of poetry.*
>   *I could scarcely forget you, he said stiffly after a moment's silence.*
>   *You will forget me, my friend, before the frost sits on autumn's window, said the girl. She went through the low door.*
>   *Unnur Ey, he whispered. But she had gone to wash the milk pails, to call over the dog, Snata, and give it the fishskin, to order the old woman to warm coffee. She was gone, some world distant from everyday life like an alien globe in space with its countless stars. He whispered something to the grass on the farm roof, something it*

*was to remember and to whisper always to the girl until it withered,
waking up next spring, remembering and whispering along with the
wind in her ears.*

*After, he went up the mountain road and disappeared into the
fog as he walked slowly down the slope to the valley floor and the
threatened reflection of the fjord in the gold morning light and the
dewy trail of the little girl under the mountain.*

The journey had begun.

Paris - Ulm - San Remo - Rome - Corfu 1948-49.

educational institutions do not care for stories about The Journey that
was traversed over a high mountain and a heath with a clever collection
of poetry in a knapsack on a quest to conquer the world, though it was
more natural to sit passive and let the world carry on. Students whined
in a high-pitch chorus: do it, teacher, do it. Read the story of the journey
never taken. Pleasure drew the teacher's mouth into a pucker. I read
it last christmas. Now write an essay about christmas. And the class,
being both radical- and literary-minded, breathed inspiration and wrote
diligently about that great merchant festival of money:

> *sleet and slush covered the central streets of the town. The snow
> reached people's ankles. Everyone was in the finest jolly christmas
> mood except little Magga in her Nissen hut. She played with her old
> rag doll on the damp floor. Her mother sewed skirts for her daughter
> from an old coat.*
>
> *Run to the dairy and buy a drop of skimmed milk with the last
> of the money, she said, red-eyed with tiredness as she looked at her
> daughter's pale cheeks. With gnarled, callused, red, and swollen hands
> she worked to fish the coins from the faded wallet.*

Then little Magga ran out to the store and the police kicked her with
their large clogs, so that the girl dropped the milk pail and the milk
puddled into snow identical in color. With that, it became clear that
celebrating christmas this year in the hut meant hunger and tears. But in
a mansion opposite (mansions in icelandic novels always face the dismal

American military huts left over from the war) the birth of the Savior was welcomed, by contrast, with a fried christmas goose and creamy mashed potatoes. Einar Magan the great merchant sat at his table feeling blessed after a huge christmas sale. In the huts, darkness reigned—desolate and empty and with hushed weeping.

Having finished their christmas essays, these prospective lawyers and ministers went out onto the school steps and had a cigarette and Coke and candy. They have brought their sympathy with humble people in artistic form. On the way down the hallway they deepened their voices, made themselves appear solemn and told the dames in the cloakroom that Nietzsche and Rilke were "out of date," along with Dostoyevsky. The ladies hang their virgin complexes on hooks and make weak protest. They are still on the sensitive Dostoyevsky step but will pass rapidly through Gide to Camus and Sartre (one must practice the French one learns). Blessed girls, they say, rescue men from tattered phrases. Nietzsche was nothing but a supple phrase-logician. At the bank there is an excellent case of a man who became a womanly maid from reading such things (yes, you guessed it: Sigurður).

When evening fixed a dusky veil on the withered earth and the trees dropped leaves that curled like shriveled parchment, they strolled enamored along Sóleyjargata. He, Haraldur Sóldal, a newly appointed doctor, led his fiancée, Todda Bomb, as the mischievous boys in the village shouted after her as she approached. (Here you can see an excellent example of the poet, the way the author uses in his work two contraries, critique and beauty, he says.) The lights sparkled drowsily in the pond like grief glittering in her eyes the morning he said goodbye to her for countless springs and went away over the lakes and moors. (Next spring she sailed after him to the big city, Reykjavík, where the formidable corruption of the capital appeared to her in the form of an opulent merchant's son on the one hand and, on the other, the drug addict, the drinker, the wretch, the homosexual, the poet Tjafsi Í. Vaffs.)

They picked their way across the bridge. Mt. Esja loomed above the roofs of the houses, wearing a thousand and one fall hues—an adventure in color.

Þorbjörg, I want you to know that in my life I have had countless women. I will not deceive you.

I know, Halli, you always loved Vala Storð.

Tell me, were you ever with Ólafur Magan?

No, she answered in a low voice.

What about the poet et cetera, Tjafsi Í. Vaffs?

She shook her head no.

I pity him. He had a hard time. He was a poet whose life and sensitivity people treated harshly.

They had arrived back home. He sighed, tired after a difficult operation in the hospital, where the powers of life fought battle with a vain hope of conquering the omnipotence of death. There was no assurance what would happen in intensive care, whether the victorious power of life could gain the patient any respite.

In the silence that came after her answer, ice formed over her innocent love like puddles on a street during fall's first frosty night.

Then, once inside, they removed their bindings, he embraced her modestly on the divan, and the night surrounded and wrapped them and remained silent about their naked bodies interacting, seeking each other's love the way a stream seeks spring water, widening constantly in the flowing river running into the immensity of the sea.

Silence.

The potato grass withered overnight.

In truth, fiction is a superstition spun in the fabric of people who *neither know nor want to know life itself.* LIFE IS NOT IN BOOKS. If the writers and poets wrote about men at work and during their leisure, fiction would be superfluous. Should a writer, however, construct some narrative that does not exist in reality but rather takes reality's place, i.e. the only true *fiction*, fantasy and imagination, then no one can understand it but the writer *himself* (supposing even he understands it). With this eliminated, nothing should be left but writing biographies. Fictions are useless to every *living* human. On the path of life, people meet others who are much closer to their problems and to real environments than those in novels. The only way to enjoy to the full

> *life's fiction is to keep your eyes and ears alert as I do.*
>
> *No, but she was many things to me, besides kind and supremely helpful when I struggled on alone in my studies. I do not know how I would have survived the program without her.*
>
> *He wet his lips.*
>
> *She was the director's only daughter, increasingly engaged in a brutal rebellion against inertia, society, and the environment; she was vigorous and beautiful, an ardent socialist, almost a communist; she had traveled a lot—most European countries—and spoke seven languages fluently; she had seen both Paris and Rome and had met Theodore Dreiser in Hollywood two days before his death, on 12/28/1945, but*

For the most part fiction is superfluous to me because of my particulars. I *could* never enjoy books if they were borrowed. I *had* to own the book to be able to enjoy it to the fullest. Reading books was a youthful thrill, I never felt the day had properly reached evening unless I had read a few pages, sometimes starting in the earliest morning. Here I refer of course to reading good books, classic works, edifying subjects, preferably scientific literature written for the masses; or, something that allows the reader access to the dream world that is the future.

> *though Ginger Rogers walked across my stage*
> *made a face at the citizens of the world*
> *no one remembers fame nor wealth as we do*
> *loving with moss-sprung tears*
> *He stroked his hands around his eyes, exhausted. He thought: We're dead, imaginary creatures in the mind of some alien god, an unchecked power that man and his science has not been able to better*

define. If god's powerful thought forgets us even for a moment, we are extinguished. One would die a clinical death. We who are alive are the largest, biggest lie; we, who are the greatest truth of life; but, my dear, you cannot comprehend this consistent example of existence. What is the soul and the life in our breast but fiction—this veneer, this remote-control power we call god?

In that moment it occurred to him that he might have plunged into political struggle, as Vala Storð had urged him to. He saw her before him smoking cigarettes from a silver case, always ready for a debate, but he wandered away from her image and her challenge: Society is the patient who needs active medical care to survive, not the old woman with colitis, Sóldal, in that hospital, Parliament, your distinguished forum, which befits your ambition and manliness.

He fell silent and contemplated his popular wife who looked at him with brilliant eyes, adoring his intelligence and education, the majestic set and manly icelandic expression of his face, anguished by thoughts of death, which lived in the depths of his being, infrequently evident in him, like the slow nagging pain in an affected tooth, constantly present but never so penetrating that he would get rid of it.

I have put you in a bad mood.

No, my darling, I just wanted to get to the root of existence; what is this so-called life, what is death?

Haraldur Sóldal wanted to split the core of existence with the deadly power of his Nordic mood. Thoughts and ideas poured out in his mind like a glacier river in spring thaw, yet he was serene. And he became aware of a solution in the distance, one like the splendor of the icelandic glaciers in its power and destruction. Glaciers and volcanoes? Were they not the very opposite of the functional life of creation? In what, then, resides the life of creation? In woman, in her body, with her breasts, surrounded by her great kindness; in fertilizing a mother's womb. Celebration lifted him to a higher level. He went to the record player and put an album on: Bach: Magnificat.

Now he was no longer tired, he stooped meek as a child to her white breast, incipient mother, white like the glacier, hot like a spring in early summer, he put his lips on her neck which quivered with love's words, and muttered:

Woman, world, earth, just a snapshot smile but no more . . .

Often I have felt that someone like me, Tómas Jónsson, possessing a scientific spirit, should be a mathematician and thermionic genius, an electronicker. Such an education was, of course, unattainable in this strange era in which I grew up: amid crushed fish, the Christian faith, and sheep. "Science hides in all ways in the spark and nature of a budding god," I wrote at some point in my Thought Pamphlet. There I opined and argued that nuclear science was the creed of tomorrow's world, especially the formula for the nuclear bomb.

We Icelanders, you should know, my Títa, cannot produce our own nuclear bomb; the nation lacks control over a vast desert, an essential. But we have sharp enough brains for the task. iceland has no lack of brains; Sólheimasandur, however, is too small for the purpose. We could instead do our experiments via electronic brain control. The country appears to be appropriate as regards size; it is well-located and suited to various scientific experiments in the fields of national science and methods of government.

No, stop, she sighed softly and looked into the eyes of her dear friend.

He pulled back out of full respect for her virginity but she pressed her body toward him, full of the winsome longing to procreate that a young woman has.

I would, she said. We should have children, she added, a life for tomorrow. I would love having children, the creation of a new era.

Yes, he said, but not until our house has its roof.

Then we must attend to the foundations in the morning, she said with joy, enthusiasm, a desire to work. What then?

And that night—the first night after the roof-raising in our new house, which we own, just the two of us, you and I—then I will take your chastity.

Every night thereafter will be an ecstasy.

My friend, you are a marvelous child. Wonderfully childish and intelligent-natured.

And I will become Þorbjörg Sóldal, wife of Guðmundur Sóldal the famous doctor, the one all the other doctors envy for his packed waiting room. What do you think the people at home in Þarafjörður will say then?

She rose from the bed, the bed of youth's impoverished station, with its worn upholstery and creaky springs, which hampered her free movement and night pleasures. She moved in stately fashion, like a hind in the forest, going naked across the floor, shielding her breasts with her palms and lifting the window curtains. Cold streetlights shone in the eyes of this proud, triumphant woman. He accompanied his hind, this young stag in life's forest. The lights in the town, Reykjavík, the progressive hope, seemed slightly distant in the drizzle.

We are the modern iceland, liberal and strong, was his thought as he kissed his wife, perhaps for the first time before the open curtain of the world.

Come on, little sprout, she whispered, smiling with a hint of fun in her voice and led him gently, with a hand on his spry back, to the bed.

Firm breasts. Loins. Eyes in the dusky room. Intense groping hands. Reef. Breakers rose within them. A lonely fish dove for the depths.

Waves rose and heaved in the red dark of the surf.

Athens - Mikanos - Milano - Madrid - Vík í Mýrdal
summer 1949.

With utmost respect for the successful conservative regime of Ólaf Thors, I consider the electronic brain to be the preferred mode for we Icelanders.

T. J. Reflections on science, poetics, and technology, Feb. 3. 1944.

Here I'm going to shoot a little into the whole story of instinct my urgent need is to trace each thread to its very end complexity that is the fertile bent of the scientist's nature you say but this is a unique example of my own mentality I say both points of view are acceptable each is your opinion the given answer

when the company received illegibly written correspondence, they would look to Tómas Jónsson's advice, expert in reading small writing.   this has been a detour and now I will continue where I left off   first it must be said that my book purchases had become strikingly costly. I never patronized libraries. Jag brukar inte gå på Stadsbiblioteket och plugga, as the Swede said. In libraries all books have the same appearance, the same binding, and dust jackets (I cannot do it, I find it more than a little troublesome to see scholars surge into the collection carrying three-compartment briefcases dressed in thick winter coats and fur hats like Abdúllah Khan, sandals on their feet and an expression on their faces as if they are going about with an aphid up their nasal cavity; wearing sandals in the frost) the appearance of the books is always extremely dry and important. Librarians stroll about in Swedish sandals made of tan leather and white striped socks made of nylon crepe, on account of the moisture (such socks dry overnight if they are washed in the evening). In the mornings they anoint Lykt-ó-nei (Odor-O-No) between their toes; nothing works. They cluelessly study their little toes, which have fungus in ways the lady podiatrist does not understand. To me it's impossible to understand your little toe any which way. The other ones I understand perfectly. With constant attention and care it is possible to cultivate the nail on the big toe if it falls off from nail-rot. Your toes should last your life if you follow these measures. I see nothing on my nails. You seem to have a normal cornea formation. I'll try a Valkyrie band-aid on my corns, apply tar powder to my toes, plug a Dr. Scholl cork between them so that air can play freely across the toe-webs, and see what happens. Onychomycosis is nothing but a fungus that grows in a damp environment. Sprinkle talc regularly on your feet; I would advise you to drink isinglass dissolved in warm water after each meal. Gelatin is also good for the intestines. There's nothing they despise so much as a little troublesome onychomycosis. I looked for assistance at second-hand bookstores where I often made affordable book purchases. A text does not lose its value like a binding, the book's external form, as it frays. I adopt a commercial model, buying a book from one bookseller and selling it to the next after reading and mending it; then I buy another book from him with the money, and sell it to the first; this is a striking example of prudence that under the circumstances is based on precise calculation   this went on and on for years and years. Any loss that resulted from this passing-between, I could consider small and manageable. Sometimes I made a profit. The method was feasible until, due to my frequent visits, the booksellers suspected me of having a sizeable collection due to my frequent visits (I had actually stopped reading and studying as a pastime), and that is their bread-and-butter. Inside their airless bookstores you'd constantly find dawdling an assortment of mail carriers, sometimes a writer, and other boring specimens of men of a similar nature who would go on tirelessly, perched on boxes (often eating Danish pastries), about valuable publications that had disappeared into crevasses and cracks from pack horses during the time of the North Post, and how worthwhile it would be for adventurers to journey into the wild beyond to look into all the cracks on the mail route; now is the moment and they could make themselves famous in the pages of the newspapers for their daring, no one since the nineteenth century has risked their life rappelling into the ravine after books and horses when the postal wages were simply miserable, just five state dollars for a winter tour. They do not risk such poor payment these days to mail carriers. Yes, there lies a great store of literary riches buried in icelandic fissures, sighed the mail carriers, bless the wealth in books in the world's fissures. I discovered an interesting chamber document by Levetzow from 1786 more or less display quality. A larger effort is needed for this. In antique book stores one generally requires a major effort for anything except jabbering. Of course these companions would try to entangle me in conversation and

get me to join them in condemning book burnings in Hitler's Germany
and the interesting Levetzow chamber document from 1786. I want
nothing to do with it. It is, however, most *interesant* in my mind when
it is hotter in Grímsey than in Akureyri, not to mention London. No
matter that the difference might be one degree—but that's okay. Yes,
temperatures elsewhere in the country don't concern me, just in Grímsey,
this distant country cut into pieces by the Arctic Circle—excuse me,
what island can boast such a phenomenon? Grímsey is unique. Equally,
I want the temperatures to be at least higher there than in Akureyri. It's
fun when it is hotter there than in London or Paris on the noon news.
So too . . . (strangely, if I end a sentence, for example, with "s," then I
always begin the next sentence with the same letter) . . . powerful protests, which Icelanders have in their blood, and condemnations of Levetzow; they had hearty verses written by the late Jón from Kotleiti and
used the verses as "a contribution to the struggle" for a fairer world; these
were the words that were very much in fashion: everything was supposed
to be a contribution to the fight for a fairer world. (Directly as a result,
you cannot help but imagine a damp basement, a secondhand bookshop
with three or four moth-eaten men of indistinct characteristics, wretched
men chewing and eating noisily in a thought protest against the likes of
famous tyrants, the Levetzows and Hitlers and saying: "This Hitler was
not a man in the icelandic sense of the word" and, because they did not
really understand, instead that he was one of the "worst workhorses in
history" and "the people made a big mistake not rushing at him right
from the beginning and shouting him down with robust verses, as the
old icelandic ghosts would have done, hehehe!" Our belief is that a button is missing from everyone's vest.) I was bored of their congress, these
people who had never agreed whether to adopt ideas shaped by radical
or conservative policies. Various sorts of restrictions have become very
popular in the dark corners of second-hand booksellers. I searched for
new second-hand booksellers, and after a few years I had threaded my
way through all the second-hand stores in town; they were all overflowing with these quirky icelandic loiterers, headed for death yet

complacent, the long-awaited death that is nourished on the concept of "iceland's leadership role among nations." Manuscripts home from Denmark to iceland, which is suffering from a thirst for reading! When it seemed there was no way out of the labyrinth of reading (my plan was to make myself immune to books by reading continually, just as you inject cowpox into humans to ward off cowpox [I managed to make myself immune to Kvaran's novels within five months of reading his books]). But to make oneself immune to books by reading books will probably never happen until science manages to isolate the literary virus, classify it, kill and inject it in its dead condition (i.e. used books) into the human brain at birth so that man as a creature will be immune to the frequent and ominous literary epidemics from Paris, though fortunately these epidemics are significantly milder by the time they reach us. Miss Gerður heard at some women's meeting that a vaccine had been found against painting and had been used experimentally in iceland. Several sick Picasso fans on Skólavördustígur were selected as volunteers; they were injected with material derived from paintings by the "Master" and then they were isolated in some museum in Paris, where only his paintings hung. The men came back to iceland untouched but the experiment was such an extraordinary strain on their nervous systems that they could not see paintings by icelandic masters or else they broke out in a rash and some of it got into their stomach and they vomited semi-digested food all over the National Museum. But I mustered all the energy I had in order to stop buying books. After a hard struggle, I managed to change this quirk in my mindset: an absolute contempt for writers and books, the quirk led me to a decent outcome in my impotence, a way of giving someone confidence and certainty.

I had realized that this was a terrible waste of time and money, that the money involved would be worth more had I put it in the bank. Thereafter, my inclination crept ever toward my savings account book. now I understand that these adjustments in man's nature sneak somehow past him in an instant I thought I was contemptuous of books but discovered the relationship between the things as they are in books and it is true what the psychotherapist Jung said in the magazine *Úrval* that a man always falls in the same well, even if you avoid wells and there are no wells around   a person instinctively digs his well and falls in   I must out of necessity discover a valid aversion to second-hand bookstores: their presence is poisonous.   no not a conclusive argument   second-hand bookstores are unjust and their books poorly sourced. They store books purchased from bookstore thieves in the christmas rush inside a small room at their home. Never in the shop. Would you like to see my home means that the second-hand bookseller wants to get rid of some stolen books, and have you take a look around his cubbyhole. This cubbyhole is a shabby closet under the basement stairs. Maybe you light upon some tome. Light on—tome—the very words they use—they strike you. How great to finally find words that fit into the idea I myself have shaped of second-hand booksellers (I created it, of course, in my own image. Note: I am invariably writing a veiled self-portrait). The same goes for writers who do not assemble word lists and make a glossary to rely on; they fall short and on issuing their works only cause problems. But is the purpose of fiction and biography to provide the reader vocabulary samples. Well, this will come later in my thesis. Recently I obtained, by pure chance, a rare book in excellent condition at a great price. Thus the wording should remove all doubt that here is a *genuine* second-hand bookstore worth consulting. No one uses such formal sentences as second-hand booksellers and collectors and then there is the exceptional appearance of books taken from the houses of recently deceased, intestate spinsters. (Most old women hoard by nature, stockpiling an incredible multitude of meaningless and useful junk. Old men do too, once they are approaching the condition of old women in looks, physical activity, and spirit. See below.)

After the following events, the second-hand bookseller stopped acquiring valuable books: some old spinster in Þingholt ate sweetened soup made from three prunes, five currants, and a clove-stem. After that she gets heartburn, spits in a fragment of wrapping paper, and gives up the ghost, legs clad in black cotton socks dangling out of the bed. In Þingholt the colonizing and colonial culture of pure virginity has reached its zenith among people who live in low wooden buildings with crocheted curtains in front of windows full of vases that house everlasting flowers. Spinsters usually die but some seem to live forever both alive and dead. Now, assume they die; so long as that happens, the dead are borne to the door shortly after noon the day before Trinity Sunday. For this reason, the refrain of spinsters is: Everything in threes. Their newly-enriched relatives (lifelong virginity requires a significant nature; women are often too spiritually impoverished to maintain themselves intact beyond fifteen years) will get rid of "all the old woman's things" on account of the sales potential of the property; land in the virgin colony is in the uppermost price bracket. They call the second-hand bookseller and give him the opportunity to see the house the day after the funeral and check through the old volumes in the attic. At night, after closing the store, the book dealer strolls over to the house, wearing black herringbone clothing gone shiny on the ass, elbows, and knees. He is led through the tiny bedroom that everywhere bears witness to her virginity: the round table with wrought legs: countless crocheted cloths; cloths on the commode; cloths on the stool-seat; cloths on the other cloths; brown wallpaper; a sour odor from the kitchen sink with its grille over the drain; the smell of cat urine in the bedroom. The bookseller yawns at the serenity standing on the open threshold of the living room and thinks: until 1930, this was how housing in this country was: a house divided into four equal parts and a shed with a protective door facing either north or east. He is shown to the loft ladder. He goes up the loose steps and is soon in a broad, low space barely the height of a person. There he rummages in countless dusty cardboard cookie boxes, Marias brand. godt smag giver sjælesbehag, he recalls and can taste Marias cookies and tea biscuits. He remembers gobstoppers and sugar mice, marzipans and toffee caramels, and sits there perfectly still within the unusable space defeated by his memories and the stale air with the intense scent of moss. He sighs and sneezes. Having found something valuable amid the junk he says: I looked through it all. But unfortunately there's nothing really worthwhile. If you want, I can estimate a price for the whole caboodle. And that's how I got a rare copy, which I had always lacked. He dusts off the books with fingers that are half-clenched from arthritis, puts udder ointment on the leather, brushes and polishes it with a cloth, and sells the books to newly-rich collectors who want to "build up their library" for display in the hardwood living room; sometimes the very same relatives who sold the dross in the first place. I can see before me the evident reason for the previously mysterious antipathy I have for second-hand booksellers. I would finally like to mention that I feel sorry for the virgin colony and its honesty, as though it belongs to bygone days in this boring town, which has been condemned to crumble in the jaws of excavators. A new symbol of virginity arises in the ruins of the neighborhood: the local bank. Congratulations, Miss Gerður.

The following reasons are the basis of why I do not read literature:

I do not read novels. They are written with secret revenge in mind, the revenge of craven writers who shrink from coming clean and spitting filth and obscenities in the faces of people on the street. I would read novels if it meant spurring on the hot, privileged rights of an artist who hides, concealing himself and protecting himself under the guise of humanitarianism. He considers himself a physician, that his publications are diagnoses of his time and therefore allowed to bring things to light, however dirty and messy they may be, the way a doctor tells a patient: this festering in your belly means you have hemorrhoids. Your colon must be removed, taken from its belly so you can heal (entrepreneurs and CEOs, with whom writers are especially angry except when they offer to pay the bill, since our country is a kind of highfalutin poetic culture: I was in charge of billing. Minor writers take bills that are all of a piece while major writers take the Nobel prize. The prime bill, a Nobel prize). Some writers are content to publish diagnostic pieces (the remedy rests with you), others come out with palliatives: 20mg nationalization, 30mg Socialism, 1mg national dance and folk songs. One tablespoon twice a day—your health improves! Still others recommend god. But what would happen if doctors publicly disclosed medical records and sold anyone what they wanted. I say: Writers are not physicians but the carriers of infection who weep from their various individual sores and bestow those same sores upon the nation. So these activities attain respectability, writers give themselves beautiful civic names: the conscience of the nation, the mirror of time, the extent of perception. The motto of these cowardly writers is: No one does not get corns; no one should be allowed to live without knowing man at his most oozing. I should least forget Sigurður's words (stolen, of course): When I read a book by a deceased author, he lives again for as long as I read it and remember its contents. Writers are always being revived. The dead must stay dead, I say. I want to beat them all to death. I have gained a new understanding of death: I kill a writer every time I read a book. Why should writers live longer than anyone else. Do they achieve more. They have no legal right to extra days than we who complete our full day's work up to evening. Nature is just; no one lives more than sixty minutes in an hour, twelve hours in a day and fifty-two weeks in a year. Avoid breaking the laws of nature. If the pull of the earth were to decrease, houses and men would lift an inch from the ground and hover in the air, we would have to drive rods into the ground so people could continue with their journeys like a ship in a storm, if the top strata was not a gaseous foam. Ólaf answered with a frown: novel characters can whine about love to writers in private; it matters little to me. All writers pretend to be endowed with compassion and true faith. The wrappings are always being embellished, more and more resembling cellophane.

One time I observed by chance three poets on the way up Bankastræti. One poet said:

> *I will be reincarnated and come back worth half what I am now.*

Another said:

Living this life is enough for me.

The third said:

In my next life I will be a poverty stricken mother of fifteen children in the slums of the East End of London. I will lose them all to tuberculosis carried in unboiled milk.

He was rather tearful over his prospective fate, said farewell, and lost everything, but the poets continued.

West End, I said and crossed the road to avoid them. This is my total personal experience with writers.

What concerns we humanitarians, we who never express or reveal ourselves to others   now I am getting to the point   except when the character is alone, adds Óli contemptuously. After a small pause he continued (Ólaf did): Icelanders are particularly stubborn-minded men who abuse others during the day, drunk, then weep at their hangovers at night, which are unparalleled among our brother nations in Scandinavia or farther afield   that is how stories pamper you readers—"people are, at heart, good-hearted"—in stories you find what is called a justification. Is not a story meant to be a mirror. Un roman c'est un miroir qu'on promène le long d'un chemin, as Saint Real said. Sigurður and Ólaf get quarrelsome about people and culture during the lunch hour. Or the basis of spring, sighs Ólaf, and grimaces. I want to say, supportively: When the maximum vehicle weight on mountain roads is lifted then but not before then spring has come as far as I'm concerned that was my thought   no   but I kept silent felt it best to keep silent on the matter   silence is prudence   it does not leave one exposed   almost invariably the rule is it that when two strong and equally certain opponents debate they are forever waiting for a third party to drag into the debate then they can both vent their anger at him together in a combined attack because no power despises another power as god does not hate the devil, the devil does not hate god, between them there is only

competition whilst they both try to get the other on his side and each is
anti-human so it is clear that equally strong enemies are not enemies
but devilfriends filled with admiration but trying to conceal each
from the other how evil his nature what they know it to be but take
note puss to keep silent a man cannot keep his counsel after the fact
is intact perhaps only in silence   how to scold a mute, deaf man

why should we also take a stance
for a while the inspection has annulled its value
unless its value is negative for the stanceless
and those who are without opinions alive from the World War
national prisons the unrest of state control brainwashing
from these it means nothing to wash like those who live
to create the world only for those who live and breathe
and everyone is created in the image of the creator
those without ideals don't destroy others' ideals
ideals move about by themselves and other ideals
die and presumably others become ideals
the godless do not lose faith in god
optimism is the root of all wars

Truly I tell you, Tita-nail, they are able to split hairs into an eternal
mid-afternoon over ideals of the soul's virtue (Sigurður) and undis-
puted facts (Ólaf) and transform the table and get ulcers from their
fanaticism.

Probably I should not remember this thing I recall I cannot obstruct
myself from remembering you can deny me the chance to speak out
loud but will never be able to wall up the holes in my mind well
I make a large cross × in the air you know with what I remain a
cross in the air leaves no mark behind I live with police authority
domineering feline nature hahaha

to be in agreement with the world depends on the soul. and writers are
the world's moral apostles prophets and failed priests. the way doctors

rebuke diseases you understand me. it may be that at some point souls were the word's foundation. that has long passed from our memory. in this shines public opportunism. it is understandable that Icelanders do not attend churches. each Icelander has a home chapel plus missionary calluses that maintain his debate on the box.

To my mind this is how it happens as it appears in the laws of earth and man:

The world is primarily the acts of its constituents and a movement across unequal but distinctly drawn lines. I'm desperate to mention this theory to Ólaf   sometimes it's the case that we are the last to get up from the table in the refectory.   in truth these are his own words forgotten by everyone but me how can he remember everything he says with that parroting mouth below his nose and eyes   I am sufficiently prepared to deny or admit if it comes to that and I get to have his friendship. Ólaf has prepared the ground, he has sown so much in me, but doesn't care about the yield. With Sigurður it is clearly pointless to speak of fraternity.   the soul's house rhymes with compass compass needle the needle points somewhat crookedly in his head hehehe Títu-totter   I never feel the presence of this legendary soul; at every moment it resists the plan. Ólaf laughs and says: no one can coddle his soul. It just is, Tómas. This resting place is our Stalingrad. This broadside I allow like wind rushing about my ears, grin pro forma and look silently at Dísa. Dísa looks ahead and pales. If she feels uneasy at our words, she searches for strength from the cactus on the window. Dísa is a cactus. They destroy you in substance, Tómas, he was saying—women. how can men offer a sane man up to such an outdated solution . . . Dísa is a spherical cactus. Yes, a torpedo directed at me. Ólaf has looked into my thoughts. I'll let Sigurður draw Ólaf's attention. I'll let him say: Universal literature— such art is the hardest of all art: love of life and men, the search for the truth. I felt sympathy for Sigurður this time. Poor Sigurður, I seldom save him from doing the same thing. Siggi has become emotional and affected in his worldview, some kind of chaos and fog. And in that vein he later opines: I do not believe in god, but I have a great need to believe

in him . . . what . . . Sigurður is the most hopeful of men; a tormented
wretch who can truly say: give me, god, the incomprehensible solution
to my problems

he lies there hungover the duvet spittle-stained old sperm on his back
and helpless now straining toward the bottle of malt I clasped at the neck
that black rascal and brown ale flows from the throat over the floor he
wipes the sweet viscous substance from his tongue with his palm howling
and keeps nothing down puking and shitting god you are yourself you
too much now he lectures not about petty citizens now is that mon dieu
donnez-moi la médiocrité the wretched Mirabeau of the table in the
refectory now drives nothing down with might and great authority and
splotches of french he lies on his back like a shot bird broken-winged
down in the maltspittle on the floor in a white nylon shirt with silver
buttons a filigree shirt he dare not send to the laundry or he will be
treated savagely

The whole town recognizes Sigurður's rakish behavior and we make fun
of him during the lunch hour for being the "most infamous man in
Reykjavík and some ways farther afield." On the other hand, it befits a
blank man like myself to evade people's thoughts. Sigurður is a useful
diversion but only in five-minute stints. To torment him calms the tension. No one should stay too long in the vicinity of a man who spews
poison; no medicine is better against him than the hydrochloric acid of
a healthy mind or else total quarantine.
You must isolate yourself from such men.
I am in quarantine from:
    a) Sigurður
    b) Dísa's glance
    c) Profligacy
    d) Any kind of dreamy feelings
    e) Rubber shoes (except overshoes)
    f) Having progeny

Jon Tómasson Tómas Jónsson from there point by point and for a thousand generations to eternity they change places the about-to-be-born Jón Tómasson for fifty years Tómas Jónsson the other seventy-six and then -son gets added to Tómas and -ss and -on to Jón century after century until one gets dizzy with -ss and -on or -son and soon the new Tómas or Jón screams his first cry of agony out in the world and catches his breath to pump it mechanically in and out of his chest cavity for forty fifty sixty years tirelessly like a device in the lungs or god knows how long no my only thought about the terrible game of conception is about strength   man is nothing but a devil with an automatic device that draws the wind into him and pumps it out of him so his legs move and his eyes roll and he moves and stares for example at houses or women and birds no I cannot think of producing such a devil with for example Gerður

    g) Thinking about my grandfather at ninety

Títa think of grandfather nine decades and still breaking the brain's bounds with life's problems and trying to make sense of it with a tobacco mix in your nose at the grave's edge   devil get away from me   mewling cat-creature or I'll pour ink in your mouth ×

×: one time Ólaf said (they were discussing literature and what they called the embellished leprosy of human mediocrity): Can you explain, Sigurður, why men and events are made simple in commie books like The Little Yellow Hen. Because the world in detail cannot fit in a single book (he says). The public understands only the simplest of life's key elements: You need to eat because you are hungry after work. Yes, but my dear sir who can repeat such simple things indefinitely, it is more appropriate to say: You have to eat so you can enjoy your new pink toilet and extra-soft blue toilet paper. The result of working and wage rises is meat and potatoes and Hitchcock movies on Sundays. It gets a bit on my nerves that commies only use a simple A to Z, and never the whole alphabet, which is very complex. They are not interested in more than two colors; the whole color palette runs together, color gets lost in their hands. Pfff, he says, you do not understand the theorists' theories. Previously, everything had ended up botched thanks to them, the delirious hope of a two-thread-system resulting in the national yarn getting tangled in its movements. They do not know that no system can be so simple as that which trusts in one true god withstanding time's attacks; sooner or later the system will split into an alphabet. The commies soothe life's journey by denying the existence of letters other than A and Z. Another thing about them is that household grievances are clothed in political costumes like with the price of whole milk. And what results from labor struggles other than people going to see Hitchcock pictures and reading Úrval.   poor Sigurður getting splashed with water I did not want to be in the way no   why are rulers made comically simple in commie books.   yes because he isn't victorious, that great intelligent poet and communist who knows everything and stuffs his mouth with mouth-knowledge in the workplace and dining areas   Perhaps they are laughable in the same way as other men are, Ólaf says snidely, narrowing his eyes at me, and on the other hand sly, he adds, malice on his face.   I would add that otherwise they could not remain indefinitely in power with their infamous conscience as the mirror of the world's time   My cheeks warmed with pleasure. His eyes paid me a compliment.   I wanted to thump Sigurður I felt very sorry for him in his doubt as it squeaked from his lips   In our capitalist society we can only be negative, we have nothing else. You know many people have distorted the path to socialism, but when we have built our society people will become more positive than ever before in history. Ólaf laughed and waggled his finger at Sigurður. Religion; my very intelligent friend Siggi, he said. This is the sort of promise a man can only make to himself in his dad's scrotum. I suspect the reason for the unusual number of icelandic commies is that they know that things will never come to the point where they have to propose anything, for what's easier than to pretend to be something if it is certain you never have to prove yourself capable. Ólaf exaggerates when he claims we have been boastful cowards from the outset of the great masked ball we call *our history*—Nothing—increasing our inorganic isolation, succeeds in effortlessly moving the geographical location of the country toward the world's central axis, no, I think we are as much on a roll as when we dress in rock giant and snow lord costumes for the annual fête at Elementary School—you could call the nation the U.S.'s foster-daughter—denying it is Nothing. Otherwise, we would perhaps be Something, because a cottage farmer who considers himself to be an estate farmer will always be a cottage farmer, and a fisherman who believes that he is the captain will get cut loose by the captain and human responsibility and he will never become his imagination; as with a worker, who considers himself a contractor. He should instead say: I am a slave, I talk like a slave, I think like a slave, I should deduce I am a slave. Otherwise his struggle for liberation would be over, he'd become free-minded, free from hassle, a slave who lazes wishfully on a soft couch. (But I say, one must not deceive himself, let your mind drift forward so a lie becomes a truth: I become what I once lied I was?) Like Sigurður who lives on schnapps and dreams, I suggested to Ólaf on the landing, never achieving anything. Do you remember what Gestur Pálsson wrote in *Should We*. No, said Ólaf.

Should we decide? all the deckhands cried out all around the ship.
We began to discuss the matter; some were for and some against.
Some felt it was safer, more reliable to decide; others thought it was downright unnecessary, "all bother and nothing else." The squabbling had gone on for a long while. Word followed word until the conversation turned into hymns and ships and the sentence was not named by name. All the ship's crew stood in a row around the ship, lay down on it to rest, and kept discussing the equipment. When a little while had passed, the captain asked again: Should we decide? Then we returned to squabbling about it, back and forth, until a teenage boy silently hefted the anchor from the ship and so immobilized them there on the tide line. And then they all went to town, slowly and carefully, as Icelanders should.

If any commie had written this story now, he would have made the ship a symbol for society and had the surf rinse it away in the night. The End.

I could sling this at Sigurður, I said, and took his sleeve and squeezed his hand as a token of gratitude. Then he responds (Ólaf) badly: Dogs sniff at the spots where other dogs piss; no careful dog dares piss anywhere except where there is already the smell of urine.   how did the first dog in the world relieve himself having no piss spot that preceded him it now occurs to me to ask when it is too late to answer good answers always come to mind afterward   Sometimes there briefly appears an incomprehensible bitterness in Ólaf, most likely because his intelligence confronts miserable, despised men. He is no exception. I think this is a symptom of intellectuals. Ólaf's behavior is questionable and bizarre. You rarely know where he stands. He enjoys confusing people as to their arguments, getting them slowly on his side but when they hang their shingle he takes the opposite view, casts down that shingle brutally, proving the opposite argument and getting everyone to agree with him. Then he will stand up and leave. That was exactly what I meant, they will say. Ólaf will grin at their approval for the way he managed to knock everyone out like freshly-caught sea scorpions. He would not throw his catch back into the sea, however, and as before sea scorpions would flock to his hook. Ólaf gobbles them up. Various kinds of rumor existed about his sea scorpions in the refectory[i] and there was not anything fishy between Sigurður and Ólaf; they would smoke together. Often.

   h) I must start avoiding Ólaf, too

Many events from this period frequent my mind. I would prefer to remember little of it. I don't want to remember anything. No one has taken away my right to be allowed to forget.

   i.
   The refectory had for some time comprised two equally large rooms or areas, facing south. They could be converted fairly easily into a single large room by opening the triple concertina doors between the two; almost the whole middle wall was a concertina door. After two adjacent rooms, the fashion was for open plan, so the creaking concertina

doors, which were made of countless small frames, were torn apart; nothing was left except the iron fixtures for the hinges in the threshold. The middle wall had been broken up so that the top and bottom parts formed plinths that demarcated the two rooms. The era of plinths reigned the whole time I ate there, now of course it has all been broken down and the house has become one great cavity. On the plinths stood the great symbol of that era, the Wandering Jew, and flowers flowed in countless braids and shoots down to the floor. Although there was no visible boundary between the rooms, except the plinths and flowers, the pensioners were divided according to their rank at work. In the inner room sat people who engaged in clean work; in the anterior were others who performed dirty work. In both, people ate at a long table in the middle of the room, perhaps set a hair closer to the outer wall. A few small tables were placed in the corner against the wall. The area between the tables was called the walkway. The small tables were for those who were eating half board, just lunch or dinner. These men came and went and gained no understanding, whereas the long table in the inner room had formed an enduring core. The walls of the two rooms were blank, painted in muted colors. At each long table sat sixteen people, fairly crammed in, people of different professions. The pensioners had little or nothing in common except a policy of living alone. They had each traveled unevenly along the path to bachelorhood. At the long table in the inner room, which in canteen parlance was The Board, there was one person less on one side than the other, at one end, because of an extensive oak buffet with an oval mirror made of ground glass. There were ledges on either side of it. On them sat solemn, great porcelain dogs who looked out in the hall with eyes so natural they resembled human eyes. The nucleus of the Board was four bank employees (I never reached this nucleus), a woman, two ladies who worked alternately in stationary stores or bookstores, a year at each place in sequence, they said, to make life varied and diverse. They were nicknamed the porcelains. Also in the nucleus were two middle-aged women and a housing adviser who

never spoke to anyone, or rarely. You could almost judge newcom-
ers by their reaction to the porcelain dogs. If on his very first day
the newcomer reacted to the dogs with jokes, he was immediately
classified as a lapsed Marxist; *at a certain period in the history of*
icelandic Marxism there developed a powerful opposition to porcelain
dogs, which became a tenet of commie faith. The dogs were smashed
and discarded at sea or in waterfalls. This awakening against Danish
porcelain dogs began with a Marxist nationalistic poet who directed
canine humor at them; it reached such a tumult that soon all foreign
porcelain dogs in iceland had been destroyed, and no one needed to
justify himself and risk ridicule. The dogs had no refuge except in
the buffets in cafeterias. But such humor was out with the changing
times and those who used it were called lapsed Marxists. The dogs,
then, had won. If someone sneered at them, he would not expect an
uprising, but the Board would respond with one voice: Such dogs are
fashionable rarities and very expensive; they are fine interior decora-
tions. If the newcomer, however, was playful and brought the dogs
over to carefully examine all their parts, the Board took to him with
open arms; he was promoted to the nucleus after a short test set by
the Board intelligentsia, and immediately after spiritual discussions
erupted, governed by two men, Sigurður and Ólaf. They knew the
whole town, *not only people in high places (at least, they would*
say: Oh, that man was at this party at such-and-such-a-time) but
also bums in the street, who lay there due to their all-round gifts,
gifts that prevented them from landing on the right shelf in life,
it was not suited to people of superior intelligence in the icelandic
bourgeois society. The Board was considerably snobbish, looking down
on we who claimed to have an all-round understanding of the human
being. On the day of a new arrival, people would dispute the situation *of this or that writer who was going his own way or approaching*
the Nobel, and then people disputed about painters who worsened
with each show having gone to Paris to discover innovations, and gen-
erally writers worsened with each book that Laxness relieved himself

of, and politics grew thinner every year, financial scandals increased and our tiny society, no larger than a New York City street, grew icily ominous. In the opinion of these two top intelligentsia at the Board, all books ought to be concise satires—Sigurður leaned toward the fellow-human-oriented lyrical rich imagery in poetry with a realistic ironical sheen; Ólaf was more for actual critical polemics. Everything characters ever did in books was really a criticism, even what was normal in the country like shitting in the open. They found indeed little of such criticism (only one author had done so in print) since people in books and movies never need to shit or piss; there is always too much struggling to improve and conquer the world and ending up in the mire seeking out booze or procuring a woman. One of the great rules for success for any man is combing your hair a certain way, back to your neck and smeared across the crown with wet fingers and also walking about at all times in a striped tie set with a windsor knot. Sigurður and Ólaf weighed in with moist sentences from a newly published Laxness novel. Their brains were a great catalog of citations they nimbly searched. In their judgment, style was the main thing in painting, employing the appropriate nature of form. They considered the symphony orchestra worth naught, and usually representations of buildings in icelandic art were in ruins, except for in Laxness's books. "Other than the lack of centralizing and storyline," they said. "The centralizing moral stands firm with the writer's perspective though unwaveringly outside the characters in their creations. It is essential that negative forces are gathered together in an epic manner in real-istic drama and the tensions that form there in order that the total influence crystallizes at the end of the story. Point Counter Point *by Huxley and* Atomic Station *by Laxness stand firm: mescal and Marxism," they added.*

The Board gaped with astonishment. Both these men were approv-ing of mescal and brewing strong beer. The result of these oddly extravagant *views by* two *stealth commies (they were suspected of being either wholly or partly so or both but they said they preferred*

*the National Defense or the Progressive Party alternately, after having
given the Socialists a chance a few years back) was a lively discussion
that quite threw the* petty bourgeoisie class *of humans who were
right at that time settling down to eat. Such discussions were meant
to prove to the newcomers that people in iceland were not entirely
mentally dead, at least not those who ate at the Board. After this trial,
the newcomer was free, and was registered either as* not the worst
*or he was not the worst. The lunch hour ended and the disputations
drowned in the rattle of chairs at 1:10 P.M. and everyone was bloated
from having* coffee after dinner, *which the inner room got with an
additional charge on their food account. The outer room refused coffee
with the surly remark: A man is meant to have nothing remaining
except for getting food after his working hours complete with his slosh
of coffee.*

*Each member of the Board had received some form of higher
education that gave rise to discussions about tests and test results,
discussions of men with grants, who had applied for grants, or who
would be receiving grants. Discussions of assorted subsidies were very
popular, especially scholarships aimed at improving people, and there
was approval for examinations. Examination proctors were highly
esteemed. At the Board, the highest educational grade was the "Simple
High School Test, Reykholt"* while the high school test was some test
*one of the porcelain ladies had completed, she worked in a stationery
store along Njálsgata that had a considerable selection of icelandic
books, Danish magazines, paper dolls, coloring books, and Meccano.
She and her friend from the bookstore were thin, small boned, with*
flawless complexions, *so like porcelain that their* facial complexion
*gave rise to their nicknames. Both porcelains combed their hair in a
way that* never goes out of fashion, *parted down the middle and let
fall flowing and untamed down their cheeks. They enriched their hair
with added vitamins and egg shampoo. No hair-maggots were to be
found in their hair. Occasionally, they went* out to dinner, had their
hair cut, colored, rinsed, and layered, deciding *there was nothing*

to it. Their hair was classically fashionable, *neither too short nor too long,* just right in the back *where the ends turned in* little curls on their nape. *The following night they'd sleep with washed hair in hair-nets and happily dry their hair in the sun,* if there was any sun to be found— *"Sun ruins your hair." Their clothing comprised monochrome angora sweaters and plain skirts, which they stroked from their thighs and buttocks with their right hand or even both, if their chair was spacious enough, as they sat down; the skirt's material tended not to crease. After sitting, they shook their shoulders and adjusted the flesh of their ass-cheeks to the hard seat, lifted their hair from their sweater collar, tossing it with a move of their heads and a delicate caress from the back of their hands which they finally stroked across their appendix. Both had had severe appendicitis attacks for many years and said that the next attack would undoubtedly see them hover between life and death in the University Hospital; their appendixes had certainly affected their bowels. The women were getting to a critical age but kept their skin young with day and night Pons creams and cleansers—"to fix all kinds of damaged complexions the cream nourishes and heals the death of the skin." They lived alone in a* moderately small and cozy *apartment, spent their free evenings washing their nylon socks and angora sweaters in moderately warm soapy water without any alkalis. Sometimes they went to the movies. They washed their underclothes daily, dried them on a rope in front of the oven; it wasn't possible to dry anything in the bathroom, they only had shared access to the toilet; they sprinkled talc in their shoes and thought—"if a married woman does not want to have children, wants to be free, she must take care to look to the negligible custom of the morning ritual that befits the móderne married woman today." An especially good vaginal salve had come on the market. In* sexual matters *they felt themselves liberal, but no more than average; they did not hate the communist politician Katrín Thoroddsen for* introducing a condom *that killed semen, which some women deemed sheer hypocrisy. "Couples have no need of more than four children:*

two to replenish society when they die and the others to swell the nation, vital if she is to come to full term in the international arena."

Although the porcelains did not know half the city, they knew several of its better citizens, if conversations ever turned to Reykjavík families. "Ah, yes, Mumi of the Engeyars, a formidable and fine soul," they'd say. "The same can be said about Óla the 'dolphin': he swam too often in the wine." Their employers were also fine souls as far as it went, though perhaps they did not pay handsomely enough, but the girls managed to augment their meager salaries via the proceeds of havoc in many marriages: *they were the confidants of upstanding souls there in their humble apartment; over simple wine they would advise on what course to take, after things had come to a pass and the couple had stopped speaking to one another.* And knowing how to clean up for men *and discovering in him slender threads, they would reject him and his minor benefits there on the cross-stitched cushions on the sofa, open their thin thighs, raise themselves up and smoke cigarettes from a Mozart Cigarette case with no interest in what was going on between their thighs—because it was not for them, but for the man who wants to vent—and so they lived. The next day they would buy soft yarn for new angora sweaters.*

One time they were enticed out to a club to dine with a certain Board man (Sigurður), but never again. After a night at Sjálf-stæðishús—"they got tipsy on wine, and then acted all shark-skinned, hard and cumbersome," was Sigurður's classification; *he said that such women should not be allowed around men. He accused them of being prick-teases with fierce lesbian tendencies because the stationery store one had driven the heel of her shoe into his groin for getting* offensively *personal with her in the little cozy apartment, when she had* simply *wanted to invite him up to their place to be lovely and chummy, no hidden agenda. "O god, how nauseating some people are. I get goose bumps thinking of him," they said to the teachers who listened attentively and could not understand it, Sigurður was a sympathetic character in their opinion. The teachers had a secret plan to invite the Board men home for tea or a wholesome Norwegian breakfast, and Sigurður could be charming when in the mood. But they were well aware he was a broken man; he became their intense* psychological study *and they, these innovative teaching women, had fun making with their independent study, quoting from the book* Stature and Character. *Sigurður had come—in a certain state of his soul—right out of this uniquely informing book by Kretschmer. They soon* psychoanalyzed *him as schizophrenic, excusing everything he did, saying: well the man IS schizophrenic. In truth, they were* not *desperate and* peppery *like Miss Gerður; they were anxious neither about ending up unmarried in old age, nor dying alone in their apartment. They had the foresight to get ownership in a cooperative apartment in the Housing Cooperative of Children's Teachers where members in good standing had first refusal. Their hope was to get their own apartment and keep it on a full teacher's salary after they stopped teaching, a profession that had changed them into some kind of shiny metal to which nothing stuck, they protested in vain; nothing concerned them if it did not personally affect them or their work. "No, one does not dread one's normal share or becoming old and weak," they said with a Mona Lisa smile.*

Two foreign girls served in the refectory—the atmosphere was fittingly international—and two foreigners studying icelandic Studies at the University ate at the Board. The presence of foreign countries contributed to the notion that the Board must not show up the nation, but display her honor in intelligent discussion and fashionable looks. But the students would ideally have heard something from the old icelandic, *which caused the Board great problems: the students wanted the sort of ideas that the Board had decided were wrong with the country, especially the cherished farming culture the students thought unique since farmers did nothing but read or write sagas. The students, prospective* Friends of iceland *and representatives for the country overseas, worked hard to be more icelandic than Icelanders, to speak a cleaner and more beautiful language than the Board, and they took icelandic names, mixing them together and reversing them backward so they were called one thing today and another tomorrow, for example Kormákur Snorrason or Snorri Kormáksson, but despite their infatuation they could still say: "there is no modern culture in iceland, only the farming culture from remote valleys, and it is wonderful." This over-hasty judgment met with a protracted chorus of o-protests from the wounded and humiliated Board. Even Ásmundur, the silent owner of the place, growled an 'o,' and Tómas Jónsson 'o'-ed, too, in his own way. "The world-famous Laxness, the worthy Þórbergur, they are from there? Hasn't Laxness established the zenith for the epic novel in world literature?" The Board became mentally paralyzed for a few days then got back on track just before Lent, demanding these people who lived in the wider world admit that it mattered that one of their great men had marked the zenith either for capitalism or communism with a novel. The Board insisted on this for a few days but the students' opinions were not shaken even on the first day of summer when a leg of lamb with fried potatoes, red cabbage, and rhubarb sauce was brought forth. One student was German, the other a Swede. The Swede always had his student's hat on, even while eating, and he proposed little or nothing by way of conversation. The Board was fairly repelled by him and tried to watch its language as best as possible, afraid of the Swede's focus on grammar and so said: I know that Urban (who sometimes wanted to be called Þorgeir Skorargeir) will sooner or later look up from his soup dish of fluent icelandic; he is just waiting for the right moment. Upon hearing that, the Swede laughed coldly. The German spoke by turns and was generous in his views: a nation such as iceland that has neither Don Quixote, Dante, nor Greek Tragedies in its language, not to mention the canon of modern literature, has no access to modern culture except through foreign books. Therefore, it loses its culture not because of external effects such as the American occupation and the defense of Keflavík, but eats up itself according to Toynbee's law. "But doesn't Toynbee say that an isolated nation can only maintain its footing if it* is endowed with internal life?" said Sigurður, "and if there is no modern culture then there is no modern culture to eat. Perhaps there's more life in the pensioners in Germany than here in the refectory?" "Just so," said the Board. That impressed the German student, who spoke eight languages fluently, taught Russian to the soldiers at Keflavík airport, and had been shelled in the leg by communists on the Eastern front during the war—but the Board could not accept his views.

One server was a Danish girl named María. She served the Board in the inner room. The other was a German, Edeltraud, who waited on the front room. People didn't really know Edeltraud, only that she had come over on a trawler with other German workers after the war and had become pregnant the first night in iceland. Edeltraud missed Germany somewhat because back home she had been able to choose from five types of coffee available on the black market. People's diets were as varied as possible if you had money to stand by a barrel at the railway station and eat hot dogs with mustard all night—"there is much more air and trees outside the city." She was in a relationship with an icelandic fishermen she met on the trawler and they were in love (on the way over the girls slept in the bunks in the ship's hold while the men slept on deck under sail stretched between the hatch covers), but when they came ashore the seaman wanted nothing to do with her, except when he was drunk. "A woman just has to wait and be patient," said Edeltraud. The loyalty and patience of this German girl earned the Board's admiration of German persistence, they took it upon themselves to never give up even though they had lost everything. Yet the Board was convinced that Edeltraud would never get anything from the fisherman except frustration; she was by nature submissive as Germans partly are and would let him wipe his feet all over her kindness, spending her savings and even ordering her to fetch booze for him from the State Liquor Store. "Such things do not happen in Germany," said Edeltraud, yet she didn't want to toss the fisherman overboard; he had entered her heart and so she would listen to the shipping news on the radio to find out where he was and *she waited for him. "She would no more than anyone else cut out part of her body and her heartsong," said the woman who usually filled in for Edeltraud on Wednesdays, when she had her day off, which she used to clean the home that belonged to the mother of the fisherman, who of course lived with her and drove everyone insane when he came back from the sea and wanted to relax.*

María had a heart out for herself. *She was very tall, light-haired and blue-eyed, and with a crooked nose, which she got when she was three, the time she fell from an open window in Silkeborg down into a barrel full of chicken feathers that saved her life. The nostrils of her crooked nose were full of dark blackheads from the sweat. She used every free moment to shut herself in the toilets and squeeze the black-heads in front of the mirror. The girl's appearance was so poor, "except for the bright eyes," that it was hard to believe that she had become so crooknosed in the land of the actress Vivi Bak, whose achievements in film and on stage wore endlessly in newspapers, along with the fact that she was on her way to iceland with a Danish blockbuster. The Board considered María's conduct polite and restrained; "she has apparently had a good upbringing and inherited the Danish cheer." A troubled smile played increasingly on her lips, which she half-opened to suck in the air as she spoke. She had difficulty understanding ice-landic, contrary to Edeltraud; she* studied the language *for three months and had only a broken version of it. Because of her difficul-ties understanding, María always placed her ears right above people and they worked out that she probably sucked her breath in during conversation because of her halitosis. The Board could not decide on the halitosis smell she had and whether she was in fact three women, one at each seating: rotten before midday, oniony at coffee, and sour for dinner. "Uvv," she drew in her breath and disappeared into her shell whenever someone said: "María dear, did you want me to eat with my fingers today." "I'm probably forgetting something, being lovestruck," she would say quietly and return with a fork on a plate. "That must be so, María dear, you are always so absent-minded." The dining matron complained bitterly about María's apathy which was so different from Edeltraud's* efficiency, *but she kept her in service out of a scarcity of options. "Getting rid of María now when everyone has gone to work for the military," she said, "I just call her names in icelandic, but if she were to move, possibly to Canada, I would probably lose half the people. You cannot assign both rooms to Edeltraud, no matter how diligent and conscientious she may be." The other teacher used every opportunity to practice her Danish with María's help. She had such difficulty getting the sounds right in Danish. Everyone was warm toward the girl. "There's something so sweet and gentle about her despite her mishaps." And the womenfolk seemed to feel she had a reliable build for motherhood.*

The pensioners received two dishes, a main course *first and then porridge. This dining arrangement had passed without incident until María came and the porridge made her laugh: in Denmark, the usual experience was a hearty soup with berry porridge for dessert. As she offered porridge dishes she always giggled. "Is María laughing?" said one of the teachers who was sensitive to ridicule; one of the porcelains lifted her hair from her neck with a light, backhand movement. After three months of much giggling María could no longer torture herself and said: I find it so strange you eat porridge after your food. But what of it? said the other porcelain as she smoothed her hair and lifted it from her sweater's collar. They were apparently frustrated by the fact that the dining hall held to rituals that were not customary in the land of* ALT for Damerne *and Vivi Bach. The Board discussed table manners with great passion, and following a Saturday vote (the result was 7: 2, the two being Tómas and Ásmundar, but many were absent, including the engineers, who normally ate on Saturdays with their old classmates from MR, '46) approved a new practice, having hearty soup instead of porridge, and they made the argument that, really, porridge was a base food, which people with light office jobs need not necessarily have instead of hearty soup, to be brought out before the main. And this achieved an end to María's giggling.*

The teachers (who taught young children to read and used the Isaac method, which is considered the best way to transition a child from kindergarten unscathed from the earlier pedagogy, *because it was easy to achieve in three months and it established reading fluency before school in the spring) were experts in handicrafts, and wanted to herd the Board to craft workshops and folk dances with Sigríð Valgeir—"who is outstanding in her field"—but the Board, especially the men, did not want such child's play and would* hit the hard stuff come weekends. *They found they met most opposition from the* engineering bloc *on the left corner of the table; they had an Olympian contempt for common entertainments, domestic squabbling, and politics—"the world will end when times run away from the technologists' control and the plebs will become null and the politicians nix." Everyone would have to sit and stand according to the orders of the* technology centers. *It seemed these men chiefly sustained themselves on strong beer. The engineers were variously preparing a new project, delivering a project, or undertaking a particular project which would, if implemented by the right parties in the right places, overthrow everything. Occasionally they would be inexplicably between projects and they would hold protracted, deep conversations about relationships in Höfn, debating certain taverns, certain men in certain taverns and their relationships with the strong beer they wished were brewed here, how in such confined relationships people changed and Icelanders could sit with bowed heads, drinking like at Bedraggled Hens in Höfn. But as many projects as they steered to their conclusion, it never occurred to them to engage in any marriage projects. They were teased—by the teachers—about this, implying they were making eyes at either porcelain lady, sucking their pipes intensely, laughing a stifled belly laugh, sputtering smoke at them from their lips, happily striking the flats of their palms on their shield-like bellies, which they claimed to have gained from drinking strong beer, so nurturing was it, and remembering countless relationships with taverns that they dived into stone sober with Magga*

*Einars—"you remember Magga; what? MR, '45; what's that?"—
and returned and* got involved *with whores, drinking, the whole
caboodle. They gave up all pretense of insinuation and said in their
Laxness voices (they all had practiced doing Laxness carefully): Are
you reprimanding us a little with women, ahahaha?* Reprimanding
with women *seemed to tickle the engineers' sense of manhood and
sexual orientation in a particular way that seemed directed mainly at*
ugly old crones *in certain taverns in certain relationships, crippled
and weeping and with vaguely husky tobaccoed voices, women who
had to screw a wooden leg under themselves or tighten hook paws
on their arms before they threw themselves down hoarse with wine
weeping on a comforter some place up in an attic rafter in Nýhöfn
and waited for* some *member of the group to take them, smelling
like fermented skate from the dirtiness. The pole of their sexuality was
centered on the young untouched honeys in their cohort, MR, '46.
Judging by their descriptions these honeys were barely earthly; their
classmates worshipped their* mystical *talents, how they tilted their
heads, how they held cigarettes and* looked at you *with every sentence
and touched their lips. Sometimes it seemed that the engineers had
achieved the bliss of "being alone with her in her room" and they were
planning to slip a hand under her sweater or clothes—"though that
is not the final stage, one wants more and more, and it costs years of
toil and word-wrestling that can destroy simply months of work, even
years, if the person is too forward." They were always too forward,
neither running nor walking in their love affairs: when the moment
of triumph came the honeys turned out to be* frigid *and many either
had a* virgin complex *or fierce lesbian tendencies that were impossible to overcome trying to "get in touch with chicks." All Saturday
night they sat in City, met acquaintances from their year at MR,
'46, talked about pipe-smoking, reminisced about old relationships
and forest walks and relationships at Gullin, a wonderful place in
Copenhagen. The conversation was often carried out question-and-
answer style: Have you run into Magga Einars? No, Magga Einars is*

nowhere to be seen these days. Has he got some woman? I don't know jack about Magga, not that Magga has changed. They sat with heads bowed over *the vanished world until the relationship of life* drove them out into life's hoarfrost *(away from the country) to oversee the construction in the herring industry. But wherever they went, they took with them, in their heads: the-once-and-future-relationships-with-cohort-MR, '46.*

The Board very much enjoyed being liberal both in politics and matters of sex; it tolerated all robust speech and plain-spokenness.

The porcelains were slightly scandalized at first, splashing their hair and stroking their angora sweaters and appendices, but tried to conceal it because they lived in the half-hope that one of the engineers would take them on *at some point after having lived outside the country calculating the strength of concrete—but their hope was in vain. They dried like concrete, became little by little harder in countenance despite the Pons cream, their latent lesbian tendencies ever more visible at the corners of their mouths. On the other hand, Ólaf proposed to María one fine day, leaving the Board astonished and sufficiently horrified to a one. Their relationship began silent and soundless and evolved; no one understood how. As a group the Board composed a "wedding poem in the old style." While the composing happened, Tómas Jónsson pricked up his ears but without submitting his own verse. Who could have imagined that he had taken upon himself the insurmountable effort of studying for his diploma exams outside school, although he couldn't benefit from it in any way. Tómas was always regarded like* any other drooling old man and irredeemable onanist.

In the outer room, the death of iceland continued in quieter, more moribund ways, with minimal spiritual trappings. The pensioners there sat stone-silent over their plates. Before dinner the engineers loitered at the empty table with their soup spoons in their hands ready to bolt down *the porridge as soon as it was put on the table. Their lunch hour was short, and if the porridge was not served* right away

after the main meal they could be heard braying bitterly in an unco-
ordinated chorus: What's this? Will here be no porridge today. We lose
a chance to inhale it after dinner.

Edeltraud would let no man harry her. She had set the table care-
fully: the second week she began to carry the porridge from pedestal to
wall, then from wall to pedestal. From there, she ladled out the food
to the porridge plates, feeding everyone at the table according to her
own system. But the engineers weren't slow to fault her system, even if
she was German. She protested and said they always got their porridge
last. "The middle always ends up in the middle," said the middlers.
After much hassling, Edeltraud restructured the sequence of her tasks,
carrying to the middle first, and then out from it toward both ends
of the table. This lasted a few days, until the engineers once again
became aware of a shortcoming in the system. They beat their empty
spoons on the table and demanded a flexible system that everyone
could agree on. *Edeltraud stood in the middle of the floor, clasped*
her fists and everything turned to porridge before her eyes. "No por-
ridge for you, then," she announced. "I will eat the porridge myself."
And they answered: "You have porridge for brains. Start at either end
or in the middle, carry to each end across the table in rotation for a
week, and then from the pedestal to the middle for the next week,
then the week after from the wall to the middle, and then across the
table each person can take his plate to hand to the person opposite."
Edeltraud stood still in the same stance while the engineers explained
their system, ready with the phrase: "No porridge for you." Suddenly
she began to sob, all turned around over this icelandic simplification,
this ferocious know-how. The dinner matron intervened, rushing into
the hall like a prow-heavy ship and striking her hands together. "Each
and every one of you can wait for his porridge. There's no crowd in
danger if someone has to wait a while," she said very firmly. The
engineers piped down, grumbled quietly, and beat their empty spoons
on their fingertips. After getting their porridge they each shoveled it
down as if in solitude, rushed back off to work with a glow in their

eyes, and farted. They propelled themselves on a bumpy and choppy pigeon-toed gait, more from desire than ability, sparing themselves bus fares and "went as far as to tramp the short distance down to the harbor," always on a quick journey to find food and from food to their workplaces. If there was any time left over after eating, they would coil themselves up to rest for a few minutes in a cloth bag by a cement stack, stretching their body on the factory floor, lying in a pile of shavings with ropes and equipment or trying to nab a chicken-nap in the back seat of a vehicle on the forecourt, feet out the door and heels up on the lubricant dispensers. As soon as time was called they leapt up, braying, their stomachs heavy and weary with undigested food in the upper duodenum, continually giving them heartburn or drowsiness, yet all the same they worked furiously. But if the rest and everything else failed in their lives, they still lived in eternal hope *of the time after their working hours, and even if that hope was extinguished in the evening at five o'clock like a ray of winter sun, it awakened immediately in the morning as the sun rose, having completed her circle around the hemisphere of heads slumbering somnolent cement- and lubricant-dreams. She woke at six in the morning, when most older men get to their feet, especially if they are uprooted farmers who suspect the imminent death of iceland is approaching after a rather pointless, sad life in pursuit of money. These men lived an absolutely positive life: the desire to maintain reasonable health with reasonably cheap food so they could put in a reasonable performance until evening, get a reasonable recompense at week's end and die a reasonable death. Often they'd get their wish, getting to die at work. They were crushed in the mud under high and heavy piles of cement bags, died on the way to the hospital, or were knocked into the ship's hold, breaking their skull. News of an accident at work aroused in them a similar curiosity and pleasure as an* incurable disease *excites in women. Sometimes one of the workers would unhook himself from his work thoughts and ask to look in the papers, once the Board has finished with them; it was fond of newspapers. If they could find news of the accident, which was not often easy, they went stooping around the table with the paper in their hands, sticking it between people, pointing to the news or the picture and saying, This one I recognize, he worked with me in the same crew. Fatal accidents lifted them far from the anonymity of the front room to the extent that they tried to interest the Board in the fact that they might have been crushed, were practically the one who died.*

The threshold had ripped out the concertina doors separating the rooms and it was fitting that the relationship between the rooms ran aground. Only scattered things carried across—what did you say— well—but of course . . . Occasionally a complete sentence stretched across, always from the interior room to the outer, like this: Why isn't security equipment installed? asked the Board, concerned about the accident from a technical perspective. "Well, it's not possible," said the outer room, boasting about their complicated and life-threatening jobs. The answer gave the Board material for a "philosophical discourse about a person with a simple job facing the giant creatures of a mechanical organism," which subsumed natural life in industrialized society and fomented new myths in the masses who assume the helplessness of primitive man, sacrificial animals over which he should rule. These workbeasts never followed their coworkers to the grave, but the repeated question was: did many people attend the funeral? "A man doesn't sit down at work," they told them apologetically. "You cannot extinguish the sun while the day shines." This sentence was their refrain and belief that one had to work while any trace of lifeforce lay in the body.

The voluntary desire for servitude within the working class was as thoroughly supported by the newspapers as possible with headlines like: THE POWER TODAY LIES WITH MAN. HE GLOWS WITH LIFE'S JOY AT MAINTAINING INDUSTRY AND THE NATION. Large headlines were followed by photos and smaller writing about the great excitement in this little box, descriptions of zealous workers rolling herring barrels, unloading salt and cement or lifting enormously huge halibut and embracing giant cod. The readers became, among other things, more erudite about the number of workers in the working class working for Eimskip, the date of birth and age of the worker who broke his leg, what region he was from, the names of his grandparents, how many children they'd brought up, how long father and son had been employed by the same company, and eventually comparisons of the living standards of people past and present were published; they'd improved, of course, for men no longer carry salt on their backs, coal is lifted from the ships with a crane. Everything was presented as a tremendous miracle.

The newspapers appeared to be in the trough with employers and their aims of increasing efficiency and a labor cult. Joyful workers enjoyed great fame as part of the "interest the newspapers and the nation have in men who complete the toughest, worst paid, and most essential tasks in society: 'SUCH MEN DESERVE EVERY GOOD.'" The papers published scant general foreign news about cloud-smoke in Arizona and new insects found in grain, which few cared about; instead they were gradually filled with actresses who were or were not pregnant, things understood or not were mixed with the achievements of the invisible men, the working heroes behind the "great changes that have occurred in icelandic employment." The popularity of the radio program We Work grew exponentially and the power of journalists around the country increased, not just meeting priests and magistrates and discussing lambing, but going between villages and workplaces, which raised people's hopes of getting in the papers. The tension and the waiting period over whether they could get into the papers made for much sleeplessness and taut pain in their whole frames. They became subscribers and bought papers in the hope of a picture, of reading something about themselves, even the same enumerations as usual in these interviews that were little more than birthdates and years, the region one was from, the farm name, the mountain near the farm, the old country place names. The life of the working class hero was lost in a soup of names; irrelevant. The leftist

papers had their part in this work madness, never having had enough
of entrepreneurs and of effort, zeal mixing with sport and the regular
column About Fish, swollen with interviews with herring kings and
their relationships with the major poets, and not to forget the factory
owners and their slave masses.

Once the Board was about to let this clamoring discourse fade,
the journalist's obligations and the role of the newspapers, you could
scarcely hear faint life-breaths from the lips of the workers in the
outer room. But when they were confident that no one at the Board
was eavesdropping and mocking their conversations about whether it
would be better to work for this magnate or another, each considered
his own salmon, admired the size and initiative, and wondered if he
would have a better future working for Coal & Salt Co. or Eimskip.
The company- and magnate-rivalry was a root guiding this boring
city. Most often Coal & Salt Co. won the competition and comparison; a man was lucky enough to break a leg in the Company, he was
automatically placed in sequence with those who approached the mysterious scales the angels keep as they appoint people to their designated
bowl, a kind of heaven. In the outer room ate two broken-legged
men who'd survived and were moving hopefully along this scale. One
was the third in line to be deemed disabled and the other the tenth.
The first was full of pride but the other wanted sometimes to waive
all rights since he had received a half-promise of joining a steamer
with some mysterious assorted work crew which would GET MORE
FROM THIS THAN THEY PUT IN. "For sure, many will argue
about the situation," he said.

These workbeasts lived in constant fear of strikes controlled by
"those there" at the top in order to maximize personal gain by causing
goods to rise in price, and so food and lodging, too. The beasts murmured about "those there" sitting on flat butt-cheeks. But all the talk
was underground, with no way of identifying who "those there" were
unless you were "up there" deciding the basic pay and performance of
the workhorses in this foggy world. Were "those" trade union leaders or

employers? No way to tell from their talk. Sometimes "those there" ran together. But some controlled the lives in the workplace with "balloons and syringes," which were sent down to them and spurted at someone or blew him up with air.

The workbeasts took care against syringes and demanded to get their money in an envelope, not collected like some unintelligible purchase that "those there" dandled to make them crazy, blurring the lines "like when kittens get into a ball of yarn."

Occasionally, Sigurður went to the workbeasts to submit "a draft of trade union awareness signaling they fulfilled requirements other than simply toiling." "You should ask for something from your life, other than working for Coal & Salt Co., even given you're the salt of the earth," he said. "Nothing is too good for the working class." "They trade more than coal and salt now, Coal & Salt Co.; it's big business," they said smugly to the ignorant blue-collar man. His attempts at persuasion bore little success, although one sentence entered into the beasts' heads that they liked to say in the spirit of the Board: "Writers should write books for the people," he repeated and cast his eyes at them even as he said it from the insurmountable remove of the threshold, as irrelevant as the Board and the people sitting there. But the man repeated the phrase several times: Yes, if people cannot have books for themselves, I do not demand any at all. He asked for nothing and had a four-inch nail for scraping the concrete spatter from inside his boots. He'd always worked in cement, and the dust from the bags gathered in his boots and turned to concrete due to the sweatiness of his feet. At night he would sit on the edge of the bed scraping the inside of the boots; he had stretched twine across the radiator so he could dry his overalls during the night. This brought him pleasure. In the basement room he giggled over the stupidity of "those there" and the Board, talking the whole meal time, satisfied as to the hardships in cement: it was well paid, there was no dawdling or fawning, no babbling over everything and nothing. He vowed solemnly while he tore and fixed his boots, to not let some syringe ferment inside him, *but instead to memorize some basic political phrases to repeat when required: This cannot continue; it simply isn't feasible; can you really offer that to the people: no, people will not put up with it any longer. With these four sentences he sailed undisturbed when "syringes" came down, jabbering about some disaster and then going back to tell "those there": "He's definitely our man." Then "those there" sat and jabbered but ran their assholes, to the inexpressible pleasure of the workhorses, they bragged about nothing so much as if "those there" ran their assholes in acquisition disputes and that* strikes gain nothing except inflation.

Their laughter burst from the basement, where they took off their work overalls in a central room and then went to eat their meals in the outer room. It was inevitable that those who worked messy jobs needed to take off their protective clothing before they sat at the table. The requirement for hygiene didn't extend to their hands, legs, or faces; as the matron said: "You can scrabble whatever that stuff is on the food with your large paws, but I do not want you polluting the air or soiling the chairs."

It was comical to see the beasts crowd up the stairs with grub-greedy eyes, often wearing strange clothes: frayed sweaters reaching halfway up the arms; torn striped shirts with round-neck collars, old dress vests with rusty buckles dangling on the back, Álafoss-brand pants with patched knees, ripped and tattered. One-time outer pants *had now become* inner pants. *María giggled at the kitchen door. "Have you ever seen a ewe in half a fleece?" they asked, laughing, but María had only seen idiotic comedy in old films with someone similarly attired hanging up an apple tree. "Such mad men," she said and turned up her nose. The workbeasts' clothes smelled of the acidic smell of people who are still largely rural men and wash their clothes in homemade soap given them by a thrifty old aunt who skims the fat from smoked lamb in her pot, collects it in a fruit can and boils soap once a year. All workbeasts live in basements or lofts. "From a loft it's a shorter way to heaven, but shorter to the grave from the basement,"* the men said, believing they would never die, but would instead continue with Coal & Salt Co. during the day then sleep with their boots and work overalls right by them at night so their livelihoods would not be stolen from the hallway; they were always saving for old age. The filth and stench awakened joy, especially coal and cement dust and grime in their faces as they sometimes stopped at the threshold, striking the Board as figures of agonizing pleasure and pity. For appearance's sake, said someone to hurt or destroy not so much as too mock: You're half-black today. The half-black started to sing tunelessly, stick out his tongue, dance his feet on the waxed floor and get tears of joy in his eyes. With that done, the moment became sorrowful for him. The animal stiffened his face, the smile cooled on his black lips, his red eyes blinked rapidly, he plunked himself down in his chair, roiling in mind and trying to suppress the memory of the fall slaughter. He could picture sheep carcasses lying in coverings across the board so the sand would not spoil them. Finally, he managed to push this from his memory and say: Yes, I was in coal. "You cannot complain about a lack of work," said the Board. "No, there's work enough with Coal & Salt. A man can always toil through a double shift to earn extra money."

The porcelains slunk inside themselves, crossed their arms, elbows pressed to their stomachs, wearing miserable expressions. They felt a cold gust of wind coming from the harbor or a draft in the automobile garage playing on their abdomens; their shoulders shook, their teeth clenched together.

No other communication existed between the outer and the inner rooms.

tómas's seventh composition book

I, Tómas Jónsson, armor myself against laxness. I have striven to create an ordered, organized home. I despise spiritual anarchy and chaotic thought. Since childhood I have beaten away any disposition toward disintegration and sworn an oath to refuse inferior or destructive company. When studying and working I was forced to accord people considerable laxness. Instead of bodily pleasures I enjoy my superiority, the power of my purity. Most people think that happiness in life comes from your image as others see it; no, it resides in your image of yourself. In their homespun faith people look for happiness among neighbors and family members. I curse my family even though it is dead and distant. People think that people like me who practice discipline forgo happiness without knowing it. No. They start to save money and set it aside before some commodity destroys their will to save. Money exists independent from life's whims. And so they betray no one in their loyalty to it, though others betray them. They have no reason to land in evil hands. Victims should have knowledge for their priests. A person should take the value of money as a model in our times when human value is reducing and monetary value increasing. The original character of money is healthy and doesn't budge if sloppy people try to abuse it. Even in fraud cases the money arrives clean, the icelandic coat of arms on its back; it's the traitor who gets taken to prison. No one is so ignorant that he puts money

under arrest. Only touchy Communists believe money is complicit with
man or else they point to its guilt and man's innocence. Soviet money
sits under a prison sentence. Rubles live on bread and water behind bars.
Not totally. They are pampered in banks that are not monetary prisons;
everything is done to increase them. But many Russians sit behind bars
for having attempted to disparage money. Money achieves happiness the
same way we do, demanding everything for itself. Its value matches its
exchange. The value of people matches their exchange. No difference
between man and money. We discuss the characteristics of money and
men the same way: value, exchange, worth, advantages, disadvantages,
etc. I'm not one for religion. I feel sure that human wretches need to
believe; fear of destruction is the basic force of existence. Would you
feel better, you calculate, perishing in belief or disbelief. In that there is
no difference. Man is sentenced to destruction. Saving lets you grow in
confidence. It provides greater security than religion. As soon as a small
amount amasses, you rejoice greatly. You are a mature man. You have the
amount you want in a book and can increase it via the interest rate. You
increase as rapidly as your financial amount. So I might have the same
meaning; so that I exist. I have therefore I am. Come evening, a beggar
has the amount in his hat. Only a few sage misers spot as evident a truth
as this. They look at life under the microscope. This truth is too obvious for the masses who see with lazy eyes, drooling in pleasure over the
Eiffel Tower. The masses waste their seed in a few short years and then
stand there destitute, their purses similarly empty. I was a child when the
truth appeared to me: Be a miser in what you take with your hands, be a
miser with yourself. I decided to invest myself in bank deposits as much
as expend mental and physical energy. I got a return on every penny I
acquired. I own an apartment. The apartment is mine. The apartment is
me. I am a somewhat dark and dank basement but I am myself.

N.B.: I'm no Dolgorukiy, although there are many similarities in our
social conditions.

Chapter I

Tells the story of how how Tómas Jónsson came, in the course of time, to the basement apartment in Hlíðahverfi

> *I cannot help but sit down and write a narrative of my first steps on the career trail (perhaps) I should restrain myself . . . One thing is sure, I will never write a biography, though I live to a hundred. One must be endowed with unspeakable selfishness to overcome the shame inherent in writing about oneself. I can only excuse myself by writing a bestseller for others and so do a good deed for my publisher—if I can find a publisher and readers who are eager for best-selling books. I'm not going to extend the narrative by describing the difficulties I had to endure to get to this world (readers know those firsthand), but rather commence with the time I acquired self-awareness or felt that I was a person. Before it happened, I felt a part of others.*
>
> *Now I am simply myself. Bound inside me were such exalted hopes that I was afraid of not being able to fulfill them. I did not want to change anything. Nothing is a more devilish yoke than the feeling of obligation that comes when subtle praise chimes constantly in one's ear. This discomforting feeling is closely related to wanting to please everyone. A person becomes slave to praise; it delays his normal movement through life and keeps him in a perpetual straitjacket. Provident parents wrap their offspring in a cardigan before they realize the meaning of this love, which they must now privilege and serve. Parental love is the worst kind of slavery: it is legally protected and children are totally defenseless against it.*
>
> *We lived out in Tanga, facing a hill that obscured views of the sea and the cluster of houses at the water's edge. There are now continuous buildings where once there were meadows I or my sister had to run across when we were sent to the store.*
>
> *I must have been sent on this occasion; I think it unlikely that I have swiped this material memory from my dead sister. If there was*

an additional errand, I cannot remember. The main business was to get a check I think from the fishing company my father sailed with in Miðfjörður; this may, however, be the wrong memory, or it had come from America. My mother's relative went there, Jón from Tanga, a well-known man in Winnipeg. He came up with the theory that the icelandic genealogy in Greenland had gone across America and across the Pacific Ocean, such mariners, and settled in Kamchatka. Anyway, I had been sent to the store, which was also the post office, and to ask for the store manager. On the door to the office hung a colored sign of a woman sniffing a rose. The advertisement is clear in my mind as I am certain she was the first color picture I saw in my life. I have ever since been fond of sweet color-photographs in the Art Noveau style from around the turn of the last century.

I, this well-sheared model child, asked for the manager and he handed me a large brown envelope with a broken seal. I opened it, pulled the money out, wet my fingertips and counted the bills. The store manager looked at me with satisfaction, then he said:

I see you're going to be observant at all times. You count your money as soon as you get it in your hands. That is a good idea.

I blushed at the compliment, and I have for some reason never since tolerated them; I blush because compliments are disgusting. After having ascertained that the amount was correct, I said goodbye, full of myself, shamefully happy. I bought something or other in the store and went home with my purchase under my sweater. On the way I counted the money again. I knew the exact amount but in my upset over the compliment I confused my counting so I got either too little or much. I sat on a rock, took a coin out of my pocket, put it in the envelope and returned. I requested the store manager and was ushered into the office, where I said:

You overcounted. You gave me too much.

Are you sure? he asked, irritated. I never overcount.

Yes, I replied. A coin has gotten into the envelope.

Do you mean to say I can't count, he said angrily and took the envelope, counted the notes, and shook it; the coin fell on the table, rolled off it, ran behind the cabinet and disappeared. The cabinet was heavy and the shopkeeper was called in; he and the merchant and I dragged it, but we didn't find the coin. After this commotion I looked and saw it gleam between the floor boards. The store manager ordered me to move, in case the money disappeared into the floor, but the shopkeeper asked him to sneak out gently and get some wire to fish the coin out. He himself took off his jacket, bent to the gap with a wire so his boxy butt stood out in the air. He poked the end of the wire carefully on the far side of the coin; we could hardly breathe. The money fell down under the floor and disappeared. The store manager was outraged by anger, cursing me to the devil, not wanting to look for the coin but ordering his shopkeeper to tear up the planks and hunt for it. While they both messed around with screwdrivers he asked what I had bought and what money I had paid with. Then he ordered me to set out the remainder and asked if I had been given the right change.

Yes, replied the shopkeeper stubbornly. He got the right change.

The merchant counted the money and found immediately what it lacked. At that very moment, the shopkeeper managed to drag the money from under the floor: a fivepence, the amount from his calculation. He stopped. The merchant smiled angrily and said:

Now, I am going to keep this coin and you will be spanked for having lost it.

He pinched my ear tightly, the custom for adults when children played a prank, and shoved me out of the store.

That evening, my parents noticed some of the money I had been given for purchases was missing. My father whipped me until I confessed (maybe this happened in the fall, after my father came home and my mother had lost money all summer but never spanked me so I did not get spanked twice; either because she was a righteous woman or because my father let her do the accounting for her summer spending) then ordered me to get back what I lacked from the merchant's clutches. I did not go; instead, I crawled under the boat and slept there for the night.

The next morning when I scrambled home there was no mention of the money. Then I realized that getting paddled and sleeping for a night beneath a boat was worth fivepence. Everything can be reckoned in money, no matter whether it is a man's life or the nation. Realizing this, I believe, constitutes healthy knowledge for a child, saving them from the pangs of conscience or sin. To kill, rape, rob, and maim are equivalent temporal punishment, worth comparable capital amounts.

The event had no lasting impact on me and I have no idea why I remember it, but I console myself with what arises from this, what a person does or thinks has purpose. Good cheer. What use in carrying the burden of intention for every single incident in our lives. We would suffocate under the weight. Probably I would just have wanted more compliments from the merchant and an additional dose of uncomfortable joy.

others have robbed me of the apartment and myself, others are enjoying a greater benefit than I am this torments me night and day
Tómas did you call   are you awake   I heard you call
Tómas
The people one associates with get more unavoidable
    do you need something Tómas
the power more interfering
    want me to fetch your morning coffee
in one's life and beliefs than one himself
    are you sleeping
Do not stare like this, Anna. I do not want coffee.
more unresponsive are many men than donkeys led by their ears if the donkey that wanted to get rid of its burden of salt in the parable had the sense to stretch its head up from the stream and wait calmly while the current dispensed with the salt and washed it off, he could have arisen

light on his feet with an empty bag freed from birth and death and enslavement by the farmer I would have done it in the donkey's position this parable features idiocy but not the desire to be freed from slavery by fraud as if the author wants to insinuate   writers are always terrified witless wretches and should therefore become priests

    well you call for me when you're ready

I have known
    Shut up, Anna. I did not call for food. I am not hungry I have also known on life's path the art to lying in a stream with heavy salt bags on my back and shoulders but do not intend to just let the stories about it lie in the salt rather take them with me to the grave

to say: here, but no further. I walk outside at night. advertisements for the movie theater face me. I am just on an evening walk, I say. And nothing can attract attention like walking alternately fast and slow and waving your arms about to increase the blood flow to the heart. Nothing is as capable of leading my body astray into bad company. I should be the model of every healthy man, every person seeking continual improvement. Still, I try not to write my name in the skies, as was said of Sigurður. With some dexterity it can it be assigned to Ól . . .

    are you a bit poorly Tómas this nice weather   get some fresh air into your lungs   Dóri is going to bring you outside here by the trash cans   maybe forgot to bring a dog today

    listen it won't be good for you to be stuck inside on a Sunday   have you taken your medication   open the door I am at the door listen up

    my heart beats irregularly painful but it is not the heart itself but the heart's nerves says the doctor sometimes I lie tearful for no reason but I also manage to beat the weeping down I shall prevail weakness you are too weak Tómas Jónsson you'll benefit from a little bit of movement

    do you want me to let Dorí bring you outside my Tómas

    you are abnormally fleshy the doctor counsels me and injects liquid into my right butt-cheek so that the flesh will slough from me in my urine I would have expected a distinguished speech from him a man who is the main specialist in heart disease yet I'll let his sauciness pass without a word I address him formally at night sir doctor you said in reply to his casual chumminess and humiliate him this way facing death is repulsive everyone dies and wakes again except the man who is stone dead and rots he continues being dead and not even his inheritance grows from his carcass a tree lives a thousand years and wakes each spring cars can be melted and new cars cast from the scrap but man's carcass is forever void and rusted an imperfect creation of a foolish god you had to be foolish with each other were expecting help from your faith damn you and repulsive and rotting they will discover eternity before the scythe comes for me on an evening walk Tómas dear do it for me Anna get out of bed air yourself for Anna your Katrín your Títa your Tómas the holy trinity I know it they shall surely let eternity emerge from precision instruments, the discovery will be made by self-educated naturally intelligent scientists they shall surely find devices more sensitive than temperament in man all the other German Icelanders in other families or half-Danish who knows if there is a good mix like Finsen and Thorvaldsen the jews, perhaps one-third of this man could have become Tómas you know were I forming Tómas he would be born in Bingen in Germany like the nun Hildegard not Tanga in the nucleus of the imminent death of iceland Reykjavík I would not have been born there

The soul inside me is called Katrín = The Pure
now indeed I move Tómas Jónsson   now indeed joy moves begins
with a drink at Hotel Borg   you can fiddle away gawping at drenched
roofs   Count the steps of the stairs stories between floors   moreover
you can count the doors on the corridor panes in the window   one
always finds something to kill time   killing time is a crime everyone can afford a generally recognized crime except by work horses and
contractors   time is gold they say   when did time make Tómas
golden   in the war in the war became time became gold before it was
a delusion   now a man kills gold time in restaurants our gold Tómas

my gold Tómas my gemstone   do you remember the story of the
black in Johannesburg who worked in a gemstone mine and swallowed
a gem   he had become so skinny and subjugated that he could barely
stand upright all his innards totally empty like a money safe they took
him by force pressed a finger on his abdomen and found jewels in this
black's intestine but my intestines were empty and they fattened him for
a week but the black would not defecate his body was seven days full of
shit and feces they were going to cut him up and take the gemstone from
the most valuable black in the world but were too stingy to pay the huge
cost for the gemstone company even though they would have discarded
the black in the trashcan after   and he fattened day by day without
a bowel movement a fecal cork in his colon then the idea occurred to
pump him with paraffin oil and rinse him out with a rinsing jug until
he got diarrhea runs and shit the whole day but nothing the gemstone
still waiting stuck fast in the appendix   remember Dóri how you
found the story funny as we played blind cards and Dísa said he read an
interesting story in the waiting room   Dísa told us about the robbery
of the Yugoslavian gold reserves you remember when the Germans came
across a car laden with gold killed the driver and buried part of the gold
in the ground under a tree while the other portion escaped down to the
shore with them in the car and out to a pleasure yacht which thieves
later stole and cast the gold overboard in a storm because they were
different Germans and did not know what was in the box but the ship
was going to sink in the storm   you sat so long the dining matron
looked at you the way an animal tamer enters the lion's cage with his
whip in the morning to spank the lions and stir them up with a cookie
box to show kids tricks but charged at a mouse in the cage and Sigurður
was drunk and asked if she had eaten lion for lunch given her expression
and recovered quickly and spun   the story shone in their faces which
glowed with sweat after the coffee as to the strange fate of gold and you
shook at the knee joints by the cloakroom   soon you were so cozy you
did not bother to pass water bloated with severe pain in the abdomen
that plagued you the whole night long   I watered the flowers you

say   but then Anna said absolutely do not throw your urine over me
in the flower beds   you reached over to the windowsill and threw your
water over the cactus   I doubt you have had happier days than the
one where you aimed your dick at the thorns of the cactus and pissed the
story was told of the fate of the Yugoslav gold reserve in World War II

so I farted energetically yes you startled and you jerked and also soiled
yourself under the covers was also the hope that I shoo that I foul that
as it creeps forward and the wet that accompanies this dries soon Anna
comes and cleans me her nursing work goes toward the rent protracted
hissing from my ass it means dry weather when there's high pressure over
Greenland but distant thunder makes a hint yesterday the thunder came
today rains unsettled yet yesterday I ate lamb sausage shoes indeed examine my toes I rise it creeps between my other toes is remarkable that we
have these dependent nubs on our feet red and shrunken nubs like the
skin-sick potatoes of Domenico Ghirlandaio it would have been a boon
to paint my toes he who painted the old man with a knob-sick nose toes
are the most useless and unusual parts of the body except perhaps the
earlobes and dick which is strange—dick like a cactus, what does that
mean—just as odd to have toes and think about this like how in Argen-
tina it is summer around christmas while here everything is submerged
in frost and snow do you see how a dick acts oddly but you get used to
a dick's gestures somehow a johnson but never the toes lambs skip high
with a hope the mind escapes harm but the dick is concerned with mental harm do you see how I wave this pointless wart-lappet-tipdick and
my toes uniformly coffee boiled the cork stopper in the thermos flask he
is older and more fool him but however you fart from drilling your farting cat at the cacti bent at the knees or dogs lifting their leg farting horses
farting and chickens farting in public now should Anna spank the man
Tómas who made this ugly shame which dries on the radiator   I'm
going to write something about Icelanders with literary runs not to the
same extent burning asses by the oven I let my subconscious work for me
indeed she comes running with a thread in an instant

A late winter night. The air unusually clear and light in the lungs.   I like this sentence, it is maidenly it hides within it inspiration, poetic flight   I tend to thread through the city's least busy streets.   this sentence is not as good but I'll let it move along though I'll get bad reviews from the critics about it, most likely.   the traffic and racket, resulting therefrom, weighs on my heart. Sigurður no longer surprises me. He is currently working without flashiness, which is to say, he is being punctual. Then one day he doesn't turn up to work. That same day he appears happy and cheerful at the dining table. A stench of wine runs off him. In the Board's eyes, lowered as they are to their dishes, one can read: Once fallen into the wine bottle. Instead [the manuscript is illegible here.]   downcast, like he is getting used to sobering up; he is shamefaced and his eyes have a glassy sheen. He vents to the men in the outer room, tries to initiate squabbles and to tickle Elinu. He converses with Ólaf, who smiles, and this unexpected drunken joy is half-fascinating, all the more so when he crashes into the door during midday coffee. That's that: Up with iceland, down with the world! At times his chattering is almost amusing. This loose cannon of a man tickles both Elin and Dísa so he can be certain they have been tickled by him. They wail almighty jesus and put on airs: good lord, Siggi, do not do that. He disappears and is not seen for many days. The glances over steaming soup: He's gone for good. But no one dares to speak up about Sigurður because of the presence of Ólaf. Sigurður's last words before he disappears are typically directed at Ólaf, on his petty suburban manner, how people are cyclical, that Ólaf is not reliable, how he wants to leave. On the day he reappears, quiet and swollen, he measures each movement carefully, pulling his arms taut to his sides as if trying to keep his extremities at bay, afraid of spontaneous nerve impulses that might sling a soup spoon or a water glass from his hands. A stillness rests on him, living in the eternal anguish of his bones. He might speak about how some people need only five glasses of wine to get down to the destruction inside; someone (probably he himself) has grown tired of the daily habit of putting thin eggshells over the despair lying five wineglasses deep beneath his feet. Is this how life should persist? We listen in awkward silence to the muttering, fractured by drunken coughs of laughter, a thirst for wine. Then he hovers for two days absolutely silent as his arms lift from his sides and his fingers begin to move freely. On the sixth day, he resumes his old character   the clock strikes ten it's soothing to listen to the clock on the watchmaker's workshop beat on Sunday mornings a great sound an electric din vibrating in the silence reminiscent of an electric guitar   worthless drudgery for this or that "is he prattling about some boring lout now?" skimping on his existence with wine (probably this is how he feels, terrified of having said something unpleasant while drunk) but no one responds. How is he, Sigurður the Book of Revelation, legible through a magnifying glass, clear as glass. He can make himself thin as glass in a window. That evening he visited me to my surprise   no need to say I hate drunk people take a detour if I see them from a distance rarely go out Saturdays dare not risk my life the cruelty wine stirs inside folk (this icelandic berserker disease) who drink purest cruelty and Reykjavík spills screaming out onto the streets filled with drunken storm-troopers headed to the Winter Palace at Hotel Borg and she claims military protection following a fruitless defense by the doorman   Tryggvi actually drinks daily. He drinks in his leather chair then passes the wine back into the bottles. But he remains fully functional. Jesus changed water into wine, he says. I change wine into water. Which is a greater miracle. Tómas, take this bottle out. I have neutralized its contents. Every minor action done to embarrass me. Even down to handling his piss bottles. For the sole reason: Tryggvi noticed the artillery in the Bank was working for me. Don't throw the bottle out, rinse it under the tap and put it into the cabinet. The bank is not without its gold reserves. This yellow mix from Tryggva his liquid gold. I'd just turned the corner of Grettisgata and Barónsstigur when Sigurður came into my arms in the middle of the corner. Directly into me. After five days came a glance. No evading Sigurður as he flows over the edge of the soup dish. Give me ten crowns, he says casually. A ten-krónur coin, he says, hardly drawing breath, if you know what a ten krónur is. I look past him at the barber shop. I see the red comb with its neon light. I feel my heart squeeze and my left foot rustle the pavement with its paper trash, which is being pushed through the streets at night like ghosts. The comb's light dies. A red light remains a while in my eyes. But I am silent. I'm dizzy a little at this corner by the yellow house. I took the turn too quickly. I put weight on my right leg. I must appear steady. I think: I should drink a milk mix in the evening instead of coffee. Two slices of raisin cake appear, each in front of a black cat on a side pillar. Blue grass. Sigurður, can I ask about the white garden chair standing on the lawn. A naked woman with sagging breasts sits in the chair screaming with her fingertips on her nipples. Will you give me ten crowns or lend them to me, I'll repay them, ha. Or else I will clock you in the head knock you down your kidney loose   everything will just leak out of me and such men seem visionaries   a need to appear calm particularly my nervous system   Hit me and beat my kidney loose or cudgel me, I say; you'll not get a cent from me. His gaping laugh against the white stars.   and this slacker mocks me now with laughter   you will just spend the money, I know, and make yourself a worse person.   these words I speak like a Christian children's book or a warm, empathetic wife there is much I do not sing Oh my dear father come with me to the tavern do not obstruct me further and he will say: Why have money, if not to spend it. You are drunk. I cannot get out of the strange situation fearing Sigurður is my husband I am his sweet submissive wife. The wine means you do not know what you are saying and doing. What is the reason for living sober. I'm on a brief stroll, I say. You escape death, but he will knock you out with that maggoty kidney. I have no time to quarrel. You cannot escape yourself, he says, I am you. And if you let me die for the sake of ten krónur then I will drink madly through you. Perhaps you want that. I will find a way to escape you, I say.   I'm always thinking about you   the blue grass and the chair have become a calendar advertisement with a scantily-clad girl drinking cola   Dísa   if you are me, flee me.   drinking humor is unbearable   Give me ten krónur. I lost my wife. I have to bury her. You lost your wife, you should sit at home over the body. Give me ten krónur first then twenty more, and I'll pay off the ten krónur debt here and now. Or do you prefer I walk the streets with a rotting woman's body on my mind.   He unbuttons his shirt and shows me a woman's body grabbing both hands in his coat collar and running his fist under his chin but I grip the curb with rigid toes   do you presume to refuse to aid a dead woman.   I become evil   Perhaps this is the biggest stain on you.   His tongue blows up in his mouth which he stuffs full of hair he has pulled off his chest   crazy horses rushing over the snowcrust he shouts and swings me around by the coat tail, a hen. Farting.   this nightmare knows what she does, does he know I live on oxygen not the air within flowers from the mouth of flowers but the tank beside the sheets and pillow he knows that I can crash to the street and break like a pot I carry disease a carcass slope as is he   could you kill a man for your ideals. No, he replies. Then let me go. His mouth is boiled and freighted with brown sores from long years of drinking wine. Are you not then a great visionary. Kill me here at the corner; I insist on it. No wise Ólaf no Ólafy-pie my Tómmy.   He knows about you Títa perhaps he has come across you Katrín dancing together whore-like at Hotel Borg he beats his fist into my abdomen I lose my breath at the house corner and my whole dinner gushes from my stomach to the sidewalk as he ambles away from the wall and I hold a death-grip on the house corner retching only white gum comes out of me and spreads over the toe caps of my newly-polished shoes   I stand firm against the house. I see where the comb of light turns on and off. I wish Sigurður had thrown me in front of an automobile, but he says: I will bequeath your kidneys if I kill you. You can hang them from your earlobes like a cannibal.   But taxis rattle along the street and Dísa passes over me like a heavy sea-turtle at low speed I hail a cab   the curtain is drawn over Haraldur Sóldal's window for a brief moment my face goes gray waves a sharp tongue between its lips like a red prick   I crawl through the door and sink into the seat. My body emits a cold sweat. And I am exhausted.   I hold in my hand a nervous wreck a fistful of white spaghetti   it was a thirty

krónur journey in the taxi, but he received just ten. I go out penniless at
night. One can then in good conscience deny a man a loan, even show
off your wallet. I had to get the money from inside as the car sat waiting
with the meter running. The driver did not look at the meter. A little
ebb in the General Thrift envelope.

DEAD IN HIS ROOM FOR MORE THAN TWO WEEKS
Last night a man in his eighties was found dead in his room.
The man, who was single, lived alone. It is believed he had
been deceased for more than two weeks. The body displayed an
advanced stage of decay. The cause of death was not clear when
the newspaper talked with the investigation, but it was likely that
the man had died of a heart attack. The tenants were not believed
to be aware of his death: no unusual odor was detected as the
window was wide open and it was very hot in the room so the
corpse had almost dried up. Moreover, cats from the street lay by
the corpse at night, so the people in the house said they would
not have seen any unusual cat activity by day. The man was called
Tómas Jónsson, a former bank employee in XII. pay grade, owner
of the apartment. Inside his belly was found a household cat who
said in healthy icelandic via meows: My name is Títa.

Continued next edition.

Subscription phone number:

so death comes to the garden I grow exhausted   my hands tremble   I
have no appetite for coffee and set the thermos away from me anyway
I can barely lift it lie supine in my bunk above the cat the cat shoots up
and scratches me if I died no one would know until I started to smell
not until then but the death has gotten so great in here he should be put
out in the corridor   I hear the woman scold a young child I should
put the telephone in my room I hate big floral dresses I'm exhausted I'm
fatigued   someone goes slowly across the gravel outside the window
during winter darkness the sky is constipated it strains str-str-str-in and

morning barely arrives it is not enough to squeeze the nipple and wish
light would come all day people are around me it is a game   I am here
alone with my oxygen tank and a cat

in my memories I sprayed insect venom that is DDT in West Germany   What has happened to me   the cat gobbles broken glass and
laps coffee from the nozzle of the thermos shits in the chamber pot up
on the table like Dídí in the old days are you not too harsh man with
her my Dídí mine do not grow up girl   I weak I dwarf   I have a
black cat soul and a soul called Katrín I reach for the pill bottle they keep
my arteries open at night increased cholesterol level in my blood they
are my friends the pills now Elísabet has come in from her piling heart
in the herb garden a great horror it is beautiful under the grasses and
rivers taken in each pail Elizabeth however is delighted a large turnip and
potato harvest a year's supply she spreads on the bag in the sunshine and
begins seed sowing immediately hardy potatoes gold-eyed everything
hangs together like a pearl ribbon around the root   if I die no they
will discover eternal life before it comes to that.   To whom   two
downcast horses tölt past the potato beds and cough a gentle cough
Elísabet wakes before everyone else and spins a single string in her knit
underwear two strings in her socks and three strings in Jónas's smock a
great pleasure it is to look at her blue combed unspun wool and Jófríðar
from Jófríðarstaður the work never fell from her hand they combed it
all and spun it at home pregnant each year they ate the whole potato
harvest for mealtimes is it any wonder if they pushed themselves forward
to regional meetings and demanded to sit up front with the milk drivers
while other women's groups stood on the platform with laments over the
need to protect themselves against dust no would young women not now
put themselves out striding the snow and mountains to get themselves
a bass at the ball something other than the servitude of the working icelandic women they are the most beautiful and most capable in the world
who can bind bales of hay up in the moorland and tie their skirts around
themselves with bloody thighs singing patriotic verses whenever they get

time to breathe and children in infancy with their dúsu their pacifier of chewed food they suck into evening after work only just returned from a moss-covered lava field sorely tired Annakatrín Annawater I cannot breathe and she hands me her water in a glass to me Tómi a tome mom she says praying

you must not excite yourself   you are creating some cursed hunchback of thought you cannot escape you grow frightened like a kid lying in your lair all day and night   get up so I can wipe you   and let Dóri lead you out by the trash cans you'll benefit from this Tómas   it always has a good effect on you

don't squash the cat with your feet.

what cat   there is no cat here unless it's in your mind

where is he?

now you say your soul dances outside you rage at Hotel Borg   can you not just take care of her I say   set a scrap of paper on yourself like wiping a kid's butt then back in your lair

Do not step on Títa.

graagh my god   there's no cat here

Do not step on the cat.

graagh my god   I think I'll speak to the renter   wipe yourself then or do you plan to just rot here as you live same as me I suspect not even the old folks' home will take you   you can have your home at the refuse disposal   oh oh you are nauseating   that you should have been an important man in banking

Don't crush the cat underfoot in your impudence

what cat now graagh

Do not step on the cat.

There is no cat in evidence

Where is he then?   now I feel relatively clean and washed in bed I am Katrín you say I am Tómas   Don't step on the cat.

there is no cat here   no you will not feel better in the countryside you are no farmer you will quickly start to kick the cows in their asses   is the water good did it refresh you

It is perfect. Just don't step on the cat.

don't be difficult there's no cat graagh god indeed simply no cat stop
thinking about mistakes you should be Prince Albert of Arabia with two
warlike falcons with outstretched wings up on head having eaten you up
from inside your head

ÆÆÆÆÆ

Oooooo

Try to avoid worry or negative thoughts, the doctor says   I do not
need his reassurance to keep on going my life is certainly safer than the
doctor's   I could send you to this Dr. Busch and let him cut you. Your
medical insurance will pay for everything. Do not go. You get a discount
for two. First know your homeland before wandering abroad and getting
killed. I've never been to Geysir. Not yet to Gullfoss. I have not even
seen the Tub at Grímsnes or the salmon running the falls into the Hvíta
at Borgarfjörður, which is apparently a beautiful thing. This would not
exactly be a vacation. iceland is an excellent tourist destination, although
the hotels in Siglufjörður are lacking. The doctor looks at the calendar
over my head. Lake Lugano, he says, it is renowned for its natural beauty,
extremely unusual. I took my whole family one summer. The hotel can
be seen in the picture, if you look closely. We were extremely lucky with
the weather. We were there when a tourist bus drove off the road into the
water. Thirty women drowned. All art friends from Minnesota. Tragic
accident. We were brought breakfast in our room. And when we went to
Geneva, all the hotels were full. C'est pour la fête, they said. We drove to
Lausanne, where the streets are either up on rooftops or in deep ravines.
And when we left to return to Geneva there was no hotel to be had.
C'est pour la conference, they said. Many bees fly about Switzerland,
continually gliding in and out of bakery doors. And if you buy the cream
cake, a large crowd of bees will chase you around the streets. Extremely
good Klees in the museum in Berne. Take these pills, which I'll prescribe,
regularly.   one needs to see his country from all sides to recognize

all familiar landmarks and place names who was killed where put your finger on a map of iceland some story happened there   Have you been to Lugano, the natural scenery is unique. There, in front of a birch, my wife and I met a light-haired Norwegian student of classical architecture who had just graduated: Copenhagen - Paris - Rome - Switzerland - Berlin. They know how to enjoy life the Norse before they go and specialize at university. If Norwegians and Icelanders meet abroad it's like brothers accidentally coming across each other after a long absence, both broken-winged at the loss of their women to the same disease, nephritis. We drank a morning coffee together. He was going to work at a pharmacy. He was going to Berne. A uniquely sympathetic young man. We recognized him immediately from his student's hat. You must go to Switzerland. A person goes neither there nor anywhere else. A man is too busy paying for his house. You have to have a roof over your head. And after to think about getting a wife to care for him under his roof.   You cannot spend your whole life taking hot water bottles to bed   shoe soles hum on the polished linoleum   if a man has a hammer and a wife then he will want to nail four-inch nails in his wife's head,   but as you know, Berne is the Mecca of the pharmaceutical industry.

My sister died. Does anything mark it or was anything erected at her demise. She was four times married and three times engaged, never to the same man. After her death I am alone of we siblings and never married but maybe to my cat. My sister was called Björg. A good name for a sister. We were six. I felt no special emotional connection with my sister. She died. Yet I went and dressed up for the funeral. A cemetery, as is best. Someone said he almost didn't recognize me. The years have changed you. I hardly know myself as the same person. Hahaha. My sister has gone to her grave. And I loped around the yard in search of my parents. I asked god not to let me die suddenly; that must be so revoltingly easy. I want to have some relationship with death, I hope to struggle against it. I listened to the ocean. Here in Reykjavík you don't hear it. I despise the lazy sea, lazy waters, lazy years. Some kind of white sun shines in the sky over the cemetery and the horizontal ocean by the beach. A lot of rain has fallen and the sun sucks the rain from the earth in a white spray. The mountains sweat. The people crowd into cars, which drive to Tanga, hidden in the bluish haze of the bone factory. I see Lóa standing with Anna at the cemetery gate. I know Anna is the daughter of my niece. I walk to the boards and examine the well-dug grave. The coffin is white in a silver-gray grave. The soil is sandy with hard grass patches due to the shells. Here everyone has torn fishskin eyes except Anna. Her eyes are yellow like piss stains. Horses in their winter hair stand by the yard and watch with calm eyes the people carrying sand in their shoes toward the crosses. Someone calls: Will you be here for a bit. I start. I look back. Someone answers: No, not this time. I stand by my parents' grave; they have their children with them under little tussocks. Sentimentality extends beyond the grave and death. I think the answer has sounded in my mind for two centuries. I used to know every face. Now I know almost no one. I am in no hurry. I walk to the town over the sandy flood plain. I thread for stones. And there on my walk I feel similar to Nick, sitting on the pier's end: he seemed confident that he could not die.   to gain wisdom in love you need sometimes to have been untrue the way illnesses are necessary to gain life experience many people have left the hospital entirely transformed by their life experiences who was it said that   someone in the refectory when we were discussing love and diseases   I sit facing Dísa at coffee anyone can sit anywhere he pleases invariably Dísa and I sit in our assigned places I face Dísa Dísa sits opposite me   Dísa   I remember only that I sat with feet crossed under the table facing Dísa   everything else I've lost and forgotten

    I lie supine on the divan my feet out past the edge   I don't move   I lie flat as a slab and do not move I lie with my head in a magnetic direction but the earth's magnetic field is constantly in motion and that stops me caring about the Guddas about the abducted Turk-Gudda and Thief-Gudda and any Guddas overhead as I lie passive in bed my peers are piling up lifelong card files to note down and try to remember the dates of the books they read but I would be ashamed to remember a single word from a book my body fuses to after reading what they call scientific essays about icelandic studies at the University of iceland but I dig in my nose with character laudabilis prae ceteris and magna cum laude but when I get up and can move my brain I'm going to write an article about icelandic Studies so that the University will grant me the status of doctor honoris causa then I will stop digging in my nose because honores mutant mores I'll get a strained groin like the professor's superstructure out of matchstick feet roaring mewling mewling with a gurning expression when I júbílea with the Gádeamuses hymning on Independence Day June seventeenth I am instructed to rest the doctor says get your blood moving with an evening walk push your circulation around the heart is lazy once the dust has disappeared from the air and settled to rest for the night on the ground don't drag your feet don't stir the dust lift your knees I know myself best what's best for me . . . I allow the disembarkation point of the infectious army of germs to gain a foothold on the beach after that I counterattack and drive the germ rabble away from me into the ocean like twelve bulls who turn their four heads in every direction in the middle of my temple

On Kimblagarr

Tómas Jónsson
an essay on icelandic studies

Kimbli is considered by many scholars to be the son of Broki, but the scholar Finnur Jónsson brings many interesting arguments against this, most of which are guesswork (like much of Finnur's work; he was not completely infallible in his research). If, however, Finnur was headed in the correct direction, wouldn't Kimbli rightly have been living in the seventh century (was the poem composed then?) According-ing to genealogical research, the names Blágarr and Garr often occur then, but these names have roots that follow from Úlfsteins Hrets (the cold), and derivations of them, especially Blágarr, may after various

shifts mean that Kimblagarr was composed no earlier than the thir-
teenth century; later, even. The name Bölvi (and indeed Mildís, too)
first appeared in Yngli's family tree. And Glámur lived out east in
Miklagarður a.k.a. Constantinople. It is probable that King Ólaf
of Norway sailed with him to Garðarríki, but it is barely possible
to guess at comparable arguments (cf. Heusler) as to what Yngli was
thinking.[i] The consideration seems very doubtful, that Vefja the Black
had had a ship in passage, as has been argued (cf. Kuhn); it is not
known that she had a ship at her disposal, though set that aside for
now, and on the other hand consider Garr (Garrdrápa I) and Mimbil
(because the English word Wimbledon and the icelandic word vembill
are derived from there (and Spanish warrior-king Wamnba, 672-);
they mean "one with a belly") said that Vefja sailed the Valkyrie plain,
which can be established with good probability. It is also doubtful
that a one-handed man was standing in front of the forces of the
Völsungs (were the names Kimbli and Mimba confused?), suggesting
that he has ceased to lie about Kimbli. Very peculiar here is the use
of the word "vilmögum," but it proves nothing about the poem's age
or origin (no knowledge has emerged about Kimblagarr since Finnur
died; we have not managed to find the author, the scribe is unknown
and nothing known of the history. Kimblagarr is not mentioned in
the reports of the Árni Magnússon Institute, the Royal Library in
Sweden or the Antiquarian Society. The age of the manuscript cannot
be determined, neither by orthography nor font; it could be writ-
ten in the later part of the seventeenth century or the last quarter of
the eighteenth century, as will be discussed below). "Hirð" probably
entered the language in the eleventh century. "Vilmögum" appears in
the Poetic Edda, so it is cautiously proven that way (was, then, part
of the poem written before Hávamál [21 v.] while the later part (42
to 61) is from the twelfth century?). There are many lexical correspon-
dences between Garrsdrápa 1 and Kimblagarr and Oddrúnargráti.

---

i.   *Sinn und Ursprung der Yngli, Halle* 1875.

Most significant, however, is the relationship of the poem to Mimb-latal: "continued to the high place   a chieftain-meeting," which obviously references Oðinn, and Meierbaum's correction "The chief continued   high in the meeting" is in the fullest way unlawful. From all this thorough scientific examination the poem seems to have been written in the eleventh century or perhaps earlier.[ii] But thoughtful people view the poem as composed earlier or later than stated here— when, then? Here, as is to be expected, there are no ideas backed by resolved arguments, only indications about simple things that inform those who wish to read a poem-fragment. The poem as a whole is lost, with no mention of it in the Codex Regius, *and little to use as a source except oral tradition recorded in the eighteenth century, though it seems Finnur had caught wind of the poem in a paper manuscript.*

As may be expected given the legion of articles, essays, and doctoral theses about the age and origin of Kimblagarr, it may be considered one of the most remarkable farts from the spring of ancient literature.

now I would like to have a soft-boiled egg one egg or two then raw I would drill a micro-thin hole in the shell and with my nail burst the yolk and suck it gently from within a man is always surprising himself get yourself a soft-boiled egg the miser says I say nothing hesitation hand you the pleasure bag what, do think you I will fatten myself on eggs by mid-morning the day has halfway stretched its claws under the divan and pilfered the eggs from the pleasure bag all these sanctions cussing make you ill do you see Títa how he struggles into the air and itches and coughs now I shall waste I will whip you and limit your egg rations because of the insistence on fattening you will have no hen eggs get yourself a chicken to drill the remaining eggs see to the paltry laying you blow out the egg drink it I've never seen such a big scoundrel you do not let the girl play her ballgame in peace

---

ii. Das Kimblagarrproblem, Deutsche Vierteljahrschrift für Literaturvissen-schaft und Geistesgeschichte, IV (1930), pages 223-645.

bima bimbam bimbirimbi rimbam
who is beating out a bimbirimbirimbam
it is Tómmas bimbirimbirimbam
when will he discover bimbirimbirimbam
his lovable strumpet
bimbirimbirimbam
let them go in peace
bimbirimbirimbam
you are planning to rush out into the corridor and tell the girl to come
here with the ball game my goodness I am going to give you one small
square of good Lillu chocolate   you are damned desperate today   I
will have to tie you down if you carry on these giant exertions with your
nail
    dad I want eggs
oh! how the cabin-runt quiets
    dad mom I want honey and eggs
    Clear off. I do not want you on me.
oarlock is a stump   the girls have not long been playing the ball
game before they all decide to head inside kicking and struggling do you
hear them

a little hand stretches abruptly upward and a red ball slips from the palm
and slams into the wall   a yellow ball rising meets a red ball dropping
from a stretched hand with fingers in a claw-shaped grasp a red ball
swings from an arm thrown behind a back sent almost simultaneously
up a green ball a yellow and a green ball whipped remains in the air a
yellow ball touches the wall gomp swings from it in an arc meets the
green ball rising it is mid-drop rejected by the palm gump as soon as the
green ball hits the wall gomp the red ball flies up the yellow sitting still
between the fingers the yellow ball must be sent on its speeding journey
from the wall gomp and heads on a downward arc the red ball heads into
it at violent speed ah zah and the balls kissing wah! in the air gump a low
crash and balls scattered on the floor wah-wah

always the violent excitement of the ball game   three balls: yellow, red, green. Three balls jumping gump-gump—gump-on-the-floor. The red ball kisses the yellow ricochets wah-wah swirls around it and the yellow ball pushes the green ball under the radiator bouncing after him and they lie there side by side gump-gump hiding, kissing, and lying stricken by panic, done in.   however much you rage you will not get to look through the keyhole until the long extinct volcano Keilir spews again are these perhaps your death spasms the small animation before a demise lava pours down the hills thickly and piles up on a grass-patch beneath the mountain   No, Sigurður *I* do not believe that he is a widower. He is no more a widower than I am, he is just like all the pensioner-diners   to hear the hullabaloo mocking and moaning in the stones little or less can be heard hahaha lie calm   you little ten-year-old boy   do you want to get mixed up in an arrest with the police do you want the house scandalized again so you shall never dare from now on to look into the eyes of any man cut off from work from a conscience that threatens you in your sleep terrible dreams from the pages of a newspaper

Immoral Conduct with Young Girl
Last night a man in his nineties was found guilty of indecent behavior with a ten-year-old girl. It does not appear to have been a direct attempt at sexual relations, and the little girl was absolutely okay except for nosebleeds and a nervous breakdown and talking in a foreign language. She was taken for medical tests. Her attacker has never been found guilty of similar conduct. The case is still under investigation.

do you want Miss Gerður to turn her big eyes to you and say although this is a moral offense these little girls are idiots around old men they do not blab now that makes me angry with you I will slap and torture you yes I will pinch your head Títa scratch at your collar do you want a full reminder I will stab you with a needle tip owowow unfortunately he felt that painful I stabbed you Títa unexpectedly in the eye now it bleeds do you have this the scraping finally Títa collapses down wretched and weak a sense of decency hides inside you   a wish I want of which even Sigurður might be ashamed   if everyone looked like you in this would the world look differently out from the newspapers no have you returned come to prowl a greater shame stay put a while I'll call you hottentot how they behave shame does not exist for heathen hottentots not among the blacktail brown and curved and with a black eye on top of everything else I gave my friend a black eye which worsens the girls' unseemly play they say you are not kind ughugh just scream ughpish in a virgin choir in the laundry room when you gape like a fire hose at the younger and more elegant but now you want to fumble along into the laundry room behind the rope to peek at the underwear and I will show you girls come see how to spank an unruly boy indeed he's going to bite you all ohwoewoewoe do not let him bite my fingers not a hard bite just you try well he always bites stops to let bite owoewoewoe I'll let her mother know this you damned Tómas what the hell have you done to the child bit me jeez jeez almighty in the navel gas furies no you dare not bite back near the lair a careful search finds the dregs of a sense of decency in you jeez a jeremías in Jesus's name

I lie with my ear fixed to the bottom of a glass my arm gone stiff holding it still upside down on the wall severe neck pain I cannot endlessly lie on my back on the divan and listen to the man lecture it is not enough to loiter all day fascinated by the disjointed mutterings of old age

everyday you sleep in but wake on Sundays, when the girls band together in the hallway. I am not unaware how they play their daily ball games while you sleep soundly and dream like any good impressionist about L'après midi d'un faune Sundays and virgins swarm and disorder in the hallway with colorful balls. Youth passes in ballgames: First with one, two, three, and four. Well, your childhood is a little distant. You never long to become one of them, you who have never passed joyful days these sixty years, you who have hung at me with your charm, irritated and troubled, because often I irritated you with rash thoughts, chatted with you in confidence and said: chérie, you are my most intimate friend. Teasing is never uncomplicated. I am lighthearted but have a heavy-hearted element. I have a myopic prick.

I take back the implement box, cover it with my fingers, mentally afraid of the jets of water. I slip into my jacket, sticking the box tightly under my arm after having wrapped it in a towel. The towel I take with me after using it and dry it on the oven. I do not care to have my towel hang in with their towels. People tend to dry their bodies with my towel. I am not paying for their laundry. Isn't that right, o my penis, o john thomas. Sometimes we get a bit over-excited, don't we? I will never treat you as badly as you do me—do to yourself, notably. Destructive impulses govern you. I am your husband. Your Pope. You strive to topple me from my chair; I have no option but to issue you a passport, exile you like some tainted substance. I am to you as Tryggvi to me. Pour out the bottle—do so wordlessly. I get true pleasure from admitting the theft and possession of your personal freedom. I get true pleasure from knowing you are being oppressed. My underling. I am honored to know you have a complete right to strike. My unique pleasure lies in suppressing the freedom of movement in your chest. In this we find the impressive image of equal rights. Inside you lives the right to revolt; inside me lives the power to quash it. A unanimously approved equality. Fart. My power over you is your profit. You cannot look after yourself without my assistance. I cannot make water without you. Herein reigns the spirit of symbiosis. Consider yourself able to live independently, a self-governing state with its own economy. Yes, yes, I know you have your book in the bank. But Títa would eat you. It never occurred to you how often you had engaged in foreign affairs out of pure ignorance, checking your advice on foreign policy without my intervention. Certainly I do not interfere in your private matters, your whims, your inventions, though I pour them in the toilet and sometimes outside the house corner. I follow approved methods of market forces. I said to you immediately, and you had the sense to understand: First a roof over your head, then intercourse. Your policy was, however, a total human fantasy: first intercourse, then a roof, if necessary. Your paths of thought follow the masses: rushing blindly into the unknown without regard for any element except your own desire. You would have immediately put yourself in the company of directionless men, perhaps in dissolute company in more than one case. I am a social being; the justification of all seducers. You are afraid of being orphaned from the company of womankind, says the Qur'an, so marry all the women you like, two or three, or four, but no more. The state here has another law, my god. I know my Sword well, that he would have broken the limit given in Muhammad's law-book. To me, you are a source of shame and fun. Were you in someone else's keeping, you could have landed up with Muhammad, and would by now have become a fleck of windblown sand in the deserts of Arabia, or a hen on Sólheimasandur, which Sigurður stole from the chicken farm at Fljótshlíð and threw out the window of the bus, "just because; a prank," during the employees' association awayday. Had you landed up with Tryggvi you'd be at this very moment changing wine into water. It would be your one wedding-night miracle. To think this imp should have landed here with *me*. Change your dwelling. I'll tell you about your service for the days to come. I'm the real deal. I see the devil in your eyes; you are planning something evil. Go to King Faruk of Egypt, enlist in his service; or Shasta of Persia, he is planning to beat you with his hands or maybe has nothing against having two of you; he does not have much of a prick. Much that is small achieves some big thing. Take the full travel allowance in each country. Here is your passport, you treasonous traitor. Your indulgence.

Vegabréf

Passeport   Passport   Pass

Ísland

Iceland   Islande   Island

Valid for all countries except the Soviet Union and its affiliates

Nr. 1/1967

Fullt nafn vegabréfshafa
Full name of the bearer   Casanova Tómasson, Jón Tómas
Nom du porteur
Voller Name des Inhabers

Þjóðerni   Icelandic, Islandais
Nationalité

Staða   leikfang
Profession   playboytoy
Stellung

Birthplace
-day and –year   Iceland
Born at on   15. 3. 1887
Né(e) à le
Geboren in am

Heimili
Residence   Reykjavík, Iceland
Domicile
Wohnort

Tunga   Íslenksa
Language   Icelandic
Langue   Islandais
Sprache   Isländich

Hæð
Height   18 cm
Taille
Gestalt

Háralitur	grár
Hair	gray
Cheveau	gris
Haare	grau

Augnalitur	rauður
Eyes	red
Yeux	rouge
Augen	rot

Vegabréfið gildir til
This passport expires on   2. 3. 1970
Ce passeport expire le
Dieser Pass ist gültig bis zum

Útgefið	Reykjavík, date 2. 3. 1967
Issued at	other
Délivré a	

Lögreglustjórinn
The chief of Police   Tómas Jónsson
Le chef de Police
Der Chef des Polizeiamtes

Gjald:
Fee: Kr. 250,—
Droits:
Gebühr:

Now choose or reject. This my ultimatum. Surrender. That is not the way. I have written the poison out of you. I do not simply write you out of a sense of duty then stick the paper in consecrated earth. Or dress your wounds with gray strings, like when a man writes away his warts.

Hear that. Hereon in there's no reward for you. In the next life—you will not become the mother of five children in a poor neighborhood god knows where—you will get to stretch out under the palm trees and turn mild, longing eyes to Mecca; your desires will not concern me. You will not return to my service. And if you accept the passport it does not mean returning home to your father's house once it expires. You are declaring yourself a global citizen or else nationless or else a political refugee. If you prefer to stay here with me you'll still receive food and shelter, no service required, but you must obey my advice in every respect. You will betray yourself in the forthcoming afterlife; you will be granted such benefits; you will dance and carouse. I reckon you will have difficulty finding a woman as companion.

Now I am going out and will not listen to your whining anymore. It is almost twelve.
    there's no benefit to torturing him further says Katrín
    he has nine lives like the cat Títa

You've set off for barely 80 years, according to the issued passport. Little notice should be taken of that document. You are in your nineties, whatever the documents say. You have reached retirement

| Starf: | Á eftirlaunum |
| Profession: | Retired |

So.

8.

I have a deep affection for Títa. Títa is the warmth in my garden. Títa is my warmth. And Títa is attached to me. This proves that Títa has many good nerves not to be found on the exterior of her body from head all the way to tail. I'm only joking, Títa. So long as Títa can lure someone in she will not be a loner. She is nevertheless eccentric and idiosyncratic. And she gets worked up and savagely rages for periods. She moans a magical, intense cry to lay claim to a home. She shows me her jaw, her claws, her red, thin, but rather short tongue; I'm going to grab it and stick it inside myself. She trots over to me. She looks suspiciously at me with yellow eyes. That's Títa: suspicious and cautious. You see, Títa suspects me of hiding something.

good morning Ásmundur.

yes good morning

i am utterly disturbed am ill-disposed to the letter þ "thorn"   it resembles me in the mirror of the bathroom   Títa is being thorny   here comes the little piss-soaked repulsive lord Flotteroy and he hands me a gnawed doll soiled with slobber   I suspect this brat is never washed   no that was Stína   Stína was always pisswet. One winter day one of the girls crept out the basement onto the stairs. She sat there, captivated by the trash cans and the rats until her pants froze to her and the steps. A boy tried to force her butt up with a crow-bar, because she couldn't get free. A medical examination revealed that the end of her colon had frozen. She died as a result. (an excerpt from the incomplete biography of Stína Sveinsdóttur which will undoubtedly be widely read by women; it concerns a girl who died because her father's patriarchy caused her colon to freeze and that led to her death.) The death announcement appeared on television and in newspapers, the obituary of a beloved daughter who was suddenly called away like a sunbeam. In the basement the beam was never to be seen playing around a half-naked child, just a downpour. Had Títa fed from her she would have licked Stína, but Katrín swung her in the crib then took a taxi down to Hotel Borg, having first pulled a herring net tight over the cradle so she could not get out get into the matches.

no Ásmundur does not want dolly.

She said Ásmundur. Why does Anna keep saying Ásmundur. My name cannot be Ásmundur. She said: Tómas is going to wipe himself at night. Then she said, the heating bill will not go down if the cold snap continues to the end of the month. I thought the woman said Ásmundur   the way you puzzle over the oil bill a mother lets her child freeze to death on the steps outside

Stína froze to death the other side of New Year   it is impossible I said afterward you believe the couple in the kitchen that we office workers live better than others   I heard the same old whining   why are someone's monthly incomes twice yours do we have less he cares about having money and obnoxiously continued   Indeed. Ásmundur comes and issues commands. Títa and Stína crept in after me. I rubbed the stick soap around her teeth, at first Stína was reluctant sputtering with open mouth and lolling tongue. It is probably tepid on the tongue.   drive the idiot cat out Ásmundur.   cats should not be tolerated in residential houses, I say. Títa has squeezed herself under the bathtub, so that next to her . . . (something is wrong with the text here)   let me force her out with a broom stick.   wait Tómas. Whistle. Títa disappears.   There's little room to move in here. I squash her against the wall, when she bends herself down the shaft drives under the tub and presses an abundance of flesh toward me.   Whistle   I am satisfied that Anna squashed past me smoking in the kitchen and drives with great thunder: drum-drummumm-drumm, lifting her heavy asscheeks from the chair: drimm.   let the cat be   nono wait   Katrín, don't keep the cat inside, if Tómas hates him, says Sveinn.

Sveinn hides behind the kitchen table wearing striped pajamas like a prisoner, slurping his morning coffee from a plastic cup swollen and wonky from sleep. Sveinn is muss-haired and puffy-faced after much dozing, after dead sleep, after the amount of money he gathered up yesterday with his hard work and the toll on his back and his knees. Yesterday was payday. Today is Sunday: all day slumber and sleep under the British bedspread. His hands rest ignorant and foolish alongside the coffee paraphernalia with dark mourning streaks under all the nails, swollen and bluish, licked with kerosene.   how can she resent him pawing at his naked body, skimmed-milk white, of a Sunday morning when he has belched out the wind from the donuts and coffee he forces the kids on her for the weekend work he has got a job once has twice paid child support payments for the twins Stína and Dóri his envelope was thoroughly stuffed for nine months his frown lightened when the seal was broken and the contents turned upside down what was hidden   anyway what labors workers perform after coming home the night-rate of office workers who go until five then work longer another job after work or night work according to the bank director's whims (something is probably missing in the manuscript or else the writer has gotten confused; I would not be surprised)   not skimping off at lunch after meat chops with red cabbage since time is not cut down to the nail   I cannot stand this anymore Sveinn says.   He elbows in, grabs the broom and thrusts it under the bath (wasn't I just writing about that?). We all tussle in the toilet, but Títa lies calm like Svings driven up in the corner behind the foot of the pot (here it should say tub for consistency in error) where we can't get to her. Rather they scram than you, my puss, I do not rent to people with children. The advertisement was clear: a childless couple. They snuck stowaways in.   We came here childless.   Fine. Could I have seen into her. He smuggled

Stína and Bubba into my basement apartment hidden in Katrín's belly. I have a legal right to finger her womb lining at the threshold door. Out. Out. Out with your urine-soaked child in your belly before it pulverizes everything into small smithereens and leaves the apartment desolate and devastated. Guerrillas. Shady dealings. Curiosity draws the boy to the door; he wades to the faucet gnawing and tearing his way forward, over the floor in the water puddling from the kitchen tap, which sprays over the cloth in the sink. The fabric is soaked through. He claws the satin paint from the walls, which I painted with a roller, paying full price. He picks at the walls and drills his fingers into every crevice, so nothing can be done with the apartment. Bubbi draws penises on the drawers and closets, stuffing all the keyholes full of matches in defiance of warnings and the announcements by the Homeowners' Association: Don't keep matches where children can get them. Do not smoke in bed (which they both do after intercourse). No rules get followed. Bottle caps rest firmly inside Dóri's jaw and he starts to choke at least three times a week. He swallows buttons and fasteners; repeatedly they rush him down to Urgent Care and pump them out or fill him with castor oil and wait until Anna finds the lost item with a needle in his feces, washes off the dirt in the sink, and sticks the coat button back in the button jar, which the kid walks over to like it's a jar of bread in a food drawer. Bubbi, you cannot always be getting into the button jar. This is ugh and yeuch, Bubbi. Katrín sits on the chair and smokes (I think I have never smoked like today ho-hum, what?, coated with throat-dirt) until she cries, My Jerí in cho, what's up with your flab (this exclamation my Jerí in cho is still popular out in the country)—and quickly fetches the castor oil bottle. I catch him red-handed with the phone. Heavily she rises up like an old seal from the skerry: half-drowsy and falling into slumber from the effort. In between: she turns the radio dial like a grindstone (she never can find a station properly) while I seethe at her with my eyes. Tómas since you understand foreign tongues would you be so kind and read this canister Sveinn found it lying around in at the surplus store. She returns with the tin and continues over to the wet kids sitting there

like a big floral haystack, which has been heated   this will be the
eternal theme I my father my mother my sister and brother family
and the baking powder blown out from the belly.   I move them
away before he opens the door and forces out a new Dóri who will
knot me up completely   I open the toolbox and take out the
razor. I rip the blue seal from a razor blade. In addition, I get an emery
board for my fingernails. I stick a new blade in the razor, set it down on
the glass shelf below the mirror beside the ashtray and the forest water
nymphs. And I stroke a fingertip casually over my stubble, turn on the
faucet and let it run until the hot water steams. I wet the brush in the
appropriately warm shaving water and stroke it across my jaw, pulling
back my face against the heat. Steam layers the mirror. I wipe it off with
a washcloth. I lather shaving cream over my stubble and smear solid
splotches on my whiskers. I follow the directions (Modo de emplear) of
the shaving cream. My beard is sore and I go over the stubble twice with
my Gillette razor at different settings: 7 for the first shaving, 8 for the
second   no a person should not own an apartment for strangers
to spawn in and lay waste to with their lustful bodies even if they are
sympathetic before he can wipe himself with his own paper this brush
its jaws its own toothbrush and dry off the whale oil with its own towel
The State ought to set up a general defense fund for this stuff. She stood
in front of me proud like a queen impregnated in her sleep by some dre-
amprince; and I gave in, I accepted the coffee, and sat down, crushed, at
the table with my legs crossed, drinking more cups than I ought to while
your snootiness softened. While I sat nailed to that chair I imagined a
penguin rummaging forward with a refrigerator on his stomach alone
on a journey over the glaciers of the North Pole. She showed me with
the fear of god an X-ray the doctor allowed her to keep of a lopsided
colon   one does not need to be a great doctor to see the wrong (my
only jee)   move your finger across the film which Katrín glued to the
kitchen window using condensation (for god's sake) and the cloudy sky
that is the colon met her spine (all asimmer). After having tied you with
a tether I threaded it down your trouser leg underneath the sock and

tied it to your big toe. She can watch me all bumptious from the kitchen door with her big open surgery that ripped when she was getting to her feet just immediately that same evening barely awake from the stupor of chloroform (awful, she thinks); and asks me to read (would you be so kind) packages and dispensers and asks if I understand the foreign lyrics in a pop song (my jee you do so much good; think of the difference) but I don't want to hang about for all time in the kitchen staring at a crooked colon (less easy to see now) glued to the window. She should have shown me the organ picture when she moved in; I would not have rented to them.

Fingers stroke the newly shaven stubble. The roots grow under the skin like a complex filigree. To shave me to a gleam I move the razor up then down, criss then cross. I cannot use the same blade more than twice. Títa you cats do not need to engage in frequent shaving your nature is subtle yet complex with darkness covering you should hang ties together at odds wind-drying on a crane the whole winter and get sent into spring like anyone else dried fish in your black jaws in Nigeria you with your thick-coated collar like a fashionable ruff she is like an over-coat from the fashion store Feldinum where Jónni the Mink Merchant employs the state to spruce up old ladies oh he is so considerate

    would you like me to take the diapers out of the bathtub   I mean it Tómas

    no it is totally hygienic only let them lie

    do you want a cup of coffee   I have a hot brew on

The method she uses to ingratiate herself with me is extremely transparent. I am facing the absolute last moment to get rid of them before she empties herself and spawns a full house. Is it enough to make her feel hostility. I send her stern mental signals. She works and potters with the radio in search of "any decent station," i.e. something light and refreshing. The antenna gets the message and the speakers command her to scram within a day, persona non grata. I have always been diplomatic. This Tómas Jónsson is innately an utter diplomat.   he comes so

smoothly indeed I cannot put it into words this indeedydeed I do not
know how to say it   he manages to be both directly and indirectly
too but in a direct way   he is a tip top gentleman   do you want
the bottle back   just a drop so so   this was nothing at all only
a shadow of a drop hahaha you use words so uniquely sweet of you to
let us see your   god this man Tómas was born a gentleman from the
old school   she wilts and sits. She draws apart her thighs heavier than
ten under-duvets. She sits diagonally on the head chair and foams: Show
mercy, now jeezee show mercy, none of your bullishness. And her arms
dangle powerfully by her sides, strung down with heavy weights. They
touch the floor. She prays for mercy. Here you will find no mercy. She
rolls her head to and fro senselessly. Green oozing foam wells from her
mouth. I can see the fists in her abdomen, squashed there after coitus
interruptus "they said that the queen gave birth to a kitten"; that was
Títa speaking from the *Thousand and One Nights*. She's widely read a
literary cat or rather a female cat who knows how to read classic books. I
set her free. She is done in, weary from thirst. From her skirt fall crumbs
like black lamb droppings, which Títa bolts down. I drag the bloody
message from her swelling body and in the evening she sits deathly pale
at the head chair when Sveinn comes home.

we have to find another apartment

what's wrong

I can no longer endure the constant mental warnings from morning
to night cannot switch on the radio and set the station without them
raining down on me

Perhaps someone is advertising vacant housing in the papers   He
is wearing his coat. She turns on the radio for Sunday Mass. They both
hold their breath and wait for the mental signals. I brush my shoes in
peace and quiet, and then the priest says, remain here in this house,
eat and drink as you are offered, for the laborer is worthy of his wages.
You shall not move from one house to another—it was too late to send
the signal: 00/3 leave my house. Worse, I found his dentures under the
radiator in the hallway in the morning as I reached for my overshoes;

one tooth was missing when I checked the gums I found it in my shoes examined the roof palate with a mirror, much to my horror I thrust the teeth into the soft gum and placed it all on the radiator. Then I went to eat, came back, took off my coat, and went to the door of the restroom. I saw a doll lying on the floor, picked it up, went uninvited into the kitchen and said as I rubbed the doll teasingly on Dóri's nose: Here is Dóri the doll. Sveinn smiled and I glanced at him and saw that his dentures were pretty much stuck up inside him, put in place after last night's bender, and teeth broke chewing his steak and browned potatoes, spiced sauce on his tongue.

Thank Tómas very kindly now Dóri

From this I drew conclusions: He was the source of the commotion in the hallway. The whole day Magnús has been shamefaced in my presence. I have made an abnormal number of trips to the bathroom—always looking into the kitchen on the way.

the boys held a little celebration for the company's anniversary and one gets battered and bruised   he says   the man can barely hold his head   I am waiting for the musician to dawdle to his feet. He slinks up right at twelve or one each day drinks beer from bottles which I set in the window to cool. What was that rustling in the night. The worst is a torn loop. The overcoat is destroyed by hanging it by the collar, which stretches the material so it pokes out in back.

Good morning, girls. You are playing ball in the hallway.

what of it

How are the walls faring.

The dear little girls stop their ball game become embarrassed and toss their ponytails

Have you started going with boys, I whisper slyly.

the walls are flecked by the balls   the girls fart disgustedly with their lips and spray their gums which is a problem for a little girl with a little hard stone

no

lying ferments early in a woman's flesh   a shame she is so coquett-
ish   I can see she has been with a boy from those kissing lips I long
to bite them   what comes next
    I jump in through the door that slammed a whole month back and
when I open it again shy little girl creatures are giggling in the hallway.
    In such good weather, you should play with the balls outside.
    there's no smooth wall outside   says the strumpet cheekily balls
don't bounce on pebbledash
    the wall of the garage.
    it is far too low for us
    i think you have grown tall high in the air.
    of course   she says, turning up her nose   that's just for little
girls but we've got breasts why not have a look

and then the door opens further on in time and again the frost has come
and autumn returned it's started to rain and autumn rain breaks cold
and bleak down the house walls and the sidewalk filled with little girls
buzzing in high heels red painted lips red silk-letters pasted on the cheeks
with an old bra on top of their sweaters my fingers crack with arthritis in
the cold and old age and misery settle when I slam the door behind me
and pray that it clicks in the latch I say grumpy and aged
    Get lost take your nuisance balls some other place.
    Outside it's pouring buckets   says the strumpet
    Raining, I correct. Go play on the second floor then, the corridor in
your apartment.
    Then the balls will run down the stairs and you do not have to search
for them when you lose them
    Yep-yep, I say, overcome by the arguments of youth.
    Lend us this ball for our ball game   says the strumpet and dives
her hand suddenly under my coat you have reached the age of having
little sense dear girl
    Any balls there.

I jerk back, she pinches pretty firmly.

yes why else are you all scrotum-touchy always whistlewhistle with your pocket-billiards and we can see into your toilet at night my jee hee we knocked and said to Anna we are so desperate would you please let us use your toilet thousand thanks and we made a teensy weensy hole in the paint by the window and can see in hee hee and didn't pee our pants

The girl has a leg to stand on. Yes, this girl is not making it up, a hole in the paint no bigger than a pinhole.   but I play my part and steal chewing gum from the radiator where they cannot hide it from me in a gum bank overnight I glue it over the hole

you are terrible you devil you imp and pussy who stole the chewing gum you damn gogo

the girl creatures that day were without chewing gum after a milk- and sausage-offensive to the store not long before gave them a chance to steal the paper- and explosive gum but the wrapping on the chewing gum is bad for the element in the radiator there are no ideal spots so the gum is not visible when you walk down the stairs until you look at more than one side then filch it from the hole and I chewed the rest to test how it would chew this devilish gray viscous damn fortunately man has teeth for this large chewable menhir

I disappear as far back in time as I came. The apartment has no doors. She stands open, empty and gaping, like a newly built house, opposite the airport, which is now in hiding there under the hill. I two-step around the naked doorless rooms. Rusty claw-fittings protrude from the light gray stone wall. The planks run horizontally only, in some places with a bridge between, with wide gaps both in the ceiling and on the walls of this sarcophagus. I stroke my fingertips down the inside of the outer walls; loose flakes of timber break away, and I see the grill at the end of the wooden beam adjacent the floor, where moisture enters in through the walls from the ground and causes cold feet. They have been left there through distraction and negligence during the work instead of being caught up with hammering nails as is the custom indeed there are no damp vents in the outer wall so the beams rot. I touch the house and draw my fingers down the wall rugged and pleasant under the tips of my hand which turns gray with cement dust. And I press my fingerprints onto the windows with this gray powder. I think: Four outer walls, nine interior walls, floor below, a ceiling over me. And all around me: the strong smell of cement-mix and drying plaster astringent to my senses. My eyes see: widely scattered around the floor wall-spoons like metal sets, some on the edge others sitting on polished paper, wall hammers and sharp chisels, all shiny from use. Empty or half-empty cement bags lie against the walls. A battered water pail too shamefully heavy for my thin arms from the concrete at the bottom, and a cement-dirty mixing trough. The floor in the living room has been beaten with wall hammers, marked white with countless blows. I say to myself, and the spirit of the apartment to me, Tómas, you move in this Fall. I tour the apartment. I touch every wall once, I touch the ceiling in my imagination, the panes with my fingertips.   no one is working inside   I love this apartment. She is everything I have acquired with thrift and self-denial and setting myself aside for fifty-seven years   where have the masons hidden themselves   I came here after work at night   I broke in via the service door

I wrestled the divan to me tried to avoid lying too much on the side where my heart is but lie flat directly on my back raise a beam with my feet so my chest is not pressed up against my heart I like this position best I sleep on my left side and so went bald on that side of my head first I am also hairless on my calves from sitting cross-legged the heart is on the left side of a man's chest cavity that genius of nature carefully protected under curved ribs no it would not be good if the heart lay stupidly visible in front of the chest and the kidneys and all internal organs hung outside you like in dreams and it was possible to see food decompose in the intestines and sink lower and lower or the blood that pumps in the veins and lungs blood cells always eating oxygen   then I think people would be horrified by man   yes I know man is repellent

I could as easily have my biography read: I started my career as an errand boy in a textile store. Or somewhere else. Meaningless aspects that describe rusty houses that charm the eye and are some of the most beautiful I have set eyes on. There is no scenery on a par with corrugated iron that has long started corroding. No sunset enters an attic's windows with the natural beauty of red rust spots on houses that are beginning to decay. Rust must ideally come from salt burns, a patch against eternal sea- and sandstorms; saltburn offers a greater variety of color than plain water or rain. An old, marked ship, its side broken and bruised, gnawed at by surf and seaworms, thick with neurotic birds on the bulwark snickering on a summer day. Later I worked my way up and became a government employee. I pulled myself up from the nameless turn of the century. I was nothing. I am called Tómas Jónsson. I had nothing but this body with its head, two arms and legs, eyes and mouth, and all my associated parts, all undisfigured except the ears. Now I have both my body and my apartment in a good place in town. My body has entered her. I dislike the jam-packed street bus. I do not enjoy being around so many people, unless we are working and isolated from one another. I do not like being touched or talking with close-standing folk. I feel comfortable stroking my fingers along walls. I take pleasure in stroking a smooth-shaved chin. I dislike the image of Héðinn Valdemarsson, "who worked so hard for the common people." My family is scattered and dispersed amid bank books. And so I will never become lonely like Sigurður, Dísa, Ólaf, and all the people in my head and be without an earthly place even if I reach Abraham's astronomic age. There are many ways you can write a biography; a person lives many shapes, stepping up stairs until he gets off the top step into the clouds where his gods are. But Héðinn never wanted to pay his workers higher wages than others. Go on strike and demand money from me, then, said Héðinn. He could have paid people more than the set rate, says Miss Gerður, and offers a good example. Now, when I think of Miss Gerður I get the smell of Knorr soups. Héðinn simply refused to assert an atmosphere of fatherly providence at work, says Sigurður. Although he might be acknowledged for giving the communist Einar Olgeirsson a whole house lined inside with silk upholstery, answered Miss Gerður. Did you not think that Einar had received that and other valuable belongings and gold from Russia, asked Ólaf; try to accept it. I am only repeating what the best people say, what's widely known, said Miss Gerður. Try to develop your independent opinion, suggests Sigurður. Rush off home to the commie Einar and look into things. O you are just a mortal man, like me and others, Ólaf, and you make mistakes and say things in inscrutable ways, even if you do know the poet and bum Stein Steinar and have bought him beer, said Miss Gerður spitefully. After having held her own she seemed momentarily confused. Then she rushed out (oh jee) and had a weeping fit and an agitated stomach. Chairs toppled. People leapt to hands and feet. Shocked faces. Troubled expressions. Silence. Friðmey standing by the toilet door and asking: Come on, Gerður dear. Can I just talk to you briefly, just one word. But Miss Gerður sits on the toilet seat with heavy sobs and cannot stand up (jeez almighty some people can be so malicious). I was about to say that Steinn simply "landed" in that poetic hell as a way to put his mark on the town, the same way she "landed" in the bank, and that he had been in the war in Spain, which in his own words was the highest ideal for an browbeaten writer, and also about to say to Ólaf, that he had just "landed" being shot in the ravines in Teruel, and I felt it was redundant to point out, the way Ólaf "landed" buying Stein beer or a person lands in one of a number of things; he did not say: I am a man eternally without goal or purpose; no need to search for deeper meaning, as each donkey nowadays does search, he described himself further, yes . . . these old women always have to go off on their personal hymns, says Ólaf, partially reprimanded over the outcome of his dispute with Miss Gerður who sits triumphant, crying on the toilet. She triumphs through her stomach pain and tears. Ólaf got no further in "setting my mark on the town" than buying beer for the poet Stein and boasting about this prestige in a refectory. I think little of it. I could buy a whole case of beer and send it to my namesake, Tómas Mann, but I would be no more of a man for it. Miss Gerður cried loudly fighting for her breath on the seat and blowing her nose in the toilet paper; the women had to use the men's room and stand guard for each other. But we all agreed at the table that no one had come across Einar Olgeirsson the commie exchanging large amounts of rubles in the Bank and at the same time we agreed that everybody could have his personal view on the matter, without it being a political opinion, and of course Einar could easily have divided amounts down into countless smaller amounts and gotten a military man, some commie in his service, to exchange the rubles in various banks, without any evidence of it. It occurred to me that he was copying my method: I have four savings books, five books at five banks, one in my name at National Bank, the second in my mother's name (she is dead) in The Farmer's Bank (she loved the countryside and cows),   I do not know if my parents are alive or dead they lived their life or death according to their own whims   the fourth is in the Industrial Bank in my sister's name, the fifth, no I have a third in the Fisheries Bank (my father was a fisherman) in my father's name, my fifth is in the Trade Bank and that one is made out to Títa. This method of depositing means I do not wallow in money. Immediately when my annual statement comes I hand Títa the one with 9% interest; there is a big difference between six and nine percent interest on savings. You know, the government has failed to provide me with a new property survey. In such a society, individuals must be endowed with more than a little prudence in their transactions with the government. Títa gets the highest interest rate, but she may not, that catskin, take anything out of her book for a whole year, even if her life depends on it. Admittedly, she may pawn the book and get the equivalent of the credit, but Títa is unaware of these terms, as set out in the annual statement. Her charming little playmate keeps his money hidden between the leaves of books. Soon he will get a book from the Money Bank. Perhaps he longs for a

different wife than Títa. He looked approvingly at Dísa in in the hallway.
Look, here comes Dísa.

Good morning, I say, and take off my shoe covers (a durable Pirelli
model).

Morning, responds Dísa.

With a noble lightness in every gesture she undresses herself, off with
her boots (she tugs gently with her index finger and thumb high on the
heel and yanks the boot with a quick pull off her stockinged toe). Dísa's
hands are white and feminine. Blue, Nordic, gently feminine eyes that
are reminiscent of two sky-blue forget-me-nots in deep snow.

Hi, we're just sitting down to eat, I say. Hi. Hi.

Up the stairs go Sigurður and Magnús, another Magnús than the
one who rents from me, Magnús Jón Einarsson of Flateyri in Önundar-
fjörður, a very modest and frugal regional type who barely speaks about
anything but the difference between dried fish here in the south and
frozen and sweetened frozen fish in Flateyri. He takes great pains over
the topic.

Do you have some hidden agenda, asks Sigurður.

Dísa and I have a lot in common, I answer and peek at her out the
corner of my eyes.

That's good, she says (my jee how good).

Inside you'll find another fellow who is a better match for you than
me.

Well, she says with a gentle, feminine demeanor.

A fellow who can go a bit loopy, Sigurður says.

Dísa's whole character is feminine. She is 100% woman. If she understands anything, she understands the meaning of the feminine (whatever
special understanding that may be), the value of feminine intuition, of
looking at things from a woman's point of view, and even of conflicts
within the feminine perspective.

I've heard his complaints, I say, meaningfully. He is called Baui.

Baui, she repeats with womanly wonder. I have never heard of or seen
him.

Of course not; he talks about things that are totally foreign to you. Magnús and Sigurður de-wind themselves with a couple of farts and move into the refectory. It is pointless to get ahead; every pensioner knows that he may only take two steaks from the platter on Sunday; along with four potatoes; brown sauce is not rationed.

It's dark in the hallway. I scent the dark for a while. Our eyes meet. Little john thomas notices Dísa's presence. She takes a step forward, stroking the flat of her palm down her stomach; brushing herself off. I hurry over to Dísa. She stands nailed to the floor (my jeez what is this man doing). She blinks her eyes a few times very rapidly (are you angry for some reason).

What's happening, she asks with a gesture (I am astounded).

Here you have him, I say.

She doesn't budge even when I pat her belly. She does not say O! but she looks like an iceberg on an ocean. You will die on a rock, she is thinking, who knows. I cannot think of a solution, so I do nothing, just stand motionless on the mossy carpet right in front of her. Hips still in the hallway. And we breathe excitedly in front of each other without words on our lips. The scent of a kiss on her lips. We stand there, each thinking calmly: what does this mean, what will he/she do. She coughs in my face (atch hoo), a glorious cough, like opal. Then she progresses rapidly up the creaky stairs, plunking along somewhat in her heavy shoes. I tremble.

With the flat of her hand she had stroked her smooth hair beside her cheeks and wet her lips with an irritated expression. I had seen her red, moist tongue tip flick rapidly between her lips and twist like a snail in a hole; she had smacked her lips, set her teeth as if to kiss. Her lips suddenly solidified, grew scales. One should not agonize over, but forget; I am unable to forget.

The door of the refectory has tiny colored panes with a thin cloth as a protection. She reaches a hand in front of herself and opens the door. She heads into the refectory (one must expect such men to attack).

The dining matron resembles the women of her station: heavy, fat, slow to react. With great effort she manages to serve dinner on time. Her extensive arms are red from tottering over the boiling-hot crockpot steam; she is always poking at the food with a fork to see if it is decently fried and so her arms have gained a paunch or two of slack flesh around the elbow joints. Nevertheless, she claims to have long been armless thanks to all this cooking. That's at odds with reality. But we know the first commandment of eating out: never oppose a woman's advice. Her name is Sína. And on Sundays she invariably gives us chopped steak for lunch. So this all happened on a Sunday. I wish all Sundays were Sundays. I wish it rained every Sunday except right as we were coming and going from the refectory. I wish I could hunker down under the covers and sleep blacked-out between Sundays without waking anxious on a Monday. The steak is too spicy for my gastrointestinal system. Dísa sits at the table. Sigurður sits at the head of the table. Magnús sits in the middle of the table between the two students; they send each other chess moves across the dishes or around his back. Ólaf rushes in and sits beside Sigurður. Dísa strokes her flushed cheeks with flat palms. She is blushing as the blue chill of a house-cold breaks out in her cheeks. She clears his throat, hav-he-hav, and soon the fat from the soft steak scales her lips. She put it in her mouth on the tines of her fork, her jaws swinging to and fro, bjabb-bjabb, as the steak mashes down her esophagus down to the stomach grog-grog. I see her before me like an X-ray, all her organs trying to digest and process nutrients from the steak and turn them into that flesh I yearn to possess, almost sixty kilograms of woman with hair and toes and all the limbs in place, all for man's pleasure. A man should never think anything, then the question posed is: How are things with the apartment. Not ready, I reply. But they promised it to me in the spring. Then you'll get it in the winter. You probably will not have to wait long to get something inside it, says Ólaf. What should one get inside, I answer ill-temperedly. And so we ask and answer the things that get asked and answered when someone buys an apartment, and then

Bjössi comes in holding a briefcase. Bjössi is a night watchman. The bag is his black soul; he never leaves it alone, he says. Yes, the bag is dark brown in color, and in it he stores all his possessions, gold watches, rings and jewelry. I know nothing about it for sure except that the case goes wherever he goes. While Bjössi eats he sticks the case firmly between his legs and clamps his knees together so no one can steal it. On the street he has it tightly gripped in his right hand; it has given his hand a leather odor. Bjössi wears a large gold ring on his right index finger. On the ring's shield are his initials engraved in ornamental lettering. Does he let go of the bag at night, asks Magnús out of nowhere; he doesn't otherwise participate in conversation. If he talks again, it'll be about dried fish. Bjössi does not answer; he picks his teeth very rapidly with a sharpened match. After that he gnaws the match at the end then works like mad at his front teeth and bores with it into the farthest reach of his maw. If he's not chewing food, he's gnawing matches, and I counted that he gnaws on average one match between courses and two while his stomach finishes digesting. The brimstone heads he tears off with his front teeth, drops them in the ashtray, lights another match and pushes the flame carefully against the heads, igniting them with a whish-piss-whish, he seizes it and rises to his feet with a repressed belch ro-bo-bo, says bo-bo-ro and is a touch queasy: Yes, that's it, be well, slamming his chair into the table, steadying himself with a ro-bo-bo: greetings to one an all. His largest expenditure is matches, which Sigurður says he lives on. We, the people, watch the sulfur deflagrate in the ash tray, noticing the stubs but not saying how tedious we find this oddity. Bjössi claims that he gnaws matches to quit the habit of tobacco. He eats very fast. But I've sat with Bjössi for ten years, five since he left off the pipe. Why not cook for yourself in the watchman's apartment, Ólaf inquires. What does a man care for such complexities. But at night he does not take coffee to go, as the others do. His job offers perks, though he flatly denies it. First, free lodging; also, no need to buy clothes. I could direct him to the 4th article: Automobile inspectors and special law enforcement officers shall receive a free uniform. Each year they get a uniform and every other year an overcoat, alternating between rain- and dust-coats. Headgear as necessary. Finally, and this is not unimportant, all major repairs and modifications to the uniform and overcoat are free of charge. But he gnaws matches and is said to spend significant amounts on women on Saturdays. Because of this Magnús had to ask whether the bag has ever been put down.   what percentage of men in the world have enjoyed a woman at night   Björssi sleeps with women as they leave the dance, and the rumor is he collects refuted arguments, i.e. the women who rove about the dance hall irritable and militant after the choice pickings have been eaten. Björssi's method is to mix in with the multitude of people the dance hall vomits onto the street at two o'clock in the morning, acting like he was inside and jostling and standing in the throng like anyone else. If he sees someone a little too corpulent for her dress, a woman tiptoeing around sore-footed and careless in the crowd, he walks up to her and says I've got my car so she goes with him though she curses at not getting a moment's peace from being fondled. They are mostly nags, Sigurður says, swearing he has seen Björssi on the pull at Thor Coffee Bar. I don't get paid in work clothes, objects Björssi. No uniform or hat (he has at least five) provided. They cost a great deal, he says. Tómas you should bone up on and learn Björssi's method, Sigurður says. I look at him with puzzlement. A used garment protects bare buttocks. I cannot understand Sigurður. In a flash, it's Saturday. I move my leg and the weekend has arrived. In this drawer are all life's Saturdays along with their lonely humiliations, their inactivity, their sleep. I wrap a scarf around my neck and set a hat on my head. Outside the air's warm. But a man could catch cold in such sly weather. I hear overshoes scrape on the muddy street. I avoid street lights while I am in sight of the house. I know how to pull the wool over others' eyes. I walk very slowly. I should have been a spy. Everyone tries to work out where I am headed and to what end. No one does. On the way to the nightclub on the prowl I am blindfolded by the women who believe that it is enough to jump girlishly and excitedly around a man in his underwear and get money off him without doing anything else; I finish up quickly, blindfold this imitation girl and drive her out to the bus station at Hlemmur where I uncouple from her, leave her senseless for the next man. In this way, the women can't find their way to my home when they come to their senses, can't demand money or threaten me with complaints, suicide, or childbirth. Five fleshy Rubens-women lie with their wet eyes on the night's battlefield. They curse and fume at Hlemmur—"yes, that one should have paid, the swine"—and do have not a cent for the cab ride home to sleep off the liquor on their double ottoman. Who would have thought that in every cell of my body lives a little lusty elf able to satisfy an entire regiment of Tel-Aviv women. I look at them from the perspective of King David of Israel marching his army forward, the chosen of Yahweh, broad-hipped and with a pleat on their skirts, to a Gazan battlefield. Baui sniffs at them. I have read that Arabs fight with their life and death. But I thrust the hat's brim down on my forehead. Oh, Daughters of Jerusalem, weep for yourselves and your children. It folds and bends, this hat brim poorly made of felt, but it still gives any countenance a criminal expression, and every woman has the lofty dream of saving at least one criminal in their lifetime. Poets want to save the whole world; women want to save poets and criminals. And if I were some damned poetaster, I would be called: A fleshpoet (skáld holdsins). Yes, you're going to make yourself into suckers, fellas. Not everything they say about their adventurous nights is true. Songs and dance music burst out onto the street from the open windows. I see heavy curtains of red felt stir slowly in the breeze from the hall, which leaks a haze of smoke as though it was the gathering of some primitive tribe. I stroll casually up and down the street. The night is moderately dark. The streets are illuminated just enough for darkness. Some man snooping about gets in my way. I ask: will the dance be over soon. The doorman denies me entry; I say it is imperative I talk to the man who plays electric guitar in the band. He stares at the watch's bracelet under my frayed jacket sleeve, its figures not fluorescent. Yes, soon, he says. I look around. He has not gone far; perhaps he is engaged in similar pursuits as Bjössi. I seek refuge near the gas station and wait in the shadows. It's safe to stand here; there's always movement from the carport. I see movement in the corner. Björsi stands at the entrance of the garage. He is wearing a light coat and puffing a pipe. Every other year a rain or dust-coat, I think, and the hope is that it has not been spoiled by the tobacco. I turn my back quickly to him, draw myself to the opposite corner. The man with the frayed jacket sleeves is there and looks at me sulkily, furtive. Tómas Jónsson suddenly feels a need to explain his presence. The guitarist lives with me. His wife fell ill suddenly and it is irresponsible of the doorman to deny me entry, he says. That's how people in positions of authority behave. Couldn't Valla take a message, says the man, hesitantly. He refused to. The man looked at Tómas with a sad and serious expression, the sort women encourage, a helpless, false guise that impresses any woman: Oh, you have no idea about his troubles, the terrible war he wages with alcohol; we have to help him. His eyes are flat gray fishskin eyes. Valla won't let anyone in this late, he says; you could try to call.   Does Valla sell hunting licenses outside the door   Ring, says Tómas, shocked, in extreme situations one must deliver one's message verbally. I should go and write about this situation in the papers, that's all that matters. The man scratches his head. I can name examples. Once I had to wait around a full three hours at the Telecom Station for a long distance connection, please have a seat and wait calmly thank you, S-iglu-fjörður; when I threatened to write to the papers about the receptionist and the poor service and asked for her name to mention in the letters to the editor section: Dear readers, I spent all day down at the Telecom Station sitting there, bim-bam . . . the phone lady was quick to turn the page, Tómas for Sauðárkrókur, booth number two. Yes, that's how it works, sometimes, says the man. Would you like to learn about a tragic accident via telephone. No, he replies, it's normally verbal. As an added bonus, I have to stand around out *here*   I Tómas Jónsson, humiliated, loitering like those "door chaser" men, as they're called; they are notorious in town but brash in their sex games and women are excited about them but also extremely huffy—"they are absolutely disgusting." Do you think it's anything more than self-promotion, the men bray. What's self-promotion and what isn't. He points to Bjössi. See, I say, for what purpose could this man be here except to fish for fermented rags, for poor women. What do you think Valla, doorman and bouncer, would pay this man here at the door to catch women. No, what we need is an energetic, progressive journalist to eradicate this behavior via a pithy article or a writer to compose a poem about these blatant poachers; here we have the basic framework for a poetic social commentary. He pauses. The man looks at me, waiting, with his sycophantic womanly eyes, but I have no intention of giving him a longer speech; I want to give the wretch an opportunity to slink away. His actions are against the law, no hunting here, the street is a public domain, I say, adding to what I was going to say. This man's name WILL be in the papers. ALL OF ICELAND WILL GET TO KNOW WHAT HE'S CALLED AND WHY HE WAS LOITERING THERE. My thoughts wander to Bjössi. He can fit anything in his stomach without any discomfort. Edeltraud carries in a dish piled with round steaks with chicken wire decoration above made from a knife tray. A woman's diet is cheaper than a man's. Still, I can report the impossible fact that Dísa leaves less on her plate than we. And yet she doesn't get fat. Strange how Dísa stays so slim. Food-greedy women get no fatter; it's as if the greed leaves nothing for the body, as if she somehow eats herself. In a drunken speech Sigurður says that the Hound of the Baskervilles has ripped out Dísa's heart and absconded with it to the island of Malta, where it is stored in fermented mare's cheese, defended by two castrated rats. More Sigurður drivel. When is the steak coming, says Bjössi. Do not bring in another, replies Dísa. Better to turn to the delicacies. She smiles to disguise her food-greed, forcing her nails into her palm, barely controlling her salivary production, her larynx jogging up and down when she swallows, the murmurs of her gut particularly appealing: grogg-durr-grogg; her little stomach sings when totally empty, and soon it gets potatoes to digest, to crush and dissolve in sweet acids. She talks little otherwise. Dísa is reserved. A man who kisses a cat that has just eaten a rat could release Dísa's heart from its shackles, Sigurður says. Better to tell me no one has acquired it for the future. While she eats, Sigurður uses terrible words but her appetite remains unchanged, it is perhaps somewhat increased by the nervous tension. I am fattening women for pornography, don't you know. Sigurður has an excuse for everything he does. You never know what lies within frail, porcelain women, says Carl Gustav Jung. To take unto yourself some other person, on the off-chance, completely unknown, to bind her with bonds of devotion and love: that is a game of chicken. She may be good enough to look at, but I would probably become annoyed with her on closer acquaintance, with her true nature. Damn her.

i) further thoughts about Dísa

Sometimes I am hunting for some insinuation from Boggi and ask: truly, you have got some knowledge there; or: Something comes to those who receive full pay throughout the year and put it aside. Boggi replies: Huh, what is it to put something aside; there's nothing but fatigue from getting into a fight with absolutely crazy children for a whole winter; and the parents are worse. He thinks children's teachers have a responsibility to be leaders for children, a model for the young. Boggi refuses to get behind teaching out in the country, "simply because of the barbarism that prevails. Much of this stems from a scarcity of teachers, but not because learned teachers refuse to teach because of the paltry salary; this country is actually understaffed everywhere except in the hospitals and while no one wants to face facts, no solution has been found to the problems of teaching; small schools in neighborhoods out in the country continue to build their poor existence around *elderly teachers* who have stuck with the job, first as a miracle and then with the slight hope of a pension or scraps from the teachers' insurance funds, or some lump who continues out of some mental calcification, which often rescues rural areas from being total teacher-deserts. I could not give so much of myself and my energy. Teaching, if I may say my opinion, is a job, but it is neither ideal nor torturous. And though I have taught for twenty consecutive years, I prepare each session conscientiously, and observe the teachers' handbook. But my god, out in the country, no—rather in the grave. In Reykjavík teachers as individuals are at least fairly inviolate in their homes, able to hide away or be left alone, but—absolutely—there is no such thing in the countryside in all the so-called WHOLESOME-NESS. There the teacher is a horror like an old woman or turds inside the body and a desire for porn; there seems to be never-ending prosecution material. Men may not have their genitals, nor may women, in case the sexes use them for "general purposes," N.B. do not even mention them in textbooks, no books at all, but you may wave them at people on the bus. In my opinion, we should not allow a person who speaks this way to keep his teacher's rights. What concerns me most: the person will not want to accommodate me at all. She will give nothing; no sacrifice and no take. Love, marriage to me, she would treat merely as a new job that she would lay the foundations for not with couple's handbooks like the wonderful *Married Life* by Henry and Fredu Thoronto, who are of the opinion that *love games and wiles* are normal pleasures within the limited framework of privacy; in a marriage, everything is healthy and clean. I can barely keep up with each of Björn's movements. How can I judge thrift. A street corner separates us. I can monitor every move of Björn's almost unnoticed. The dance music falls silent. Only the heavy chirping of intoxicated voices carries out the window, which is now driven fully open. People jostle down the stairs. The hall literally vomits out on the street: intoxicated adolescents, intoxicated men, intoxicated women. People throng close together near the front door. A woman expels a scream. Someone has groped me with their hand jesus. Now Björn seizes his renowned inner passions. Tómas Jónsson crashes into the field from where he was hiding between the cars. A girl sits in a back seat and shows three men something that no one can see with much leg kicking, hand gestures, and there-you-go-not-so-ohs. He elbows forward. The less drunk escape through doors taxi drivers keep half-open on their cars, blue and glossy and worried about leather and sweat; they want a fare for a long journey, hate running little errands. A drunk woman bawls at a figure in the disorderly crowd, What kind of sick puppy are you, feeling someone up. The words are directed at a brute in the crowd. A beefy hulk in gabardine clothes, who turns and pees a jet scattered by the wind in all directions so the women have to try to avoid it, complaining, cursing, laughing, and trying to protect their coats (Jeez almighty he got piss on my chic new coat I can't believe it), two beef-cakes in leather jackets storm over one giant and another hulk and the giant attacks the rude hulk and slings him still peeing into the mud where he lies on his back, genitals hanging out his fly continuing to pee in short bursts though the head is senseless and the women navigate around the brawl (no, this is absolutely not possible are we not all Ice-landers are not we having fun calmly restrain ourselves the hulks and giants should not be kicking the prone figure's balls, they only do that in Finland). More giants eventually come along with some other guys and wade in high-handed; they hit and punch, countless icelandic fists in the air and between their legs the muscleman lies passed out, somehow still peeing in the mud in new wingtip shoes, all the rage (fashion is the law). Overcoats flicker and vibrate on their owners, the wind rushes constantly at perms so the women hunker to shelter by the walls screaming and shrieking with short breaths as they hold to the mussed hair on their necks with both hands yelling as if their lives are at stake: *car, car, here, car*, god where the devil are the cars, you there, don't drown me already. There's Björssi, supporting a middle-aged catch to his car. She is abnor-mally quiet, almost too tranquil, eyes old as ice and blurred, too drunk to resist in high heeled shoes. Perhaps she has been *stuck* at the table all night and found that while others were having fun she was *terrifically single* at this party whirling around her in all the ways we were expecting, she found that you *could* never go out with Kalli and Jóna, Val and Tóta because *they* looked after *themselves* like sheepdogs and not the opposite. Kalli and Val. Oh, no. He shouts: car, car, you, car, there. And the car brakes and he jumps in. Man. Two guys run up to the auto workshop. And back. The driver jerks the car back and the guys jump from the workshop. The driver curses but avoids driving over their stretched legs, which kick in the mud. No doubt he thinks my agitation has to do with being drunk. No, follow him in the green. They drive through the streets and turn the corner, where the car stops in an empty street with sleeping houses all around. The doors swing out like wings; a man leaps from the front seat and unwinds the window, the girl half falls onto the sidewalk, after her slinks a man who lifts her up and pulls her panties up her white thighs under the street light and supports her stumbling into the door nook, a mash of feet from the car. Then three lights in the house turn on. He pays the fare and the girl pulls free and comes at him swinging her hands and strikes the bag into the air: go on, idiot, perv, get. Everywhere Saturday night is in full swing, it shines from drunken eyes, it's in stomachs, mouths, houses, feet, in the air, even in the sticky hum of tires on the street. The city cleans its bowels from its workdays, its blood and its thoughts of work, and climbs drunk and purified over the bounds of Sunday, unconscious like a newborn baby. The city center has become incapable of joy, a dangerous place to walk. I get to the house after a strenuous hike. Bjössi works here as a night watchman, barks at thieves, locks and unlocks doors, dusts mats. Here's where I humiliate myself in the XII. pay grade. Here stands the building. Within touching distance. Light shines in the basement window. Through the back door, they have gone down the stairs. Now they lie motionless under a feather duvet and an Álafoss carpet. The street police drive very slowly past. The car's window is open and the police speak into their new carphone. The car pauses so I can observe how they talk in the phone. I stare at the technology. Then the car disappears around a corner. Bjössi's voice. A taxi drives to the house, a girl staggers. She focuses on walking ahead. I barge out. Between Tómas Jónsson and the girl, a sharp conflict erupts. I strike out with the bag and yell. What does this man want, I hear her scream. I have not become an attacker. Bjössi slams the door. I grab her waist, soft as boiled sheep's head, but she drags my body after her outside against the car's right buttock. I thrust a forearm between Bjössi and the girl. The police car continues its circuit. Do you want me to call the police, my driver says. He calls and the car stops at a suitable distance so we can all see how they talk on the car phone in full regalia. I run and then I stop running. When I feel my legs can run no longer I wander aimlessly along the street until I startle and stop. A bottle has fallen from an open window and broken on the pavement. I could have died, no more liquor for me, says a girl. Come on up, friend, it's just me and three meathead giants having a party. Louts. Louts crowd to the window and threaten to urinate on me if I continue to snoop around the house. Then they tug her away from the window. You can lie by the window with me and look at me all evening. The girl comes back and swings her arm and throws me thirty timeless roses. I do not know if this is the same girl who visits me and who I long to touch, I lift my hands and see my fingers are bloody meat, and the girl sails on like a cipher. You are awfully shaky-handed today, Tómas, says Björssi, one might think you were hungover, if we didn't know you were teetotal . . . If it were not known that evil blood congeals inside. Does Björssi know if I drink liquor or not. He cannot; I drink my liquor in secret under the covers. Is my private life a hindrance to him. Did Björssi not come to look for it. Oh, I am not hungover, I answer quietly, it's just my old heart. I am often filled with admiration at my self-control and the great power I have gained over myself. I can never have enough of repeating old glories. A complex but eminently manageable god lives inside me. I have divined a demon. I sense things even before the gnashing of teeth. I dream before daybreak. How could a Birthday Book know aspects of my personality: willpower, self-control and calm in any situation are fundamental elements of who I am. How could a small book in an inferior format have known me inside and out long before I knew, everything it has taken Tómas Jónsson seventy years to discover about himself. Most likely a man is not fully born until he dies. How does everyone know all of everyone else's individual make-up, but I never know anything about any one. Does man, as an individual, only exist to the extent that he is a context for other people. In chapters, I do not recognize even myself: What is Títa doing, a cat, prowling around Hotel Borg. Who am I. Tómas or tómmas or some other Jón Tómas. My quiet is unique. I must be so carefully made because I'm an Icelander. The last purebred Icelander. Do you each day feel you have a bad heart, I ask Björssi and seek help from him. The sound of empathy in his voice fills me with pity. O yes, I have long had poor health, this is not as incidental as many consider, I say while sugar cubes melt on my tongue. I wanted the bird from some legend to come grab my heart and put it in mare's cheese next to Dísa's heart or any heart. In the cold, Dísa's nose becomes as colorful as a puffin's. The human heart has long been a difficult assignment, says Ólaf.   no he says nothing just stares over the table at something distant probably an airplane out the window treetops in the garden like he sees a dream flutter in a cave among the kelp and algae or wind and the suction in a grounded ship   medical science has found a new drug that stimulates blood circulation to the heart, says Boggi.   no she can never talk beautiful words from her lips she just talks about regional studies and the perfect method of reading instruction taxes and percentages   no drug can benefit my heart, I say. Dísa retreats behind her eyes, finishes her cup and clasps her hands. She rests her chin on her knuckles. Her knuckles are hard and white from effort. She inspects the cactus, but perhaps she sees me out the corner of her eye. A person should have steel health and a steel heart in a sturdy steel body, says Ólaf sarcastically, in a steel world inside a steel lung. Everything from stainless steel. Dísa. And deer all around a steel deer Dísa, Dísa.

f) though I have lived through twenty years of war and wasted a lot of power and won no victory—I must take my mind off Dísa

And you must also know how to give up in the right way. Or to pretend to conquer. To whom should I tell skirt-chasing stories about me and Dísa. Because I lack the goods and travel money to go to Höfn, the stomach, heart, kidney, and interest in engineering. In vain have tried to bring charges relating to the biological warfare I have often been subjected to—to the United Nations. Mr. Tryggvi Lie, the chair there, has not so much as answered my letters. Yet biological warfare is damnable. In this respect, having the free right of complaint is covered under the equal rights in the Human Rights article. This Tryggvi Lie does not exactly have bags under his eyes from worrying about me. Tryggvi probably has eyebags of concern for the skiing in supremacist-crazy Norway. And who would know—unless it was he who ordered the doctors to put germs in my medicine instead of genuine drugs. I DEMAND PURE MEDI-CINE. I refuse to take medicine full of fish that will swim constantly around my blood vessels and jump waterfalls in my arteries and lagoons of blue veins and swim up and down the salmon run of my heart

IX. class A

> Tri-x-y poisoned ×
> Dísa is trapped in my brain.
> Poisoned ×, purged myself of mental ×-er of Dísa.
> Let her
> rot from me.
> Respectfully,
> Tómas Jónsson.

now finally the darkening day moves slowly over me has come halfway to evening as rest invigorates my body I ease my blood pressure carefully in my heart my nerves' high tension after a day of much energy production I lay myself totally limp my thought bound in the calmness of a cow field gliding through the night pasture the meadow green field not where grass grows but where ideas enter the green colored paint   rest   the couple rushed to their door separately after great and hard bickering the tom-toms gibbering no longer in my intoxicated and muddled head   I wrote to Dísa of myself   I am empty   I have become oxygenless

> then we come to the arrangement and separa-
> tion of the various kinds of fear that form the
> primitive under the heavens' dome with water
> and with man's flesh with the innate execution
> of your actions and gestures to the creator: fear

of authority of weapons of machines then fear
of life itself most frequently because it is most
linked to man he is covetous and reckoned
within the elements of the body the fear of life
and he steers people and dwells ever within the
flesh and people that part and he is ever connected to the sub-divisions of the mind because
all this is fear never one part two- or three-part
absolutely must he . . . (here some of the manuscript is missing)

Here is a simple example of the formation of fear:
    we are not entirely equipped to gloss
You have become forgetful in your sarcasm, for example, of what you did
June 1. Say that it's necessary for you to remember all the incidents that
occurred in late August that year. Your thinking will become (perpetually?) concerned with the forgotten items. Both during sleep and while
awake visions will loom over your head the whole month of December
(in this case, the vision becomes a gallows). Finally you are able neither
to understand nor explain the differences between reflection and image.

    you think in dreams everything
    is natural you come to think up
    many solutions all insoluble
    finally you reach a higher stage
    of human experience, which is
    to not distinguish between fact
    and the desired so the myriad
    mosaics of your mind remotely operated
    a crowd of unrelated words in chaos
    o there comes a man in harmony with terror
    that lives inside and destroys you
    with forgetfulness finally arrives

that which shall come you are come
completely out of this world and yourself
an empty mess Tómess Jónsson join in
now my Búkolla while you are alive

An incident never has a reliable outline. Your thinking is no longer material. There are two kinds of memory: assimilated memory, which increases without dissipating, and indexed memory, which increases in order, rather, to keep everything analyzed separately.

do not read so fast we hardly have a chance to gloss

some person seizes terror
she is not able to pull away from
the webbed card index of memory
objects and cannot say: here are
firm memories of horse rides
over Kjöl here an excellent view over
the mind's subdivisions the journey there
and here white-eyed Lóa and here cannibals
savages and here difficult teething
but what she looks around wildly after
sees no end has lost all environments
in the existence of fear within the human

From forgetfulness comes the existence of anxiety and from equally obvious causes and the forgotten situation it takes physical shape in one's stomach.

he is everywhere at hand
is in everything
is in nothing
all of us thrown into forgetting
and we are born only to be forgotten

Man is the element of life, and anxiety is the element of life and of man. It is the A-Division of the mind that hosts terror. She is housed there one's whole life long. Thus ends the insights of Tómas Jónsson, a lecture 8-22-57.

Dísapoem, which also could have been written about Miss Gerður, Lóu, or other women from the author's timeline.

namely Hell
neither have I seen your sagging breasts
nor under the clothes that shelter flesh
yours are like armor: dress socks
panties garters and garter belt
except in Miss Gerður's mind then
how you armor your frozen way
my covetous prayers wish neither
clothes nor the persistent dismissal of your slipping
staple—my cunning desires for fleshly relations
with such an excellent monstress as you are

here ends the award-winning and acclaimed volume of poetry by Tómas Jónsson

Finally, we shall look into what we are: a various group of names chosen by our neighbors. Who knows whether the body corresponds to its name. You, Tómas Jónsson, walked from the front door of the house early in the morning and returned in the evening christened with another name: Tómmas. Too much. A man's name and nature are often two or three contrasts. Earth and man don't always fall into an embrace (although this may happen among teenagers and old people). Doors and flesh look truth in the eye: the door is eternally a door, flesh is flesh. No one flies away on wings of stone, which the bird casts. No one holds another's hand like a rosewing. I do not kiss with a nettlekiss. But someone said:

behind your back I draw composite images; they are natural. Who was that great fool. Who thought anything was natural.

probably it would be possible to send them a written eviction notice   writing letters to people who live in the same apartment seems beneath Tómas, but not tómmas (now look at that I'm just a hermaphrodite). I am forced to show tenants some human dignity, these uninvited guests who have settled around the apartment and made it their lair. I could take myself overnight to a hotel and write a difficult eviction letter from there without getting black bruises on my conscience.

Tonight (2-22-54) I dreamed a somewhat puzzling dream: I felt I was headed home. Someone invisible came to me and offered me his company. I see you are nightblind, she said. I considered her offer half comical, since I was a little deserted rock off the coast. In haste, I calculated my geographical position (I thought in every respect the way a deserted rock would in a dream) and felt it would be best to relocate one nautical mile closer to land. Turbulence settled on me. I sailed toward the country and woke up. Here ends this asinine dream.

Tonight, however, (12-4-54) I saw a deserted rock through my binoculars. The deserted rock was me. On this flat rock nothing grew but bladderwrack. I looked around in all directions from the lighthouse and from the seaweed cluster rose a snow-white seal's head which stared long thoughts at me, its eyes strangely gentle and womanly; then it yawned three times. White foaming crests rose around the skerry. The seal called out to me and said: Please do not simply think of me as a symbol of someone else important to you and your life. Do not be superstitious or a wishful old woman. I'm just a plain old seal with remarkably gentle and womanly eyes. Good, do not take my words too seriously. Everywhere a tomb a mast = Tómmas. And I woke up.

tenth composition book

I could declare to the State that I am taking sick leave. Like other folk, I am entitled to paid sick days. In all my working life, I've not missed a single day. I often go to work sorely ill. You never get the flu, which is going around, said Miss Gerður, the plague never lays you low. We are each entitled to twelve sick days annually, and most people probably take them, whether they get ill or not; I feel no need to give them to the business, since it gives us nothing, says Sigurður. The morning he got promoted, I am the first to insist that an insolent man got promoted. The branch manager wants to make him more dependent on the business with this appointment. Títa, I put some milk drops in a glass for you. I told the housekeeper not to stir the milk in the coffee, but to leave it in a separate glass. Do you have an empty shot glass, I asked, the milk sours the coffee overnight. No one has undertaken to provide a roof over my head, free; most of my life I have had to struggle for one. Certainly, one makes money on rent, which is necessary so I can pay my mortgage installments on time. Katrín and Sveinn should be out on the street. I need the storage cubby back. I was planning to make toys and sell them at christmas bazaars. I would begin small-scale production of pretty toy cars. I am opposed to big industry, especially heavy industry. I could sell the cars for a decent profit over christmas. Or I could write christmas books. Around these people, there's barely room to stroke one's own head. She has filled the storeroom with rubbish. You cannot move for all the boxes and tins, wrenches, spare parts, and oil cans from the

American military they bought at the Defense Force Supply Store. We are collecting these things in order to sell them, he says. Somehow you have to support your family. Maintaining family is an eternal dilemma, I answer. It's a devilish challenge, he says. That's life for most folk, I reply. When we meet in the hallway he initiates a conversation. The formula for dialogue with Sveinn goes: He says a short sentence. I repeat it in a slightly altered form. These discussions continue until thirty phrases have been spoken, combined (15-15), then Sveinn is drained and sighs: Yes, so it goes. I say: Yes, that's true. After this great mental exertion he lies down on the couch, crosses his legs, and falls asleep under a military blanket. He is a like a guest in his own home. But his wife stalks bulkily across the floor like she owns each item, each cabinet. She spends her life traveling between the radio and the telephone. I do not know why they have put in a phone, probably so the husband can report that tonight he's going to work overtime. I never hear her say anything on the phone but this fleeting sentence: I'll leave a snack on the table for you. Yet she seems to use the phone endlessly. She is constantly ringing out but holds the silent receiver to her ear; very strange behavior. I could believe that Miss Punctuality was one of her friends in this town. If the kid fusses, she gives him the fridge or phone to mess with. He'll listen to the sound, astonished, and forget to scream. Sveinn's work clothes hang in the closet, glassy with ointment, instead of hanging on hooks in the laundry room, as I have repeatedly told them: the radio and newspapers have urged people to leave their special work clothes at the workplace. It often occurs to me that we here in the apartment are rapidly approaching middle age. Here there is a kind of reverse development. I would not be surprised if I woke up one morning and ran into Henrik Bjelke in the hallway with a commission from Frederick the Third, King of Denmark and its colony, iceland, to "possess the apartment by law and by right." I would love to see the expression on the couple's faces should the home become something other than a place where Sveinn eats, increases his breed, and sleeps off his fatigue from carbonic acid poisoning. Today the house is blissfully free from the electric guitar. Each night the phone rings. I pick the receiver up gently and place it against my ear. I listen breathlessly to the other end of the line. The connection ends, and I stand on the cold floor and spit on the handset. iceland Telecom is apparently the accomplice of these thugs. They refuse to check what number has rung and claim the telecoms laws prohibit that. Now they are checking whether I am at home. Stalking me. The couple would not stir even if I were injured one night. They sleep like cows in a cowshed top-to-tail, heads to feet. Títa would eat my innards, stuffed as they are with steak and soda crackers. When the electric clock on the corner of the watchmaker's workshop buzzes two blows, the phone rings. I hear the guitarist come home. He waits in the dark hallway until a knock is struck on the door, then opens it and, short of breath, begins by the coat hooks. The girl on the third floor is in cahoots with him, the strumpet who previously played ball in the hallway. I look around the bedroom. Slowly and quietly it turns to day. Things come rapidly into the light from the darkness as the time of the day grows on the window blind. I open the closet to examine the coat hanging on a coat hanger. I'll not let them run along my hallway. It is enough that their behavior keeps me awake. They can remain in their own rags. My gray coat hangs there no longer. Its time has come. The third coat I have had in my life. The first coat was a gray ulster coat. I bought it at Geysir. It was light gray with white stripes. Then I had a darker coat. And this one here is dark gray in color with black stripes. A thick coat. A warm coat. Somewhat too thick to stroll about in in summer. My shoes last me a decade. I wear shoes from the Bata factory in Czechoslovakia. By now Bata factories have likely been nationalized by the Soviet authorities. Perhaps large factory complexes with water slope roofs. My shoes. Slightly frayed shoes, but sturdy and good. I would not be opposed to visiting the Bata factories. They produce the world's best shoes, all made from various leathers. There is a difference in seeing them versus icelandic barges, made in some dwarf factory and named Imperial shoes, no less, undoubtedly made from inferior leather. No, Czechs know how to make shoes, so that they do not scuff. They sow shoes from the finest Cordoba leather. The giddy people on the street saunter about in domestic Imperial shoes that have one thing in common—that their leather uppers slide about in wet conditions like a slimy commonwealth of rawhide. I despise people who let themselves be seen in the bank wearing Imperial footwear. Well, Títa, you nodded off reading. Do you know the story of the stork who invited the fox home to eat. You should not lap from the neck of a thin glass any more than the fox should. Here is a can lid. I picked the lid up off the street especially for you to lap from. One day I stumbled on it half buried in the mud between some tire tracks. I would not collect the lid while it was light; instead I waited for dark, and when it was sufficiently dim I went out to the trashcan at 16A, checked the air as if I were looking at the weather, drew a króna from my pocket, let it fall, then picked it up and put it in my pocket along with the lid. No. I hid it inside the palm of my hand, stood still in the same position while the shaking trembled my knees and I calmed myself. I hurried away, and after that I made sure no one ever saw me by the trashcans at 16A.

my puss you have many things

A person would probably have heard the news if I, Tómas Jónsson, an employee in the XII. pay grade in a state-run business, was observed picking dirty junk or a can lid up off the ground by the trash can at 16A. It would be interesting to know what people in the neighborhood think about me. They likely believe Tómas is an unsociable scientist, an odd twig or something similarly eccentric and icelandic hahaha

I throw up over you
A forty-year-old man's childhood is far behind, but around sixty
he approaches youth anew, though perhaps that is too early to just
reminisce and live only in memories. But my lifetime is so uniform
and impoverished, I am indeed so isolated from fat, so calcified, that
I justify myself living night after night and whole winter days in
Thoughtland. True satisfaction lies in refusing life, falsifying events as
best as possible, making true in fantasy how it is morning in a warm
bed when, incredibly, you are lying at night under a cold blanket.

Oh, this town—this cursed distended city—has always had a devilish effect on me. She crouches down on me with her revolting limpid sky. In dreams she is tolerable: as a nightmare is. Like a nightmare I have been on my own since I first aimed to be an expert on ecstasy. And I doubt that anywhere in the widest world can be found such a dull man as me. I am an unbearable devil. I am scum, a disfigured night-creature with white cracked teeth, a glowing tongue, hairy on the outside, not dissimilar to a tufted rat that runs over a naked body in a dream. To give an example: I'm so boring that no one has ever wanted my friendship. People prove this to be so by avoiding me in the street, spitting yellow erysipelas spittle at me on their way from the office of the city physician, without giving me an apologetic smile. I have strongly noticed malicious sneering people recently come from the epidemic clinics the newspapers publish regularly from January to April each year. I seemed heavy as a child, I felt happiest in the company of bacteria and viruses. Look at your siblings (Björga), it was said, look at how pure their expressions are, how they radiate joy like a christmas child, but you leak surliness all day. I see the devil reflected in your eyes (and truthfully the devil gleamed there, I was bored of Jesus with his stiff frozen expression and repellent tenderness). Nevertheless, I longed sometimes to be—for a moment—the one who told jokes and entertaining stories of strange people and strange events (or, for example, to be a sentimental singer and sing From the Heath *so quiet everyone got goose bumps): the devil puts his fingerprints on the cyclist's windbreaker; an uncanny fish swims out of the taps in a high-rise building, where a grouchy woman shuts herself inside the room because there is no balcony in the apartment and she cannot air the bedclothes; coral grows on a man's head; mind connections emerge between a man in Norðfjörður and women in Stykkishólmi; a salmon carrying a woman's snow-white hand is caught in Soginu. Whenever I have tried something like that, and rehearsed and prepared it, my words have become so exaggerated and violent that listeners have said: Oosh, don't be so repulsive. At exactly the moment I most wanted to gather a good, harmonious group around me and be the life and soul of the gathering. Fortunately, this pretentious desire of mine was fleeting, wrapped up in a fivefold joke about myself telling a series of stories so hairy the women would get goose bumps and sweat between their breasts or pucker together their thighs for fear a hairy and invisible hand would touch them down there. "He had barely come through the door when the atmosphere of the party lightened and each story added to the witty stream from his lips well into morning; we rolled about laughing." I dearly wish such comments would apply to me. But I, wooden man and log, serve no purpose while men die laughing other than to be a metal plate reverberating joy through frozen lips, while torment cries inside my mind. Somewhere I read that comic actors were usually dull and boring in their personal lives. I told Katrín this after unsuccessful attempts to create opportunities to speak up from the swamp of drowsiness. My sense of humor is considerable, attentive to play and the improbabilities of life, but Títa, Katrín, and Annakatrín look at me with eyes that say: Let's see whether everything he has to offer runs aground, Tómas Jónsson telling his stories. I stand in the center of the floor, nervous agitation affecting my words, an uncontrollable fear at not being able to get the soul to smile his heavy lips. She offers a double-edged smile with her teeth, as if the tongue might trouble me; at most she is smiling politely or coughing nervously from anxiety, giving a hollow cough for appearance's sake. I flap my limbs, a cord of fire around my forehead, and rush into the first and easiest of my trifling stories. People smack their lips dry in their mouths out of pity and change the subject before the atmosphere becomes suffocating, sometimes starting to sing national hymns, recalling memories from their school years and talking about their teachers in geography and natural science. Alas, this city with all its navel-gazing, boring men is most tolerable in a nightmare.*

I sneak home immediately after work, go into my room in the dark and lie still for a few moments while the anguish of the day disappears from my nerves. One time, I was so distressed that it almost meant I would need great courage to speak to someone without being addressed first.

No doubt people think I have discovered some system whose implementation will transform the world, that I am creating a new religion, and that Parliament has given me a fellowship. Oh, this nation lives indefinitely in pubescent fantasies of hope. And while I was young I thought that someone would pay for me to study, as happened with poor, promising farmers' sons in books. Time passed—nothing—but I said, you will meet your fate in a similar way to Jón Eiríksson, the king's Special Advisor; you are a slow-burner as he was and to prove it soon your Ludvig Harboe will come from Denmark to the colony in the heath-blue north and send you to Niðaróss-by-Hafnar where you will complete your bachelor degree and from there your way lies directly to the academy in Sórey; but the difference at Moltkeum between my days and his is that I will not get invited to become a private tutor to Prince Friðrik, heir to the Denmark of dreams.

There are plenty of historical analogs for your crown prince and crown prince Jóns both called Frederick I would never have given up in the fight for the nation and seen her removed from the limits of the colony or else I would have taken myself nonsensical out of Löngubrú it is better to be living with a dissuaded head than half-dead with him dented no a corpse has never saved any nation in reality truly Jón was disgraceful a traitor to the nation and a coward of the first degree Jón and I were both hairy nosed those who love nothing have nothing to betray commies like Sigurður cannot therefore be considered national traitors the commies neither have nor love any homeland commies do not even love Esja and Hekla they just love wine and no danger that he will at some point become a wretched traitor a schnapps traitor or (here everything breaks off abruptly in the account . . . undoubtedly something has been kept from the reader . . .)

Nothing can be done except it is immediately whispered about. Tómas was seen collecting the can from the street, says the staff in the house. The best sons of the nation have, therefore, the infamous rabble as a bone of contention. The old woman at the milk store will *write me off.* The men, who spend Sundays hanging around the garage all the livelong day, go silent if they see me. That is bizarre. Maybe they think I'm a nuclear physicist who disappeared from Bodø or Pontecorvo.

did you know where Pontecorvo was

there is no word about it in the book

you should know something more than what is written in books   do you know who Carlo Ponti is   ooo and that he lived with that sex-bomb Sophia Loren

Pontecorvo could create another kind of bomb my Títa

that is not in the winter curriculum

(What follows here can be omitted from the textbook.)

not all of life is found in the curriculum but before Napoleon considered invading Moscow he studied carefully the winter curriculum and learned by heart with his indexing brain all the underlined sentences he went to the examination recited the dates and names wished that he had come up with something good but while rattling off his curriculum fluently several spirited lunatics who were not part of the curriculum escaped from the Moscow Asylum and set fire to the city Napoleon shouted deeply offended and hurt to the teachers this may not stand it is not in the books but what about how the city burned and Napoleon sloped away and got frostbite on his balls which later led, along with the swelling blisters, to his death, in his memoirs he writes in war lunatics are the most dangerous Hitler learned this first commandment of military theory and removed all the lunatics whom he pardoned until his troops were flooding over the plains of Russia and everywhere they came they went to the asylums first and killed the lunatics but Stalin found a solution he let the Russians eat garlic though it was not included in the curriculum and by eating garlic the Russians defeated Hitler and what

does it matter if Goliath moans in his death throes it does not count
killing an armed giant with a stone that was not mentioned in my book
in my curriculum my invalid defeat is just as poor as anyone's defeat
you shout just as an art historian at an exhibition these paintings are not
included in the art history curriculum of Taine whom I studied ignorant
critics nor are diplomats in London featured in the Russian diplomat's
curriculum and increasingly an awful lot happens in the world of art and
politics beyond any critic's curriculum no matter how men shout and cry
and insist they follow their curriculum by the book

I have my suspicions as to why the kids lean against my window Sundays. I draw the curtain. I am not about to let people look in on me.
What they don't dare do themselves, they send the damn kids to do. I
have to have the screen covering the window the whole day, even though
such behavior might arouse suspicion. When people walk along the sidewalk I see they focus their sight sideways into the window with pursed
lips and fluttering eyes, always spying on me, especially after the event
in the laundry room. I was simply straddle footed so I could piss down
the drain. I was coming home when I was seized by a sudden urge to
pass water there just one time at eight in the evening. I had never used
the laundry myself, which I had equal right to the same as any other
apartment owner. I stood astride the grille and spurted and tried to spurt
straight down the holes, when the foolish girl came in on me and made
me jerk, roar, like I had been startled, so I spun around and some of the
stream swung into her, causing her to emit a shrill cry and leap to the
side of the washing tub screeching, where she crashed into the mangle
and fell with a great tumult and lay on the floor among the pots. I
rushed to her aid in the dark, and it never rains but it pours, because
Valgerður came in just then, arms full of dirty laundry that she was
going to soak, and screams like her life has been threatened: What the
hell are you doing with the child. I struggled, bent over the girl crushed
between the tub and the wall covered with blood from her nose. And
when I straightened my back thunderstruck by astonishment over this
new affront, she pointed screaming at my open flap; Baui was out of his

hole, dangling carelessly over the bloody girl. She screams: What is this meaning of this, and she brandishes a laundry paddle threateningly at Baui and I. She takes the paddle to the empty basin and makes such a noise that the whole house whips down the stairs to the scene and prays god almighty to help them and demand a medical examination of the girl who is prodding at her pussy eagerly.

behind the laundry tub Unnar's virginity lay buried

They furiously rub at and brush the sidewalk abnormally often these days, but can see nothing through the window. Gossip women do not have eyes that can emit infra-red beams. But their thoughts hover around me. I have thoroughly checked that it is impossible to see into the basement room during the day if the window is covered. It is close to dark inside here, and the cellar is largely buried. The windows are all but level with the earth so prying biddies have to sneak by bent-backed (acting like their shopping bags are an excessive burden). The most diligent of the gawpers are little old women who resemble roaches or diving beetles. But I make sure never to turn on the light inside unless the screen covers the window. If it is dark outside one can see into a bright room, but not from the bright into the dark. And the old ladies clean their fanciest clothes at night. Now the overcoat disappears in the gathering darkness. It is nearly total dark. Tonight, I will break up with my lodgers. I will not allow anxiety to torment me anymore. I arrive at the locked apartment. I ring the doorbell to make a reasonable argument for eviction, at his disposal. No one comes to the door. I look around and lift the rug. The key lies under the corner. What if some thief plans to rob the house. He'd deploy the same method: ring and if someone comes to the door he would ask for Guðmund.   Nonono that's too common a name   He asks for Hildiríðason who is of course back home in Eglu. (This is probably suitable for Egil Skallagrímsson's Saga.)   Apologies for the trouble, says the thief humbly. Burglars need to be polite. And if no one answers the door the thief turns on his heel and looks around.

No matter how inexperienced he is, he knows not to begin by breaking the door or trying a skeleton key. He looks under the mat. To think that people in the nuclear age still store house keys under the mat. In some respects everybody still lives in Old Testament times, despite all the technology. This alone should be valid grounds for eviction. To further emphasize the matter, I might add that the thief ate all my evening meal and drank my coffee from my thermos flask so I have none for morning and he spread smoked horsemeat on my rye bread. And in an extreme emergency I might have to sacrifice the thermos, sell it at an antique sale and also the other cup. I have two but can no doubt manage with one. The thief likely knows it.

the writing desk is headed into dusk I can no longer see my writing I am going to place in the cabinet the neck tie hanging on the back of the chair like a lazy worm I have certainly written warts and all about Dísa and Miss Gerður tonight have thought about them it had not occurred to me that the divan is a double a person rests better on a broad divan than a narrow one I ought to splurge on a rest best pillow for myself Helgi Tómasson the psychiatrist at Klepp the Reykjavík Asylum should receive a Nobel Prize in medicine for inventing the rest best pillow it has cured ricked necks for many people with muscular rheumatism, but how is it Helgi's invention at Klepp is the sole scientific feat of the icelandic people no we have two Nobel Laureates Finsen and Helgi the French encyclopedia Larousse actually gave him to the Faroe Islands and we Icelanders have no man in the book that is shameful but I lie on the divan often comfortable despite things with Dísa without her becoming aware her I snuggle down with Miss Gerður and a large number of women I meet on the street and bring home for debauchery and I have been with pale-skinned women in skirts the victorious winner in the women's 1952 handball tournament all but one of the ICE Unit and all the Mothers Society and the newly created icelandic Association of University Women many of the most famous actresses in the world Cleopatra and Queen Ingiríður in her national dress the Greenlandic

Eskimo I am reliably the only man who has touched the female Nazi Ilsu Koch Josephine wife of Napoleon awoke beside me here suffering from a cold I stole all the covers in the night she said Isabela the catholic was here briefly from Spain during the summer and asked me to redeem her from her lesbian tendencies and sitting in the chair with her naked I shrugged off a marriage offer from Greta Garbo Florence Nightingale I had to throw out just yesterday are you not fond of this milk and the cow's milk Títa is so picky you are she is still fatter and better nourished I could lure Presidents' wives and deprive them of their expensive Díor dresses I undress the weird fashion on the street outside painting beards on them in pictures and putting them in uncomfortable positions at sunset I sleep on the scented thighs of the King's daughter, Giohare from Samandal, where cows graze on goats' hair and kiss open-mouthed virgins at the slaughter everywhere the State mandates dos and don'ts except here on this rough divan blanket where it is enjoyable to masturbate totally freely and fuck according to one's choice defenseless womenfolk earlier or contemporary in history or not in her at all because darkness does not restrict me even though martial law is in the house I am the boy at Haföldun who sends the girl on *Favorite Songs* to the patients on State Radio are those there in the red coats the song the marzipan man Presley sings I am a thought that disappeared to secure a wife in my night-temper I seduce small-maidens in churchyards and known-maidens the most famous virgin old ladies as a death-comfort I take the trouble from death which faces all maids I am a criminal thought I cause this great disgust that a woman gives to man after two years of marriage becoming lazy in her loving always hungry nibbling at food all day lying with others and birthing grassy-headed dull-eyed children who suffer from constant earache like a ship captain's daughters I cause creaking in a freshly-washed woman's hair under the comb because I am the eternal tómmas who Sigurður and Ólaf agree has never lived anywhere other than as a thought-fetus but now this fetus lies quivering cold, sensitive and exposed like a snail that has lost its shell no one knows me except maybe an out-of-town woman who mistakenly looked for the loony cart and sat there all day and night in the bus station at Sundlaugvegur and passed a poor night's sleep then continued her journey on the bus the whole next day until she got back the memories in her head and remembered that she had promised according to a bet she lost with her cousin to eat a half portion of fried fish with mayonnaise at Matstofa Austurbæjar or a faraway farmer or a freelancer who keeps a pet lamb in a meadow to disappear to on summer evenings I'm forced into man but at the same time I am all the noble and distorted and the human kernels in men's breasts, which god has begun to move away from the assault of passion only man is in man together with cars houses furniture and sunsets that pours diagonal rays over the ashtray and cigarette music tin that plays Mozart when the cigarette is lit and birthday celebrations grapple with the smoke so they can listen to the Little Night Song until throats are sore and painful and I wade in them like a giant in ground mist and arrive shining on the line to let myself gallop an electric current to the nipples that explode afterward I put them in the money box hahaha   everyone suspects that Tómas Jónsson is a wizard of lust in secret ellipses . . .

Every great men is ripe for persecution. I am convinced the curiosity and malice of human beings whets my job: collecting modern folklore and
     Tómas
          now she comes right up to the door they heard me laugh   don't you want to come out and visit with us   we're playing cards you know you are always welcome to join us

The Black Sheep
a folk tale

As is well known, iceland was occupied during the World War II, first by the dirty British, then later, by request, by a select American army. This request for military protection of the population, however, was made with one condition from the icelandic government, and it has remained in military protection contracts since then: that in the U.S. force there must be no members of the negro race, or, as the provision states: in the U.S. Defense Force there should be no men of black stock who, mixing with the ancient icelandic nation (which must always be its own acquaintance though it is chosen and of norwegian royal descent) could in some way endanger the particular characteristics of its national population of pan-Germanic and Irish descent.

    It is believed that the U.S. authorities immediately acquiesced to these requirements, provided no other hindrances or conditions were set for the occupation. Our wishes have not been followed in all respects: occasionally men with dark, if not black, skin color and sheep-wool on their heads surfaced in this country. Black men were not in the permanent garrison, but came with the supply ships that provided food. And so one time a negro ended up here in a ship cabin and he was granted shore leave by the customs authorities, chiefly so people did not gather on the pier and delay the unloading by gaping, as was common. When a pretty sizeable crowd had gathered the authorities released him into the country and a group followed the man at a distance (this was a common method for distributing the population and it later became a tradition to have one negro at every ship port, which worked well). The story says that the ship stayed briefly, one day; some believe it was only in the region of a few hours' stopover. Anyway, shortly before the ship left its mooring the negro came back to the pier accompanied by a girl he got to follow him, but had not taken due to scant time to have sexual intercourse. Men do not agree on whether or where he had sudden sex with the girl. Some say they were in the back seat of an automobile and pulled the seat forward and had their heads and legs sticking out the open door. Everyone, however, agreed that an automobile had driven the negro to the ship's side, but some want to maintain that he put the woman up against the mudguard to show off in the protection of the harbor surrounding the bulwark.

It is amazing that no eyewitnesses agree, but it proves the old saying it true: everyone sees his own sight.

The girl, who had or did not have sex with the sailor, was called Anna and she became pregnant after this ended. After a nine-month gestation period the fetus ended its stay in the womb; the girl had birth pangs while she was hanging laundry, but the contractions were mild and at long intervals.

Grandma, with whom the girl lived, knew no better than to give her soda powder mixed in water to intensify the pangs, which led to nothing useful except the girl got rid of her wind without getting rid of the child; her belly swelled, her suffering increased, and then after three days in an awful state of health—the sickness at times passed from the girl or appeared in her in quick fits—she lost consciousness and was at death's door. Then the neighbor women took her off her grandmother's hands, engaged the bakery van to come and drive her to a hospital in Reykjavík; she could hardly stand, and in the end she had a cesarean section and the child was taken howling from her by force; it had—according to the official reports of the event—changed its mind right away during the first day of labor pains; suspecting serious consequences if born it decided to remain in the womb as long as possible; the child had hovered to and fro with its decision to make its fate visible or hide itself away without taking a definite decision.

And the doctors, holding the child up by his feet and shaking and shaking it to activate the organs' functions, diagnosed that the child manifested some kind of perversion. It was born white in color, but in the hands of the doctors, to their great alarm, its skin began to darken until it became coal-black, which they thought was caused by contact with the atmosphere, unless some color gene had the peculiar property of changing according to temperature or circumstances.

The chief physician of the hospital was well familiar with the Government's provisions in the Defense Treaty. For this reason, he quickly rang the Foreign Service and explained in his best phone manner the scientific premise that the color genes had undergone a transformation because of exceptional chloroform levels in the air in the operating room and the toxic gases formed in the womb and the interaction they had undergone.

Here in our hands lies a dark-skinned child attached to an umbilical cord, no longer white, although the windows were open wide, the doctors eventually admitted.

The ministry employee who answered demanded further explanation of the phenomenon, ideally a report on the incident before a decision could be taken on the Ministry's behalf. The doctor then had to explain the difficulties with which the woman had had to struggle to birth the child. The negro child had too large a head for the icelandic woman's frame, and it was clear that stubbornness and reluctance were innate in negroes, especially in making decisions. The doctor in charge of the birth said:

With regard to the above considerations and the fact that more male children are born than girls, and that regional physicians out in the country are hardly prepared with the special equipment necessary for a successful caesarean section and to pull the child from the mother by force, there are dangers in this journey: if the nape and head size of the population grows disproportionate to women's hip width.

It is not promising, answered the man with whom he was speaking, if we are of one dimension but negroes are broader across the crown and we will collide with each other and stalemate together.

The doctor was unprepared for this coarse icelandic humor given the danger of the moment; his tongue was tied, but when he recovered he stressed the urgency of the need to try to find out, free from any pretexts, what action should be taken.

Hold off on any intervention, the office worker Tómas Jónsson answered. Let the woman lie unconscious while I send out feelers on the matter; a meeting of the ministry will take place.

The mother has not been brought out of her anesthesia and it is imperative we take a decision right away, the doctor said, exasperated.

Hold tight, said the office employee in soothing tones. No hurry.

We simply cannot wait. The mother cannot tolerate an extended anesthesia. It could be done before she wakes up; we could notify her in good conscience that the child is dead and has been taken for autopsy. Do you understand what I am saying?

Between these two men, the resolution was agreed: cut the baby's cord and then off it.

The doctor came out of the phone booth with sweat beads on his forehead. The head nurse wiped them gently from him by applying sterilized gauze. He asked for a cup of strong coffee, set it down at the table's edge and took a sworn oath from everyone who had assisted with the birth. The umbilical cord was severed and the body was thrown into the milk bucket on the floor and bled to death. But there was so much strength to the circulation that the umbilical cord swung to and fro around the pail rim like a jet from a powerful water hose and it twisted and buzzed on the floor not dissimilar to a wriggling articulated earthworm. The body was burned, with its limbs cut off, in a special oven that hospitals have, connected to the central system. After that, everyone had a cup of strong bitter coffee.

"Thus, with snares and sleight of hand, the tendency toward racial hatred and discrimination that would otherwise loom large within the nation, and which other countries must confront and seek a way past, was erased. Had it not been, the birth of this one child would have brought upon our defenseless people the threats racial fanaticism creates"; so read a secret report to the authorities on the matter.

The government reacted quickly to put an end to unruly protests (the first in the country's quarter-century of military occupation) that were provoked by the poor handling of one black man's arrival and the breach of conditions and provisions designed to protect iceland from invading forces.

The head of the U.S. Defense Force reacted angrily to the government's claims, sending word that he would charge the individuals concerned with murdering the offspring of an American citizen, and threatening to bring the matter before the United Nations, *presumably after its founding, which clearly violated iceland's proposed Declaration of Human Rights and would hinder the admission of this unarmed nation, the most cherished in the world, into that fellowship; the threat was never carried out.*

Despite the considerable furor, the child had been cremated, so there was no irrefutable proof that it had been anything other than the brainchild of the office employee who answered the phone (when the Ministry was forced to further defend itself by saying that the report was drawn up drunkenly and was a bunch of nonsense, one could only foster the idea of a black child drunk); he was fired. After a heated meeting in a back room of Parliament, the apologizing for the report stopped (the case was made a principal issue) and the government went on the offensive, sending the chief of the defense force his first and only letter of insult proclaiming the national mood. The letter, of which Tómas Jónsson kept a copy, included this section:

". . . you Americans should have adopted such ingenious solutions at the beginning of slavery, and castrated the blacks so none of that dark race outlived their life. A sizeable herd of them were taken so as to get something for your ancestors in Africa. Had you applied an equally radical approach against the multiplication of blacks, you would not only have been able to prevent the present and future chaos of racial tension, but also, with time and pillaging, managed to clear the whole of Africa of blacks and thus with that removal and your descendants have removed the old colonial troubles."

It is completely unknown whether the military administration answered the letter; by that time Tómas Jónsson had been let go.

Recorded following the account of a bank employee in XII. pay grade.

have I moreover been yes deprived them of their automatic right to lie undisturbed yes in my mansion or is my sanctuary become a cash cow no I have some money saved in general no and again no knock on their door yes to seek out friendship no rather to inquire yes what about I am

engaged in nothing here no I just sit with idle hands behind a locked
door

who knows what happens while I
loiter apathetic old age concentrates
or fasts your resolutions to nothing
distributes anticipatory thoughts but as
flickering sparkles strewn by some hand
sentences which I had thought
irrelevant written on the black table
the stamen was hard the table black
on the walls of the mind I came there
to knock at the door of the body that soars
on wings around me like
a dead satellite that works
systematically to resolve
indiscriminate thoughts all scattered
about the seventy-minute days not
my thoughts inoperate at the origin
I tómmas am only the
receiver for remote transmissions
an occasional inactive aerial and
I say that your life lies is in winning or
losing in the lottery of chance
I lie still as if entirely as if a dead thing on a table

The Corpse's Brutality
a folktale
Shortly after New Year, Katrín Jónsdóttir's parents came to Reykjavík
via the Stykkishólm coach to seek a remedy for their infirmities: he
for his sick heart, and constantly suffering from hay fever (some said
he was left unable to breathe due to an infection transmitted from
the sheep); she for rheumatic pain in her lower back. Katrín met her

parents at the coach stop and accompanied them home on the bus. That evening, the couple would not touch anything other than boiled milk and pretzels. They turned in early, rather knocked about by their journey in the bumpy vehicle.

Katrín lived with her husband and seven children down in a cellar, which, following the laws of storytelling, was very unhealthy.

The apartment was jam-packed, so the couple had to huddle in the same bed as three of the children; they slept head to toe. Despite their age the children still slept together and loved in a half-aware way according to farming custom: in outdoor work, with milk pails, at cowshed stalls, and herding the sheep. That is to say: cooperating—in an honest manner.

The dark room was illuminated by a naked bulb that hung from the center of the ceiling. Inside the bulb was a finely twisted filament and it lit when a black switch was flicked down.

And because the children were readied for bed and asleep long before the couple, according to Reykjavík city police regulations, they undressed to the brightness of the hallway bulb.

Next morning they awoke habitually at six. In bed, while they were waiting for signs of life in the hallway (Katrín ordered them to lie still and not start pottering about until Sveinn dragged himself to his feet), The couple whispered about their visits to their doctors, of which they were afraid. At half past seven they heard Sveinn. He went farting along the hallway and groaned with contentment after this morning breaking of wind. Then the couple got out of bed together and said their prayers:

As I leave my comforter
my intention is your bequest.
Living Jesus care for me
and lead me on the right path.

They both broke wind after that and the prayer felt relieved of their concerns; they were filled with courage and boldness.

By just past nine, after the children were at school or up to no good out in the street, and the youngest child sat carefully tethered to the foot of the bed, Katrín followed her parents to a new doctor, whom everyone had faith in. The outcome of the trip was that the woman should return the next day, two hours before normal visiting hours, to place her body inside a light-box. For the man's heart, they would need to take a graph.

Throughout the day the couple sat nervous and anxious in chairs in the kitchen and had little or no appetite. They were almost perfectly still, except when they had to lift one of their buttocks, and as uncomfortable as they were they did so as much as possible, since they considered it an antidote to idleness. They said little and were barely bold enough to look out into the garden at the trash cans, which they found very interesting and probably full of useful stuff. Each of them carried inside their minds their worry over the cow in the cowshed, whether it was being milked at the right time. The children played games on the floor and inside the kitchen cabinets, but the games were unfamiliar to the couple. Nevertheless the woman made fumbling efforts to get on well with the children, without success; they squirmed away from the caresses and touches, getting a bad smell from grandmother and struggling against grandfather's "hot-hott-horsey" until Katrín made a decision and said to her parents:

Children should be free. A person should never force children to do anything; it causes them emotional turmoil.

She did not know what to do with her parents. Rural conversations, always ending in low sighs and a chorus of affirmatives, were for Katrín symbols, like an oil lamp or a coal stove that never came to life; she wanted to get moving, to be lively and fun, to have polemics about people and topics.

We like to be around you all here in the kitchen, the couple explained when Katrín suggested that they move into the bedroom or all stroll down the street to see the glass-eyed cat.

So they loitered there the whole day.

Before the couple went to bed that night, the woman removed some grease paper from her clean knit underwear and put it on the chair at the headboard.

What coffin do they want to stick me inside while I'm still alive? she asked in the dark, worried.

Something invented by learned men, the man said.

He tried to seem calm, used to coming to Reykjavík every year to get things fixed. The woman raised objections until the man said, exasperated:

What is this, woman. You will do as you are told.

Then she fell stone silent and went to sleep, certain of her husband's protection; she asked god to set over her a wall of powerful angels before she took her rest. She was happiest when her husband firmly rebuked her and told her to stop this and that: get out of the barn, scram, get lost. The woman smiled contentedly, even in her sleep.

Sometime in the middle of the night, the woman woke when the man sat up suddenly with a snort, then wheezed through his nose; as the woman was about to help him he fell back on the pillow and gave off a protracted belching sound. She was going to fumble out and get him some digestive medicine for his gas but she dare not look in their bag because she would have to turn the light on at the switch; though it "was simple enough to look at, it was still complicated," and Katrín had repeatedly insisted "no wandering my house in the middle of the night." And so the woman, concerned as she was, merely wrapped the duvet around her husband's clammy body, calling upon god, asking him again to put a strong wall of angels over them; and she thought:

he has relieved himself with his belching

Then she belched, lay back down and fell asleep.

At six in the morning she woke up, sat up in bed, combed her hair from its plaits, scratched her head carefully with the comb, over the crown along her part, and plaited her hair again, staring distractedly out into the morning darkness and silence. When she finished, she swung the plaits up on the pillow, folded her arms on her chest and did not stir.

The woman was not in the habit of thinking much; she felt that ritual blunted the body, which needed to preserve all its strength throughout the day, but at night she thought sometimes about god and why He allowed man in some countries, not all, to have many wives; she reckoned such households had to be happier, especially in rural areas, since not all the work landed on the one woman. But now, up with the dew and sitting in bed, she found unacceptable omissions, lying still with her feet apart under the blanket, staring ahead without looking at anything in particular. Never before had she been able to hold her sight still for so long on the same spot. Her eyes were active and efficient like her fingers and toes. To her surprise, her thought started to work unprovoked. She giggled foolishly, and at first she thought: great raven eyes winging in flight across the lava moss and Magnús in the mossy lava; she gasped in the calm and continued thinking, which led her to come up with: how on earth do people live without hens; her third thought considered canned food: how could food be locked in a closed canister with no lock, and how could no ravens be seen on the streets when the eternal poison for foxes was meant to eliminate the ravens, but not vixens, who were clever enough not to eat vixen-poisoned food. This was more than enough thinking for now; she yawned, smacked her lips, and pushed a finger into one of her breasts; there was a hole in the breast and she gained a strange pleasure from fiddling in it with her fingers.

At half past seven the children woke with protracted wails. The woman got out of bed, filled her mouth with sugar, and stuck her wet tongue tip in them, one after the other, appeasing their fear of waking up. She changed her underwear in bed, reminded herself to get the man to replace his underwear after the doctor's visit, put on knit underwear again; so that she would not forget, she tied a string around her index finger.

He is due for a change of underwear, she thought.

Now she stroked her head, cheeks, shoulders, and hips, rubbing hard to convince herself that all her body was awake from sleep. She praised god for not depleting her health during the night and went into the kitchen; she ate porridge with her grandson and taught him to start the morning with a prayer out on the steps.

Breathe the outdoor air three times, your mouth open wide, she said.

The boy didn't know how to take in the morning in moderation; he breathed really quickly until he got faint and staggered on the stairs. Then she took out his prick and let it spurt out over the steps in a thin arc against the stone and dented tankards. She taught him to shake off the drops, "the way men do."

With the clock almost at ten, Katrín said annoyed:

Mom, I wasn't expecting dad to park himself in the bedroom all day long.

I do not dare shake him.

What's that, woman, thinking you cannot torment him awake; you are not a serving maid.

The woman then took off her shoes and walked into the bedroom in her socks and shoved the man. He was dead in bed.

Katrín rushed to the scene with a double pocket mirror and held it up to her father's nose and mouth. The glass revealed no haze, though she stroked with her finger. She held the compact at his nose and kept it there awhile up against the nostrils, but couldn't force a sneeze.

They knew he was dead.

Katrín had to borrow a phone from the milk store and call the GP, who listened to the corpse and after this was done wrote out a death certificate.

The remainder of the day was taken up with the complexity of "planning a journey" in order to get the body back to Tanga. Katrín called Sveinn for help, but he refused to leave his job for something that was not beyond two grown healthy women.

At the coach concession the women were advised to buy a coffin for the body, place it inside, and wait until the bus could "take it up top," some time in the next few days; there was a separate waiting list for standing room. The woman found this an unhelpful offer, especially in such unusual circumstances, and Katrín comforted her; the driver suggested:

You would lay him out for a wake for the week.

Mom, we have no space for a body in the house, said Katrín, think about it. My husband will be furious.

In modern novels, girls in the dairy line represent resourceful, left-leaning, clear thinking. When the girl in the nearby milk store learned of the trouble facing the mother and daughter, she said:

If you are in a cooperative, the Association of icelandic Societies should be obliged to provide storage for you.

Katrín borrowed the phone and explained to the Association what had happened:

I do not know anything more than that my parents always sold first-rate milk. I do not understand how you cannot provide cold storage for Mom in such circumstances.

We are not exactly dealing with milk here, was the answer, but we shall do our utmost to convey the body with one of our partners, on the first trip possible.

This Association is conducting itself like a bunch of fanatical capitalists, said the shop woman. She gripped the receiver so that what she said could not be heard. Ask about the cooperative's vehicles.

Katrín asked, but when the person asked into it she reported that they were not able to put the extra labor on a driver, and the best solution would be to have the coffin ready at any time of day for when the trip might coincide with a delivery to the co-op in Tanga.

Forget it, they said to one another. They are just prevaricating. We have to rely on the bus.

The one "miracle" the shop girl achieved was to have the coffin

230 |

delivered to the morgue at the hospital, and after that the women went home to wait patiently.

The very next night the old lady woke up suddenly, crazy in the head and with no idea where she was until her hands touched the bed and felt the night-sweaty children, who now slept in each other's arms. The woman lay there, momentarily still tired after sleep, then combed herself, cried, and after repeated attempts got back on track with thinking intermittently about two ravens on a telephone pole. She tried to make them fly, but the ravens sat still. And then to her great astonishment thoughts streamed from her mind, mainly regarding this fatal incident which she felt was too normal to be true.

nothing normal can be true   she thought   a man rises up abruptly, belches in his dreams, and lies down again it is impossible that that is something as unnatural as to be dead he is dead contrary to the wishes and prayers to god that he be allowed to live as long as me   while health and strength last

Very unexpectedly she became beside herself with anguish and mental agony—as with an earthquake, when the earth moves in waves and the kitchen table slides about, or when landmines from the war explode and cups are thrown around in closets. Her thoughts fell silent:

come to think about it the wire knot the doctor did not stab a needle into a cow in a stall I never saw the doctor's hand operate the needle on one of the fingers of the body and pokes his eye I had never seen it one still has to get used to Ólöf on the pillow Bína with a needle poking creatures healing creatures

The man had often told her, standing with one foot in hot water in the cleaning bucket before she washed the floor, the other in her lap while she washed his white varicose feet, that his heart had come to a stop with a flash in the hay barn; at first he had become speechless but then an idea flew into his mind, he sat on a hay bale, bent his head between his knees and clasped firmly, maintaining this fixed position a moment with his knees and hands clamped around his forehead and

nape, so that the heart pumped again with a jerk. He stood up, felt
dizzy, but survived.

*   liked hot water no he was not too good to yes to use cleaning water*
for a footbath no he was not the kind of man to die without knowing
it no life secretly hides he does inside the corpse in under the skin and
she sat on a chair facing him with a heavy foot in her lap and dried
between the toes yes yes apparently unaware of the kissing of his toes
after this foot bath my dear she clucked and so sleep

*   She started to believe these thoughts. She did not come to any*
conclusion, and yet she needed nothing but a chance to think.

*   Take things calmly, Mom, Katrín requested.*

*   But her orders had the opposite effect. After lunch, the woman's*
anguish reached the point where Katrín gave her a sedative, since she
didn't want to touch her food.

*   Take this, three pills on an empty stomach, she said, reassuringly,*
and your cares will be gone, you will get your balance back.

*   The old lady swallowed the pills eagerly and drank some water.*
Katrín stood at the opposite table corner observing the effects. As soon
as her mother's eyes became blurred she smiled a victorious smile. The
remainder of the day the woman dozed on the chair with her arms
crossed over the back of another chair. She felt like she was inside a
telephone pole. The children came up to her and prodded her broken
nails; they painted them with water colors and her whole hands green
and the woman did not move one bit.

*   Stop painting her, Katrín shouted at them, otherwise she won't*
know she's the same person. Would you still recognize yourself in the
mirror? You'd at least be startled.

*   The old woman went to bed entirely unaware and passed the*
night in shallow slumber.

*   The next morning Katrín was going to give her mother more*
sedatives, so her concerns wouldn't trouble her, but the woman flat
out refused to take any more pills. Her suspicion that life still lurked
hidden inside her husband had become a conviction, one she came

*to feel sure about while she was in the telephone pole situation. She
could not dismiss what the telephone line had buzzed in her ears:
without doubt there's plenty of life still there under the skin in the
ears in the eyes*
  *The woman demanded the body be checked by a physician who
was trusted by responsible people.*
  *I do not want to live on suffering murder on my conscience, she
said, resolutely.*
  *Katrín went to the dairy and said to the shop girl:
  The death has begun to prey upon mother.*
  *(Reader, your suspicions are correct: the cashier was none other
than Todda Bomb, Haraldur Sóldal's fiancé.)*
  *Todda called her sweetheart once Katrín had called a GP who
made it clear that no one in their right mind could doubt the man
had died of a heart attack. The response, hardly worthy of a doctor,
aroused resentment in the neighborhood. The rumor spread rapidly,
resulting in hostile divisions: for or against there being life concealed
in a corpse. What GP dare be snappy and inflexible when answer-
ing a woman who has conviction and faith that life lies hidden in
her husband's body. They asked god to help them and the basement
apartment filled with fervent women offering advice and wringing
their hands over the GP's irresponsibility, caring only about collecting
money from people and not bothered to give effective treatments let
alone examine women with a machine which uses steam to destroy
unwanted pus.*
  *What medical implement is a tube with a sucker, they jabbered.
Why not just invert a glass of water on the chest? Have to examine a
graph? People have no need for all this, and who pays for it?*
  We pay, with our health insurance and our doctors and our taxes.
  *The bustle, quarrelling, and panic in the apartment led to the
woman feeling pain in her heart and screamed protracted moans,
lying in bed with three hot water bottles:
  He knows he should be ashamed of himself.*

*The women grinned triumphant at her bedside, at the head and
the foot, by the wall, by the door, the closet, on chairs, and with their
butts up against the antique sewing machine. By and by two or three
went into the hallway to whisper:*

*Truly, she does not have long left, they said and smirked and
shrugged. A while since a woman has "gone the way of her husband."
Widows have become so healthy and unconcerned with obligation.
Modern medicine prolongs life and a neglected heart encourages a
desire to outlive one's husband so you can finally blossom and go out
dancing.*

*The women were busy washing the woman around her mouth
and nose with cotton soaked in schnapps and had bound her feet
facing the North Pole with cords knotted to the ceiling so that blood
would go to her head; just then the girl at the dairy came and said
she had "arranged matters" so her mother could examine the coffin. A
taxi was waiting outside to transport them to the hospital.*

The hospital carpenter showed them the way to the basement.

*I cannot have on my conscience the live burial of my husband,
sighed the woman. Bury me alive instead.*

*Yes, but Mother dear, said Katrín, if he wasn't dead to begin with,
he will surely have suffocated by now.*

*I have thirty years of experience in this field, interrupted the car-
penter, and know of no case where a person has woken up in his coffin, and that is not perhaps surprising since, in the past, corpses were
bound under the throat but nowadays the mouth is glued together
with adhesive plasters, or the corpse would lie there open-mouthed.*

*I never saw him press the needle into the soles and he never poked
around in the eyes, replied the woman.*

*Mother, Dad has passed, said Katrín, this is all about you; leave
him be. He is taking his rest.*

*While the carpenter unscrewed the coffin lid, the women stood at
a distance and held hands.*

Call me, said the carpenter, when you have had your ceremony.

At this very moment some nuns who were carrying a coffin waddled across the floor to lay the tree-wood there in a corner behind the
canvas screen. They came out from behind, dusted off their layered
skirts, and stepped out of their wood shoes, which clunked on the stone
floor. The woman watched them then approached the coffin with slow
steps. She stood over it, listened, stilled her breathing and put her ear
to the rigid breast. She pulled a pin from her tassel cap, closed her eyes
and stabbed him in the sole. The body did not stir. The nuns were
waiting at the door and raised their white kirtles. Katrín looked at
them apologetically and snorted and twirled her index finger beside
her temple. The nuns smiled and shuffled their feet. The old woman
bent over the corpse's face to kiss it a last kiss and stroke the neck, as
one does with a corpse, but Katrín turned away and went to find the
carpenter. The nuns walked out smiling in their crisp blue aprons.

Well, Katrín sighed.

In a few words, the carpenter explained to her how everyone who
dies in the hospital has to have an autopsy.

I am much more than a carpenter. I sew sheets to go around the
bodies and I label the toes, so there is no confusion about the candidate.

He laughed and added:

It is so neglected. These are the things that make the mourner
sorrowful. Sometimes I have to shave the poor wretch and trim them
if they come to me looking awry. Some of the winos are significantly
greasy.

A person in your line of work must meet all sorts, said Katrín.
Gee, I couldn't stand it. I'd go mad.

They talked for a while about hospital conditions, how Katrín
had wanted to be a nurse, that caring was a rich vein in the female
character, but now she only wanted to move to Mallorca or Spain.

I'm not made for this cold climate, she said.

The old woman lay her head down in the coffin, and as if overcome with grief she emitted strange sounds from her mouth, mumbling and sobbing and struggling to break away from the body.

Stop, Mom, Katrín begged, tugging her black satin skirt at the back.

She was trying to haul her mother away without looking in the coffin but the woman did not stir even as her skirt was tugged. The daughter stooped, defeated, grabbed her firmly by the shoulders and said:

Come on now, Mom.

Because she could not help keeping her eyes from the coffin, she saw a thick line of blood running from the corners of her father's mouth, down his neck to gather in a puddle on the base of the coffin. She gave a low sound and the carpenter hurried over to the scene.

What is wrong? he asked.

No one answered. Katrín squeezed her eyes shut. The carpenter went around the coffin and came to the realization that the corpse had bitten the lips of the old woman while she was kissing it, and it had them in its teeth. With dexterity, without doing further harm, the carpenter managed to break the grip of the corpse's teeth with a screwdriver instead of a chisel and free the woman. Her lips hung in shreds from the corners of her mouth like red pulp, and there were bits left in the corpse's mouth. Katrín and the carpenter supported the woman into the service elevator up to the first floor, where the nuns received her and led her into the office, from where she was taken to ER after the receptionist said:

Unfortunately, all general accidents fall under that department.

And you should have seen the poor woman's mouth after. The doctors had to cut the tatters from the remaining parts of the lips, sighed Miss Gerður, and stitch them back together. Sóldal, this renowned expert, did not even try to graft chicken meat on, as is done in such cases. No, her mouth was an open space. You could see her dentures, and when she took out her false teeth her tongue moved restlessly like a piece of blood pudding in a hole, and her uvula dangled. Absolutely awful.

Recorded following Miss Gerður's account.

Those who listened to the story Sunday afternoon debated whether the corpse was awake. It was like a con. Some felt it had been caused by sudden muscle spasms in the jaws, but Sigurður argued that the woman had been bitten thanks to another unrelated story, published in the journal Writing and Art. *A few years later I heard the same story over several cups of coffee outside Kjalarnes, with the exception that life remained inside the body and Sóldal pasted the so-called heart-cans on its skin, on either side of the neck, so they looked like sick thyroid glands you see in pictures of African pygmies suffering from iodine deficiency. One can was a pump that propelled blood around and the other was a suction device that drew it up through the body to the brain. The equipment was invented by an uneducated person or at least by someone self-taught. His name was Tómas, and he was reckoned to be a Jónsson.*

The old man, who had been a corpse, reportedly lives in full swing, for which he can thank the woman's spirit and his own trickery; she should be applauded for her innate instincts about corpses, too, and last but not least Tómas Jónsson deserves thanks for his creativity.

Their persecution, their dissimulation, and their inquisitiveness give me strength, support and justification. The defiance and contempt of the public is fuel for the artist's engine and genius. Now they discuss my sudden weeping fits. What fits. Am I not even allowed my health. And to be made to go manage it in some damn complex, The Spa Center. Will nothing remain, finally, except a large dying torso with dead, dangling limbs. Tomorrow I will smoke you out like a fox from a spruce. I'll remove your gas cans from the cubby (it is illegal to store gasoline in residential dwellings so you can have no complaint), pour them over the carpet and chairs while you sleep, then set fire to everything, scurry into the toilet, turn on the shower bath in haste, stand still in the seat-bath as you burn and turn to ashes. I need to preserve the apartment to conduct certain experiments. I will say to the creatures, i.e. you: My sister and brother-in-law are moving here and they have no roof over their heads, and they are demanding to live with their brother. I had to borrow from my relatives to pay for the apartment. Now everyone is gathering in the city. Forces conspire in a wasteland. No one wants to keep doing the things he is already doing. Rural folk no longer want to stay in their farm lairs and watch the sun disappear into the glaciers and darkness fall gentle and quiet over the valley, which sleeps an extreme slumber in the blue reflected glow of the slopes where lambs ramble nightdrunk in the dew by the streams, and the wind dies in the arid canyon. (Here I have succeeded thoroughly; chic style, nothing coarse.) No, everyone wants to get lost in the throng and live an oppressed life. To become wretched. To suffer from muscular dystrophy. Mentally and physically deformed. Enfeebled. Men complain and whine in a thinly-veiled complacence. These days, whining and cruelty pay best. Losers are rewarded everywhere, on the radio and in the press, and they act without consequence in movies. Everyone discovers he is needy. Why should people not pursue the renown that follows from inferior behavior. For my part, I say: I am a wonderful wretch. I need everything from everyone. And then all I do is write memories. I'm disabled enough and mentally paralyzed so that people get interested in my poor life. I'm going to write the first book ever with the intriguing title: *How I became a mental and physical invalid without also becoming a jerk.* Buy the bestseller by Tómas Jónsson, a book about a jerk that is being translated into seven foreign languages. The author describes with sensitive self-understanding and openness and unprudishness his mental suffering; he is an old, sick, and friendless invalid in a basement apartment of which he has been robbed; he is an invalid with shit on his ass. This gently written book is full of subtle understandings and awareness, full of sympathy for the underdog. The book is a warning to all of us who are not yet confined to bed. This is a book for the entire family, good for learning about life and the fate of children. A bold book. It will awaken many questions in its reader that will remain unanswered by the author; each must answer for himself. Is Tómas actually really disabled. Was he stripped of his apartment through trickery. Is he a dadaist. Did he rape a ten-year-old little girl down in the laundry room. Is he perhaps a homosexual. Is he a murderer. Who is Tómas. Is he all of us. Is he a symbol of the modern icelandic nation, mentally and physically disabled and ill-fitted with military clothes from the American base. About these and other questions, you will break your brain reading our must-have christmas book this year: *How I became a mental and physical invalid without also becoming a jerk.* Read the book about the man who wrote about his genitalia (the way people once wrote of warts) as a small but lively wart below his belly and wrote to Heads of State. *Tómas Jónsson Bestseller*—our christmas book this year.

The Soprano Katrín Jónsdóttir
a folk tale

The opera singer Katrín Jónsdóttir was esteemed as the pinnacle voice, above any other icelandic singer between the war years: her voice was vibrant, rich, masculine, and strong. She could with utter confidence be considered our most famous and most adored singer, without disrespecting other singers, an icelandic national singer in the fullest sense of the words, an uncrowned queen in the field of voice. In the years before World War II, she sang and earned renown among German music halls, where she sang with such enormous joy and to such large audiences that she was given the nickname Unsre Katharina. And there is a story, originating with a well-known Icelander who once was her contemporary abroad in Paris, that she did so well on stage in the City of Light that people went out into the street to watch her, esteeming her a marvel—and this from jaded, cosmopolitan Parisians not usually considered stirred by the trivial. Katrín seemed a leading light, a noble spirit in her art, her whole appearance and facial features classically icelandic, pronounced but genial. Her nose was raised high, and preceded her everywhere, on- and offstage. For certain, suitors streamed to her from all over the world, great men and princes who lay beseeching at her feet with crowns of state, covering the opera stage with orchids at the end of her songs, and it was not uncommon for her to receive two hundred floral baskets (by comparison, icelandic actors usually receive at most three or four on their sixty-year anniversary, plus half the takings from the performance). Katrín traveled everywhere in a private car, which the count of Bavaria gave her as a courting gift, but to the afflicted and passionate suitors she always said demurely: I am already bound with inseparable bonds of love to my native northern land and to my voice. The magic world of vocal chords merged surely with the unambiguous serenity of icelandic glaciers, gentle streams running into birch scrub and truly global citizens—but Hekla's hidden fire lived underneath, so that when Katrín threw herself with the strength of an eddy into Wagner's works, it was almost guaranteed that the abyss would stir and she would descend into the great violence of creative ability.

Katrín Jónsdóttir is earning plaudits overseas, declared the front page of every icelandic broadsheet.

But despite all her great victories and fame—"Tonight the roof was nearly torn from the Berlin Opera in enthusiasm," wrote Hugo Weiss in the Berliner Post, giving the singer five stars; there was almost a full house—Katrín remained the same sweet shepherd girl who sang for the Elf Festival at home in Dalasýslu and who, reaching the age of confirmation, wearied of her zeal for echoes alone. No one knew that she had for some time been infatuated with the larger world, all its promise, fame and glamor. "I sing," she said once in an interview with the renowned critic, Ludvig Gryphius, in Brunschweiger Tages-Zeitung, *"because I feel like my voice and my zest for life does not have sufficient space in my chest, out, out, my breath—I want the world to enjoy and benefit from what little I can give it."*

Even as Katrín stood at the pinnacle of her singing renown, the State collapsed and so did the value of the Deutschmark in Germany, but people came driving with wheelbarrows of banknotes to buy tickets to her singing spectacle. Hitler came to power and the great fame that emanated from Katrín had this effect on the most powerful person in the nation: he could barely fight back his tears.

Her fame had reached his ears because Göring had by chance bought one of her records on the way to the Chancellery, and since Hitler wanted everything in Germany, both young and old, and nothing escaped his eagle-quick eyes, he asked what Göring had in the envelope under his arm. He said, like any faithful and honest man, he was holding a record.

Let me hear, put it on the gramophone, said Hitler.

And after listening speechless to the song, he could not say anything but shouted in enthusiasm like Faust in the poem by Goethe the German Giant (in an expertly rendered icelandic translation by Jón from Kaldaðarnes):

Now, fetch me this.

Hasten to your work.

Göring replied, out of pure gentleness:

Maiden-fishing is important work.

Half a month will give me time

the opportunity well to whine.

Hitler was in bits at the song, so impatient and captivated by the voice that he could not wait and commanded instantly that he would have Katrín or no other woman on this side of the grave. He had never been with a woman, and so his expectation was all the more intense. He looked at Göring full of scorn and said in the spirit of Faust (translated by the same genius):

If I knew a moment of peace,

I would hardly need Göring,

A straggling child, to allure and seduce.

As this conversation was taking place in the Chancellery, Katrín was in Hamburg singing to a packed house every night.

Our Katrín Jónsdóttir is achieving wonderful things in Hamburg, read the front page of all the icelandic broadsheets.

Without hesitation or a second thought Hitler ordered Göring, his lifelong friend, to immediately have the yacht made ready. His ship was berthed at moorings in Vistnar but Hitler furnished himself with some sausages for the journey and swept a black cape around himself. Late into the night the large wagon was furiously driven, a hundred and twenty kilometers, along the new Autobahn to the coast, Hitler asleep in the back seat; the Führer arrived at Vistnar early the next morning, took a few amphetamine tablets and boarded.

Now the story turns to Unsre Katharina.

After being called back five times and receiving 102 flower baskets on stage at the Hamburg Opera, being praised with greater exultation than ever before—she had to sing six encores, including Sofnar lóa, which she often used as an encore, a clear contrast in its gentle music and simplicity to heroic Wagner—then she took rapid steps to her dressing room and stripped off the Valkyrie costume while newspaper music critics competed to write their praise epistles: "Katrín Jónsdóttir, the icelandic singer who graced the stage of the Hamburg Opera this evening and whom the German public has named Unsre Katharina, is a true genius in the use of her voice. She has the full power of interpretation in the roles she undertakes and she combines technique and creativity; her acting and all her gestures on stage are exceptional. Her performance of the difficult role of Sieglinde in Valkyrie was richly dramatic, her voice shining and clear as the northern sky in her own country . . . one discovers iceland revealed in all its glory . . . with the greatest splendor. We salute this Norse guest from the land of sagas, the true heroic blood . . ."

While newspapers frantically printed and distributed her fame among hungry readers, Katrín lay calm in her bower at Hamburg Castle, which she had been specifically invited to use; she rested a moment and refreshed her vocal cords with the most expensive and best Liebfraumilch available in Germany. On all the bottles was written: Especially bottled for Katrín Jónsdóttir.

As soon as it was dark that night, once Katrín had emptied three bottles of Liebfraumilch, she jumped up from her tapestried cushion *and ordered her special servant and assistant, Mohamed of the Asra tribe, "welche sterben, wenn sie lieben," to have her rowing boat made ready at the hall steps.*

Now let the night unfold, she said.

With full secrecy, Katrín threw over herself an oilskin made of thick bullskin, which she had had made back home at Skagafjörður, and put on her black sea-shoes from Snaefellsnes and hid under a sailor's hat the light braids that reached to her waist.

And so she could roam, disguised and unrecognizable, she ordered Mohamed, the ferryman, to row the dinghy silently out from the river's mouth. It was dark everywhere; over the murky sea there was neither a glow of light nor the pale moon shoaling in torn storm clouds. Katrín sat in the stern, silent; she looked, exotic beauty full of longing (Verfremdung), at the black waves passing in a dark play with the cheeks of young boats. No words passed her lips to the ferryman the whole way, but when they came out opposite the Kílarskurðinn canal she stretched out her white hand, adorned in rings engraved with obsidian stones, to indicate that he should stop and bring in the oars. Mohamed obeyed her command, avoided looking at the woman, avoided her beauty like his own death in a poem, drawing away in a humble retreat, wrapping himself in furs and falling asleep in the dragging keel to dream of an Arabian half-moon.

Hojotoho. Hojotoho.

Heiaha. Heiaha.

Hahei. Hahei. Heiaho, sang Katrín goading the sea and turning a tough face against salt wind; this was her custom, greeting the natural elements with this Valkyrie song, slipping out at night to the ocean's vastness along with her loyal ferryman to practice her opera roles, wearying her icelandic energy in the excited storms and tumult, sometimes up until morning, fathoming the dark forces of her soul and mind in harmony with the untamed forces of nature. And she began a song that sounded like surf din, singing tirelessly the first and second parts of the Valkyrie, restlessly. Small-fledged clouds in

*the North Sea matched the song with deathcold waves, lonely and
foaming in their eternal restless rage, their desire to break apart the
land. Having worshipped her and offered her his arms, the wind was
determined to steal her to him, his nature eager to apprehend her,
absorb her body, dissolve her into its form: water oh the water water.
But Katrín laughed at death in her greed for existence, and sang:*

Hinweg. Hinweg.
flieh' die Entweihte.
Unheilig
umfasst dich mein Arm.

Waves. Ocean. Her best audience.

*After the song she drank another bottle of Liebfraumilch and
then began the finale (not in icelandic translation this time): Eight
Valkyries in full armor gather on the mountaintop on their return
journey after victory in battle. Brunhilde enters with Sieglinde, who
is overcome with grief after the death of Siegmund, killed by Hund-
ing. But Brunhilde believes in her way of life and offers encouragement in song:*

Denn eines wisse
und wahr' es immer;
den hehrsten Helden der Welt
hegst du, o Weib,
im schirmenden Schoss.

*And she gives her Siegmund's broken sword. New Volsungs will be
born from the hotbed womb of Sieglinde, the most majestic champi-
ons on earth. With a whetsong, Brunhilde reignites the life force in
the chest of Sieglinde, one of the most beautiful scenes in the history
of opera, characteristics that later came to crown Wagner's works,
especially Götterdämmerung; Sieglinde sings of joy:*

Du hehrstes Wunder . . .

*Katrín did not get any further in the song, when, just a stone's
throw from the rowing boat, which jumped on the excited waves,
red sailing lights kindled, and moments later a spotlight fired on,*

swinging in flashes of light like thunder sparks over the desolate wave crests until the beam turned on Katrín. White beams blinded her in the ravenblack night, silencing her singing; black whales sank in the deep, birds flew off; but the dark Faustian voice could be heard calling (again in a brilliant icelandic translation by Jón from Kaldaðarnes):

You, noble and beautiful, may I offer

you my escort and support, good lady?

I am not alone, Katrín was about to answer, but she realized at once where these lines of verses came from and she answered them playfully:

I am neither pretty nor fair

and alone I will ply my way.

She woke the ferryman and ordered him to row hastily away from the cone of light. But she was not able to escape.

Then the Führer himself came on the yacht deck, and through his well-organized intelligence he came to terms with the strange behavior of this icelandic Valkyrie who let no one set rules governing her methods and customs. The Germans' gold teeth and leather jackets gleamed in the dark; they commanded the ferryman not to move from the keel section. The gangplank was slid hastily from the pleasure yacht into the rowboat, so Katrín could not refuse to come on board and sit at the Führer's laden banquet table. Eel was for starters, the finest Mosel wine to drink, and then delicacies were borne in, each better than the last; Liebfraumilch flooded the visitor's lips as she engaged in passionate conversation about the arts and philosophy.

Initially over dinner there was much conversation (Hitler had the wine brought out immediately to stave off shyness and reticence) about the difficulties a true artist faces on her career ladder; in particular, an artist from a small and relatively unknown nation like iceland, how she might overcome each obstacle, breaking narrow bridges behind her with persistence and determination in order to become great and tower above a sea of mediocrity. Hitler knew such difficulties well, and he talked about them from bitter knowledge, but Katrín became aware of his complexes and neuroses gathered in his subconscious: a fear of having to exist defeated and at a lower rank in his contests with the world. As the evening passed, his neuroses surged back up from the time of his infancy the way virginal milk floods about his neck and stomach, unaware of anything good because of the sheer force of trying to keep suppress his depths under his gestures, overcompensating by being pushy with the servants; he harried them out with the dishes, found fault with how the sandwiches were arranged on platters, and so on. At first he tried to stay measured and drank little; doctors had advised him to avoid wine because of his temper, but later he slipped downhill. Drinking with Unsre Katharina was an outright exception.

Promise to look after me, he had asked Göring in the toilets before they sat down to eat. If I get tipsy, take my glass from me and turn it upside down.

Hitler plied Unsre Katharina liberally with compliments, and in conversations conducted in confidence and sincerity they were agreed that art was 99% hard work and diligence.

It is surely a burden, said Hitler.

Or a boon, said Katrín, playful.

With the arrival of the steak the conversation moved to talk of food. Hitler asked whether Katrín had a robust stomach or had found it difficult to get used to German food. Indeed, the first few weeks she said she got an itchy rash over her body which she thought was caused by digestion, though her doctors said that was to do with her liver.

And how are you faring with German food nowadays?

Splendidly: though the icelandic diet involves more basic foods; the German one suits a singer better.

One does not need to eat as much in warmer climates as in colder.

After the steak, Hitler asked for news of iceland, which he had always wanted to visit.

I want to have some authority in the matter, he said.

His desire did not stem from the influence of the Nonna books on him in his youth, though he thought fondly of them; what motivated him was an inner desire reaching back to the beginning of time.

The icelandic sagas, their essence and worth to men, tempt me. A pagan calm devoid of Christian moralizing. That's it . . . Eddaic poetry came to mind immediately when I saw you in the floodlight and you looked at me, he said, and recited aloud from one of the poems:

Why do I fear
Freyja's eyes?
I feel those eyes
Burning fire.

At this little witticism, they laughed heartily.

Remarkable, said Katrín, you have the correct pronunciation, and icelandic is an extremely difficult language, the oldest living language in the world.

She told him that not only to flatter him; Hitler was quite fluent in icelandic, and could get along well. Katrín lifted the spoon and Hitler said skeið, Katrín lifted the fork and Hitler said gaffall. And so on usw. o.s.frv.

Upon completion of a truly satisfying dining experience, Katrín could not help but show him a hint of icelandic hospitality and invite him and Göring home for a coffee at Hamburg Castle that very night.

Let's drink coffee and cognac back home, she said. It would be compromising for me to be seen with someone else in public. But I do want to thank you for a lovely evening.

The pleasure yacht berthed and Hitler and Katrín went together along the tunnel of trees. The moon came up and struck silver decorations over the withered garden in the pale glow over Reinbek and the surrounding area; silver frost beads glittered on chestnut trees and elms, the gravel on the path skittered and crackled under their shoes as owls wailed in bittersweet mistletoe.

The industrious city slept as Katrín showed Hitler and Göring into the blue room and asked them modestly to excuse her while she slipped out and changed clothes.

The two companions sat in deep chairs with silk upholstery and— nach einigem Stillschweigen said Hitler:

Ich bitte dich, lass mich allein.

Single-minded lust was running through him.

Nicht jedes Mädchen hält so rein, said Göring—herumspürend, like Mephistopheles.

The duo were unusually literarily inclined this evening. Katrín and Hitler stayed on alone in the castle. The servants slept, and the St. Bernard dog yawned lazily on an icelandic sheepskin rug, and on his back wriggled a swarm of little kittens. Katrín fetched them steaming coffee in floral espresso cups with gold trim. And after the first sip Hitler moved right to the chase, asked for her hand and turned himself so that it was unavoidable she could see his feelings for her made evident in his pants. He ground his teeth before her on the floor and said:

OoOoOooo, and he shook her hands as he tried to have her touch him in the right place.

I see that you are direct, acting as you are, said Katrín. I appreciate such personalities, but I will never give myself to another or get married except to my native land and to my voice.

A powerful soprano sigh escaped from her lips.

I want my love alone in my bosom, if things go wrong I'll die of grief; she added with melancholy expression.

The words were barely silent on her lips when an internal tension wracked Hitler, who approached Katrín deformed with rage, one of the blood vessels on his forehead swelling like a fat earthworm in a cemetery. First he tried to get her into marriage with a lump barely suppressed in his throat, plaintively begging her to promise herself to him, but when that was not enough he turned to threats and anger.

He seized Katrín, who was almost straight-backed at the sofa's edge, took her in a death grip so that she jumped and fought her way from the slippery silk material of the couch and flung herself, knees open wide on the panther pelt on the floor. In the tussle her dress rode up to her thighs, she gave a suppressed cry and used the icelandic woman's defense, trying to drive him off with her shoe heel and puncture his scrotum, and kicking and scuffling on the floor among the quiet and large St. Bernard, the kittens, the shining and broken espresso cups; Hitler almost managed to subdue her under the big oak table, but she received a lucky break when he ended up ejaculating. That placated him momentarily which gave her an opportunity, since their business needed to end in one way, with a crushing defeat for him, yes, even though he was the Commander of one of the most powerful and industrious nations of the world, facing a human being who had made the expensive choice of devoting herself to art and giving it herself—her only self—whole, both bodily and spiritual energies.

The ejaculation during their unsuccessful wrestling increased the Commander's castration and neurosis, but Katrín stood over him goading and triumphant.

Save the world, and with it my love, he said, crushed, lying on the floor with wisps of hair stuck in his eyes and white foam falling from his mouth. Or else I'll destroy it in a burning rage.

She was silent; she sniffed disdainfully and looked at the Commander, this boneless heap on the carpet.

Are you so deeply mired in the world of the Valkyries that you would choose the world defeated at your feet, even if in a terrible state?

I require nothing more than to continue to serve my art, she said.

If I cannot win you with goodness, I will conquer the world with evil, Hitler hissed unthinkingly, without guarding his word or explaining his actions. Never before had it occurred to him to wage war.

Good, do what you can, said Katrín indifferent. It's all the same to me.

Is your singing voice worth more than that the ears of those who listen to your singing remain unburned? Scorched ears cannot hear; burned mouths full of dirt will not call you onto the stage.

I am not a politician, but an artist, she replied in a whisper. I cannot; anything else is impossible.

Do you prefer war or love?

I find my peace in struggle.

You would rather that the world and its houses collapse than the curtain on stage behind you? You need not forsake it; I am not so selfish in my love.

I could never move between home, husband, children, and theater.

You claim to know me so well. I will not place a burning sacrifice on any altar but Wagner's.

She pointed forcefully and his lips parted in anger.

Katrín, he said, you are a true artist. That is more than I could be. But the world's corpses shall therefore hear you singing in the theater of death, and I suggest that man only submits to woman in desperation: should I lose the war, you will also lose your victories.

These were his final words.

Art is long; life is short—Life lasts only in the living, not a moment longer, she sighed in parting.

His face black and blue like a newly-strangled body, he hastened on his homeward way from the castle and proceeded quickly, directing the bow of the yacht to the Kílarskurði canal and thence to Vistnar. Once they were sailing he is said to have talked with Göring and looked over the railing toward England, which was invisible in the dark night:

After this miserable defeat, it feels not enough of a remedy to conquer this dirty world.

Of course, it will be easier than the victories over the icelandic artist, Göring is said to have replied.

At the isthmus, beyond Kílarskurði, he beat his fist in the direction of Poland.

The next morning he woke up on board hungover and senseless, horribly guilty and regretful; but there was no turning back.

my good god what did I say and do in my drunkenness I cannot taste wine   he thought desperately   I remember nothing

In the ship's toilet he made unsuccessful attempts to recall the night's events, looking at himself in the mirrors while he brushed his teeth because he feared he had bad breath from the acidic wine on his tongue.

who are you   he thought and looked carefully into his eyes   and whispered to himself: what kind of wild animal are you, Adolf.

Sensations of fear traveled around his mind; he sweat and suffered from waves of heat, half-deranged on into morning; then he ran himself a hot bath, took his B-vitamins and salt and soothing medicine, settled himself in bed, and called for Göring.

What happened? he asked, trying to conceal his fear with complacency. Did I achieve my meeting with the Norn?

Göring unfolded it all for him, giving a solemn oath attesting to his attendance, his humiliation on the floor and the ejaculation that had caused him deep pain. By nature, Hitler was not bad so much as sensitive and stubborn. What he took upon himself had to stand unaltered and he never compromised on anything. In short, he was a product of the time.

A glossy Mercedes Benz drove him furiously along the Autobahn and speed appeased his nervousness. The driver sped at a hundred and fifty the whole way between Vistnar and Berlin. All the while the other vehicles stopped on route and near it; ambulances were on hand in every small town and at all intersections.

His first work in the Reich Chancellery was to send a telegram to his border army:

Corn blossoms are on the flower. Gilliflower is fragrant at night. Now morning has a meaning for us. The night approaches the garbage can.

After that he called his mother.
I have committed a great sin, you must forgive me, Mom, Göring
heard him say . . .
   This happened on August 31. The next day, on September 1 in
1939, the Führer's armies advanced into that pigpen, Poland.

Dead silence reigned at the Board in the refectory after Ólaf had finished the story of the icelandic soprano who one night in late August held the fate of the world in her hands, but chose to cast away a decent man who changed into a wild beast with the pain and caused millions of deaths with his unbridled temper, as Miss Gerður put it. She did not want, this magnificent woman, to sacrifice any of her calling to art or her freedom even though she would be with the Führer and was offered the luxury of Berlin's Reich Chancellery.

Although I have often heard this story, said Miss Gerður, I somehow never believed it.

Hang on, said Ólaf. Most peculiar of all is that the words of Hitler became prophetic when he sent Katrín, via the icelandic Ambassador in Hamburg, Dr. Wiesbaden, the first corpse of the war, a symbol of victory and a shame pole. He brought Katrín the package on a gold bar, and when she opened it and saw the contents Dr. Wiesbaden said that he saw her startle but she said nothing.

No, she said nothing, that was very womanlike, chorused the Board and smiled pleasantly.

Despite everything, Ólaf continued, the fatally wounded Führer sent Katrín over to England on a Danish ship, which shows a new and unexpected side of the man and his merits. And we should also note that five years of London fog had the same effect on *her* voice as the cold on the Russian plains had on *his* communications routes; simultaneously Hitler lost the war and she lost her voice, returning home a broken woman and founding a singing school at the bottom of Hverfisgata.

Total silence.

Legend has it that Katrín was on stage at Covent Garden mid-aria when something came over her; she suddenly lost the thread, her voice broke, there was a knot in her vocal cords. And at the same moment it was announced over the speaker system that the war was over and the British rushed to their feet with screams and celebrations. Now they were singing, not her: There will be blue birds over the white cliffs of Dover to-morrow, just you wait and see. There will be love and laughter for ever after to-morrow, just you wait and see . . .

It turned out that one of the vocal chords had torn right by the nodule and she said to herself: Now you have sung song permanently out of your throat.

And so they both waited, defeated eventually.

What was not revealed here in iceland was that a small locket with her picture was found in Hitler's ashes in the bomb shelter; the Russians stole it.

It was a picture of her child, I heard, said Sigurður.

No, that is a myth, said Ólaf.

This folktale is recorded based on the Ólaf's account. I have heard many versions that do not agree, particularly as to the Commander's solemn pledges, whether they were made before, after or during his visit. I remember some laborers who were laying a road at Bratta-brekka, intelligent men and attentive, wanting to argue the case that Hitler had sworn a costly oath in the presence of his General Staff before he set off, then got drunk in his seat, as they say, to give himself courage, and so had cause to say: Either I conquer the world or this woman. And from that the language developed according to the laws of tragedy: an irrevocable pledge that cannot be resolved except by death. One of them in that scattered gravel, a knowledgeable, observant farmer, said he had noted that men with gridlock symptoms had such temperaments. Anyway, the root of the evil was the cynical woman, not willing to be friendly to a man.

Dísa turned fire-red at this and perhaps felt it was a threat.

Society is clogged up by invalids who don't trust themselves to do difficult work, instead lying purring at home on their divans, brought low by nerves. The best work is torn from the healthy and given to the sick. If people do not care for such hand flapping they get money for being sick. That's paid better than any domestic work. Into the invalid's path gets pushed countless grants and awards. In the hospital he receives free food, housing, and services, which calculated in money would be a pretty purchase; on returning home he gets sick payments and better, you are on the payroll of your employer, the State. If you are lucky enough to lose an eye, you can live a lifetime on benefits, you get free housing, and good-hearted people club together for a TV so you can have something to do with your remaining healthy eye. No wonder television aerials are only on the chimneys of the homes of rich people and invalids. If these people get too lazy to breed, they are pushed into it with grants for intercourse. The state pays for every child produced. Other kinds of production are left to sit on the back burner. Whole families do not work at any other production. The expectation is that the nation's foreign exchange earnings are small. The population's libido operates with a State guarantee. Yet the sex-weary have a plan to kill all middle-aged families via masturbation. Between sex and disease, which sustain family members in their lairs, a life gets emphasized while constantly being advertised to people in fish houses and on boats. A lazy wrapping replaces lying feeble, as swollen water streams in from all sides. Every effort is made to increase the per-capita population. Although the country has never been so many as now, neither more nor less than 180,000 residents, it is argued there is a sexual problem. The Icelandic Women's Association recently issued the following challenge to women:

> *Icelandic Mothers in Cities and Rural Areas,*
>
> *At the fifteenth National Congress of Icelandic Women the following proposal was adopted, submitted by the Women's Association from*

*Bíldudal: We icelandic women in Bíldudal call on other icelandic
women aged fourteen to forty-five years, anywhere in the country,
from sea to field, to apply themselves earnestly to increasing their
contribution to the population growth in our hardscrabble country,
to demonstrate tangible citizenship in this work by moving the native
country toward its 200,000th State inhabitant by 2000 A.D. The
nation is innately fertile.*

As soon as the government learned of the challenge, demonstrating
the great patriotism and labor-mindedness of the Women's Association
of iceland, it sent out the following notice:

*At a joint ministry meeting of the Government of Iceland, it was
agreed to provide a special award to the woman who brings the country to its 200,000th inhabitant; as a gift, the mother will receive an
engraved silver shield but the son or daughter will get free flights to
Copenhagen, back and forth with Air iceland, with a week's lodging
in a first-class four-star hotel and 20 Danish krona allowance per
day during their stay. Furthermore, the person in question, according
to special ministerial license, will be granted the priority of holding
the honored title iceland's Favorite Child, both in official documents
and in daily use. If married, the person in question will be granted
10 days' free accommodation in Mallorca with her spouse. The even-
tual burial will be public and conducted at State expense. The title
iceland's Favorite Child shall not cause difficulty according to laws of
the land. The same provision applies to twins.*

. . . while newspaper columns constantly rage against those who have
something: we, the people who make a detailed timetable for each coming day; we who with energy and dedication have tried to make strong
apartments and homes and a homeland against the imminent invasion
which a domestic invalid society has spawned for itself. For example,

Sveinn gets income for his five children (he was also fortunate enough to get support payments for Stína a few days before she died), plus he works three jobs. What do they have to complain about. Do they want someone to make a film about the painful life of those who only own two cars? Do they expect a bestseller to be written about them? (I have lived a life of fascinating material, said Anna; Svanur even began to write about me.) Do they not have a car, a radio, personal effects, and a standing lamp? Would it not be fortunate, if someone sidled up, I do not know how, and broke his knee cap. Would he not get a new plastic knee and a duty-free vehicle on top of everything (being declared a disabled invalid), which he could then sell for a decent price. Would it be right if I bought a vehicle and left my bank empty of savings, other than the compulsory savings of teenagers, which are of course indexed for this invalid against devaluation. But my money may deteriorate in inflation. No one thinks about that. The new, young and hardy generation of lapdogs does not, of course, have the sense to save for themselves. Besides, it's high time these lap dogs got a salary for going to school voluntarily. As it is said: salary for birth, salary for sickness, salary for fucking, salary for learning, salary for suicide. And probably god will tempt them with high wages, all these people who are believers, "just in case," or they will stream over to Hell; better bonuses there. Those over sixty remember two times, the past and the present. We. Afterward this rabble intends to turn my apartment slowly and silently into a universal American Keflavík airport with a military radio. You will not take it. Life is hiding inside me, although I am an invalid. I see you before me, an image: the one with a broken knee-cap, the one with a twisted colon, under the headline: A couple with five children going out to the street because they need to look for a bite in the garbage cans. The picture shows: a standing lamp, a refrigerator, a washing machine, a car, a carved couch, two night tables, a queen-size mattress from the Furniture Store in Austurbæjar, two radios (Telefunken brand), one with a built-in turntable and cassette player, so you can record the voices of the children on their birthdays, the other a portable Jumbo you can move from the living room to the kitchen and from the kitchen to the toilet, so Anna can get the dirt off to a mixture of Negro music and "light classical songs." (When will a radio station come out with a request show called In the Privy amid this "flood of shows"?) And in addition, a veneer crockery cabinet housing a Junghans electric clock, a television and a carpet . . . "corners in the middle" is the style of their couch. The newspaper readers will sigh: god, who can be so cruel as to drive such poor and needy people out on the street just before christmas. I think this will give the "leftist" students in Reykjavík schools good stuff for their christmas essay—written, of course, Hans Christian Andersen-style. Det var saa grueligt koldt; det sneede og det begyndte at blive mørk Aften . . . Stína could become a model for Little Girls with matches, frozen piss-wet on the stairs. "Good" and shortsighted parents saved me the trouble of chasing her away. Are there not songs and sympathy in "crying injustice of justice." Become a homeowner and you must insist on an X-ray of a woman's oven-womb before leasing to a childless couple, so it can be ascertained THAT THEY ACTUALLY ARE CHILDLESS. Or do the poor have full authority to act impudently, with anarchy and aggression.

Damn it, I probably never let myself accord Ásmundur Steinsson's knowledge a role in my skepticism

Ásmundur had his residence on the site of the refectory's (perhaps former) location. On the second floor. I am familiar with his life history, which is fairly similar to, or could be like, mine if I continue to ignore the value of housing and property.

many people have identical histories I well know it yet there is no reason to follow Sigurður's commandment that it is best to have nothing but the state and nonprofit organizations because then nothing is taken away in tax nor other ways which is certainly true and indisputable but impossible because though man is alone and has nothing he always has something that never disappears unless he is absolutely executed, only the dead man has nothing

Take this example: young girls strolling outside on a moor. They find an old trash dump and "claim ownership"; greed based on exclusive rights comes quick to humans. On the first day they collect all the largest and most beautiful pieces of broken glass from this "outside toy." A week passes and the little hussies are happy with the broken glass until the end of the week when they grow bored of their assets and so the gold in the heap accumulates in their eyes; on Sunday morning they rush off and go to the heap and take the "best" broken glass remaining: the inferior becomes good when there is nothing better. Over and again the same thing; they tire of what they cherish and visit the heap weekly, monthly, or annually, always finding something to take. This little dump has become inexhaustible. They always discover something useful and valuable. Coveting is in man's blood: to find the big in the little by reducing assessments of quality and value. Of course, the value of the pile decreases in the usual sense, if it exists in reality, but not in the mind of the tiny girls. That does not happen until someday they need to piss. They sit on the pile and now it doesn't drip from them but gushes out past their shoes. With that wonder of nature they examine by chance (or instinct or whatever one wants to call it) under their dresses and see: a transformation has occurred. In an instant the dump has become a useless rubbish dump. They abandon the outside stuff and margarine tubs and seek out a man for under their dresses and a real play space, i.e. a nice house up on Snob Hill or at Boulevard Bingo with Danish model furniture "frá dør til dør D.F.D.S." fit for the Queen, and they take possession of an eight-bedroom sunny apartment with views and a rock garden where they cultivate natural outdoor plants.

ideally I would never give a thought to Sigurður   but Ásmundur   his story is a bit special and of all people I could tailor to myself were I not Tómas, son of Jón, do you want to listen shall I

death alone is beyond the understanding of mortal
living men
why should man complain about his science

eternal life never gets disproved or
proved by experience
life must commit suicide in the search to know

writers and priests and philosophers
are useless in thought
and with the outcome
their ignorance attempts to gain
significant value

no one can disprove anything beyond
understanding
no one prove anything beyond his knowledge

in a nonsensical search and soundscape constructed
existence an assignment
for the gods of poetry and religion

and call politicians cunning
the writer and the priest
bluff god when they need to lull to sleep
the waking

each country hypnotized with regalia and verbiage
they speak with affectation
I lack words I need a writer or a priest

to take wing and provide my thoughts flight

and the historic reality
floats away on winged words of deception

that masterly Tómas, who barely trusts bragging
writers and priests and philosophers
and the lying words of power-sick politicians

tell you Ásmundur's story, Títa.   It goes like this:
Ásmundur "the glove" Þórsson had with perseverance, dynamism, and
hard work, which had been preserved in his family for two centuries
alongside depression and psychosis (he came from a very priestly country), managed to build an impressive house at the intersection of X and
Y. He was born at Görðum in Garðahreppi (I didn't care to get the
correct birthplace because his materials and earnings there are gone and
lest it comes to his mind to improve his situation by bringing an action
for damages against me), son of Thor Ásmundursonar (the formula for
first born sons: Thor, then Ásmundur, then Thor, then etc.) and Her-
dis Einarsdóttur (who came from the most ambassadorial and writerly
country) in 1881. He grew up around farm work but his mind was
summoned early (like meltwater) down to the shore and out to (the
silver shining) sea. While Ásmundur was completely healthy and sane
(depression entered the dynasty in 1821 with Þorhalla from Efrabæ in
Flóa, who seemed an awfully strong character of a woman) he lived in a
small bedroom chamber in an attic no larger than the floor area, so that
his sea bag hung behind the door and a couch filled the whole room;
it was otherwise empty. In the room, he could not stand upright comfortably except under the skylight, which was no significant problem,
because he was mostly lying down while he was on land. Ásmundur
pursued the sea, first in open boats, later on trawlers. He was esteemed
among the trawler fishermen for three things: thrift, magnanimity, and
never taking his toll on voyages abroad. (N.B. to take the toll in fishermen's terms has an ambiguous meaning a] to purchase certain amounts

of duty free goods for domestic sale or one's own use, b] to take your toll on women, as in physical sex.) And yet a woman was the reason he met with an accident that led him to lose his honor and employment. It is not certain how the accident occurred, but one of Ásmundur's hands was ripped off and also a toe; from that time on he was crippled. There are different stories about this; in their aggregate we might find a trace of what we call the truth:

1. He was standing by the capstan while the net was being hoisted up, the wire got looped and cut off his hand. Ásmundur startled, although he did not react, and the result of the muscle contraction in his leg loosened his big toe. For some reason this upset the balance in his head; some believed him heavier on one side because he slung to when walking, and his gait was not unlike the motion of a wave. Some people call this disease "touched by jellyfish" (since the muscles vibrate like jellyfish).

2. He was unusually food-greedy and his hurry to eat led to him inadequately removing the bones from fish before boiling. The body was full of bones, which he swallowed and which rattled about him; they either dug into his blood vessels or pricked out of his fingers and toes and sometimes out of his body so he resembled a sea urchin or hedgehog if he did not pluck the bones.

3. He suffered significantly from a mad strength and the berserker disease. One time he and other crewmembers were at the circus where they saw a strongman bend a thick iron rod between his hands. When they returned to the ship, the sailors were sitting over a beer and gin with some british tarts in the dining room. One tart was particularly outspoken. She was of tall build, slender, pale in the face, small-mouthed with teeth that bent inside her mouth. This and the short torso were all characteristic of english women. (As morning flutters in, they dress loosely, in a sky-blue and pink nightdress, fresh from sleep, to go have bacon and porridge at the breakfast table. English writers call this coming like a sunbeam into her husband's life. In England it is the custom to establish a marriage at the breakfast table and in english poetry the woman is

like a beam and when she dies she visits her husband as moonlight so Britons sleep by an open window, but in the process they go about with their fly open, and with this there's more to lunatic folk in England than in other countries and the women are untouchable and distant, like a colony. This womanly demeanor is the result of a maritime national mentality, the opposite of the seaman, whose woman is there just as "a piece to stick it into" and Ásmundur was like that to a certain extent but he was also a sailor and seafarer who would dream about woman as a vast ocean, as sunshine, as moonlight. He went whole months without her and therefore she [he] became wet dreams after the english national spirit.) The tart in Ásmundur's story could both sing and demonstrate judo moves. She went berserk in the dining room as Ásmundur's comrade told her about the strongman in the corner, but when she began to flex her muscles they urged Ásmundur and her together, and said:

It doesn't do to save money or strength; neither is useful untouched in a bank.

Long into the evening Ásmundur resisted taking on the girl. She called him the dead muscle-bank, one that gives no interest, and then taunted him meanly, and he beat his fist on the table so the glasses jumped and the ginmilk splashed on her dress (she drank gin with milk like tarts do because they are pretending they are not drinking alcohol, just milk). She jumped up in a rage, demanded that he find her a new glass, but he refused to serve a woman at the table and said:

I'm no hooker's bartender.

The girl poured abuse over him and settled into a boxing stance, and the women cried out an english wail, a quick yet protracted eúúú-sound reminiscent of the name Ésu.

She's challenging you to box, said the sailors. Ásmundur would not listen and stayed seated.

You don't dare fight a tart? asked the sailors.

I could crush her head, said Ásmundur, and crumpled a beer can between his hands.

Eúúú.

The sailors translated his words, but the girl grabbed the other beer and crushed it just as forcefully as Ásmundur. For some time they competed crushing beer cans with great joy and resounding eúúú-shouts. Ásmundur's temper rose; he laughed and slobbered. But the girl was not satisfied with the strength test. She insisted Ásmundur get her a fresh glass.

I never will, answered Ásmundur stubbornly, sticking out his head as deer do for an attack.

Either he gets me a glass like a real man or we will come to blows, interpreted someone who understood her language.

I will never fetch a glass for a British tart, said Ásmundur and remained steadfast, his chin tucked into his chest.

At that answer the tart became deformed with rage. For safe-keeping, she scratched three artificial moles from her chin and cheekbones, put them in her purse ready for the next customer, and spat on Ásmundur's nose a grayish beer froth slightly darker than coal smoke; it leaked into his mouth.

No strongman would allow himself to do this, said the sailor. Ásmundur shot up and struck the woman with a fist; she flew from the blow like a beam and grabbed him in judo hold, swung him in the air so he and all his limbs slugged powerless to the floor where he lay out cold. When he woke up that night he dragged himself to his ship's bunk with the glossy beauty spots glued on his face as a disparaging gift from the girl, as if he were the ship's hooker. The next day the sailors found a shriveled toe on the floor, and since anything can happen when drinking they each checked his own foot, and when they saw Ása's foot they made fun of the toe and the beauty spots. Because of the irony that had befallen him, he hid the injury to his hand. He tortured himself with work, and the worse the agony got the more heated grew his confidence and pleasure. He hid the injury under a full sea-glove as his hand swelled with a violent rash of blood boils and abscesses he cut into from time to time with his gutting knife in secret over the shit bucket (this happened after the sailors on the ships stopped needing to sit with their asses half out over the railing to shit before toilets were introduced) and in a strange way he enjoyed seeing the pus-streaked blood well from the cut into the bucket. The sailors thought he had hemorrhoids and teased him because they believed that only those who take it from behind got hemorrhoids and Ásmundur stopped touching the tumors which made matters worse. Finally, his lower arm and armpit gland were so inflamed the arm lifted from his side, which made Ásmundur combative on deck.

He has grown mighty, the sailors howled, this man who struggled to wrestle rags.

One day out at Halamiðum, the sailors were chopping fish down in the hold, one of them was stood apart from the group, chopping away. Ásmundur snuck up behind the man who was totally unaware and so drove his tool into the swollen hand; the sailor tugged back, thinking it was caught in the hold's opening and stuck fast. The tool did not want not to come free and so the sailor turned to have a look, and saw spurting pus and putrefied blood splattering in his direction.

I was lucky I was there, was how he put it and laughed heartily at this turn of events. Ásmundur turned pale and tottered, but five nearby fishermen saved him from falling, took him under the shoulders and dragged into the dining room. On the floor they cut off his coat and the evidence came to light, blue veins that seemed to stand outside the curd-white skin like the dark roots of a peculiar abscess flower (his hand) with its five swollen stamens. The first mate cursed before he issued his diagnosis:

This is not an inflammation but idiocy and folly.

Upon diagnosis the Captain said:

Fisheries are not required to cover the consequences of stupidity. He walked down into the dining room, stood astride over Ásmundur on the floor in a puddle of pus and challenged him to show that seaman's pluck he knew Ásmundur had inside, and bear the infection, at least while the trawler filled itself. Ásmundur's assurance quickened slightly at this encouragement, which indicated a degree of faith; he thought there on the floor and said:

I will do my duty.

And he kept on thinking: I stand with you against sailors and abscesses   And after he said this he salivated. He was rolled on his stomach and his pants pulled down. The first mate wiped one of his ass cheeks with cotton and, having pressed with a finger near its bottom, injected him with morphine. Half an hour later Ásmundur stood on deck like a new man, half as work-mad as before. He was sedated while the morphine supply lasted, but they needed more from home, and they would not be done until the trawler was full of fish. Ásmundur became beside himself with the pain and the first mate had to take him below deck and tie him to his bunk with strong straps. The trawler sailed with fish and the half-dead Ásmundur to England where his hand was cut off, and the heads cut off the cod were sold at market in Grimsby. On the way to the hospital, lying almost unconscious in the hamper, he said:

She used illegal wrestling holds against me; it cannot be taken seriously. And before he went to sleep thanks to a dose of anesthetic he said:

Five. No. Five times no.

He was stubborn in nature and would not even one time accept anesthetic let alone a woman.

Now look at this and consider the sequel:

Ásmundur comes stumbling into the refectory from his place. He fixes his eyes on his chair right by the door as if it is a distant goal. And when he stands at the table he swings himself into his seat. With a peculiar hand gesture he manages to wring his paw, clad in a black leather glove, well-polished and gleaming, up on the table's edge. A hollow wooden sound resounds through the dining room. In appearance it resembles a dead beetle, the stitching on the gloves somewhat frayed; it lies oddly stone-dead on the white cloth, and probably it would be more tasteful to carry a neat stump than this lump connected via straps to the stump. There is something disturbing about the black glove motionless right beside the soup dish as afternoon music sings from the radio; it is like a crime thriller or something at an antique sale, dross mixed together with the past, things that once had their uses, but the hand is old and dead, this icelandic fist. Ásmundur does not get food from the common platter, like the rest, the platter that is passed among the plates, but rather morsels of the dining matron's meat; she picks bones from the fish in the kitchen and carries it to him like a small child. Humiliation is Ásmundur's agony; he is chock full of memories from the past. His face weeps self-contempt when María puts the plate in front of him. She is Danish and the pain is for two reasons. He feels terrible and he wants to hide from our attention behind a grimace. He sits at the table like he is the matron's economy measure, her method of reducing the pensioners' appetite. This residue does not make you physically sick, but it does lessen the hunger inside.

4. The story goes like this: it often happens to a *heavy* man that they get the love of a cheerful woman who plays with him like a cat with a mouse in the hay yard. Ásmundur is said to be that type. A marriage incurred by such a man can only be blessed compared to one where the husband closes his eyes to the past and is able to enjoy the game, knowing that a backsliding wife would become obsessed by guilt as often as she gets dressed, particularly concerning the enjoyment of sexual partners prior to marriage, which they regard as a sin. In this fine state, a man enjoys his wife more than if she had always been loyal to him. Coexistence with a loyal wife is characterized by mental inertia; she has a chastity bonus. I have every right and reason to be grouchy and twisted. I am loyal and reluctant. Ásmundur was sure he could never win the favor of women, that he was too faithful a man to be an option. There is poison in the eyes of women who do not consider marriage a direct biblical command: Go forth and multiply. This sort of woman is harder to find. Instead we have: Go fulfill your wishes. He had enough sense to suspect that he would never get near a spouse except by sharing her. And so he decided to pull together his money and build a big house. Very few women can resist a three-story house, deposits in banks, or companies. The house was built from scratch in the midst of an economic crisis. He sought a woman's body to accompany him and their relationship would exist among words

and sentences such as: "stand upright except under the ceiling window" and "mostly lay down while he was in the country." One day, it was like in a storm that some anxiety seized him and he had difficulty breathing. He bolted to his feet and involuntarily opened the skylight to breathe some fresh air. The room was so small and the air so heavy it seemed emptied of oxygen; he felt he could not breathe, so he breathed out of the window such that his head protruded from the roof while the rest of his body could not be seen from the windows across the street. Since the room was low to its ceiling, his chin was past the window frame. While he breathed and his body replenished its oxygen, he occasionally saw a girl's head emerge from the roof window in the house across the street. These lonely heads appearing on two red roofs often looked into each other's eyes. Some evenings he saw sticks lift up to the window and hang lingerie and underclothes to dry. The girl seemed to wash underwear inside her place and dry them on the stick. In Ásmundur eyes this resembled a standard flag that flutters from a ship's rigging, but though he knew semaphore he set no meaning in symbols. This indicated only that the clean female had the same kind of little, narrow attic bedroom as he did. Now one time he was standing with his head up out of the roof and staring at the washing fluttering. And before he knew it, the clothing had fallen from its stick, swinging in spirals over the windy street and landing on the roof right in front of his nose. He is startled to see the garment tossing before his eyes and manages with some presence of mind to capture it, and he sees he has some women's panties. Time passes and he waits but there is no sign of the girl's face in the roof window and he does not know what to do with the panties. His shyness means that he does not like the idea of going with them in hand down the stairs and across the street, so he stands guard all day in his window, food- and coffee-less, making sure the frost does not bite him; he is used to standing on watch in all weathers. In the evening, when darkness had fallen, it seemed to him a globular hump appeared in the window, the girl's face looking out the roof in search of something since there's nothing on the end of the stick. He puts up a hand and waves the panties several times in the same way as a shipwrecked man on a raft. The hump scans around without making any sound so he starts to holler. The face of the hump then looks across the street. Then it disappears down the roof. Ásmundur is about to give up hope but at the same time the girl reappears with a flashlight and directs it to his window. Ásmundur does not hide away but rather exceeds his ingrained reserve, waving the panties vigorously as he shouts:

These flew over to me.

The light flashes over the roofs and the girl cries out:

I'll be right over.

A few moments later there is a light knock on the door. Ásmundur pulls open the door; a young girl appears in the doorway and says she is called Fía. He gets embarrassed but invites her in though he has few conversational topics to bring up, so he talks about how she made a good choice with the flashlight, which she willingly hands him; he sees it is a rectangular flashlight with two conflicting polarities and a mirror lantern on the side. They look at the flashlight a considerable time, testing it together and she says there is almost no way to get new batteries, so she makes these ones last by putting them out overnight on the radiator.

The compounds inside them ferment, you see, she says.

They do, yes, of course, he says.

I was stupid enough to buy it from a trawler fisherman who sailed from England.

I'll buy some batteries for you, says Ásmundur.

They speak of "things you cannot get in this country," for most of their time, almost all, which saved them from having nothing to talk about. Many trawler fishermen owe their marriages to "things you cannot get in this country." The girl discusses how different life in England had been: there you could get all things of all kinds, whereas here there was nothing to be had. The topic peters out and then she asks for her clothes, the panties that were drying during the conversation. Because the frost has worsened, she asks Ásmundur to turn around while she slips into them; she has nothing to change into and often goes without panties except in August.

That time of year it is dry enough, it's feasible to dry something in one day, she says.

Ásmundur turns and looks out of the roof window while she changes.

I feel like my clothes sought you out, she says. I hope that you let yourself imagine something.

Ásmundur imagined many things during the rustling that took place behind him, and from the shallows of those imaginings a marriage proposal rose, the way a house gets built on sand. It became clear Fía was thrifty; in no time at all she had him bequeath her half his property.

If you find yourself scared of *me*, she says, remember a woman will not run from half a house.

And thus began a marriage story marked by hope for neither happiness nor unhappiness. Ásmundur's wish of inviting a woman into his house had been fulfilled; he believes a woman is a property's protective coat of arms. He had a professional paint a rose pattern up the staircase, rented out the second floor and part of the basement, but lived with the woman in the roof apartment. This was a manifestation of optimism. Ásmundur had a younger brother named Markús who was a scoundrel with a pageboy haircut and a slender mustache like a fop. While Ásmundur endlessly hauled cod from the sea, his brother pulled haddocks on the divan in the apartment and made his home in . . . (This part of the manuscript is missing.)

. . . hook caught under the ring . . . he was hanging, dangling in the air, swinging to and fro in his boots and anorak; they cried:

Take off your ring.

. . . did not want to not let go of the ring. The wire snapped the finger and the ring off him, and after his return his brother reported it to Fía as that he'd wanted to get rid of the trappings of marriage so he could have a girlfriend in every port . . . Fía besieged Ásmundur with questions about the causes of the accident. Then she ordered him in the future to report his movements to her, not that there were multiple ports to discuss; the trawler only ever docked in one place in England.

He thinks you aren't worthy of him, said Markús, the wicked brother, who was descended from the priestliest country but was in *revolt* against his family.

We are a match.

His words fell on good soil. They spoke heatedly, and Márkus said he had never felt a *warmth* with any woman but her—never before such spiritual understanding.

You are different from any other woman I have met, he said. I cannot define what it is, but warmth does not quite capture it . . .

They talked *sub rosa*; he told Fía about his commercial enterprises and about women and how some women *shaved* their genitals before intercourse.

I am probably too sensitive. *He* cannot stand to see *her* in daylight, because of a fear inside that started after the dog bit me in the groin when I was a child. From then on *he* has been afraid of any opening, and if he is shocked he imagines it as a pair of gums. So women and I have never properly fit together.

This stirred Fía, in truth it aroused in her great pride as the savior of this unfortunate bachelor. After having shut the window and turned off the lights she undressed under the covers to see if they fit together. He buried himself in her sweater and wept in the dark after he kissed *her* for *giving* him so much and her altruistic breast was delighted for the short time *she* received *him*, stock-still, without being pushy.

I have to sacrifice myself and save this man my god he has had such a hard time he needs to be cared for, *she* maintained.

Oh *she* is so good to *him*.

Fía's confidence grew, *she* "had never in her life received anything but ingratitude and shame" so her body had been completely unsatisfied. She got orgasms with Ásmundur, but the soul's weight from Markús—and so she did not feel guilty, but generous.

god is good to allow a man *this*

She thought a lot, in the kitchen and in the bathroom and even in the hallway and in bed, as Markús dressed her warmly in ever more sweaters and dresses until he finally had her tied up. His crying fits increased, he complained and cursed life, and not even she could care for him during the fits. The weak disposition of Þórhöllu from Efrabæ in Flóa was now surfacing in him.

Everything will be all right in time, Fía reassured him.

Then stop letting my brother dishonor you, *yours*, and *mine*.

Ásmundur is on a trip with the trawler. Imagine the sea glittering in the expanse, variously in moon or sunshine, variously gray or blue, maybe green. He thinks often about the gap between his fingers, how he is skilled in woodwork and widely read in literature, and it occurs to him to whittle a finger to replace the one he had lost (he considers cutting off more fingers so the wooden fingers would be identical in all respects). In order to replicate the original finger, he singed the tree finger with hot nails where there had been a bruise under his nail, and in private he admired the construction and expected that Fía would, too (he had gotten that notion from books). One time when the net had been emptied onto the trawler deck and the artificial finger sat motionless within his glove, melancholy seized him; he reached into his pocket for the dead finger, seized with minimal fuss a wriggling cod, put his finger in its throat, and released it back into the sea.

I guess not all of me will end up in your jaws.

This is the way he thought.

His first task in Hull was to buy black gloves, and on his homecoming he tried his finger in the thumb before he pulled the glove over his hand; he placed the wedding ring on the outside of the glove. Thus adorned, he came out of the bathroom, and once in the kitchen Fía mocked him for his ingenuity, leaping away from him with cries and clambering up on a windowsill.

You devil! I'm afraid of you, are you trying to become a man with metal hands?

After that, Fía was quick, together with Markús, to head down the stairs to tell Sigurður and Ólaf about "the way things have developed." That night, before Ásmundur went to bed, she put some black twine and embroidery scissors in a white envelope and placed it under his pillow. Egh, I've got goose bumps. I'm mad. Eczema has broken out over me just thinking about him, she said and stamped on the stairs as though she was beside herself with disgust and itchiness.

They stood without moving by the coat hooks on the stairway leading to the attic: she, Sigurður, Ólaf, and Markús.

Hello, Tóm, how are you, Fía called out to me. That's enough chitchat for today, Tómmas.

Can I chitchat with myself?

Perhaps I cursed the stairs, but Fía could be agreeable, the way tarts are when wrapped in thick smoke, coughing and throat-rattling, styled in uncombed perms, always a cigarette between their lips. She was pretty enough and neat, if she wanted to be, with a small mouth like a pinhole under her nose, her eyes bright and tense, nimble as a snow bunting. They critiqued the situation among themselves, the dinner matron and Fía, who slept on a pallet on the floor for the week after Ásmundur had searched under the pillow with his fingers, found the letter with the twine, cut open the thread with the scissors, and knew in that symbolic way their marriage had ended without any struggle on her part—though he lay in bed, his soul in utter turmoil. Ásmundur stopped going to sea.

But because I felt pity for him, I arranged for a food service for my husband, on the condition that the costs would be taken from his share of the apartment. Markús and I do not need much space; we are both slender.

The matron knew the stipulations well for when the attic apartment was all gone. Ásmundur had eaten it up past use but she had continued to feed him and now he lies in the trash-storage with his mental and physical capacities slightly inflamed. The Board carefully discussed his situation before he managed to eat himself all the way down the stairs. At that point, no one had seen this mysterious man's eyes; he just floated or existed in thin air and then one day, very unexpectedly, he was sitting at the end of the table, silent like a rock pillar, and Sigurður had to give up the seat he had held a long time. We estimated that Ásmundur's trip down the stairs with a knife, spoon, and fork took about seven years. No one knows for sure, no one knows how square-meter amounts convert to meal costs. His stay among us in the refectory will undoubtedly take much longer. The second floor is much more valuable than the penthouse. Here one must, however, take into account the overall deterioration of properties, depreciation, and the recent significant devaluation and increase in the cost of food. It is much more expensive to eat than it was a year ago. The worst of all this is that the apartment's valuation was confirmed in writing before the war. Devaluation had not been taken into account. Ólafur loosely estimates that if Ásmundur does not have any food other than Knorr soup he would eat up about 1 cm^2 per day. How many milimeters^2 with each soup spoon or soup dish. Depending on how many spoonfuls are in the dish and whether they are heaping or half. On average I estimate there are five, well-heaped. Ásmundur eats soup twice a day and porridge in the morning, but can anyone survive indefinitely on a gurgle of empty soup.

I just calculated this on the spot, said one of the students out of nowhere. Supposing there are on average five spoonfuls per plate, then the equivalent for each spoonful—

But no one was listening to him. However, I was full of curiosity. Only old Tómas pricked up his ears. He seemed like his whole life he would be the sort to shoot up a hand and say:

I've got the answer, teacher. If the Russian chess grandmaster Mikhail Tal moves his queen to G 5 he will win the game in four moves, without a doubt.

Tómas has hit upon my child-like pretensions.

A lifelong, young adult middle-aged old man, he pretends to know better than anyone else—always in all cases these young intellectuals know that if Tal places the queen on G 5 the game is won in four moves

Tómas blinked. He opened his crunching jaws and put the spoon between his tongue and teeth.

Example No. 1: Ásmundur has a three-story house, one hundred square meters in size on a three hundred square meter freehold lot.

a) How long does it take him to eat each story, if the upper story is valued at ISK 200,000, the second floor at ISK 300,000, and the basement apartment at ISK 150,000? His board is estimated at ISK 23.30 per day.

b) How many cm^2 does he eat per day? Assume two main meals and three snacks. The ratio between the main meals and snacks is 2:1.

c) How many of these cm^2 does he eat with a soupspoon, if the ratio of soupspoons and snacks is 15:1?

d) Calculate each apartment separately using the same numbers.

Such an example might occur in a math textbook for school children; it is no wonder that children become such angry devils if they get this sort of question, says Ólafur.

Dísa enjoys the humor and laughs:

I see that you bankfolk are not all that strong at problem solving.

The Board rolls around laughing.

And if you had answers, they would not be worth copying in an exam.

Ásmundur continues to chew on his own little morsels. Ólaf wittily says to Sigurður:

This man's work is just like the communist's subversive activity: he eats away his own property rights.

When Ásmundur stumbles to the table everyone falls silent. For some reason, everyone is frightened of the jewelry that adorns his dead finger, a ring set with a shiny stone. Some are of the opinion the entire hand is cast in gold, which I deem impossible. Ásmundur lost it long after one could go to the bank and demand the equivalent of one's account in gold. I was once tempted to tell the Board a story about how everything gets destroyed from the inside and covered in dust, about an Englishman who was granted vacation from his dedicated service to the Crown, and stayed in England. He began his work as a poor man (yes, I know this story is somewhat cliché) and was relieved of his duties after the summer vacation, having then reached an advanced age, and he returned to India where he was going to pass his days in his house, but when he stepped over the threshold, it crashed to the ground because termites had eaten the core lumber from the inside and nothing was left standing except a coffee table with ivory edging; all the rest was dust at his feet. And you know why the table stood alone in the ash heap. Because the termites could not get into the wood. The Board started giggling to hear of this tragedy. I fell silent, and after that I decided to not speak up. In my silence I had the idea Ásmundur could protect his property by taking tranquilizers. You cannot spend while sleeping, you need no nourishment, you do not eat your house, and you never feel better than when sleeping in your bed. It is not enough to lie down. Just being awake and keeping your eyes open consumes energy.

What did he eat at this meal, asked Sigurður. The roses from the rose tapestry; linoleum on the landing; brass braces on the edges of the steps (Edeltraud polishes those Sunday mornings).

He does not need to worry even if he eats himself all the way down to the basement. A widow lives there. But who will feed him when he gets to the garden. Ásmundur eats with his left hand, which is evidently cumbersome, and you can see the struggle in the fierce convulsions of pain at the corners of the mouth. Maybe he needs to know the food has reached his stomach, since he seems to hesitate with each spoonful. The house shrinks beneath his feet.

what am i eating now   i think it is the damn toilet bowl

Today he eats a door-frame, tomorrow it will be part of the internal wiring or a key from a lock. One spoon: groms-puff-groms; and the vicious circle narrows. He puts the spoon away in disgust; so long as she lies there dead, the property stands intact. He has tried to go hungry, has lain all gassy in his bedroom cubby without any food for two days, the dining matron plunks herself down, through the door abusive language can be heard in the dead-silent dining hall, the pensioners gulp their soup down quietly and hold their breath. The matron plunks back through the room, sweaty and hot, her face flushed. People stare at her, but she sails heavily on, her buttocks rising and falling. And we know what food will be served the next day: salted meat and beans. All the doors will be allowed to remain open, doors that otherwise are closed (the kitchen is kept closed so our appetites do not increase too much), and the salt meat and bean smell will flow through all the parts of the apartment.

Alone in the room off of the dining hall, tormented by hunger and anguish, Ásmundur will bury his nose and face in the pillow and wage a hopeless struggle with the great banality that is the smell of bean soup. Thinking of the smells, of the steam, something invisible will win him to this great struggle. The body's needs are stronger than a man's temperament: the sound of chewing; water rolling along the tongue. The swollen stomach yells out its motto: food, yuuum, food . . . he sways and sweats and stumbles with a terrible expression from his lair toward the destruction inside: a spoon and a fork and red salt-meat sprinkled with yellow beans. He barges jabbering on (no other sound emanating from his body except stomach growling).

Well, what's this, man. I'm just cooking.

And several square millimeters disappear inside him with the spoonful. And this is why he sits last at the table fighting with his appetite. The same method is being used against me in my apartment.

Tómas, don't you find it awfully tiring, always eating at the refectory? She is crafty, her conversation sly. This great pile shakes from belching.

Are you going to have anything nutritious today Tómas at least get some milk soup inside you.

Ásmundur's mental anguish gives me stomach cramps, even though his anguish is probably only in his head. For days I remain listless. I force myself to pick at the food Anna brings me and leaves on the chair.

you can choose whether you touch it, but refectory food will never be as nourishing as homemade food that castrates the soul, sterilizes it. Anna is simple. An invalid.

yes but good Tómas you settled the rent with us

In front of her swelling stomach she dandles a child in light-blue satin clothes, blue boy with long blond locks that fall over his ears. I do not answer. Dog.

isn't refectory food usually some unhealthy nuisance cursed nuisance why worry about my health

isn't the Board bad for your stomach

she thinks that my rapid trips to the bathroom are due to diarrhea caused by food poisoning no it just feels good to clean one's intestines occasionally for example fortnightly a sedentary person needs to void themselves at intervals

She stands with spread legs in the kitchen doorway as though she is offering herself

in my mousetrap

She thinks. Roving eyes. She sucks on her teeth.

usually people's stomachs weaken and they get cancer from too much refectory food

you are unmarried she thinks when you are all done for the state will own your belongings confiscate them   at least I am involved with you she thinks perhaps I will name my next child after you my tómmas   I think for her many are feeble because some rise to their names and chiefly those who do not marry go to their aunt go to names kiss names   a bachelor so you will inherit his name, baby   I would never get any peace because of this damned name of course you could benefit well from it I think ahead for her who never thinks anything do you not know we are second cousins

I really enjoy Mrs. Helga's food.   excellent, plenty   lots of meat especially burgers and sweet buns for sure do not doubt it

She looks at me approvingly. I picture a certain landscape close to Skeiðarétt and see bleating sheep before me I have enough sheep to think about being close to her and bringing her with me. She will get no inheritance even if she baptizes all her kids Tómas. Now she is preventing me from entering the toilet.

will she desist does she know I stole the castor oil glass of a boy named tómas tómmas in my head and great-great-grandfather his great-grandmother suggested to him once a year that he should clean out his belly and gut

Katrín studies me with her eyes. Katrín's gaze strokes invisible hands around my collar of hair and my bald crown and belly and searches icy fingers down my back. Yes, I always have cold hands. I stand in the hallway rigid, stiff, and stubborn as I face this floral mountain. Her foot sticks in the doorpost. I clamber over her foot. Leave the corridor. Have you nothing better to do than mess with me. With a sweep of her hand she bangs her flat palm on my back so I trip into the room. She laughs snootily.

now go clean yourself up   you've got pinworms

she holds a long squirming tapeworm between her varnished nails it wriggles kicking about and yawns wide.

god, I'm sleepy.

I double lock the door. And with the help of a compact mirror I examine the back of my head in the large mirror. I stand bent over the round seat of the white bath chair. On my head are red blotches. She receives a toxic telepathic message and, exhausted, collapses on the kitchen stool.

I sail into the fjord convex white hills on both sides the sea is white like a sheet at the bottom of the fjord a blank spot   an oil barge heads toward a submarine heading under the mountain and pumps thick crude oil into its tank and reverses out

Katrín sucks on a cigarette in a director's chair. With an innocent expression I open the door. Today the doctor came in and injected me

in the right thigh. It has started to bruise. As soon as he saw the swelling
the doctor said:

Best to rest it.

But his eyes said: never speak directly in the presence of the patient.

You're 79 years old today Tómas and headed toward eighty
I am no older than I want to be.

Nothing to fear, your health insurance will pay.

He injected some burning liquid in my eye, rested one finger on my
pulse, dug his fingertips between my ribs, tapped on my stomach, and
left. After a moment, I lifted everything up and was able to chant:

I sit in the right seat
swing a rock with agile feet
I squirm from joy so itchy
my wool sweater gets stretchy
that is a beautiful song with superb lyrics by Charles Baudelaire

After that rejuvenating song I slid into slumber. I woke up rather chip-
per. I stretched for my composition book and was able to write: Katrín
lets the house go south. Rubbish is scattered about the floor. Dóri swims
in the trash. She bends down and scratches her kneecap. She stretches
out her right leg and examines her red toenails. She looks carefully at
her feet, fetches warm water in a pail, slips her feet into the water, flexes
her toes in the water, and smokes three cigarettes, listening to the radio.
She puts on deodorant. And then she thinks about how *she* could make
some additional household income without the municipal taxman coming along.

Examined in depth, I regard myself as a very dangerous casanova. I live
a double life, visible and invisible.

An office worker in the XII. pay grade doing harm at night.
I can see the newspaper headlines
The wife of a senior official accuses a detective.

The indicted, Tómas Jónsson, denies the charges.
no I will confess it all and let the State feed me in prison
for a few months
Woman Blames Man for Flirting with Her in Public.
Importunity on the Streets Constantly on the Rise.
*Woman in Seat Number Fifteen at Concert at the University
Cinema Alleges Sexual Assault During Performance of Béla
Bartók's Sonate Pour Deux Pianos Et Percussions.*
*Government Employee in XII. Pay Grade Throws Blood Sau-
sage into Double-Paned Windows of Apartment after Sexual
Quarrel with Women at Þorrablót Winter Festival in the
Boatshed.*
Are Sexual Matters Taking Over from Politics in Public Places.

This would be a worthy subject matter for the Charles
Baudelaire of iceland.

Rvík 27/2 1968.
In an exclusive interview with the newspaper the couple said they had
not gone to bed for private reasons. All the lights were turned on in the
house. The outside light blazed and also the decorative pairs of lights on
the trees in the garden.

We were not situated in the floral living room, nor in the corner
room, rather we were sitting in the hall when, without warning, broken
glass rained down on the carpet, and a blood sausage smacked on the
piano . . . hehe. Who would believe it in the office, *me* in a newspaper
headline.

THE MAN IN THE SHOE COVERS
KEEPS APPEARING

The man, dubbed The Man in Shoe Covers, made an appearance last
night about eleven o'clock. This time, he disturbed the home of residents
at Skálabraut 2 here in town. The facts are these: Jónína Pálsdóttir, a

housewife at Skálabraut 2 who is well known for her vigilance pertaining to the treatment of the insane, which she learned about in England, was sitting inside with her husband in their quiet home, having an icelandic dinner. On the table was Chicken in a Basket, which is currently the popular entrée at The Boathouse; the couple had brought it home about nine o'clock.

We eat late on Saturday evenings, said the lady, and pitch dark; we rarely eat out, but instead get takeout.

They had barely settled down when there was a ring.

I said, innocently enough: Magnús, would you see who it is.

But Sigurlaug herself went to the door. "I'll play host," as she put it.

Hardly had Sóldís Paul opened the door when a man in shoe covers forced his way in and

snatched the chicken from the warming tray.

I was not scared witless; I just gaped. The feathered chicken in the shoe-cover man's hands as he wolfed it down. I practically heard its wings flap in the thief's stomach. I did not utter a word, so we just stood listening to Hugo Wolf. As surprised as I was, I immediately knew the man was insane. What should one do in such cases? The man was yelling. But when it became clear he wasn't leaving, having gnawed the chicken bones and scattered them all over the floor, my husband seized on the idea, as a last resort, of throwing a woolen blanket over him, like you do with fire, but that failed. What do you make of this, dear readers: the man pulled a gray cat (Títa) from under his coat and threw him by the hind legs at Valbirn. I expelled a half-choked cry as the cat landed on his face and hung to his eyelids with its claws. I asked god to help me, the eyelids torn, and I saw my husband looking with confused round eyes at the chandeliers. Then the visitor showed me an abomination unfit to have in one's thoughts, never mind to print in a newspaper.

Go away, I yelled—just think, all this with Hugo Wolf on the gramophone—you sodomite. I was bewildered. I grabbed the pot with the newly-bloomed month rose in it and threatened him. Oh jesus, go away, god do this for me, go. You cannot defile yourself in front of a married woman. I ran out into the garden, ran three times around the house, overcome with nerves. The eyes of the stars were sparkling. And when I finally stumbled back to the door and flew over the threshold inside the house, I said to myself: I shall never forget this, as long as I live. All my senses were disconcerted. The visitor was wearing black shoe covers. Pirelli. I trembled like a sapling in my black evening dress and my husband took me by the shoulders and said, Pull yourself together, woman. This has come from the innermost places of your mind. I took three Valiums and drank some hot water. I saw the chicken untouched on the table freshly roasted in its feathers. My husband made me a hot water bottle and I took a nap. In the dream I composed psychological, bodily poetry:

the rain pounds the window

the rain is a key to observing

from the gutter a waterfall

on the roof a small chimney

And if this is not a nervous breakdown, then I do not understand the concept of psychosis as it is everywhere discussed and how people always say, "Yes, I think he suffered a nervous breakdown?" From that time, I have been under medical supervision. My eyes go in different directions. Do I have psychotic visions like the painter El Greco?

The case is under examination by the police detective force. Those who might have been close to the house at Skálabraut 22 about nine o'clock yesterday are kindly asked to identify themselves to the police. Miss Gerður is suffering from a severe nervous breakdown. Her mental state is almost at the null point.

Tómas Jónsson.

this is the eleventh book

(. . . and what follows is written [happened] without any purpose [what matter whether the act or event involves a purpose so long as he or she happened; *that* something happens is of the greatest importance] and the text and material are composed from three different manuscripts; in particular, one marked III., which is obviously the last composed, was used as a source . . .)

Upon completion of the adventure in house number *22*, Tómas Jónsson was exhausted and deprived of oxygen, talking to himself and dozing in his thoughts: When will this mania of mine stop I who have come so far past the age limit it allows I should be burned-out my nervous system quiet in the body lie lifeless think not anything no stirring only rest why should T. Tasso have written La Gerusalemme Conquistata   barely in the air

I rise and walk a short distance from the house. I head across the street. At the end is a small and attractive square. Raised Square (just think of X-square; yet not the one Marguerite Duras wrote of. I think she was not a good woman by nature, quite the snob). Everything comes naturally to my perception and moves slowly.

waiting out a shower
a small square wet from a rain shower

some old men actually a few months old feeling whole agile and quiv-
ering have broadsheet newspapers underneath themselves and sit on
the benches around the oval-shaped square spring has come   chil-
dren jump and play in the sunshine   the sunshine jumps in the
children   the sunshine and children jump over the yellow skipping
rope   girls stop playing ball in the hallway   never again
hear the sound dumbt *of a sponge ball on the stone wall the girls*
jump by turns over the rope when it reaches the ground in its swing a
cathedral clock strikes (a square must have a striking clock) the heart
of the world strikes three blows that sound and stop over the square
today it is Saturday today is not Saturday today I consider Sunday the
surroundings an atrium natural light visible yellow and red blue and
a woman moves quietly across the square on two legs one in front and
one behind she holds a laundry basket in one hand and a scrubbing
brush in the other Tómas does not recognize her face (I can see the
woman is Miss Gerður I know she is Lóa)
Gerður-Lóa:

> *now the blessed spring has come and girls skip outside in the sun-*
> *shine   the girls are dressed in white gathered dresses which*
> *swing while they run as dresses do on lively girls but not like wings*
> *they carry green ribbons knotted around their hair on their necks*

girls:

> *jump over and out and again and in to the new*

Gerður-Lóa:

> *skip up and in to the new*
> *they jump and arrange themselves in a line behind the back of the*
> *girls swinging the rope waiting their turn again so they can jump*
> *they jump from either the right or left right or left by foot they*
> *jump they skip in white dresses and*

spring:

> *skip skip up skip spring skip to spring*
> *joy shows itself in a very slender cruel scream*

Gerður-Lóa:

hahaha all girls brought up today are awful
girl:
  you lose
little girl:
  I'm next
girl:
  no
little girl:
  I always have to turn but never get to jump
girls:
  yeah now it's starting to rain   run for cover from the downpour
  Tómas looks at the cloud bank gradually moving past the chimneys
  and speeding toward the square the bank sails low travels far
  across the sky not like an off-white column of steam from the
  muzzle of a horse and it swallows the sun not the straightforward
  smoke from a chimney the city cats do not wear clouds the city
  does not open its mouth to the rain the square drinks no raindrops
  like a thirsty dog the din increases   and runs   and rattles
  the handle of the laundry basket heavy rain strikes it constantly
  increasing with heavier murmurs I am going to get up and lock
  the window but I rest exhausted in the heavy murmur of the rain
  it cascades over the house roofs like five hundred thousand million
  soft sponge balls
Gerður-Lóa:
  we might possibly escape
voice:
  Tómas, this is spring rain
Lóa-Gerður:
  here is candy for you girls are awful terrors in groups not so sweet
  today
girl:
  since Saturday
    yes today is Saturday and teenagers drinking beer

girl:

    if you drink coca cola then you don't rust inside dad says he gets
    rust from the working women in their cars with coca cola
    the coca cola queen cries coca cola tears (big mistake) but the wind
    cries rain tears and Tómmas cries the tears of Tómas Jónsson

Lóa (who is no longer Gerður):

    doesn't that little strumpet want candy

girl:

    she gets mixed up a little and never really dares accept the general
    laughter among the girls in the hallway the rain sound increases
    now it fills the whole world I know this is Miss Gerður Tómas does
    not see her face covered by the dark scarf

girl:

    her mom has forbidden her from accepting candy from strangers

Lóa:

    that so

girl:

    yes

Lóa:

    why

girl:

    gimme candy

Lóa:

    there won't be enough for you all if he changes his mind I only
    have five pieces she will receive him later
    Tómas knows that Miss Gerður snuck the menthol candy in his
    desk drawer he freshens his mouth so she never offers him another
    then I know that is Dísa

girls:

    give it to me
    no, me

Lóa:

    this one runs here and still gets wet to the flesh

girl:

> he is her boyfriend
> I see through this strange glass she points a finger at coquettish girls
> who are becoming adults and stroll with their fiancés almost every
> night to the movie theater to see breathtaking American block-
> busters and to be enchanted and to cry with sympathy for the star
> Joan Crawford (I do not love the set of her mouth) who did not
> discover fortune and love in riches and palaces but who killed the
> man and committed suicide the public's favorite entertainment
> is to cry over love tricks and the drinking of tycoons (she is also
> not expensive) laundry women and harbor workers understand so
> very well a sorrowful princess on a throne of chickens gaping with
> wonder over the stupidity of men in the windows of the moon the
> pepsi-cola king Lot lay with his coca cola pussy in the first book
> of Moses and they had cola-pepsi kids who ought to fill the earth
> like sand does a beach (this is of course drivel of the worst kind)

Tómas:

> Puff what pouring rain I'm dripping

Gerður:

> Squeeze yourself further into the shelter, man

Tómas:

> I have an errand in the house opposite I am hardly drenched
> though I ran this distance across the street

Gerður:

> get away from the showers do not let yourself be seen in public the
> first few days after the event it is best to seem quiet I know she
> wants us to have a ball game

Dísa:

> except with a bouquet of flowers for his girlfriend that is totally
> fine for you Tómas instead a wet bouquet of yellow flowers chol-
> era-sick flowers which I do not recognize dandelions or buttercups
> he knows no other species of flower except those which poison sleep

Tómas:
    what else
Dísa:
    one should never say what else rather else what nothing
Gerður:
    else what except nothing it pours down on us some more
Tómas
    I would compare it to what gets poured from a bucket
Gerður:
    this is a good description it exactly describes this rain   it is
    a bucket shower
    Gerður poured a white milk bucket over Dísa's head and wretched
    Dísa cannot talk a hollow noise sounds within the bucket her
    mouth is full of broken glass she attempts to talk
Dísa:
    you choked me you are no person
    with quick gestures Gerður sketches a mouth nose and eyes on the
    bucket with black chalk
Gerður:
    Now you can breathe see and talk from behind your blinking
    blinkered milk bucket eyes
    Tómmas won't venture out into the rain though the house rises
    there its roof the most kissable lips
Tómas:
    like a cloudburst from the looser breasts of women (sings)
        Sunday in London
    (their song they learned in English correspondence)
    bloodshot eyes complaining the scab of morning
    while the pub's decrepit personnel wash the sidewalk
    all the buildings in the streets have shut their windows
    the streets are unconscious from noon onward
    Sundays here are notdays

if you were a lion would you be able to saunter to the zoo
spend the day in brothel in Soho shouting
drinking beer at a pub washing yourself in the sky's soot
used to icelandic whores, women who keep you in dough
you examine two-thousand-year-old churches and castles
a beggar and London at night
NO. No.

always there is no summer vacation here no Sundays nothing
except Mondays and knowing breastless women

Dísa:

the rain is the grass's mothermilk and cordial for herbs and beloved
to farmers who hang from cow udders

Gerður:

not the rain that falls here on the gelded grass of the city
I remember the farmhouse room at home
I remember christmas when christmas was holy and Christian and
everyone got a tallow candle at christmas and you were blessed in
the true faith of god and the country with lambs it was wonderful
to sit in the spring I recognized every mark on the sheep in three
counties and the trail of the old river in the snow and the mud
flats I loved my country autumn evening sun trails and lifeless
winter sky
frost blue.

Dísa:

perhaps the rain is good for the grass in the street areas

Tómas:

undoubtedly but the grass it does not mind
it just grows outdoors in nature under the sun
here we are not in the country with fields cowsheds healthy air
and windmills once they arrive

Gerður:

the beauty of flowers travels farthest in autumn

Tómas (thinks):

> *pointless small talk is worthless good for nothing makes me uneasy*

Dísa:

> *are you from the country Gerður*

Gerður:

> *yes I come from the blessed country*

Dísa:

> *Flowers are their most beautiful in autumn if autumn comes so*
> *long as I am also from the countryside*

The girls sing:

> *Lóa is a corpse from Flóa*
> *she lies buried in a hole-a*
> *the fox has a man*
> *Tómmas is his name*

Tómas:

> *well girlfriend that must be funny hahaha but entertaining clever*
> *Tómas speaks as if he was a little girl I say but clever me is told I*
> *recognize someone Lóa who I rented a room to I do not remember*
> *all that I do not remember*

Gerður-Lóa:

> *Tómas is surprised to find he does not recognize us Dísa*

Dísa:

> *girls do a lot of things for fun*
> *more than teasing old men*
> *they poke sticks in buttercups and dead rats*
> *and say yukyukyuk . . .*

girls:

> *he is her boyfriend Jennier and Jenni she is shy no good can ever*
> *emerge from behind a washing machine her mom says she shall*
> *become a world-famous singer and sing for Hitler and gain formi-*
> *dable praise and money but have no voice Jenni-sister sing Jenni-*
> *sister sing her mother forbade her from drinking cola and getting*

anything good from a man in a basement in the afterhours he is
terrifically boring
a skirtchaser in the basement
Dísa:
  why can't the poor girl accept things
  I seize her mouth and her words creep between my fingers like
  white pinworms
Sister Jenni:
  my teeth are rotten
girls:
  hurhur boo-hoo as if you cannot sing with rotten teeth
  to my relief she has not divulged the secret Tómas swirls a finger
  around his palm she stands by the window and plays with balls
  she has a ball game on the pane the pane rattles loose and broken
  glass rains down over us cold icepicks green and yellow balls like a
  falsehood on Dísa's lips dancing on the pane
Dísa:
  I set eyes on her in which window is she standing Tómas
                 in the third to the left on the second floor
  now she must be following me Dísa:
             she is an excessive pricktease Tómas
                        perhaps you do not see her
  half under the laundry tub now she stirs the curtain moves the
  washing on the clothesline do you see I am nothing Tómas:
                 you have a veil over your eyes take
  it off
  she hurries back and forth around the stage throwing up her
  hands and shouts: I'm a housewife at home I am a basic woman
  of the earth I am the first woman my hole is a cleft open deep and
  a lonely figure growing bracken and wood cranesbill
Gerður:
  I will not take the veil from my face

Tómas:

> come here, stand by my side you see her it is her birthday today I'm
> going to fetch flowers my flowers
> (*I cannot be silent talk endlessly torrentially days and nights asleep
> and waking my autonomous nervous system is broken and my
> tongue rages constantly in my mouth the words flow from my
> salivary glands I am condemned to live in barren words the doctor
> should put a sound damper on my mouth people cannot sleep in
> this house for the flow of words*)
> come here

Gerður:

> do you think I see the pencil sharpener how much fun it must be
> to sharpen and have a fiancée
> new cloud   new wind   more rain

Tómas:

> Better to have a fiancée and fiancé alternately have you gained
> one

Gerður:

> yes once but I never saw him
> the first lady fights for the cause of a goose-bumped toad in the
> presidential enclosure   citizens and ministers eat chocolate
> from silk bags this is the first time that they do not understand the
> problem which deals with a major poetic melancholy come from
> visitors on the top balcony

Tómas (his voice unchanged):

> he must have been a peculiar fiancé if you never saw him

Gerður:

> he spread a handkerchief over my face do you recognize the story I
> sensed the taste of bark in my mouth a tree grew inside me and I
> baked little blonde sweet pastry girls

Tómas:

> with one of the hidden people

Lóa:

    not hidden he was made of steel

The girl:

    Tómas Tómmas I see your mug one could let things occur sporadi-
    cally Lóa are you married then

Gerður:

    No you could end up with your foot under the car like Ásmundur
    my daughter would be ten in autumn

    Gerður snatches the bottom of the jacket and swings me around by
    the tail as is done in private in henhouses with lazy chickens who
    do not bother to breed so the last egg scatters away from me shiny
    in the sun (what nonsense)

Tómas:

    no cars are visible anywhere along the street

Gerður:

    they came before but they least expect I have no daughter
    the first lady bows to the President and whispers: here this place
    has a deep and dark fate
    the President answers: yes my dear, this is pretty much from too
    much from many much game pieces let that go the costume is good
    and takes exact aim
    lay for me Tómas and I shall hatch   you will see you will not
    regret it

Tómas:

    drove cars over the egg
    the drunk man walks along the middle of the street in the rain the
    police inactive in a shelter under the roof peak and do not care
    even though the man is breaking the traffic regulations and the
    street lamps have red pupils

Gerður:

    probably they are also waiting for the shower to stop
    here's Sigurður

Sigurður:

>*I stroll in the rain's rain because in the middle of the street hello to*
>*you Lóa an ugly washerwoman like my old lady Tómas*

Tómas:

>*do you recognize him Gerður*

Gerður:

>*I recognize everyone who has business along Hafnarstræti drunk*
>*or sober*

Sigurður:

>*like my old lady fie an ugly woman ugly she who hangs by her feet*
>*up in the attic in the house of sleep Tómas*

Tómas:

>*do you think he will attack us*

Lóa:

>*no he will not lay a hand on me he goes past and sees a scar*
>*through the veil let mommy kiss the scar where he hurt himself*
>*buss buss buss Sigurður indeed*

Sigurður:

>*the old lady at the sewing machine and sews me battles with pins*
>*in her mouth like needle-words and at her feet and now the roof*
>*leaks down to the sewing machine under the dripping ceiling*
>*drops penetrate and fall directly into the hatch and the sewing*
>*machine rusts but my old lady does not move from her spot such*
>*wifely squabbles are continual like a leaky roof as Proverbs has it*
>*and falling onto her the drops startle the flesh and frighten the*
>*house she says a rusty machine is my punishment, but if I do not*
>*get a shock from the machine then there is no punishment Tómas*

Tómas:

>*so it goes*

Gerður:

>*no*

Tómas:

>*who then Lóa*

Lóa:

> *I do not know but one morning he came I was kneeling on the*
> *floor on my knees growing hard lichens and green calluses from*
> *washing the floor and wiping the table legs at the door I heard*
> *a rustle I did not look around but sat on my heels because I*
> *knew that I would be raped this time no dragging he lumped me*
> *behind the counter threw a handkerchief over my face and lay*
> *on me like a bag there between the mail basket and the radiator*
> *I never let go of the washing cloth after he went and I lay still*
> *for a long time finally I rose to my elbows the handkerchief fell*
> *down from me onto my shoulder I went out shortly after Gerður*
> *came and said keep the cloth as evidence yes he forgot it and a*
> *child inside me and I was going to keep both in me I shall keep*
> *the child and see if it resembles any of a number in the office as*
> *it ages*

Gerður:

> *I have a fresh memory of the smell from the cloth I can indeed*
> *recognize people by smell Tómas*

Tómas:

> *you could easily have pursued him with the two folded pieces of*
> *evidence in hand Lóa*

Lóa:

> *who is going to care what brews and ferments in my belly for weeks*
> *and how in nine months I get no child support I imagine him*
> *descending from a foreign ship in my mind I picture him coming*
> *back to search for his lost blood (where is my pure, lost blood) and*
> *find me grown into the floor where the dreams stop always a series*
> *of identical images however I turn my mind   public life in*
> *bygone days   said the prime minister   now no one needs to*
> *experience it men just read stories and watch films no one needs*
> *to live anything any longer for everything can be seen in films just*
> *watch enough often a kind of torture device for the eyes*
> *the horse struck me in the face and my father let the riding horse*

beat its hoof flat in my face because I was grumpy from holding
the reins while he went somewhere and that's where the scar came
from it is hardly possible
nothing is noticeable through the blue veil
but in the cold it becomes a bluish bruise like a dead birthmark
and broken teeth and snot frozen in an open nostril
I could bend down to my beloved with the tender blue scar and
mutilated teeth
do you eat hákarl in the States
she did not die
my daughter
she was in a white dress with her eyes gone strange
Sigurður:
well now it is raining from the sun
Tómas:
that one is drunk like it ever rains from the sun
Gerður:
most likely it rains from the sun as the sun shines through the rain
on the grass
metal sounds
now shining pearls rain down
angels in a Grimm fairy tale break the leaves from the savings
bank's trees in heaven
the shower sails on
now the sun goes gray from rain
would you listen to the conclusion:
away from the rain loitering under cover of the box and taking
shelter against the torrent wind
I wept
do not stand there child without protection and she ran over to my
car humming along the street
and when he disappeared some mush hung among his cervical
vertebrae

she ran away on both feet to pull up a few buttercups
they lay crushed in some story or other in the paint on the sidewalk
I disregarded them
the wind blew her dress over her face
I pray that she escaped across the street
she claims to have been detained I continue to try to meet with
him
this daughter of mine is a horse
he sees her in the angel's place grazing in the pasture
she both grows and matures the daily bread has a good kernel
men have to have horses and mares
she learned to sing and play the horse piano
nor could I give her all the world's comfort I long for her to return
to me through the fence but she needs extra time with him, she
will come back the same way she left he says initially he kneads
me some specially prepared dough when the dough sours she will
be reincarnated to me he will bring her to me again he says: your
belly is not scales fishskin tongue you have no cat tongue inside so
we sing:
him: do you know how to bake bread
I: yes I know how
him: so you can make cake
I: yes I know how
him: are you quite sure
I: yes I am
him: or maybe you are just tricking me
and then he says you must bake sweet pastry boys in the oven and
I tremble and stand baking day out and day in but nothing bakes
aren't you trying
Miss Gerður expels a splitting cry that ends in a mothersick laugh-
ter and a coughing fit
Gerður:
jeez I do not have the words

Lóa:

> *I am not filthy there's no dirt between my toes only this scar repul-*
> *sive who wants to put their lips up to the color of a dead lung*
> *except through a handkerchief or in the dark maybe not even*
> *once after a few years will my belly become a sarcophagus I know*
> *cases in which the woman carries a stillborn baby in her belly*
> *until she rots from inside out some do not care that they decay but*
> *after death there's no flesh and where there's no there's nothing but*
> *houses and manmade structures and they are uninhabitable even*
> *a sense of loss without flesh*
> *sounds of rain   the rain flows*
> *as if that transparent wall never were*
> *but the sidewalks cast their drops upward   carbuzz*
> *er þetta a metaplay*
> *yes answered the dramturge*
> *I just hope he does not fall down groundless*
> *like the weather in spring the summer does not come before August*
> *usually*
> *the so-called life of this man rises off him like rain he loiters and*
> *looks for shelter in the doorways and prays for it to be short*
> *still drops fall the sun dries them if she can see*
> *come in*
> *the city a white sheen between sun and rain*
> *Lóa spreads the handkerchief Ásmundur goes to the food table*
> *wearing black gloves on the handkerchief is marked in large letters*
> *T J with marker ink*
> *no it's not me either Sigurður or Bjössi but not me*
> *over the cloudless sky god drags the angels by the hair they have*
> *strewn golden coins on the floor over the earth Grimm fairy tales*
> *and gaseous clouds cats hiss in anger at the moon's windows*
> *(Where is my lost blood, I cannot find that which I will never*
> *find again)*
> > *wake*

cautiously I release the sleep from my eyes I lie crushed under the heavy
death of sleep and dreams something heavy but warm lies on my chest
and inhibits my breathing I need to pee badly I lie on my back a considerable time with closed eyes I do not move to the left but am lying dead
straight in the direction of the North Pole for the sake of my well-being
given this presence lying on me a pet daring hardly to stir crippled limbs
fearing to upset the pleasure the very short bliss after the nightmare after
I suddenly wake up Títa has crawled into the covers and lies in my dry
body sweat inside the armpit and breathes the rat odor from me inside
the twilight day has tilted the window is open to the sidewalk my face
dirty with sweat it has not rained or frozen I startle a cold shiver I have
slept it is good to sleep I rise to my feet it is good to stand on one's feet I
close the window carefully I belch belching is good I open the door into
the hall and grab Títa's tail I hesitate a moment sometimes in life it is
good to hesitate and then make a decision what difference affection and
cruelty I sling the cat with all my strength against the wall but he does
not disintegrate no he does not fall like rainwater to the floor but spins
in the air and the cat's asshole lands on the phone he shakes himself and
trots into the corridor dreams hide subtle accusations and they charge
me with foolish lies shame and judgment all parts of a man are vulnerable while he sleeps I piss nothing is as good as getting to piss in peace
and quiet when you are bursting it is good to have an empty bladder
awesomely comfortable I wish I could fart then I would be very happy
O it is so good to be just a moment in time the course of the blood that
I lost long before now

my 12ᵗʰ composition book

Miss Gerður's story about the cleaning lady is trivial nonsense. I had no idea she had a daughter. As a stay against the insidious whispers about me it would be wiser to place the blame on the janitor, who gets to control who walks around the house. To me it is irrelevant whether Lóa attended a séance. So too almost every man after god is no longer interested in a relationship. I may not be confused about events. I need to separate waking and dreaming events. But via this means she meets her girl and the medium calls it a reunion. At Gerður's initiative, there are office whip-rounds to cover the cost of private sessions with the medium for the washerwoman. The sessions are a kind of visiting hours at the maternity ward. The medium dandles the child and shows it to her against the glass. She will be sitting on a chair inside a large sealed cardboard box and looking through a round hole, sweaty from the heat and nearly choking from lack of air; then he lets her crawl out the box onto the divan, while he covers her in a plastic bag and ties it about her neck. It is not enough that the medium lets her go through this get up: we have to pay him to put her in a bag. No, I will not, Sigurður says. I tell you, I have often played the medium, for good money, for example for a recently deceased service woman here in Reykjavík—of course I reincarnated her. A good job, well compensated. At the time it was my only work and so one where I did not need to squabble to get paid. You did not need to go on strike; indeed, it would have been difficult for the medium to have to explain to the woman: you know, the deceased, she's gone on strike. I reincarnated at least three times a week, according to demand and how fit I felt. Specifically designated days, Saturdays, Tuesdays, and Thursdays. Thus employed, I made the remarkable discovery that it is rare for Reykjavíkers to have sex more than three times a week. We in the reincarnation business came to understand more than the average man. I will never forget a confident woman lying above her divan under a red lamp, which hung from a long cord over her belly button dangling back and forth. When I stripped to my underwear well lubricated she rose halfway up and waved to me with a handkerchief tied around her right index finger. To conceal themselves they usually had a sweat-cloth over their face and I remember how he sucked at it when they gasped. I'm sure no one has been able to reincarnate as thoroughly as I: no woman ever complained. I want to tell other men about this possibility, reincarnation; for little effort they can get some extra money . . . hearing this, Bjössi grew uneasy on his chair. I know, my Bjössi, you have for years played a cathedral priest who in the prime of life death took from his congregation, a congregation he keeps together still, now he is silent. Bjössi turned to the rest of us and I continued, saying: When his wife asked the medium how it was that the cleric grew in number each year, he said: In the realm of the dead, men age and fade and their apathy toward sex increases just as here on earth. There, asexuality is a sign of virtue. After this I reincarnated as a cathedral priest and never went to mass. Sigurður laughs his drunkard's guffaw all over the blue coffeepot on the table, as pleased as the residents of this town with his jokes. They know this is nonsense *humor*. They are always jabbering *humor* like he is the salvation, a lifebuoy for people drowning along the path.

Lóa must have dragged Miss Gerður into the toilet, weeping and trusting *her alone* with the secret. They blocked up the bathroom with their whispering, running the water continually so they could not be overheard, and if the frantic beating on the door reached them only said *just a moment* so other women had to use the men's toilet and be on guard two at a time until Sigurður thought to take a chair with him and stand on it and peek over one of the cubicles and stand there until both were driven off cursing at him for his cheek, what exactly did he mean by this. The dining hall on the corner of X- and Y-street was watched attentively by everyone concerned, because it is as fixed as death, the way they walk back and forth on toilet trips and run the water, whispering and taking collections. Yes, he gives her hope. The medium can give her a wishing well of hope, but she cannot live on hope, no one lives on anything but his earnings. I will not dispose her assets. I do not contribute even my loose change to this widow's fund so she can have more time with the medium and be serviced by reincarnation via Sigurður, a wino. And I do not care whether Ólaf would say that the deception brings her happiness so why shouldn't she purchase it. Yesterday we discussed the agonized mother of the tiny, deceased creature who caught cold. This cleaning woman follows me, and I know what she wants. I see how she lies on her knees on the bag and divides the floor into eighteen equal tiles, wet, soaped, semi-dry, drying, and then she moves on her knees with great dexterity between the squares on the bag over the slick floor and her feet move behind her like a propeller, she strikes her toes on galosh's sole on the floor and she whistles like a compressed air machine with her dust cloth. When she goes under our desk she tells a story for you to listen to so there's no suspicion you are simply loafing. Who would value the joy of heaven if the dead catch cold there. Of cold, we have enough this side of the grave. I've been sorely sick with sinus colds for more than two weeks. Pitiful woman. Miss Gerður sighs. Somehow I find her icy. Ólaf narrows his eyes at Bjössi. But lust and darkness do not demand beauty, Ólafur says, nonchalantly. Bjössi seizes the irony and asks: And you have experience. We kick against the floor and raise hell, all except Ásmundur. Despite her ugliness I have bedded her in my dreams, examining my monogram marked with red thread on the handkerchief. Dreams are defamatory. A sea spray of dreams blows over a man and in them women sail like weighted ships. They stalk you, unbidden. Dreams fetch the world its blame. Not me. In this matter I have a clean record. But why is the housecleaning lady called Tóta in my sleep. Is it because I once wrote a poem about a Tóta. A person is rarely safe in his sleep.

Tóta

O if I should come back to visit you in your sleep[i] the
way you floated around naked in my dream one day
Lóa

[i] I am hindered from getting free of the flesh's shackles
its bone marrow and life blood bound & deemed to
lie as cold dreams which one dreams back endlessly
to oneself

O if I should come back to visit you in dreams
visit you in wet and sorrowing dream

book 13

i pluck the garments from my body   i fold my pants across a
hanger, carefully creased
in twilight
i put socks on the chair their tops turned down hanging off the chair's
edge
i tremble slightly with emotion
i do not know why i tremble undressing is pleasant
it is, however, unpleasant to be standing in the middle of the floor stark
naked without clothes or just for example wearing a single sock
or one shoe
still evening has not come
today a beautiful thought occurred to me
o days that never come to night
they come those nightless days
some days pass by without those alive coming across anything that can
be considered beautiful sometimes weeks pass sometimes months or an
entire year
then you die
after having caressed and cursed   loved   feared and turned all your
actions around death
to alleviate it
to alleviate man
i shall go to bed

i grasp the medicine bottle
now it is late night
tonight i will not enter the same sleep
that happens to those who lie down and doze at lunchtime
when should i get this coveted power over myself   i am a long time past
the age when an ordinary man has acquired power over himself (in this
i resemble the people stuck forever in puberty) so sighs relieved   my
wait little more than setting up a feeding trough
reaching the age when a person should be asexual and possesses unwavering calm and self-certainty asexuality brings   no need to seek out
anything from anyone
my blood will run still and silent through its channels
this morning I met in the street a young girl with a round mouth red
and flourishing
which she pursed like a delicate asshole
then that rose-red hole opened and four teeth appeared
connected to a sick heart
the left side of the chest under the dome of the ribs
in one apartment in a house in Reykjavík in iceland
which pushes atop the world's body
there cowers this shriveled meat as if it had been bought at an antique
sale and hurled on the bones with a trowel
the invalid nation in a tub
i lie wide awake
powerfully i search yelling for sleep
my mind wanders about sacred and sluggish like a cow in Bombay
where the passage of days
god allows me to look at the next day's light
probably i will never terminate the agreement only masturbate to the
thought
self-pleasure to the plan
i trace my life back to ancient Norwegian kings
i lie awake at night

bedridden sweating clammy like a new body
though i shut myself up in death which comes to everyone though I
want to be free and independent of anything and everything and also
death
in this abominable approach of death and pleasure
of the fatherland

fourteen

Today I have been rummaging in old newspaper trash. I have whiled away time cutting out from the papers everything that somehow surprises or interests me.   everything is natural   most clippings discuss the natural *bizarrities* of life, the world we live in. Here we are of course discussing an issue closely linked to my nature and my pastime, my collecting urge. These sixty-two years I have lived (today the doctor said it was only forty, but his views regarding my age are irrelevant to me. I am of the turn of the century generation. I have decided so. I'm that great generation. One is what he decides he is). I collect not only money but also other valuables that daily surround me: word-of-mouth stories, legends, lists of film screenings, buttons. I have in my possession probably about fifteen hundred kinds of button. And yes I collect memories, too. The total collection of each generation is extremely diverse. She (my generation) has come to use for example countless pencil types and colors that are unpleasant; colors are another topic entirely. I give to my field in that I never make lists of people's political opinions or sexual conduct; the embassy sees to such recording, and has a number of people in its service. Because of national enmity and the nation's centuries-long isolation as a land people insist on every kind of research and report-making, not just about tooth decay and ulcers, which foreign universities have studied in recent years, but much more. This likely stems from the situation of the country, which will be of ultimate importance in the forthcoming atomic war.

Sometime long after World War II (the date is missing. I'm going to say that today I feel exceptionally good. It is easy for me to explain events in a very entertaining and simple manner and I have thought and planned everything I'm going to commit to paper here) there was a dig for a few new houses in the city of Warsaw, which is almost in the center of Poland, as many know, when the teeth of the excavator (what some call a crab) broke through the concrete shell and fell down into one of the many cellars buried under the ruins of the city. No one knew that there was a bomb shelter, since all the public records were destroyed in a fire in early 1943. In the fall the excavator broke the brick wall and revealed a deep pit under it. The men working the job thought nothing of this at first; their over-arching plan was too prominent in their minds, a bold course to resurrect a wasted city from the ruins into new life under the red fluttering silk flags that rose so vividly from the rubble still fresh before people's eyes. Soon they become aware of movement in the ruins and see to their surprise a long-haired creature, man or woman, resembling those humans the infamous Soviet artist, Gerasimov, rendered so wonderfully at this time in his work reflecting a historical Marxist perspective. The creature came, or so it seemed, out of the ground and attacked with an inhuman scream the excavator and the city of flags there in the vicinity. When it had taken several steps in daylight and sunlight it grasped fumbling about its face, staggering uncertainly about the uneven ground, kicking up dust and stones with its feet; it ran into a flag pole and fell down exhausted on the brick pile. The men thought they were hallucinating, but still immediately got down from the cab of the excavator and carefully approached the creature that was howling loudly on the brick bed. They were afraid to touch it with bare hands for fear she would be radioactive—this was exactly when strontium fear was emerging—so instead they poked sticks at it. One of the men went back up into the cab and moved the lift to the creature then the other pushed her so the bucket's teeth spread around her middle. Then the red brick bed and all was lifted as high as a man off the ground and dangled in the air against the pale-blue Warsaw sky while the men considered the situation and examined the creature by telescope. Many things came to light in the convex lenses, particularly concerning the crown of creation: the screaming and crying amounted to something that resembled a singing voice or an incomprehensible language. In the telescope one could have seen, dangling two feet down from the bucket, a spewing head and two arms swaying in the air, seeking a grip. The men screamed:

The devil take it, this is a demon.

And the demon was observed by the most talented professors and linguistic experts at the University of Warsaw, many of them maimed, some with one eye, and approximately 30% of them construction craftsmen. That badly they had fared in the war. Now they were summoned to the scene, to the ruins of the Jewish neighborhood, and wielding crutches and artificial limbs they addressed the creature methodically, each in the language of his expertise, even in Esperanto, the language of the future, as it occurred to the scientists that here had arrived, according to plan, the long-awaited man of the future which the socialist system anticipated according to Marxist teaching. And so nothing was more self-evident than that he had sprung from Polish ground like new potatoes, since all Poles trace themselves back to pure potato farmers. Now the Here And Now had arrived; no going back. What was more natural than that after a bloody war the ground had recovered. She had become as fertile as before or in a way more fertile since many had gone into her as a source. Yet everything came to nothing and amounted to absolute nonsense until the professors thought to simply address the creature in Polish. The bystanders shouted:

Long live our native land, Poland. Long live scientific Marxism and the knowledge that Polish is not a Slavic language but a mid-European tongue. Long live the collective leadership of this country. Down with mousehole perspectives toward agriculture. Head in a nonsense direction to peace and carry out the impractical.

To this cry came an answer from inside the flag, a smattering of Polish:

Is the war over. Long live Poland.

Once the shapeless mass lay on the ground again they dove over the subject, stained with feces and urine, crying and hugging and kissing and fighting like flies over cow shit. Folk dances broke out, summoned from the city. And while they jumped around in leather boots dancing and braids swaying in the air with healthy faces full of the energy of youth and ignorance, the newly-formed Youth Wing of the Socialist Reconstruction across five boroughs listening to the terrible story of the living creature which turned out to be a man, how he and his wife and five men had gotten trapped in the shelter and stayed there buried alive all through the war. These people of Judah, families who had somehow managed to accumulate sufficient reserves and hide from the German Nazi genocide, which loved cleanliness and Beauty but hated everything ugly and distorted, dirty Judah, and pornography. How can you be what is called anti-Nazi if you love beauty, who else but these good people have tried to work to clean the world of ugliness. How can it be ugly to want to abolish anything ugly and criminal and to desire to abolish crime. Nazism was a longing for Beauty. And it was a point of consideration that the people had had enough food reserves for two years' dwelling there. Up above, there were complaints meanwhile that scarcely half of humanity had the bare essentials you should expect in an affluent country, at the most food in the fridge for a week. Not many of them could lie about in laziness and sloth, as the man later described it, a burden of taxes and duties, damn it, worse than the life available in a cellar. The food there was chiefly canned food, as is to be expected, but they had some smoked pork left. How did these people come by food during their years of hunger and deprivation (which perhaps was, when all is said and done, not as terrible as is often claimed); there was no explanation. But an old icelandic proverb speaks to this: during a fight, no one is your brother. This is all the more true when the struggle is for vital sustenance. Even innocent animals fight over bread crumbs.   I laugh at how despicable human nature is.   In this shut-away hiding place, the sarcophagus of hell as the newspapers put it, a woman had had children with each of the men in contravention of the laws of her faith. The youngest child was said to have never seen any kind of light or flickering, just the familiar brightness of a candle stump they eked out and never lit but for ceremonies; they on the other hand remembered the daylight like she was some viscous pulp but they concealed this from the children so they did not get IDEAS since people are healthiest without ideas. When the excavator's jaws broke the wall and light flooded in and clattered through their cherished silence and peace, harmonious, reconciled, then ideas became connected like doors that had long had stuck locks: They saw the light, heard the sound and rushed around, wandering momentarily out of their senses from joy in their wax clothes and falling, blind as posts, about the dust of the ruins. The youngest children displayed that tranquility that mistrust and the total absence of thought in the brain provides. The dark mass in their heads had never experienced anything like it, and that saved them from blindness. In the hiding place they screamed, terrified, and refused to obey the head peeking down at them, shouting:

You are free. Come up.

They loved their dark hole, feared the dancing, the dance, bright braids of almond oil, floral raw-silk dresses, and high leather boots, but most of all their fear was aroused by the flowers that grew on the edges of their hole, sending out a faint aroma. They felt this as a stench, as frenzy and rage. For three days they defended any attempts to entice them out. They used firearms their parents had taught them to handle in the dark. Without a gun, a man is alone and vulnerable. A gun is a man's best friend; that much they knew. In the end, things were made difficult for them and they were driven out with tear gas and caught in cod nets that had been stretched around the opening. Thereafter, they were driven to the organization assigned to bring children up in optimism, life practices, and Marxism. After their re-upbringing they came out full of an enthusiasm they had not previously known. Vocational training took over, the possibility to advance in life. They chose to work in a pit which resembled the place of their youth and was well remunerated.

Now they have all gone to Nova Huta district, to single-family dwellings with gardens where stepmothers, cornflowers, marigolds, and sunflowers grow. Before sunrise they are driven to the mine and after sunset they come home; both take place in the dark. They have this to thank for their sight: that they did not come out of the hole until their retinas had accustomed to the brightness. One permanent sign of their stay is seen in the way they sleep with heads under covers and keep rotting wood beneath their pillows, bringing it to their nose if wakefulness and boredom find them out. With that intolerable smell their home appears in their minds and the boredom dissipates. I'm going to finish this piece with an afterword, perhaps a moral. Everyone knows the following: it is estimated that thousands of people were buried alive in the war and it is not unlikely that people still live in sealed-off basements. Polish literature (with which I have of course had no acquaintance) was heavily influenced by this single incident. Polish poetry and fiction teems with people who lost their vision and their belief in the day, who acquired an animal nature in shelters and began to see with phosphorescent eyes and so to breed and so to thrive and to eat various things among one another in underground burrows of the temperament. These folk must have established a full society with its own rules and prohibitions, laws, and religion. For a thousand years this crowd, perhaps, will endure before digging up to the earth's surface to see if there is truth to the legends that people walk on the earth overhead, as creatures unlike these people used to, people who observed another nature, transcendental like in the stories of the ancestors. After a thousand years we will reach the hidden people in the stories, the mind's embryos, in the same way as the hidden people were the mind's embryos, the brainchildren, of our grandfather and grandmother. Or, as a philosopher said, we are all god's brainchildren. From all this, but especially because of the rooted superstition among Polish farmers, any farmer on his way to the beet or potato field will say, when he finds the grass on top of the bed with roots nibbled apart by worms or harmed by animals:

The mole men have been hard at work.

The previously referenced event was a literary windfall. According to Dr. Janos, it saved Polish literature from insipidity and emptiness and gave it momentum and deeper meaning. The transformative re-upbringing of the "people from darkness," as it was named by Polish Marxists, most importantly, the description of how they were to use it to optimize life in the country's mines. (In a way this also saved the mining industry.) Efficiency in the coal mines was a ray of hope at the end of the widely read book *How Coal Was Delivered from Servitude to Nature*, which has been translated into eighteen languages and become popular in the United States, a miracle given how hard it is to enter the American book market. But it is so striking about the Polish national mindset after the war that everything connected to people and labor has been named after underground activities. People in Poland believe, even though the country is the people's republic led by the dictatorship of the proletariat, that under the earth and below people's feet are concealed creatures that suck the essence and strength from the economy so people have barely a zloty between everyone. This popular superstition—or delusion—is used by the government as an explanation for frequent crop failures. Poverty is not their fault, but rather is someone gnawing the roots, something Marxist theory cannot address. I pause a moment: five minutes have gone by while I think up a new disgraceful irresponsibility for man. I, Tómas Jónsson, think: thus humankind can be turned upside down when part of it digs into war living in lightless and closed cavities where it pushes pebbles into its nose and mouth and chokes itself spiritually. It is unforgivable if we persist and give into our bestial impulses and continue to breed down inside a dark sarcophagus. Under the feet of each honest and diligent person, not only Poles but all of us, life is cut from life by a can-lid, the umbilical cord crushed into pieces with a pointed, stone tool bound with a thong. Thus it has been and will ever be. Through my consideration we can obtain evidence that people in hell would continue to breed if it were not contrary to the devil's law. So wise is the devil and so humanitarian that he burns in his kingdom's bath the people god in heaven throws away. The devil does this to prevent overpopulation in his home. (Anyone who kills another person should be condemned to eat the victim in order to stop the devil.) If these five people held back from their animal nature they might have reached a higher stage in the cellar and not been duped out into the day. *That* would have been world news, had they been found after seventy years safe and sound. Could then someone skilled in ditch digging lift the stone from the tomb and rob them of their fame. No. With his offspring his wife dispersed life, shortening one end of the thread but extending the other in order to make the whole thing thrifty as a miser does with himself. With this shrewd high-level explanation *I* vaguely imply, in my own way, that people have never dared kill newborns for fear of the dark. How can a blind man or a man in death's shadow fear the dark. Maybe they see white suns flicker on convex surfaces and slide forward in the dark race of life. Whatever the case, the darkness and interiority they experienced was not any better than if they had lived the whole time on the grassy earth and managed there to establish thirty Polish potato gardens. *I* would never would have rushed blindly into the daylight; I would have calmly allowed my eyes to get used to it and called up into the opening:

Bring me some sunglasses.

Sight made the Polish blind fools. Poles have always been significantly blind.

Sight brings human's eternal darkness, all save a few individuals (influential ones) who refuse the versatile existence of the light that reveals, and who struggle to live on in a dark prison undisturbed knowing in their wit that freedom does not exist except as a delicious propaganda or some prattle about patriotism.

I am forced to say:

There is no great maternal feeling to be found in an invalid woman. Gerður groans and scrapes red nail polish from the thumb of her left hand with the nail of her right index finger. Indifference has been employed there as it has here. The people blinded like moles became aware of the long-awaited: light and sun. They ate with greedy eyes and for their long wait were rewarded with darkness. This is entirely horrible. I must say that the Nazis must have hated the Jews more than excessively if they could behave this way, sighs Miss Gerður. But what is right to believe. I do not know, one may thank his blessings for having been born in iceland. If we had not been born here, who can say that we might not have been born in Poland and have been one of them. No, people here, who have enough money to live, become much more incomprehensible in the world outside. And think of another thing: despite the warnings of doctors, Icelanders continue to smoke, knowing the dangers of smoking, that you can get cancer and coronary heart diseases, which is actually something international. Diseases are international. Man perhaps has nothing in common with other nations except getting sick and dying. For example, a single mother in Madagascar might waste away from the same disease as a woman on Báragata. She was deathly pale but no longer hated me; she had probably got past that stage.

Behave yourself wisely or I will kick the back of your knee, I said.

He limped to Katrín, bent over her, and pulled off her blanket.

Where are her clothes? he said.

She threw her dress behind the couch, I said. It's lying on the floor. He picked up the bra and ripped panties and limped into the living room. He came back with the dress in his hand, put the clothes on her body, and spread the blanket over her again. He did it mechanically like the first time.

How much did she drink? he asked.

She appeared with a half empty bottle and poured it down her throat within half an hour.

Miss Gerður reads in the bathroom.   how terrible if a scientist manages to construct a machine so it becomes possible to see all types of people via a television screen   she thinks and grows thought-ful   she has heard if a man is planning to stop thinking about and loving a girl the best piece of advice is to imagine her sitting endlessly on a toilet bowl with her panties down twisted around her feet   after

Gerður pisses she dries herself with toilet paper and if a man goes to the
bathroom and sees crumpled tissues floating in the water then he knows
who sat there before him   she never flushes   her pants should not
get yellow   she stands bewildered on the floor and holds the string of
her pants   my good god can it be that all men have imagined me sitting here indefinitely on the seat   though I enjoy reading newspapers
sitting there that is an overstatement but something is fishy here   I
am not leaving   horrible just horrible   one can have little faith
in humans while they let blind impulses control them.

If I rack my brains, consider my life path, if I make a detailed comparison of myself and others, yes, I find myself to be a very valuable
pearl. I am frankly the Gemstone of the North. I will never stop being
discriminating. Never . . . I would run myself into the road before I
made a blunder. For example, I would stop drinking wine before I lost
my judgment. I must be a special challenge, a luminous star among dead
planets. One needs to consult others like an energetic man. Certainly I
have never come across anyone like me at the Board in the refectory,
someone who could speak to me as an equal, except perhaps the students
who talk among themselves in silence, through numerical puzzles and
complex chess positions and pay each other for friendship with the correct solution to the riddle over a soup dish or a hand slipped behind a
back . . .

    it is ever more fun to be young and able to be a carefree fool

(I cannot now remember if I said I sat between them.) I do not remember hearing these young generous and studious men discuss any need or
lack of need via words out of their lips. Wavy-haired Gunnar 2 seems
be more engaged than Miss Gerður or Gunnar the Engineer.   what
does Oddný Sen intend by traveling from iceland to Amoy in China is
she going to tip herself now a moment perhaps higher into old age out
of the divan at home   where   overwhelmed by memories from
days of youth gone by or perhaps she places her tortured brow against a
cold water pipe when memories rain over her like Chekhov's characters

do with hoar-frosted tree trunks O nymphes regonflons des SOUVE-
NIRS divers or does she set her palm on her cold breast and open her
mouth speechless from painful memories of this and that I think she is
a mysterious woman   I really have no interest in turning this into a
speech praising myself. But Tómas Jón . . . if you surrender your name
and play with it you become a tome some maize an empty ohm mas
mas = too much on a johnson   son is a unique suffix in a row of
ordinary people's names. I suspect that Sigurður has let a few words slip
out about his respective history.   To spell it out I must maintain
too much icelandic jabbering nonsense on and on until I subside like
an inflatable balloon that has developed a prick of a hole   to me the
much-discussed breath of life in the chest flows from the prick hole of
the mouth and when the thought has gone the torso lies down in the end
on the earth a ruptured balloon dead too much empty no mas deprived
of life   there were many fierce debates about the news at the time. He
(who?) reckoned that in 1942 something similar happened in Hamburg
on the Rhine (Hamburg is not on the Rhine but the Elba, if I remember
right) and Sigurður (that's the name that comes to mind, whether right
or wrong) told a story about (personal names in stories do not change
anything, only the material and exposition) a respectable German who,
during World War II, solicited the love of a prostitute in a basement,
entirely matter of course, then an air strike took place; a British bomb
fell on the roof so the house collapsed down to the basement, and he
lay on top of the girl to protect her from plaster falling from the ceiling
and they were buried alive. The man became terribly afraid, as might be
expected, a married man who didn't come home for dinner (what would
his wife think?). But the girl comforted him and told him not to be
afraid since there were plenty of supplies of canned food, so much that
they could live on them until they were dug out of the ruins, through a
third world war, if it came to that, and they had no need to be anxious,
they had plenty of toys to enjoy, everything that has over the sweep of
history proved most desirable for humans to survive. Her words were not

ridiculous. Being walled in and facing death increased the need to play in these sexually tame people. Undoubtedly both would have delighted in the circumstances indefinitely were it not for the canned food and the lack of condoms, leading to what he most feared, that the tart would get pregnant and bear him a child; he was not about to be blamed for another person being in the cellar. Months passed and they lost any sense of time in the eternal darkness; nothing bothered them but the strong stench of the used condom which they could not wash thoroughly and use again, since there was scant water other than what dripped down the crack when it rained, and then they would say: Chances are, summer is ending warmly. They shut away the odor of feces and urine which they voided from themselves in the clothes chest in the corner. No help was on the way. They cursed the stench where they lay, and the girl could not see anything but starvation unless they resulted to producing their own provisions, which the respectable German refused to accept for fear of the consequences—but she talked to him with German perseverance and worked on him, suggesting the scenario that they bury the bones in the chest coffin. Nine months later she gave birth to a child, which they stretched out as food supply for quite some time, bringing home to him the horror of war, brought close to them in a more disgusting manner than they would have been able to imagine. This was not so much because of the execution but the eating, "since this exceeds the sin of merely killing one's neighbor to live," as the man lamented. The girl cursed his speculations, she thought of it as a need to produce milk and exploit all the possibilities for life. She set the man at her breasts as she had read women did in the days of the Roman Empire, regularly in the morning and evening and at noon (as they did), and he regurgitated the milk to her, not all but every other drink, as it came. And so life persisted in the worst conditions—until a bulldozer cleared the ruins on top of them one day and men in leather jackets set handcuffs on their wrists and accused them of infanticide (the police had begun by examining the chest and found bones, apparently a child).

November 21, 1967, at half past eight in the morning.

Dream.

I sit on a plane listening to the buzz of the engines. On the radio news, a report that hundreds of Loftleiðir planes departed as scheduled late at night with passengers and goods to America the bulk of the aircraft flying to Newfoundland to fetch Danish miners who then stayed a single night in Reykjavík at Hotel Skjaldbreið and ate steak and eggs on white bread I sit in the right plane after a difficult takeoff from a desolate airport where a couple with their daughter loiter alone in the spacious passenger cabin and having ordered breakfast at the same time I dash to break wind within the jet which rages with a vengeance and a devil mood besets the runway with its wolfhounds and its feathered rats I am heading to New York to look into the exchange rate for króna I am paid seven króna per dollar and into the bargain I get a light with perfect electrics a woman in the flight cabin gives up on our bearings she is insane and hairy from crown to soles we then find ourselves on a blind flight over the wilderness of Canada and the woman is totally lost and Western Icelanders goggle up into the clouds and yell to the Loftleiðir aircraft which yawns its mouth and screams back totally schizophrenic I plan to shout at her within this uninsulated machine of mine that we are crossing the ninetieth and first-degree northern latitude but I know being up high there will shortly be a plane accident and we will land jackhammer-crazy in a desolate airport where I see potholes and an ill-lit runway flowing against us a track on a desert island owned by Air France we come into an empty passenger cabin and meet the family I do not want to know these people especially the man who howls in agony on the cabin floor, but the one accompanying me steps inside the blue glow and makes a necessary friendship with the man within iceland's trade relations with other Arab states he catches the man's arm away from an old French porcelain with a blue pattern in the weekly magazine

Time *there is a picture of Kurosawa lying off-frame on a lush field with a knife driven high up in the chest cavity murdered by his fiancée who runs buck-naked outside into the eye of the ocean Kurosawa's hair is rich and thick but without any stubble on his chin the image is blurred like a faxed picture in a newspaper he clutches at himself in spasmodic death cramps in front of the film studio the side is made out of ties instead of trellis and strings are strung between the pillars and the dangling tassels of thick withered grass are not dissimilar from those that barbarians bind around their calves for decoration at a sacred dance I peek into the temple door to watch the lumbering bull walking in a row over the flaming floor within the temple yard which shines with gold dust abnormally bright the bull continues to budge forward over the floor lazy-eyed in this all is infinite perspective and the temple dark and cool rises between me and the bull the decorated lines on a Chinese bowl bodies sick with death sway me from death's power inside the temple I am hurled to and fro in a sacred dance pink lotus flowers pass slowly along the floor and arrange in open rectangles in from the walls in the middle of the floor flowers are arranged by the invisible inviolate virgin hands this is a funeral feast and lotus flowers should trap me under the midtower where I am burnt and my ashes thrown into the mouths of the flowers I value the noisy eating their lips grabbing me in anguish I dance and am hurled about the floor in violent clashes with death with upheavals that splash putrefied flesh in my face like a foul water of bones I take my dance with death through the narrow channel my god almighty between flowers out from the temple yard and lay exhausted by his side on the kitchen floor in failure I strike an unexpected knee nowhere no more nor less than in the belly of the virgin mary who explodes no quarter will be given me now I lie dead in the veil of death I feel my flesh is dead and I desperately snatch at my balls which are dead and shriveled hard on the outside like a walnut the soul cries out in anguish a little ark blown away: I do not want no no my mother stands at the kitchen table and eases the heads off fish with some blunt tool not a machete*

she knows I'm dead and a sheer stubbornness and a whim inside me
does not wants not to burn her face deforms pale with agony the head
falls from the fish and bounces along the floor with swollen bloody
gills then I know how I died before in Sússa in Imbra in Mala I move
my finger over the file of the newspaper I choose again to die in Sússa
in a hot climate there where the dunes are dry and with beautiful
views over the plain and as I make my request I wake and the picture
of Kurosawa who was murdered by his fiancée with a knife out in a
cornfield whispers to me from the pages of Time: *death is a matter*
and problem of style and the body looks at me with the blurry eyes of
a newspaper photograph

They are set about one foot apart and tightly tied to execution poles with
dark circles around their mouths like Canadian Eskimos who have eaten
human flesh in an extremely hard winter. Six shots penetrate their hearts
like tin cans and the woman's belly hangs down pregnant like a condom
full of water or Rembrandt's picture of Christ taken down from the cross.
In this there is an argument without context, I remember Ólaf saying
sarcastically, but when will you stop offering childish commie examples,
watered-down shitcakes from Bernard Shaw plays. I have never come
across the story except in thinking about Sigurður, and I cannot find it
in my National Saga collection. If it took place in Hamburg, the city isn't
located on the Rhine (here part of the manuscript is missing)

however reasonable a man is if they had not eaten they would have died
but neither does that change the matter the right and rational or the irra-
tional and wrong person will be half-dazed at this repetition and I take
back my word my spoken word will be taken back from me we must talk
endlessly so (tom)mas whom everyone complains about don't sit next to
me and I write down every word that flicks around your mind between
the clock on the watchmaker's workshop striking two and three today
when the mind's sediment is highest and slowest to get rid of it and
neuroses afflict the body the senses becoming asexual and healthy empty

like most people   the doctor says   now hear every word clearly
from Tómas's mouth I am held by these demons I'm going to continue
listening a moment with a water glass hearing aid up against the wall
and my ear set to the bottom he must take this into consideration he
knows how to strike from me the interrupted parts of the ripped apart
or run out into sand he may not require   I write words in the order
they arrive he can connect the items to his best ability I just send him a
tape recorder   my handwriting becomes completely illegible raven
flecks I continue while light lasts and then slumber on the divan and
rest might take me to sleep and dreaming dreams that is what is most
remarkable he says

At some point I want Sigurður to again prescribe me: dare to live,
Tómas. I do not remember the reason, but the challenge had some purpose, perhaps drinking; I insist on hearing the tone of voice. Strange, it
is usually easier to remember an object's smell than the sound or shape
or meaning or thought it raises. A moment's smell persists even if the
event is lost. This has a lumpfish smell. He continued: courage is the
audacity to try everything life has to offer. I want him wheezing this in
front of me; I want to feel the spittle on my face, so I can take the
opportunity to pull my handkerchief slowly from my breast pocket and
wipe my mouth. I stand by the coat peg and put on my overshoes. Or
stay on the steps to look at the rose pattern. Sigurður demands things of
others that he does not insist on from himself, I say to those nearest me
(Ólaf, who is cool inside), there is actually nothing so bourgeois as being
a well-known loafer and chancer. And nothing more unbourgeois than
being an honorable man who has received no recognition, like you, my
Tómas; that's what I want to say aloud. Dare him, then, says the man
and takes slow steps down the stairs. Strangely, Sigurðurur enjoys special
protection from his counterparts, although they constantly sneer at him.
If something gets said they take his cause *against me*. It's no life when
you drag yourself to the grave, just a mild lingering death, he says. No,
Sigurður's life is no life. But if my point of view is higher than his, and

each of us lives beyond life's expectancy, I will not judge. In all likelihood men in this country have never lived a life. But the young generation is truly industrious in its fucking and drinking hard liquor and we are preparing the country and the economy for this health-insured generation. But fucking cannot be the goal of life even if it might do some good in moderation. Yes, this country is so driven it gives itself no time to live, it stopped *CARING* to be driven, it becomes *MORE DRIVEN* than any other nation, this *DRIVEN NATION* may be *ENTERPRISNG* but does not bear much fruit, because that *DRIVE* never becomes anything but *BEING DRIVEN* for oneself, buying ships and boats not with money but <u>DRIVE</u>, continuing with that DRIVE, standing in place in **HIGH DRIVE** and singing a DRIVEN complaint: you cannot advance no matter how <u>DRIVEN</u> you are without displaying more <u>DRIVE</u> and effort. He visited me that second time, accompanied by Ólaf. And Sigurður is not drunk here to advise me. At least, I let them in. I lay on the divan. People usually understand that I am lying calmly on the divan with crossed ankles, come over for the sake of curiosity after I move into my own apartment, whenever that is. And they said as they looked around: You got yourself a nice little nest. Yes, I guess you could call this a nest, I say. Sigurður plonks himself in a chair at the desk. I did not invite him to and I risk him prodding fingers in my memo books. Some people who visit sniff into everything while they're here, pulling books from the bookshelf, examining pictures and papers, fiddling with small items on the table: the finery. Sometimes browsing books, plucking a crust from the bread, picking the crumbs off the table with their finger and licking them, holding up the table knives or messing with the children if some are around. With such a guest the best advice is to start your visit by *giving a tour of the house* while he gets over the worst of his tension. It settles things to have something to talk about: I see you have a Japanese cork picture, the view is great from the bedroom window, the living room sunny, I like your sofa-bed but you have no microwave oven. Everyone has one these days. One should never invite newly arrived visitors to sit immediately, but allow them to move about freely for the first ten minutes, and once he has finished speculating about salary and whether there is going to be a strike, then a heavenly calm comes over him. Ólaf perches on the divan corner. And it is easy to track their facial expressions. Sigurður fishes up a brand new cigarette pack and takes off the wrapping. I reach for the red floss and clean my teeth with it. He sits there (Ólaf); I did not trust the seat with his weight. At the time of this visit, an old math problem is fresh in my memory; I recall it shortly before the conversation began. Whatever the reason, I have some antipathy to this math problem about two cars that set off simultaneously at various speeds per hour, one from Akureyri to Reykjavík, the other from Reykjavík to Akureyri, and one must find out where the cars meet. It remains beyond me to know how I got through that example. Sigurður was doing the same thing and said: You don't need to prove whether you are as steadfast as you pretend; he launched into his stubborn argument without set-up. I was utterly opposed to it. I do not remember being bold, but noticed the wine drops on his lips before endless arguments about what one dare and dare not, whether Picasso is a better painter than Miro, who is more the author, Strindberg or Ibsen, where Laxness is in order of world-famous writers; does one need to strive to do this or that to make himself a creature, to test whether a person is in reality a creature, whether Icelanders have stagnated in a strange adolescence of small nations with thick skins. One could categorically answer yes. I remember Sigurður as a likeable, proud young man, but somehow he became a Columbus egg. And what use was that egg to Columbus now it stood broken at one end of the table. It broke and was put in the trash. Are savage tests the touchstone for human virtue? It does not occur to me to tell him. I withdraw this thought. One can withdraw one's thoughts. You cannot judge whether you are a criminal until you are in the criminal's position. Let him call me Tómmas; I will call him Girth, Sig-a-sig with whom Onan sought refuge, for shame's sake. I glance at Ólaf, who in turn dares Sigurður against me with his eyes. His eye expressions are feeble, not unlike the color of the sea during gelding season, January to April. I lay on my left side, like now, and hold the pillow under my armpit, supporting my head on my hand. Maybe not, I replied reluctantly and felt my mouth distend from the emotion. I rolled onto my back and clasped my fists over my chest, which is good advice, in an emergency it's possible to raise index fingers to the rafters and fiddle with them by one's lips. He baited Sigurður into quarreling with me. And so we err in judging others. On closer acquaintance, you find out a man beats his wife with a frying pan, refuses to buy her medicine, and flings soup meat at her on Wednesdays. You would be wise to avoid me, Sigurður, I said calmly and licked my salty palm. You have no idea how I live. Tómas knows nothing about Tómas. He stamps his feet and screams to throw me off balance. This is an old but weak trick; I'm prepared: I just lift puzzled eyebrows toward my hair roots, make a dumb face and kiss my fingertips. You should not think I'm some bipedal Book of Revelations like some people are when they are in a certain mood. Ólaf egged him on with his eyes. Stop pampering yourself, how mysterious you have grown. I understand that both were satisfied with the visit, because Ólaf unexpectedly took my cause and I fell silent. They talked about the Tómmas who *objekts* and in arguing with Ólaf I gained, tómmas, of course, too much of an urgent victory. I was nowhere a bystander.   Sobbing was going to smother me   I ran as fast as feet can   they were fleetfoot and ran him down in a short time   we will sit on him in hell until he pisses   they sat themselves down, butts on my belly, and awaited developments   I heard people shout for me at dinner   I heard shouts for me at midday coffee   but they sat fixed and patient and talked of sailing ships   the day faded up in the sky and I blew up from inside and they felt it through the buttocks and moving energetically on my belly when the urine sprayed they cursed their soaked asses and sprang to their feet and saved themselves screeching at the stain behind   for sure we need to try everything to convince you that man is nothing. A strange thought. Sigurður and Ólaf want to blame the man who returns a day's work up to evening, little worthless wretched behavior, and prove to him that all men are sprung of the same innate laziness.

Sigurður's mouth widened by half and the cigarettes would not stay in: police, lawyers, judges, and the whole system of criminals thank this success. I will not pay tax and support disabled people and those unfit for work dragging out a life as bill collectors. From where do you get extra money. I have long stopped charging for my evening moonlighting. Do you think that I can charge if I go out at night. I do that as a physician. Do not say anything about what you do for any purpose other than fundraising. I guess you do not put two and two together, you walk both for your health and to fundraise. Well, so it is. I am not free to do what I want. He leans back in the chair after this confession, and I point to the rafter with my index fingers. Ólaf giggles on the divan corner: Did you come here to fuck with the man. Yes, you are fucking with me I say, you fuck, fuck you just enough no mas and proud of it. Sigurður waves away a hand: What is this damned life. A tax that erodes man's power, and finally in the grave a bank deposit of death. It is best to be an invalid and a loser, then nothing gets demanded of you. He distributes cigarette ash all around, but Ólaf puts an empty ashtray into his palm. He opens and closes the box each time the ash piles on the cigarette end. Trust a chancer to suck constantly and puff smoke from a cylindrical holder that flames on the tip, blowing it from him, tapping the ashes off with light strikes of his forefinger and sucking the cigarette holder again after awakening in the morning and before falling asleep at night; so on year after year. Well, that is devotion to cigarettes and not promiscuity. If you're starting to get sympathy for criminals, it won't be long until you become one. Sigurður needs to think to himself. He is quick to judge. He asks:

Who does not seek where sympathy can be found.

I mentally squeezed his hand. How fortunate, having yourself as one of your truest admirers. Finally you will straighten your inner self and society through your tastes. From me he'll get no compassion. With tenacity I fail to write Sigurður away from me. Nevertheless, I wish you hearty congratulations. No, a man must put his heart into something. Now I have had enough of this visit and renounce it and change the subject.

The cashier position I was forced to turn down because of an ingrained contempt for men who embezzle; this would tempt me to draw money to which I was not entitled yet still be innocent. I make myself imagine a number of similar cases. I fear one thought altogether. I stand guard against every thought. This is what makes me purebred. Also this: I do not allow myself to think dirtily, since I least want to turn myself into a person who commits illegal acts, infringements, or the like. I use Sigurður for this. I do not trust myself to withstand risk, yet I yearn for the risk that accompanies positions of power. Sigurður probably never believe this. With the loquacity of a great skua he speaks commandingly and arrogantly, an equal opportunity offender, of course (no need to take that out) bodily inspired by alcohol. Alternatively, the wretch sits silent and distressed. He is a bold coward, and his trademark is:
In this message-in-a-bottle lies turbulence.
An honest man gets neither studied nor investigated, he is a nuisance to nobody, he shies from crime. But a legion of doctors and scientists orbits around the other type, asking: What does biology tell us at the moment a crime or an offense is committed. This is what the researchers are trying to ascertain. Yes, yes. Books and books about the ugly, miserable, nasty, the lowest of humans, and the healthy component of the nation hungrily absorbs them, this useful, debatable issue, in an enthusiastic devotion to criminal nature: this beautiful work of art about ugly behavior written with a sensitive understanding of and sympathy for the underdog, lost in the struggles of life; this book about our fellow man, the outcast man. Deviant delights gussied up in many fine words. Each underdog here has murdered his adversary. All society's aids spin to protect and assist him and find a place for him in Hotel Prison. Instead, people should write best-selling books about good and healthy people. Write best-selling books about me, Tómas Jónsson. Don't leave it to me alone to make myself famous and wealthy. Crime can be beautiful or artistic. Is it artistic to rape a young girl in the laundry room. No. But it is newsworthy. The deed becomes beautiful if it is placed in an intriguing

costume. Stop discussing them and look at those who use their time well at their desks during the day, working with drive and perseverance and adding additional employment in the evenings at home on the divan. When there is liquor on the one hand, there is always enough money to be made from spendthrifts. Stop publishing accounts of such men, mask-clad evil men and silk-gloved thieves who get rich and rob those who have nothing except honesty (how is it possible to rob a moneyless man; is it any wonder that I should ask). They are certainly different and numerous, but they make for absurd artistic subjects. Being honest and loyal is more complicated than being dishonest and deceitful. Fill newspaper columns with *unartistic* writings about sincere men, how they scoop up herring in the fishing grounds, how economical contracts are negotiated in trade and commerce, how an enthusiastic young man takes profitable projects to the minister until he makes a promise to herring-workers. Yes, we must do this if the press is not entirely a lost cause. A man who gets fat on waste does not seek out healthy food. People are as liable to eat garbage as are pigs in a pen.   I beat three resounding whacks on the table   I should be a politician   I take off my glasses   I drink from a glass of water and efface the pensioners from my mind   I sit on the divan   I'm tired   my speech is nearing completion   applause rings around the hall   I stagger to my feet with difficulty   soon I stop being Tómas I've grown tired of being Tómas   I could just as well play the fish   I walk to the door   I turn the key in the lock and hide it under a shirt in the suitcase. I lock the bag. I hide the little key to the bag. I hide it blindly so I cannot see the hiding place. I am the key to greatest courage. Fortunately, this composition book reveals nothing about me. I lay prone on the sofa. Fatigue passes through my nerves. I want nothing but warmth and rest from my routine, but man is now a completely hopeless struggle. Judging him is not in my nature. First I must weigh up everything that comes into my mind, say everything my tongue thinks to say, see everything my eye brings to me, smell all the smells the nose comes close to, hear all the sounds that hearing perceives, find all the tastes the

tongue can taste, feel all the emotions that feeling can comprehend, then
I will have achieved being an imperfect human, not perfect like a corpse:
Man is what's uttered as he dies.

So strange a man wants to fly onward sometimes (not just sleep) like
threads in a river that hesitates a moment and seems to refuse to flow
out to sea accompanied by other water and try to turn back against the
current, returning to the source. There are such threads everywhere in
life and nature.

Alas! I would buy an old bike and ride out of town on Sundays. I often
see adults on bicycles. Young people find it easy to balance, although if
they fall off the back they quickly get to their feet and keep pressing on
as if nothing happened. Old people find it harder to balance, and once
they have lost it, they will rarely return to the saddle. A serious problem,
sitting on a bicycle, navigating a healthy balancing position. Keep both
hands clamped on the steering, pedal rapidly with your feet and adjust
the saddle between your buttocks.   for pessimistic people never get
outraged since they lack the requisite optimism   Before I am able
to offer any resistance Katrín has come down to the National Theater
cellar. Restlessness in my sleep competes with the balance of waking.
Kata sneaks to the table in the dark nook. I place my arm swollen from
sleep around this woman swollen from sleep. We yawn in each other's
faces and smell each other. Then we kiss. She sneezes and I stick the
tip of my tongue in her nostrils. With a soft gesture I place my palm
gently on her womb. No woman stands with someone a few times then
touches them in a dance. I have locked myself inside and do not come
out. The key is lost. She drags home at night from the Theater Cellar
sorely tired to me, waiting for her sleepless and patient, and saying, like
people who frequently interact: Other people are very tiring and boring;
I cannot be bothered to go through this. She does not drag my dog-body
after her. He sits at home confined to bed. Someday she will discover
herself asexual and howl indeed moan from her gills and try to ration her
energy in the morning each day. Overcome with exhaustion she will quit
work in the afternoon and lie down with a headache. Finally she will

get overwhelmed and collapse on the sidewalk. From the nearby tobacconist's the police are called and come to the scene and shame her with a rough arrest into their car driving her either to casualty or the basement. The newspapers publish large headlines: Woman Found Lifeless on the Steps of the National Bank. No acknowledgment of what is an open secret: the woman is taking cash for herself using forged accounts. In the office there's grumbling, raised voices: This cannot continue. It is not possible. She will be terminated with a year's notice. Something must be done about it, says the CEO, something cannot continue. The woman sits fast whatever happens. No denial passes her lips; she even hails from a most priestly country. A whole clan supports her: One Tómmas is in the Ministry of Justice, another Tómmas works in the Prosecutor's Office, a third Tómmas is involved in police investigations and all these great Tómmas Tómmassons hail from the most priestly of countries. god knows it is useful to have the backing of such Tómmases here in Tómmasland. The termination suffices. I will drive the woman, since she must determine whether she goes or does not, says Ólaf. No conclusive evidence is found against this fraud apple of ours. First we need to find a party to charge but the prosecution becomes involved. No, such a thing cannot continue. Anyone in his right mind can see that. The woman is far from popular. She comes crashing in on Mondays—often barely sober—and distracts others around her by driveling about herself in the card catalog. Oh, she has such a hard time. Ólafur the office boss comes to his door and says, Listen up, something has to change; this cannot continue. This person has been unable to work for a long time because of the flu, she is not entitled to more sick days than you who never lie sick and who show up on time. No this is DEFINITELY not acceptable. Our fraud apple looks without appetite at fourteen pencils, an eraser, a ballpoint pen, and paper clips. Everywhere around her the sound: No, this cannot go on, anyone in her right mind can see that. The government must fall. This is DEFINITELY not acceptable. The other day she complained bitterly of anemia. Would it not be splendid to stroll outside at night or sit a moment in the sun and bright snow, I say tentatively.

Instantly she flares up and is about to tear me apart, fussy and arrogant: You go freeze in a cold sun, you anemic nonentity, you Tómmas. I loiter powerless in front of the mirror in the bathroom and look myself up and down. I do not like her pushy manner. Her vituperative reaction results in my never speaking gently to her again. She is not of my generation. She is not as grandly vigorous as the turn-of-the-century generation. I thrash her as soon as she creeps home to my body in the night, drunk and panting and barely speaking; I squeeze words from her mouth and assail her life with blows and strikes. Little by little she is written away from me as superstition says you should do with a wart: bury a leaf in hallowed ground. Everything takes time. I write her from me with this novel. Writers try to write many warts from society. The writer is a destroyer of warts.

Now it is necessary to show self-control. I take a clipping off the table and run my eyes over its columns. My vision stops with hydraulic brakes of tears as my eyes carefully read the newspaper account of the girl in England with a congenital hole in the heart. Blood flows unsystematically free from the shackles of her body's blood vessels, it swells within their cylindrical bodies, it subsides sometimes twice a day. The refectory examines the picture of the girl from all sides and the Board, sighing, circulates the newspaper, sighing. The most famous experts in the girl's country, Great Britain, study her and propose a ban on her exposure to anything that can make her pregnant, even the thought of a man. The little lamb escapes this medical prohibition all the way to Italy; at the beach she meets a young, handsome Italian. The morning papers publish the news: *Young English Girl with a Hole in Her Heart Gets to Know an Italian.* The Board is breathless over the story. Hopefully the couple have some sense, says Dísa. Miss Gerður moans: At the very least they should take precautions. The Italian gets her pregnant. He agrees to bring her home into his house through its dirty kitchen door. No-no, the Italian does right by his impulses, nurtures her in a Christian and Catholic way. *Girl with Congenital Hole in Heart Not Expected to Survive.* We had no option, says the prospective mother to the journalist, weeping with happiness. The refectory gapes. Now I'm excited. They must flush the human out, it should not be injured. Miss Gerður gets a twitch in her jaw and speaks fanatically about the responsibilities of life *itself* and the nature of sex and how god is lenient when the time comes. I am a great believer in destiny, she says in that particular Nordic, proud manner and adds that if the girl is going die then she will die, period; if fate intends her to live, then she will live. It's that simple. The young miss makes a point of keeping her clumsy spinsterhood in tight reins via a liberal babble about understanding *man's weakness*. I feel *nothing* is wrong, I'm just excited to see and find out. Over the nine months the young miss's sad eyes meander through the newspapers, but nowhere is there a word about the girl with a hole in the heart. Maybe, it was not the heart, but the heartNERVES or heartCHAMBER, she says. The case has dried up, maybe they destroyed the fetus with gamma rays or injected her with new marrow. So the news comes as a shock: *Girl with a Hole in Her Heart Gives Birth to a Healthy Baby Boy with Help of Leading Experts at St. James Hospital in London.* The birth went well. No, this is definitely propaganda from the Holy See, laughs Miss Gerður, or the Italian Tourist Board. No one can tell *me* that a woman with an open hole in her heart can bring a child into the world. The birth is pure propaganda. The young miss sits with a sulky expression over the newspaper alone in the refectory over an extra coffee. She rambles on with a blurry expression and forgets about the girl. Miss Gerður sitting alone at a big long table, nothing important in the papers. Only ads for rising fish prices, new volcanic eruptions, earthquakes, shrinking glaciers. Then the birth of a child without a navel in Holland and Kennedy is elected president. I throw the clippings away from me. Spring comes and summer. The sky is like a dirty milk bottle. Evening. Days. Kennedy. The sun rages on grassy areas and tries to beat some green straw from them once the frost has left the ground. No dice. The grass areas reveal no color, waking after a yellow winter. The trees shoot out buds and the buds die after a few days. Everywhere children are being born without arms. "It pays to kill a president." The grass areas continue as earth beds. A loon choir in Akureyri sings:

nine power plants newly opened in the country
but the nation undermines its center of gravity
sluggards sit firmly in the forefront
no one suspects where industry is headed
things CANNOT CONTINUE ANY LONGER

I discover a great truth. I will discuss it later. In a miraculous way I found the essence of existence. I know what it is, but I will not let anyone have access to it. I am not so stupid. Great, dark forces are hidden within the figure that is Tómas

look at me
see icicle fingers
freckled scab bald
the swelled belly
genitals miserly soft between the legs

no one suspects what lies under a coat. (I lie coat-clad in my lair. I lie under a blanket wearing a coat and shoes and overshoes)   where was I going   not the least trace of thought should survive me on this side of the grave   everything I say and have said is done in order to give a false impression of myself   everything Tómas knows he guess-es   when Tómas rests under the green turf many yarns will have been lost in death's ocean   (Now he is *entirely* carried to the grave, this adored and famous storyteller has run his course. A full bowl of water lies pulverized in the earth under our feet, this earthen vessel of life, Tómas Jónsson, never recoverable waterproof from the earth. We mourn him, we drink milk to him, Tómas, the absolute opposite of a wandering rabble)   or is he just a constantly jabbering delegate not saying a word of sense and in this respect comparable to Sigurður or whatever he is called   I hardly care to remember him by name. Someone asks me, I hum after an improbable pause: Sigurður, who is that. I never heard the man mentioned; I do not know any Sigurður. And I walk away, somewhat stiff-backed; I work my fingers like mad on the calculator for two hours continuously. I cough and clear my throat. Or I complain of a runny nose and gobs of spit: Your sputum is nothing, you should see mine, these meadow-colored globs. Just since this morning I have gone through two handkerchiefs. The third will soon be covered in these small globules. Your cold is still in your head and nose. I am sure all your sinuses are full. Next it will go into your lungs and I am still clearing my chest since the flu. With this cold, I set a new spit record. Look at this, it came from my last illness. It's nothing compared to this morning. That was such substantial SPIT. Yes, I see it. I have broken the icelandic spit record. You never get such purple spit from your throat. I always get *that*. I walk away from people who want to stop me on the street to talk about their colds and their mucus or ask for the nearest pharmacy. I have an inalienable right to avoid people. Now I'm going to tell just one story before I stop. I'm no Anton Pavilits Antonovits who was buttoned into prison December 25 1932, alleged to have refused to give his sister Admotova Antonova his address. I believe he let her know the house number but kept mum about the street name. Ingenious. Some valid reason as a basis for the refusal. But this Admotova was irresponsible enough to accuse her brother of *knowingly knowing the truth about Stalin*. That'll come up later. My memory has undergone a pleasing regression lately. Yes, one gets older and one's memory develops autonomy. Young people's memory is largely dependent on others, always bound to specific subjects. Nowadays I remember something as a glimpse then forget it immediately but it shows up later, totally of its own accord, independent of time and place. I know it well. But if I *want* to remember something I summon my unconscious to inquire, she goes on the prowl, gets employed in eclectic tasks, and returns the results when she is in the mood to finish the research. I know that ignorant people call it confusion, but this is actually exactly what it is to be *un*confused. I have no doubts about my sedulous unconscious. Here comes a crone holding a newspaper article. So. A man is full of newspaper articles and radio news. Our heads are full of all kinds of characters, large and small, and countless wavelengths. Admotova's legal hearing in Moscow draw the attention of the free world. A woman named Admotova Antonova had rented one square meter under the chandelier of her brother's new three-square-meter apartment on Slava Street. These apartments they shared with Anton's wife, their son, and the furry dog Gontsa. And they all subsisted on one cabbage soup and bean dish a day. No part of the house was heated; there were no creature comforts, no running water. NOTH-ING. The house was gray both inside and outside, dark and bleak as a Russian winter sky, windy like the Kola Peninsula. They (the couple) slept together in a hammock, Admotova on the floor, and their son under the dog (imagine that translating over here, offering it to some sixteen-year-old, some handsome icelandic teenager who sleeps under a Dralon® duvet, no it would not translate THANK YOU very much). A deathly cold prevailed in the Soviet house though the residents attempt-ed ineffectively to warm themselves with a Russian carping and shaming, with fights, vodka, and sex. Twenty years of the USSR had this one effect: making *people themselves* quasi-animals. But to prevent housing congestion, the government sent the police at night to disappear people without a trace. Russians call it night cleaning; we call it political purg-ing. The house was never cleaned in the other sense; they did not own any cleaning implements except the weapons the secret police brought at night. But the human creature is persistent in the face of suffering and people formed the only organization that was free, collaborating to rent nightly space for three kopeks per week, shared equally among all, even the dog; they earned a living through theft. It was always thought the wisest dogs in Moscow lived around the Kremlin, thieving and snooping for bones in trash cans. They stole the bones for their masters. Specially trained dogs went for high prices on the Moscow black market in the years 1925-1937. It was possible to buy dogs specially trained to steal everything from sewing needles in locked apartments on the fifth floor to dogs able to carry out bank robberies and car theft (now these dogs are the cornerstones of the famous Russian circus; they have been retrained and their talents directed in new ways for the benefit of the nation). But this dog's life was not without risk. The authorities took precautionary measures. For example, dogs faced mortal danger if they pissed on the street lights, and foreign correspondents were often witness to little waggish dogs barely lifting one of their hind legs as they noisily ate, wearing a sly expression like small dogs are wont to, and sending a weak stream an adequate distance away from the post. On the other hand, up jogs a large, single-mined dog, right to the light post, sending a huge jet from under the proximate hind leg in contravention of the fact that the authorities had wired electricity to the street lights, so the dog ended up burned to ashes by the electric shock as the electric current streamed through the wires on the post and from the post along the spray to the dog. There was no reason for that to continue. Animal lovers hit upon the plan of erecting small sticks in gardens for dogs and strays to urinate on. The police tried to prevent this, of course. Over time, sticks in a garden became a sign of national disloyalty. Nevertheless, a piss stick resistance movement spread throughout Russia and from there comes the saying, Piss sticks in the garden is a political concern, which Kruschev used a lot—the Russians, as is well known, do not speak in poetry like us, but rather in proverbs. Well, yes. During the darkest years of Stalin's reign, colorful fountain chamber pots for both dogs and humans were much in vogue. They took their name from their likeness to drinking fountains. They were identical except that the arc of water ran in the opposite direction from a drinking fountain, and then automatically from the pot's basin into the pillar that held it; the pot could be raised or lowered depending on the size of the one relieving himself. If the bowl was not in use one could remove it from the pillar and the pot thus turned into a decorative cudgel ornamented on the outside with bunches of grapes. All hand-painted, varnished, and greatly splendid. In Russia, people always piss behind the floral column, the proverb goes. And in the morning they swapped places, pouring from the cudgel into the common toilets on Slava Street (and as a rule always urinated before going to bed). They often had to stand waiting in a line for hours together. (Do not think that electricity had been run through the street lights only to kill dogs, but also wretches and drunks, which Russia crawled with, to stop the ugly habit they had of leaning their shoulder on the lights, a caricature with pocketed hands and a cigarette sagging idly free from their mouths, worn deerhunter on head, big toe poking from shoe, clothes crumpled around a sorely-used body.) While people loitered in the L-shaped queues prescribed after the death of Lenin (L for Lenin), dressed warmly in tattered smocks in winter, the pot's bottom often froze, and the State would pluck from the poor an additional kopek as a fee for the chamber pot. Well. In the middle of the floor, Anton demarcated with white lines a square meter, which he leased Admotova. He demarcated her space there so the couple could use the wall to sit in the evening after returning from the enslavement camp. Admotova could never step over the line; she had to jump from the doorway over to her box and sit directly on the cold floor until sleep overcame her. Thence foreign reporters would seek her at all times until the idea was hit on to string a hammock across the room's walls, then she murmured to herself: now the time has come and Babushka leans on her right ear. She slept in contempt of her brother and sister-in-law mating in her sight, and the son and the dog, against the wall. She said, sighing heavily: Things fare badly for Mother Russia if a couple do not have a bearskin pelt to mate under. Hope fares poorly when some are dogs and cats and drink tea, and others are floor lurkers, and the world is divided into two hostile entities. (Admotova was the first person in history to define the world as two hostile entities.) And she sorely envied the couple for the polished-copper teakettle in one corner. Facing this was a fixture covered with an old bearskin pelt (see, they were not completely broke; they had a bearskin; one's thoughts can often be insolent and totally wrong). Behind the pelt Anton kept his toothbrush in a birdcage hanging from four-inch nails on the wall. It is certainly a global phenomenon for a tenant to steal a toothbrush from the householder if it is lying in public view. My experience is not unique. That's how a new toothbrush of mine was ruined, once. Unknowingly, I did not bring it to my room, but left it in the bathroom one morning and in the evening when I entered heedlessly I saw it lying on a glass shelf; as I slid my finger on the bristles I felt that they were wet. Everything being normal, they would have dried during the day IS THAT NOT SO. If I attempted to use someone else's tooth-brush I would know to dry the bristles on the radiator or I would sneak it immediately after the owner, brushing my teeth quickly and leaving it in exactly the same place, so no one knew whether it was wet from me or him. Anton hit on the same idea, but differently, because he poured caustic soda solution on the bristles (tenants also sneak the householder's soap, razor, perfumes, comb, and toilet paper if the roll is loose, for example on the cistern). Do not blame me if some things are getting mixed together in my memory. I waited for her, awake, as she slunk into the toilet. Admotova snuck behind the pelt and Anton heard it with his ears, only pretending to sleep, a little rustle and movement in the dark. Night on the rainy mountains. She returned whining almost immedi-ately from under the pelt, groaning from the smart and holding frostbit-ten fingers to a mouth sick from scurvy and Vitamin C deficiency. One of Anton's eyes witnessed this in the gleam from the street lights. The other eye was pressed to the net in the hammock all night, which faced down. The first eye stared straight up in the sky and could afford to give up the luxury of sleep. During sleep a man's nose sleeps, the ears only slightly. Sunday. Admotova with her singed burnt mouth, her jaw lead-ing me to think of an uncouth word choice. As I jerked into the hall the hundred-kilogram woman peered sideways at me, eyes burning with fury, enraged, a contrarian with her kids. The caustic soda ruined the bristles. Now I appreciate that soda can immediately clean a brush. Sometimes a solution arrives too late from the unconscious. She did not boldly sneak my toothbrush any more, though I left it deliberately under the mirror. She perhaps sniffed at it; I do not know. For many days, she had a fiery mouth. And though she colored her lips one could see sores flowing out the corners of her mouth. She saw the trick in the quadran-gular open kitchen door. The couple rejoiced that she (who?) died in a snowstorm at the corner of Lermontov Street while Anton waited in a long L-shaped queue in Red Square. He visited the Tomb every free moment, fearing that otherwise he would lose the apartment. And when he stepped into the vault, who should be sitting on the marble bench except Admotova, who was observing the trials of her body. She looked up, saw Anton and shouted: Where do you live now, you pig, comrade brother Anton. (This probably happened long after the death of Stalin, when the S-shaped queues were prescribed in all photographs.) That said, Admotova lived at full tilt, working during the day cleaning streets and removing snow. After night fell she sought refuge in the tomb, which was well heated although a coal shortage prevailed everywhere in *the state of happiness of communism.* Admotova had a devilish foresight and cunning; in winter she made frequent visits, which she hinted were the result of a love for their glass-coffined leader (would anyone be opposed to having Jón Sigurðursson in a glass coffin or Jesus). No guard dared shoo her off and even announced her presence to awake the attention of the masses who hovered around Red Square half frozen in the hope of some residual heat from the Kremlin's doors and windows. Admotova was not one to mourn when others froze to death. She felt it was cold or laziness in snow shoveling, she muttered, mouthing: Now old Babushka is less cold in the c-l-a-w and she immediately and without preface set down her spade and pick and headed toward the tomb. There she was seen shoveling snow, this Russian national character, in all Western newspaper photographs—to the right of the stairs. Where does Comrade Admotova mean to idle her time away, the foreman asked. The mausoleum, she replied and in a calm manner let light flicker the idealistic fire of Leninist Marxism. If you are cold you will work yourself warm, said the foreman obstinately, there is plenty of snow here. I am not troubled by cold, said Admotova, bridling. The foreman was stricken with fear by the answer and remembered that Russians MAY NOT be cold under the USSR; it was forbidden. But he feared the precedent Admotova could spread among the ragged rabble who worked along Skálholt. He was silent and dared not declare his hostility at her trips and her labor treachery. It could have cost him a visit to Siberia. Admotova got to sit in the tomb daily calculating pay rates and overtime wages and respect for the leader's face, constantly knitting and spinning, her work never set down. It was a great delight to see her wool-work. Sometimes she practiced writing her name and would give it one of the foreign delegations. Her handwriting was fantastic, she managed so well reversing R-to-Я. By and by she rose stiffly from the bench and stroked pro forma the dust off the coffin and polished its silver braces. She of course immediately recognized Anton, who moved slowly in a line parallel with the coffin dressed in a black smock and with wrapped legs. There was no doubt that he had emerged from a photograph of Red Square in winter, but not a photo in a USSR paper. I do not recognize you, he said, you are from a totally different Soviet paper than me. And a fight broke out there. Don't crowd the coffin! shouted the watchmen, who overpowered Anton and carried him into police station no. 139 on Gorky Street. At the trial, staged for the benefit of foreign correspondents, Anton offered the mitigating circumstances that his eyes had been frozen and therefore could not have focused on Admotova. She appeared on his retina as a cubist reflection, he said. Nothing could be seen except the broad struggle of light and shadow on the surface. The mouth lies, howled Admotova, "the eye is the part of the body that is most resistant to cold; really has no one felt cold behind the eyelids," says Aristotle, and Leninist Marxism has never contradicted his theory. The theory is right. The case was sent to the Ideology Studies Council, which agreed with Aristotle's theory. And Admotova was afterward recognized as a frequent guest of the tomb so that opinion fell in her favor and she claimed the toothbrush in the bird cage as a documentable possession of hers along with the wall space and the tea kettle. Authorities and protesters boasted of victory in one of the most notorious trials ever, and their echoes came to iceland and "crystallized" as a legend that presented Admotova as a precedent liable to trigger an uprising among shoveling women. The party made a secret agreement in which she would come nowhere near shovel and spade, or tomb, either. Okey-doke, Admotova, dear, they said. You just lie quietly at home during the day and sleep and drink tea on full salary; the city will pay. A woman, Grevilovska (the name is related to the word "grefill," which means both a pick and the devil, two things that merged in this woman, a woman who shoveled with an icepick and who had a devil inside her mind), found out about Admotova's secret; Moscow is a city with eared walls, just like any other that considers itself closed-off and monitored and ruled by police (gossip can spread from Moscow to Kiev and thence to Pacific coasts via serving girls in just five days) and it was known Grevilovska meant to take advantage of the rumors' speed and reach the tomb unseen, but when the officers saw her they let ammonia into the heat pipes and connected the refrigeration machine and Grevilovska froze to death on the marble bench. And then a message was released: that Lenin's embalming fluid was best preserved in hellish cold. Now the temperature in the tomb is at freezing point. Nothing thrives there except cold bacteria. In the opinion of the icelandic delegation, the Asian influenza virus originated there. But the truth about the mummy is concealed from many men, even the Russians, which is that the glass coffin does not store *the actual* body of Lenin, but a detailed simulation produced by Tussaud's Waxworks in London. Everyone knows that famine and devaluation prevailed in the Soviet Union when Lenin died, the exchange rate dropped, and to solve the devaluation, a proposal was made by economists at a secret meeting to sell the *true* body of Lenin (who had five substitutes so it was uncertain whether the real Lenin died, since the substitutes were brainwashed, blindfolded and placed together in a locked blacked-out cabin, so that when they emerged no one knew any longer whether he was the real Lenin or not). An American collector bought the carcass with substantial capital, on condition that he did not display the corpse openly until a century had passed from the leader's death. While Tussaud's analysts were in Moscow, Stalin took the opportunity and also had a form made in wax (all pictures taken indoors are not of him but of his likeness). Here in iceland he was never thought to have died a *natural* death, but a waxwork death. It is said that the *real* Stalin fled his own tyranny to Peru and now cultivates a garden. After the trial, Anton was sentenced to sit in the center of the floor in a chalk triangle and obliged to hold his wife in his arms as she held their son in her arms as their son held the dog Gontsa in his arms and the dog held his paw to the chandelier, condemned to watch Admotova treat herself to hot tea. (There are legends at the refectory that Stalin gave Roosevelt Lenin's actual body at the Yalta conference, a symbol of Soviet friendship. But that is of course purely a Tall Story.)

N.B.: These fragmented legends, plucked from every direction, are recorded from oral sources from around the country, totally unaltered by any artistry. I do not have time to sort the items into a clear scenario (cause : effect), to construct a raftered building and finish them with a well-made final sentence conveying the opinion that fiction is the writer's spiritual sexual intercourse with the story content and the reader, hopefully resulting in orgasms for everyone and everything; soon I am going to die.

Memo: If it should turn out that my life lasts quite some time, I'm going to write a novel full of contrasts with the situation in the Soviet Union, obtained on the one hand from *The Morning Paper* and on the other from *The National Will.*

Remember: Character sketches. But above all: fine icelandic *humor* is lightweight and comprehensible to people.

Meanwhile I remained distant to myself, neither generous nor spirited work finds her way to worship at my door. Precautions are necessary. I have made a detailed record of where and how things are in the room, as much in the drawers of the table as in closets and bags, so I can perceive the slightest turmoil. I think it pays off, though my time is wasted in inventory at night. I've drawn almost invisible lines around the feet of my alarm clock and the condom pack in the bedroom drawer. I keep three condoms on hand in case I need to use one. There is hope yet. I exercise discipline and mostly leave myself alone nowadays mostly except perhaps in the evening, if a lack of character shoots through me. Baui cannot take a joke; I irritate him with an old negro woman and get nothing from him for a week. The old woman is long dead so there's nothing to get angry at me for. I do not recall where her image is displayed; on a pack of cocoa. No. I remember she was a singer, black and strong, immensely ugly. I do not want to deny the fact that sometimes I even consider my desire to become a fleshly woman for a short time, maybe just once or twice a day. Ideally I would have been a kind of gender-tuner, with a gender switch beneath my belly or in a secret belt around my navel. And when I would put a finger under my shirt and press my navel (I am always in there digging lint out) I would appear to others as a big, light-haired, sex-bomb: in the street, in the bank, in second-hand bookstores, the men's toilets. I would play this game until everyone got furious and felt they were hallucinating. No, the human creature is poorly equipped by the hand of nature. Everything is immutable: trees bear leaves, leaves are green; all humans walk on two legs; snow is white; seasons come in an unwavering series one after the other; no law breaks itself. Fashion is not drastic enough, even the makers of prosthetics are so conventional that they construct a prosthetic in the color of what it replaces, not bright or dappled as it could be, and leaves need to rot or wilt so that the green does not disturb the peace. Only the presence of death disturbs man. I would enjoy the greatest popularity as a world-famous female scientist. I think that must be so. No domestic Icelander excels in science. On the men's market there is *too* much supply and fierce competition, but there is an *open way* to fame and fortune for a gifted, talented woman. People may doubt my talents and abilities *as a man* but were they in the cylinder of a woman's body they would probably say: She is singular. The requirements for women are less stringent. Generally, it is said: He is lazy *for a man*; he is ugly *for a man*. As a woman, he would have probably been considered hard-working and handsome. I do not know. But there is no doubt that often I consider becoming a woman. Yes. If the truth is malleable and the human body, too, why could not those feelings become tangible and manifest either in the form of a woman or a man. I would be a world-famous woman in the field of nuclear physics. No, as I have said: everything about a person is a bound substance. I guess the nation would strongly oppose such a woman on its coat of arms. I guess the newspapers would not catch the news:

First Self-Taught icelandic Woman Splits Atom.

The mirror would display an image of an ancient woman with an ax; it would be popular and unoriginal. Some unique news: in this basement here in Reykjavík yesterday a self-educated woman managed to split the atom with improvised equipment. But the icelandic Association of University Women has been silent over the event. We cannot recognize this woman without stamped documents from the university, says the head, Tómassina Tómasdóttir, in an interview with the newspaper; she has no certificate and no scholarly woman's female features *from birth*. We cannot demand prospective members lift their dresses for admission to the club. This woman does not have a *genuine hole*. All this sounds marvelous. Now it is woman's time. The time of man has passed. With overuse of himself and his exaggerated features man has managed to run through the ages of achievement, to make himself a *totally known entity*. Woman, however, is still at the stage of the unknown. She is an algebraic creation; she is x. All great men will become women secretly or apparently. With old age, this becomes clear in men. Notice how great professionals in various fields become old woman with age. Shave the beards of the great men of the nineteenth century and, lo: there you have, evidently, a strict grandmother. Women would get a significant boost if great men could change themselves after becoming inoperative as pollinating animals. Examine photographs of Ibsen and Einstein (and countless others), shave the beard of the man in the image and clothe him in a black satin dress, if he is a foreigner (put the domestic ones in national costume), spread dandruff and hair that's falling out on the shoulders and collar, and you will see: out comes the old *woman* in them. (Is it a coincidence that the icelandic authors usually choose *old women* as the subject; is it just a romance for old women or a latent desire to be a woman.) Variously these written old women are strict stepmothers or lively . . .

well, you know. Place a hamper full of crochet and crafts in Churchill's lap, take out his cigar, and see the correct image: a grandmother sitting in an old wicker chair, busy with wool work, good-natured, witty, and a bit obscene. I could resist the temptations of the flesh, so I would not need to drop the first year of high school—due to childbirth. As is commonplace, like the Society of University Women complains sorely, the subservience of woman, their compulsion to lie flat like a skate, plaice, or flounder, fish species that are bottom fish and monochrome, white below, black above, as women are viewed mentally and physically. Women are flatfish. What trial of strength would it be for me to stick my tampon in each morning, *carry out the self-explanatory details of the contemporary woman's morning routine*, a precaution women's issues continually hammers on about from A to Z: geld yourselves with a stopper. All female swans are females. If drowsiness sinks over me or I get sleepy from the test-tube steam then I, the scientific woman, would swallow the anti-baby-pill and be independent enough to freely stroke my own head. Sometimes I would use the old tips, rinse myself occasionally with a weak brandy solution. A proof that I *could* resist the temptation. I take my dreams as witness. Make your judgment on them. You would be difficult judges: complicating dreams and confusing them in rhyme with your cross examination. My dreams have never

but eventually these countless examples became contradicted are dreams there to confuse men the prosecution bench from then on they do not distinguish that which happened awake or in a dream the human spirit reached its highest level absolute anarchy and has been convicted of the same stage man arrives at after extended alcoholism and drug use and infatuation with sex with mergers

Had she (the laundry woman) been examined immediately after the rape subtle analysis might have revealed some particles of Ca-O-la talcum on her thighs, since I spread this type of talc on my groin morning and evening. I get a heavy sweat around my balls and the sweat irritates the skin and gets into my rectum. I suffer from night sweats too so I stroke my palms firmly on my thighs and my chest wrinkles with old dark sweat underneath. My thighs rub together, red patches break out, ulcers on my testicles, if they are not well taken care of. In the investigation now I would innocently ask what relevance that has, but in a dream of course I would be equally guilty after as before. Self-torment is every Christian man's atonement. I am directed to a seat on an oak bench. Two policewoman guard the door.

why did Göring laugh in the well-known image of the Nuremberg trials everyone laughing and the police at the door pursing their lips to hold in a laugh what could be funny in this place with the war crime tribunals I've never been able to find out about why it does not fit the trial in Nuremberg but there's no explanation for the laughter which is what alone awakens people's curiosity   why does the British encyclopedia know neither about the laughter nor that the British royal family is of icelandic descent it is no encyclopedia that damned   was the photograph of Göring published in a newspaper to make curious people crazy at this legal torture: at what did Göring the murderer laugh what allege that led the judges and everyone to join in a court of laughter before the death sentence was pronounced and the executions began of Göring and his fellows for crimes against humanity is that what humanity is then a lying spot on the tongue of the guilty and innocent is this one and the same or is world history funny like the material in the writers' novels praised as genius because people either laugh or weep on each page of their reading

Come, says the judge, swear on the Bible. He rises slowly from his divan and goes to the table where the book lies. Place your right hand on god's word and say: I will tell the truth and nothing but the truth, like in a radio play. This man is a pagan. Those present look around them as the words come out. Miss Gerður sleeps red-faced on a blue cushion.

The judge tilts his cheek to his fellow judges and whispers: If the man is without faith or just superstitious then his oath is useless. Does the woman tell the truth asks the man gruffly. So, woman, out with your tongue. He keeps his buzzing tongue fixed on the tip with bitten nails and watches the black spot through a magnifying glass. This is just a wart, I mutter through my throat. I am writing about my warts, genitals and limbs and tongue also so that I do not lie in the novel, Tómas Jónsson, Bestseller. I ONLY WANT TO BE A TORSO. The judges put their noses together. The court is emptied. After careful consideration, they deem me truthful. He is confirmed and baptized and inoculated in the Lutheran faith. This will be a relief to god, they say, self-righteous and dependable. Their decision is hindered because I have sworn a false oath. The effort is over. You believe in god *at heart*, my love. Indeed, I say. All hymns make me emotional, no matter how loathsome I know them to be, or badly sung. And I'm relieved that someone made the decision for me. Or semen was found in her. Analyzed in the laboratory of the University. I ejaculated both on site and later in a dream. And also dreamed the event. I dreamed it long before. I ask: Have you ever been forced to do another's will during sleep. No one forced you to rape or carry out the atrocities committed while you slept soundly and innocent

fifteenth book

The soul is a man's wife. The soul is called Katrín. Katrín is my wife. Katrín means The Pure.

16. notebook

You are an adulteress, Katrín. You know no moderation in fornication. I become faint at our eternal squabble, stamped by you day after day, week after week, month after month, and year after year. I use all handy measures against you, so you restrain your own presence. I have hardly taken my eyes from you; you're gone. After a lifetime of marriage, I have been able to read deep into your mind and get to know you. I see your reaction. No, I see not feminine intuition but rather asexuality. I need no longer have your presence. We are divorced.

22 August 1957.

My days have become quiet. Nothing of import during all this time. A lack of news leads to well-being. Days should ever be thus: uneventful and clear. A man enjoys living alone in a house, never meeting anyone to speak with, pottering away at carpentry in the storage room, cutting out rough materials for a novel; ideally I would prefer that to bone laziness or confusion or whittling little images of you in words. Craftsmanship is a healthy practice. If a life is lived in craftsmanship then a man finds pages for the heart's proximity, the blood's folly. I feel people have not immediately departed from me but come to an internal balance and harmony with the environment. People are complex creatures. All rooms are formless and empty, but Katrín bustles in the kitchen in my mind. Her child is very calm and sweet. You do not know it exists. Maybe it does not. So should children ever be.

She is stuck at home in the evenings. She is always baking and washing and straightening or ironing snow-white linen and pillows, but I lie on the divan asexual and tired and carp after her: Katrín, aren't you coming in, my dear. Won't you rest and lie down, I want to talk to you a bit in peace and quiet, my dear. Títa puss can listen to us. When we lie close to each other in a bed that smells so clean and fresh, then we will feel desire, an intimate connection. Don't you feel things have changed. Don't you feel much better after you stopped carousing. You must not be angry with me, my dear, if I say what I mean. It is terrifyingly uncomfortable to let cats watch us in bed. Science has proven cats dream. We live in an era of reconciliation and attempts at mutual understanding in international affairs. One of the many things that is unbearable about icelandic literature is when the sheep speculate about the people, the dogs offer intelligent expressions, or the forces of nature conspire to carry out the poet's thoughts and character in the story. Compare:

The storm was determined to jostle this noble old man out of the abyss.

Cats never sleep. Birds sleep on twigs. When as I open my eyes Títa is awake. Cats take pleasure in watching a couple reconcile in bed. Yes, in bed we will desire each other, experience an intimate communication. I eat one egg, hard-boiled, each night. I boil it in the kettle on top of the element. Grogg-grogg-grogg sings the jumping egg as it boils and jumps. It simmers in the cauldron and jars against the element. The child in Katrín's womb screams fierce with hatred at the womb wall. I want out of your paunch, Mamma, it shouts. I put my ear to her paunch, little tambourine, and listen to the forthright demands of this nucleated child. We listen to the unrest and power in the unborn. I want to see this damn world right away. I think it is going to be an industrious and enterprising subject if it is equally solid with its fists in reality as in its mom's womb. A child is scarily senseless. But we're going to hold it still in the paunch as long as possible, so it does not dissipate. Get lost and stay in the paunch, I say, you will not feel better elsewhere. The luxurious life these kids have now, lying in their embryo pose and flailing at the paunch and needing nothing to stay alive. We laugh ourselves helpless and embrace around our laughing boy. Yes, my friend, I say in a mock scream and pat the paunch with my palms and give the stone a little seal-nip, a man has no need to leave the uterus. The stone cries and laughs. We laugh accordingly and Katrín says: You are quite the record. You are homesick. All evening, household joy prevails. We nap embracing variously on the floor or carpet, the divan or inside a wardrobe, and inside Katrín the stone sends out tiny suck-cracks. That dynamo of a stone is scary, I say, not at all bleary-eyed, but worked up and whacking away even though it's long past eleven. I find her rather worn out, actually, answered Katrín. Then we bed down together with her and look at the little chicklet snoozing between sheets. I want to bite and squeeze the little chicklet but the doctor advised me for stimulation to take a teaspoon of port wine morning and evening. I drink a full eggshell and it passes comfortably into my body after the eggpunch. I drift into a bliss condition but never get to kiss the stone inside Katrín. I also eat a lot of vegetables. It's my duty to look after my health carefully. I stopped buying food in the refectory. I take a packed lunch to the office with me, which is on the increase; just some snacks. Here we do not have snack bars. The main meal I eat in the evening follows the Swedish model, easily-digested food, rusks and boiled meat. In the morning I eat a Norwegian Breakfast. I set off. I tolerate my neighbors better. I have neither met nor seen Sigurður in my rambles around my mind. He is rumored to be out of work, and no one knows where to find him. Has he gone sailing. I chat with Katrín privately and in confidence about horses, that everything increases except the bank account. And so we write with style and practice written forms: I go down to the pond. I see ducks on the pond. I throw bread crumbs to the ducks. Ducks eat bread. I have written all the warts off me. Good day. Good night. The weather is as it should be. There is no longer any winter in iceland. This country is becoming an absolute America since the American defense force came; it protects us against cold spells.

1 July or September 1957.
I miss my presence; that is, the presence of Títa. Any other presence, especially touch, feels uncomfortable to me. She was an extremely agreeable and sociable cat. She cleaned herself so well, always licking her paws, belly, and ass. She made one ashamed. For a time, I had sauntered all alone past her farm of an evening in the weak hope of glimpsing the cat. Sometimes she slumbered peevishly at the window or waddled soft-limbed around the garden amid empty food cans, scraps of wood, human crap, even. Weeds grew and birds fluttered with quivering wings breathing in cold air. I would sometimes venture to the window in the dark in the evening and draw Títa's attention by scratching the window pane. She detected my presence, mewed, and spit in the flowerbeds. Outside was a single band of twilight. I called to her, behind the garbage cans, and fetched her leftover fish. Then one evening I took her. I long to return to the chivalric era, when splendid men pillaged splendid women and rode fast horses. I do not feel comfortable around empty fruit tins. Katrín does not like cats, but I find cats soft on my body. I have to conceal Títa in the workshop with its wooden smell and sawdust or in the shavings bag along with blocks of wood and surplus art. In the evening I found a solution up along Laugavegur. Of course I had never reconciled myself to the bus. The houses rise around in a tempting row. Foreigners who come to Reykjavík do not recognize the same city they have been to before. Some people love cats. I much prefer them to dogs. Dogs often have filthy behinds, but the cat is a progressive. (I am not revealing any new truth here.) Others prefer dogs, wanting to have a guardian but never to pay an employee a salary. Títa will not let anyone force her into submission. A dog's instinct is aversion. On the way home tonight I perceived that the world is divided into character groups, not political systems: dog and cat groups. The groups are in all political systems. (I am not revealing anything new here, but everything is still new under the sun.) I feel like I have become a new man affected by new words. Every day renews me toward decay, toward the aging and death that

is perfect and new with characteristics that awaken surprise as to how well one gets used to it. Very well indeed. The basement is consistent with itself, buried and reeling in the corners. Here I am, where no one comes. Admittedly, I have for years been eating myself down from the upper two floors, but the basement will make me prosperous due to the rent increases which never fail to align with the króna. One should never chain up the thing he wants to freely enjoy. These days, people are waiting eternally for devaluation. They come down hardest on me in the form of Ásmundar. I am a prepper in a basement nest. My last stronghold. They will have to carry me out dead from here, dressed in black, an inoculated, satanic Lutheran. Prayers stream from my lips. Reading prayers is pleasurable. After the loss of my sexual appetite (I last had her in June) there is no satisfaction like prayer. I do not masturbate out of political interest, which is for teenagers through adolescence until they get married. The strumpet Jenní went directly from a ball game in the corridor to marriage in the attic. Jenní is what they call infatuated with her sweetheart. They are newly betrothed and he has a car and she says:

Oh it was so much fun last night, I went on a driving tour in good weather and he began to show me the bustling rats on the Reykjavík rubbish dump and kept saying: No, look. I was so enamored seeing the rats and asked: Are rats that fertile, and he answered, so funny: Rats do not use rubbers. I felt thoughts of rage, which seized me there in the car, the two of us looking at rats. Then he began to tell me about his father who was dying.

It is said that a dying man feels sensations and regains consciousness just before his last breath, before a howl rises from his lungs and the body topples on its side limp and clammy like a newly-plucked dead hen.

It is nice to be asexual and have no living relatives and not need to grieve for anyone.

In the evening I take out the books and check my dwindling balance. I don't spend long on this. I discovered a suitable pastime that carves away the taxing day. While I work, I change minutes into amounts, working out how much each minute adds to my balance. Time is an endless sequence of numbers. Eight hours are valued at a certain amount of krónur. The remainder of the living day a man sleeps to gain himself the energy to be able to suck up money. The friction of meat morsels in the stomach produces electricity, which powers the heart to pump blood into the body's arteries, which sucks in air, which cools in the lungs, and the brain is triggered to move the finger and pencil over the paper. It's like with the windmills at Holtstöðum in Flóa. They were kept running all the livelong day to fill tanks and so Guðrún had light at night to eat and to wash and comb her great and long hair. For their other needs Jónas and Guðrún did not use light; however, a hand lantern burned every night in the hen house so the lay-shy hens lost the thread and eggs poured the whole solar circuit in a volley through the egg hole, even though the law of hens is to lay only in daylight. Here you can see clearly the disposition of chickens. In the evenings, Jónas sat in the hut and noted down numbers of eggs produced, the wind direction, and weather. They are exhausting themselves so they can fall asleep in the dark, he said, putting his arm around Guðrún. Remember to let the hens have some shell-sand tomorrow. They crushed me against the wall. I discovered a moss roof through the slits in the panel. Flies found me and the chamber pot. Disgusting house flies smelling the urine stain and avoiding the fly-catching-trap. Jónas slept with his nose out of bed and breathed in the urine stench too tired to be able to fall asleep. Grandma said it was hypnotic, the smell of sour cow piss. I always believed this because I knew it first hand, breathing in the smell of the night pot, then falling into slumber above it. I need no sleep if you let the chamber pot stay there. Guðrún ferried it to the lair. Cold fingers, which kneaded parcels of butter during the day and powdered dry skýr, looked in on me naked through the knitted underwear until I fell asleep crushed tight by my panel wall in the country and swamp marshes, irrigation ditches and the rain that flowed constantly over haystacks and cemeteries that great, drenched summer. Now, in fall, they get energy from Soginu. Much changes. In the last letter, she said that hens would hardly leave their boxes, so eager they were to lay their eggs. This laying generation of hens

June 30, 1957.

Yes, this laying generation of hens, deemed to be above criticism, so I'll take up the cause. No, this laying generation of hens, whatever anyone says   today I came across the cat within the paper trash in the yard. The fish-dumpling cans were missing but in their place the yard was full of refuse and cardboard boxes. Once out of trash cans, you can see how everything is constantly changeable, shaped by wind and rain, the effects of which have grooved to my mind. I remember seeing from the window on the third floor a boy had caught cardboard box on a hook, and it was strange to see the box dangling on the hook and the boys beating it with a long stick. By sheer coincidence, fish bites were in the bag. I keep fish in waxed paper. The day was in twilight, and no one there to see. The city resembled a well-taken photo. Títa posed on a cable pole made of a driftwood tree that had turned its tree root up to the sky and its lone star, ready to jump if a snow bunting sat on the sandy snowdrift. Títa, I addressed her. The cat swung from the pole, flying with drawn claws and tightened abdomen through the air to shoot between the barrels; from there she stared at me with eyes glowing in the dark. I opened the bag, pulled the letter from under the composition book and unwrapped the fish. She was not so frightened that she refused to advance, but pawed at the fish. Every time I tried to catch her, she shot behind the barrels and rummaged into the mud. I tried a long time without success to set hands on the beast until my subconscious came into the picture and sent a message: put the letter in the bag, you ass. The letter was nothing but the word "leftovers" and I would have to succeed the first time, or she would be afraid and I would never see her ever again. I put the coat collar over my head, lying with my knees on a semi-dry cardboard box and holding the bag open with my fingers. Títa inched closer and closer. Kis, kisakis, I whispered but the whispering terrified her so I broke off and struck myself on the mouth and scolded myself so my mouth grew still and open and stopped emitting sounds. My knees were waiting, stiff and creaky, and I squatted there with my coattails gathered in my groin. She came with small steps, crawling with her belly full of kittens low to the ground, suspicious, but was no match for the enchanted composition book. She raced into the bag and was headed quickly back out with the spine in her mouth, but I captured her double-quick, closed the bag frantically and allowed myself to fall in the slush on my elbows over the bag, the lock held, but my buttoned coat inhibited my free movement, and I fell into the trash cans. Someone peeked out a window and beat on the pane because of the noise. We rolled in the snow, the cat in the bag, I in the slush, and could not rescue ourselves among the paper trash. A bleary child's voice (Dorí) called at the pane: a man is stealing the cat and the trash cans. My legs saved me by leaping up with the trash can lid in hand; I could not let go. I ran in curves, there were no obstacles on the way, neither fences nor redcurrant bushes, the house was unenclosed, its fence fallen down, and the flowers had lain lifeless a few months. The route lay through an underpass by a square of houses out to the street. I was satisfied after I had run around five houses, then I took the mother to a nearby vehicle and left the bag behind the front bumper and ran for the house corner to rid myself of the lid, then turned in a calm manner back to the car and retrieve the bag. You might be thinking that the car drove over her, but you're wrong, it did not move. One night I'm going to check the route I took, after it is safe to (something is missing in the manuscript here) . . . I set Títa up in the workshop. I firmly expected she would be with me for a week, no more; she needs food, which costs money, but I was sure she would stay with me and it would be like a winter holiday for her, in a box on a radiator. Alas, a lot of painful mewing from her bag. On the way home my mouth hummed a silent tune I heard only in my head, not my ears. No one and nothing got in my way except thoughts about Sigurður. I pushed them from me as unnecessary and when I saw someone in the distance I headed right across the street. I do not have tuneful ears but I remember the song the musician was playing on the guitar as agreeable but neither my tongue nor my vocal cords can achieve that characteristic electric sound, no matter how the air is pushed from my lungs. It was a great relief to drop the kitty on the floor. I shook her from the bag with the composition book and uneaten food. All this occurred and I decided to use the stuff in it that I was writing about Tómas Jónsson. Now I understand how a journal enriches one's life. Each worthless item gains value if it is brought into words on a page in a composition book. I say this even though I am not a literary fundamentalist who thinks the word is god. I understand just in my own way why Jónas wrote in his journal about wind directions and eggs every night. In order to get the Nobel Prize for Literature. *He is well deserving of it* as they say in the press, but all too few of those who deserve them get them, my Títa. Fifty years passed without my understanding what Jónas was doing in his writings. A new wind direction was a significant event in the life of this pious man, so smooth was his marriage. Jónas was not unkind to merchant folk who rode out on Sundays, though I used to say: Now there's one scurrying from the countryside; or: I do not enjoy farting horses in a horse paddock. I confused pudgy animals each glossy as a wet balloon, sweat-marked, with dark and sad eyes. On their necks, surly heads; the horses tossing their light manes trampled and whinnied and kicked. I remember that Jónas jumped off the wall and rolled about the horses' backs, they threw him to and fro like a feather sack. Jónas could not get a foothold. He could not press himself between horse and harness, so tight were they packed in the paddock, lips stretching to catch a breath. She whispered in the dark, hands cold since her fingers had only recently finished with the butter, and touched my dick: my love, you should not stroke this. She is coming, your mother, soon enough, to bring peace to your home at night. My Tómas, you were not exactly active, but were gentle with the animals and the master of the house and I will miss you forever. You did what was asked of you. I have kept your letters in a special envelope and send you twenty eggs 10 + 10 carefully chosen eggs. This spring I will reach the age of ninety-one, god willing, and everyone is good to me. Our Magga is married. You did not snare her but came here with your wife, you will have enjoyed this fun. This is the twentieth laying hen descended from the proud Italian cock. Do you remember him. Jónas is the same, it is fun to be married even if not to the right person. Enough to do some good. Magga has gotten fat.

Surly horses and aroused cows present no surprise for Tómas Jónsson. He treated the countryside like one big udder. Magga's daughter rushed giggling over the farm's dirt floor, fat and careful because of the merchant who slumbered Sunday afternoons and let his genitals dangle out from a hole in the bedspread in order to provoke the merchant woman who threatened to splash water on him from the barrel. Jónas wrote patiently: We finished mowing Stórastykkið today. An excellent growth. Four cables. Eight stacks. The same result as last year. In the morning we mow Flötina. Today we began to mow Flötina. An ideal growth. Ten cables. Twenty stacks. The same amount of hay as last year. Tomorrow we go to Hornstykkið. Today we mowed Hornstykkið. A poor growth. Nine cables. Eighteen haystacks. Less than last year, but better haying. Tomorrow we drive to Áveituna. Every day was like that but exciting and new. On Saturdays he wrote in the book: finally, early mowing. I put my palm on Guðrún's breast. And December 31 each year he signed in ornamental lettering: Now the year has passed. Total: 52 palms. An identical figure to last year. I have nothing to worry about, and I am in full swing. Autumn lay over the countryside. He was never bored, not even in the rain. He was never overcome by nostalgia when he opened the wooden lock and water flooded the irrigation. He drew the wooden bolt from the loop in the water gate to the irrigation gardens and came home with wet crotch, mud splattered, to eat skýr and fall asleep with his nose over the urine-stained yellow chamber pot. Yes, my Tómas, I wanted to come and see the blood sausage competition this year. Jónas has grown tired of skýr, but eats porridge and a chunky slice of blood sausage; his children eat skýr. After eight hours of staying in bed, he woke up, yawned, belched, ran the night out through his butt, ate skýr, stuffed his hat on his head, and a new day began under the cow's teats. The rain dripped from the roof. The cultivated land now withered, Magga's daughter giggled a homely giggling and between laying eggs the hens darted drenched about the cowshed mound and thrust their dripping heads under the wet saddle, which was used as coverings on the skin; the hens wore silly expressions and their brains swelled. Títa investigated everything here and adapted immediately to the apartment. I addressed her under the light bulb in the hallway, the light on me as I rubbed my hands: Be welcome, guest, to anything edible you find in Tómas's den. Be welcome, your clit too. The hens' ovaries ached after all the laying and rats squeaked in the feedbags in the storehouse. I lifted my head and examined the carved bed rail under the rafters. At some point a dexterous midwife lived in this town. She invented forceps but never got recognition for her construction. She was married to an ironsmith and Jónas said: he used it to pull a glowing horseshoe iron from the fire; at the time it was not customary to retrieve children from the mother's womb with forceps, my dear. Magga's daughter giggled and bolted down dried cod heads between meals and fattened happily. She was a master at tearing meat from sheep's heads and grappling giggling, sly and mischievous out by the farm's walls. The merchant gravitated to her at any opportunity he could and she would crawl around him   when no one could hear he said one sentence from the ten he used with her:

Have you hit puberty. Poppa's here for you. Meee. Am I to go lambing. Homely Magga stiffened up, blinked in awe and tried to be in his way in the haybarn and bull stall. Then he said boldly:

I would not even once want to kick my heel in your pussy or poke into your patch even if your body is for everyone.

She threw the cat into the silage pit. Last night I forgot to mention that I came across Bjössi near the head of the street and of course he had the briefcase under his arm and news of the refectory. Ásmundur's ground floor now flows rapidly into him from his soup spoon. He will probably need to move into the basement before the year ends to extend his days. A lot of talk about Ása, he said. But I fear nothing. I just concluded Ásmundur is rather obnoxious. Yesterday we talked with Katrín about the future. With the support of god assisting me in the future as in the past and present. The ever-beneficent god. Give, almighty god, that I may enjoy the light of the following day. I hope he leaves me his grace to sleep soundly in these dim coming nights. Good night. I kiss your image, O god, in the dark. The bull sat behind the cow, he said. The mare flung the foal. Do you love dogs. And he stood fluttering behind the cows in the cowshed and locked carefully the clicked-shut door and the coins. Magga lay on the chimney and looked down and said to me: Best wishes, I'll kill you. You are so bullish, Tómas.

June 29, 1957.

(Addition to yesterday.)

In the night saw a rat stagger across the sidewalk with a needle in its brain. Who stabbed it. The wretch stumbled and rolled paralyzed by the curb near a roof drain, and tried in vain to scratch its way out the slippery gutter. I tied a cord around Títa's neck and sent her out the window and waited with my hand on the cord while she ate the rat. Now I cannot kiss the cat's nose for several days. After eating, the puss licked herself, but I regret when thinking about this day that she should have been corrupted and the hourglass runs toward eternity and so eternity is, in a sense ruined, irredeemable because I witnessed the life of a rat and its death disappearing into the belly of a cat said to have nine lives. What need it another animal's life to nourish its own (clock strikes twelve midnight).

June 30, 1957.

. . . merciless. Had I the chance to control time I would stop its journey. I would obstruct the respiratory system, save my sight, breathe for example only every other day but unrestricted every Saturday afternoon, I would see and hear unstintingly on every major holiday, christmas and Easter, for the glory of life, of all existence. I do not want to wake up in the morning light with the upheaval of fear, referred to as nonsense but still there in every man at the day's arrival. And if I could stop breathing, I would definitely do it and lie in a winter-long coma with a pillow under my heels. I would never need fear my words again and that my sight, hearing, and breathing are not fit for their characteristics i.e. making speech, seeing, hearing, drawing breath. My eyes stare back at me bloodshot and swollen. The word was and never has been a god.

I know that life would be welcome without words. Be silent, heart. A lifetime of words is extremely precarious. They blur with use. Although it is possible to rejuvenate a word you can also kill with it. Tell time to speed its journey. Order the flesh to wither quickly. Issue a hurry-up to the decay so one becomes senile and apathetic. Let light shine where rotten blood constantly renews. You let everything return to source, to water, lava and wind.

If you do not want to rot, rot you still will.

Everything turns into its opposite and renews itself in a paradox.

Tómas Jónsson

17. composition book

Accident strikes as an oppression habit denies;
the happy one seeks
nothing more.

Guðmundur Böðvarsson

The evening is warm. I feel a passionate desire that has become rather rare: to saunter along the downtown streets. Few people are about. Probably they are at the movies. I have not been to work for a few days, but no one wants to know why. Only rarely did I use quiet afternoons to sneak out the house and crawl the streets to my satisfaction. Now I take care to come home before the evening shows let out. Even the door handles nauseate me, how people push into cafés at closing to eat cream cakes and drink coffee. One giggles, half-bent in an overcoat, strokes some snot from a nose in the cold and discusses the film. I despise snot unless it is large and hangs like a spider from the tip of the nose or dandles up and down after respiration. These are very rare. Usually only clear water or moisture runs from the nose. Snot used to be SNOT not clear water. On Sunday morning I walk along the streets while the city sleeps off its hangover. The streets are empty until noon like a moor with birds and landscape wherever you look. No one to see except the man in the flight cap collecting empty beer bottles from the streets and stuffing them about himself. His face red and raging. He has good clogs and clean work clothes. He sells the bottles at Lækjarbar and gets coffee in exchange. I stand at the glass door and see him drink and devour Danish pastries. He does not seem to save any of what he gets from bottle collecting, but just buys coffee with the returns. Last night's cigarette smoke still streams around the window. I hate going past groups waiting to be let into the movies. I don't venture out until the clock strikes nine, and the people sitting in their seats are feasting their eyes in the shadows. The movie houses clear the streets. Cinema is an excellent trashcan. I go look at the building where I work during the day. It is square and long. I look up at the walls in search of the window where I work. Many windows are in a row on the side. I find the right window. The building is about the same outside as it is different inside. My desk cannot be seen in the window. I cannot guarantee this is the right window. I count the panes to the right and left on the third floor and my fingers almost meet in the middle of the wall. My window should be the fifth window from the left and the third from the right. I could have overlooked so I count from the roof to the ground. As I do I always leap past the fifth and third windows which I find strange. There is no light inside. The front of the building is not illuminated. On the street there are few souls about. I go to the door and touch the handle with a handkerchief. I push the door. The door gives after I push with my knee. It is heavy and oak. I head in and stand breathless in the hallway. Everything is quiet. The building unoccupied. This is a public building. I open a door to a room. The door closes by itself. The door has a spring that closes the door after you. I walk to the stairs along the walls surrounding the rectangular opening that connects the four floors. The building was built out of bold optimism. According to the plan, an elevator was going to be where the stairs are, pausing on four floors. It was to have space for two people on the way up but not down. I do not turn on the lights since it is night. Because it is night it is not possible to see how the stairs wind up the stories and touch the platform on each floor, then resume on the next. The stairs go up the stories, one after the other, until they are no longer. The roof takes over. Stairs never rise up from building roofs. At the handrail on the third floor I always think: if you fall here you would be knocked out on the floor. Due to the stack of cardboard on the ground floor you would probably escape unharmed or just badly injured. Of course, you would crush the boxes and fall stably to the floor. I keep Títa in the bag and whisper to explain thing as if her eyes. Títa is curious to know how things are organized where I work. In theory this is called field study. I was fleeing a few rain drops that fell on the road. Outside it is beginning to rain. I sit on the stairs and decide to wait off the rain. After some consideration, I saunter up the stairs. When I go upstairs I run my palm along the railing, like when I go down the stairs. In this there is security; one might stub toes on something. I reach the third floor. On the way I grab at each door but they are locked. I always want to touch them all but did not get to until now. A person always finds some adventure. I sit on the platform by the door I've walked past for many years. I lean my left shoulder against the wall. It squeals under my clammy palms as I stroke the lacquered walls. It is dark in the hallway. Streetlights shine from below and signal vague shadows through the window frames. Maybe these are what's called window dressings. I do not know what the crossbeam in the window is called. Maybe just the crossbeam. I rise and go to the window. Someone might come in by chance. I variously stride or saunter. The streetlights are dim and far from the window. The light on the right is near so the shadows are clearer on the wall to the left and break on the door placard on Ólaf's office. If I was in charge, I would bronze the placards. Someone makes a racket in the corridor below. I'm not frightened of the dark. A door slams. Often it is the CEO who drinks and boozes at the office after work. At least, they did so in my time. They would store glasses of water in a desk cabinet and rinse them in the toilet, in the wash basin, white at the bottom from the mineral material that settled in it. This is not a urine stain like in a chamber pot, but, what I would call a wine stain. They drink hard liquor in what's called a mix: beer or water. From here I stand at the window on the third floor and hear the sound that must be carrying either from the first or second floor. The possibility that it comes from the second floor is negligibly small, since then it would be heard clearly. Someone is running about the first floor. Do not go down the stairs. The sound comes from Bjössi's flat, the watchman's apartment, which is one room and a tiny kitchen. The front door slams locked. Again the hallway becomes quiet. I'm locked in the building and ponder things.

In the morning, newspapers publish a law that sets high fines if you let an apartment stand empty, due to the housing shortage in the city. An infraction carries a steep cost. I, an autonomous apartment owner without debt, had not planned to launch into the housing market until prices in the country fell, inflation ceased, and things returned to a balance after the world-famous World War which made us money-rich and dignity-poor. I thought to myself, the high cost of living cannot increase indefinitely, or so I reasoned. It was growing even as I thought it through: surely conditions must improve. It seems that nothing can stop it once it is accidentally jostled into motion. Is there not a law governing inexhaustible unchangeable energy. The high cost of living became terrible. I decided not to wait for an improvement. I brought out all my possessions. I gathered together every króna. I decided to save whatever could be saved. No one should take anyone else's share to justify their lack of income, not even you, mayor, who besets me with hard conditions even though I have voted for you and your party in good faith ever since I got the right to vote. I make my mark even before election day, so careful in every respect, as soon as voting begins at the polling stations. That first day I go right from work and vote in case I die before election day, die very suddenly, then what would happen to my vote. I do not care if you have a corpse's vote so long as it lands in the right place. When I take my leave of my life and voting rights, I want to be sure my vote ended up with my party, the mayor. I had tenants in my house and know what comes from taking strangers in. At first they act like tenants, refined and discreet, but then they trample on the master's bench. Finally, you cannot move without coming across their chairs, table, the long shoehorn in the shape of a negress, shabby reeds in flower vases, candlesticks with glinting birds that dangle on a chain and spin in a circle when the flame is lit. You come across a comb with shaggy hair; gnawed pencils; an dirty laundry bag. No piano appears, played by children with tremendous talent. The tenants multiply and the landlord gets smothered in child rearing. You cannot hold with their custom of talking constantly with full mouths in the kitchen doorway, covered in ketchup. You are driven from your house. As soon as you are carried to the grave an unknown woman sinks to her knee, not from grief, but to pour Lysol where your footsteps were and scrub the floor with a strong alkali soap. Your brass name card is removed from the door and another nailed in its place, cut from the lid of a shoebox. The box that was your house becomes a dwelling place for robbers; contracts get trodden all over despite agreements assenting: This is splendid. The day after the tenants arrived I could not get into the workshop; the woman had hidden it under dirty laundry and giant bedding. Barely two years later, the kids had demolished my construction tools. Everywhere my body was squeezed by boxes, helpfulness, and idling in the toilet until I scrambled to my room like a snail in a spiral shell. I rarely risk myself in the danger area of the corridor except for the most urgent of needs. I got no peace on the toilet, a storm raging at the door, the rabble always needing to shit at the same time as me or piss or squeeze a blackhead on their nostrils in front of the mirror. I can't even scratch my head freely, but freedom is intolerably restrained. I have no one to blame. The couple wanted a contract extension despite their promises to get out with all their things as soon as the war was over, lodging ended, and we all stopped fighting for every square meter once new houses got built. I did not want to extend for fear that they would appropriate the apartment in posterity for time and eternity, not from greed but friendship. They moved temporarily, but asked to leave some of their possessions, as they had no confidence that the city housing problems were solved. The next morning, the newspapers announced the rule against flat owners letting housing stand unused. There is once more a shortage in the city; tomorrow I expect a commission from you, mayor, an order on paper insisting that I take on new tenants. It would be better to get the old ones back, having their possessions in storage. What about my rights in being deprived of my storage. I am vulnerable, I am writing you this letter to lay out the facts, but you turn a deaf ear to the town, powerful enough to be deaf the way I am blind when it comes to it. You do not need, as I do, to scratch away with your pen, and fill composition books to defend yourself, mister mayor. You are beyond explanation. In your hands you have the power to make laws and rescind laws at will. Your maturity and justice have obtained such over-maturity that you shun them in the name of power. Promises and decisions prevail against you as lightly as the little man gets a sore throat. You cry out countless contradictions as you opine about individual rights, no doubt to make sure people think of you from multiple perspectives. Your head is that shop, Nora, its glass cases full of small objects; in order to see them you look past the glare of helmets or lines of the Bible. I know shamefully well there is neither truth nor justice but I do not know how to define their nature. I was taught that truth is a concept. How can it be a concept if it leads to me not being able to keep my own flat in my own possession, instead needing to rent it out, mister mayor, a concrete compartment where I can sleep sheltered from rain and wind and avoid neighbors and not need to wear my warm overcoat or be a wolf disguised as a sheep—instead, I get some unrelated woman (in my own apartment!), a husband who works for a home—theirs!!—so they never need to carry their children outside and leave them under the lava rock as it is said we to do. I was born long before you, you little stooping man (I've seen pictures) who saw his first light from under the white shade of a hanging lamp that hung from a rose-patterned cap in the ceiling of your parents' very own compartment. You remember the plaster and the copper lamp and the oil burner you did not want to throw in the rubbish dump. I am an old man who has practiced self-denial and integrity. Now you overthrow me with threatening letters and seals. I could stop you, brazen and playing tricks with words, but the seal remains in your hands, you Tlaloc raining documents and papers. I am an annoyed animal in an apartment I own but over which I have no jurisdiction, worse off than a fox in a wild hole. Who would demand an animal take animals of different species into his den. Animals build their own holes. Am I then subordinate to animals, right below them. What would it take for me to have a home free from unrelated generations, a wife, a husband, children, Ásu and Ása. Ási has an ace. Ass, says Ási. Ása, Ása, says Ási. Ása has an ace. Ási has an ass, says Ása. Ása the wife of Ási works outside. Ási eats in the cafeteria. During the day the couple store Ási and Ása the children at the orphanage. In the evening the family meet in their rented box. Does Ása have an ass. Ási has an ace, says Ása. What's new, says Ási. You're new, says Ása. Where's the newspaper, says Ási. On the table, answers Ása. Let's just go to bed, says Ási. I am exhausted, says Ása. Ási turns on the radio. On the news, says the radio, two sheep were found inside the Hrunamanna news booth, in excellent health despite living outside. Is the newspaper on the table, says Ási. Yes, my Ási, the newspaper is on the table, answers Ása. Will you read it, asks Ási. No, my Ási, you read the newspaper, says Ása. What's on the front page, asks Ási. It was three sheep, replies Ása. You never listen to the newspaper, says Ási. There's never anything to listen to, says Ása. Leave me to read, requests Ási. If you can, snorts Ása. Don't hog the paper all night, says Ási. I am not keeping anything from you, answers Ása. What do you have in your hands, asks Ási. Nothing, answers Ása, but here. The compartment is equipped with amenities. The divan is splendid. I come to visit and Ási lies on the divan like a skate. Anyone who comes: Ási the family man is lying exhausted on the divan.

Formula for Visitors

Knock three to four blows with the knuckle of your middle finger on the front door at chest height. Respectful blows; then wait a moment. If a woman opens it a crack and looks round, ask: Is the master of the house at home? While you wait for a response, moisten your lips. Yes, I think he's resting inside his room, the woman says. Then, press your left hand firmly on the doorpost, steady yourself, kick off the shoe on your left foot by stepping your right toe on your left heel. While you take off your shoes the wife will watch your movements by the inner door in the hall, which will open after you've taken off both shoes.

Go into the corridor, knock gently on the room door and look around until you hear an answer from within: Ye-es, come in. In order to see you in the doorway the husband leans over the divan edge and bellows. He rises halfway up and stretches out a little hand, greets you, then lets himself fall back onto the divan with a sigh and stretches his legs. If he emits unpleasant odors, take a chair and sit at the head. Let silence reign a while; take a newspaper from the side table, rustle it, flatten it. If the question is: What passes, answer the sluggish: Nothing—or at most: Nothing special. Be careful to be on guard and do not say anything particular. If you are offered refreshments, drink three cups of coffee and eat cookies from the center of the plate. Then squirm on your chair and go, after giving thanks for your welcome. If there are children in the house you should of course pinch them gently on the cheek and ask: Whose are these handsome kids? On the way out the hall it is right that you promise you will never visit anyone and instead on Sundays rest at home on your divan.

The kids rush in and run a double circle around me on the chair. Get lost, he howls from the newspaper. He is rather tall and stocky, his pants smartly creased. His neck rests on poorly made pillows. Feet crossed, his heels sink into cushions at the couch arm. What are you up to now, he asks through the booming. I look at the radio and ask him to repeat what he said. Yes, I have to turn it up to drown out the din of my old lady and the kids. They are lively and energetic. Ási and Ása rush in again and run twice around me on the chair. Both are taking piano lessons and Ása is also a violin maestro. Both have ballet three times a week after school and are taking a candy class where they learn to choose healthy candy from fifteen different jars on a candy shelf, some of which are unhealthy traps. It occurs to me to trip them, but I resist and look around the room. Yes, you see the cracks in the concrete, he said. Criss-crossing. There are worse cracks in the bedroom. We walk around the room in our socks and look thunderstruck at various wide cracks. We stand on a chair and follow them with our fingers and he lifts the floor carpet and points out the cracks under it. Some fault in the base, he sighs, the concrete dried wrong and molded or the mixture was off, too wet. You try to save and this happens to the building. He drew my attention to the veneered doors, showed me the paint on the windows; cracks everywhere. Even the glass in the picture frames began to burst and my cup was a fine network of dark defects. One lovely day everything here will explode into the air, he sighs, and we will just have to hope there are no bystanders and we can escape to safety in the United States. Sweat breaks out on his forehead, pearls in his wrinkles. Everything goes to hell except for America, he says, and where will we be then. I recognize Ásmundur, eating his possessions, lapping them out his soup spoon. In the end, he laps his own death from the spoon's bowl. Everything we have gets eaten up over time. Since early childhood, I determined to avoid this, faults becoming flaws. I offered my willing shoulders under heavy burdens. Sigurður calls us beasts. I am proud to accept that name. I boast at being indentured. I shed no tears over music albums. I do not get goose bumps listening to pop songs. I push away icons and blurred images. I am a realistic man who clings fast to the reality of things. Things are loyal though I avoid *finding something out about an object*, I just love looking. In my eyes a chair is just a chair, a house a house, a flower a flower. I do not destroy one meaning to find another. I do not answer the four ultimate questions:

Which party will you choose on election day. How much have you deposited in your bank savings. Do you say evening prayers. What are you paid as a monthly salary.

The answers to these questions are private. I want to live in peace like a useless stone. In my eyes, my apartment is my peace. It is justice. Truth, too. I can hardly believe this evidence myself. I say to Títa, earnestly: these are all concepts. That's what I was taught. You and I are concepts, too. But only in a sense. In my eyes, we are things. If I say that, you will send me a threatening letter and protest: No.

Everything is both material and interpretation. Interpretation is material and material hides interpretation.

You give off a decent heat, my Títa.

I spoke to god and asked him to make me an imbecile so I could not understand my misery. I wrote about the vices that accompany my life. I could not tolerate Katrín's presence; she claimed the best advice to save the apartment would be to rent or sell it at a high cost. Such salvage is our common problem though we chose different paths. Two parallel lines meeting nowhere except in the apartment. Maybe I will lose it because of a remote-control force too strong for me. That's you, mister mayor. The evil and capricious Aztec rain god requiring ever greater and more frequent human sacrifices for each drop of water you send us. We are continually offering larger portions of our flesh without you letting rain down from the clouds from your carved oak chair where saturated air lets sweat pearl in your high temples to no avail, mister mayor.

Respectfully

Tómas Jónsson.

September 27, 1956.

Tonight I scrambled to bed immediately after dinner. I cooked for myself. I ate on a chair in the corridor and hooked my toes around its back legs to stabilize myself. I do this because people look into the kitchen. There's no screen, not even cardboard. If I turn on the light and sit in the kitchen to eat is like being in a field, seen from the street. I do not like the cars pausing, people sticking their heads out the window, looking amazed at me and saying: a man sitting eating in an empty apartment. I eat and digest my food in the dark. It is difficult to balance the chair in the dark. But man adapts to his circumstances and find measures, such as hooking his toes around the chair's feet. Kids hammer on the windowpane. Evidently others in the house find it strange that the apartment stands empty. I am not especially worried about other people's opinions. In everyday speech, I am referred to as a brute. The creature in there, the rabble says. Never eats anything but sausages. I am okay being called a brute. The fines for not renting can be up to one million. I lay on the divan. Very tired; brutes often are. I checked my ears in a pocket mirror and said to Katrín, do not go getting used to sitting at home at night and not going carousing. She steamed up, flustered. Fiery and unruly, she attacked me, in the diaphragm this time so I belched or hiccupped three times then drank icy water from the brink of the cup and clamped my thumb and index finger over my nose. I finally managed to stop hiccupping, but then I vomited the water on the floor and splashed in it with my toes. I begged Katrín to speak mildly; I cannot stand the eternal shame. She raised her voice like heartburn, but I said: if an icy harbinger comes for me in the likeness of a swan, saying death has had his eye on me, I would answer: I never did anything I could be ashamed of and if you give me the chance to relive life I would take the offer. I regret nothing, she said, and will die because no one has managed to discover eternity, and even if they managed it, it would go to someone other than me. So speaks a bully. You are a desperate soul, I protest feebly. I know your plans for me: you are selfish, sly, devious, and seek to break me with your authoritarianism. Ever since that day, the moment I first felt your presence and heard your rustle in the hallway, I have cursed you.

Then I addressed her again and said: Get lost, Katrín, follow your old nature. Sell yourself to a stranger, to the highest bidder. Become some foreign shore, its porpoise, deserving to be blown up with dynamite so you do not pollute the atmosphere with your whoring, decaying the earth and malforming the sea. People will grab your nose when you pass and ships take a detour and avoid your beaches. You fiery island that birds avoid. Migrating birds shit on you and fly away screaming in disgust. And other whore-friends throw stones at you despite signing agreements about loyalty in adultery. Because compared to your sins, all sinners are sin-free. Only stranded fish love you and the flies that beget you buzzing black worms. Your eyes are full of reptiles. Your nose exhales gunpowder smoke. Your genitals are a lice sanctuary. Neither curious shells nor seaweed arouse you. No gust of wind blows worms from your scabrous belly. Your lousy ruins taking donations from the American army like a hen with featherloss under an earth ridge. You are just as licey as before. Fly off to where frost lives. Boast of your riches of ice, where nothing stirs fixed roots.

o katrín o katrín a military base in your belly

do not shout after me: Too . . . much, Too . . . mas, Tomb-ass, Tómmas. The truth that some born alive might be undesirable, instead lead falls from your belly or gray stones that mate amid an intense erosion of wind and produce vegetation-free gravel. I come to agree. The gravel increases its kin through mercy and irritation. Here will be your end. Your belly hard as corn. Humanitarianism manifests when nothing gets born, neither thought nor flesh, maintaining the act of thinking generation to generation. By contrast, life gets saved from death when being no longer exists. Anxiety is worse than death. Anxiety humiliates whereas death is exalted by its absolute perfection. The dead cannot suffer. The corpse is the most evolved version of the body. It was madness to birth something as tender as a body in this apartment. The farmer does not strew farmer manure on a frozen brook. No man sows grass in surf.

memories and the gravel bed uninhabited except for low gravelbed vegetation   and people flocked there at night to breathe the clear evening freshness   skirts swung their light fabric   hats lifted in the farewell of a calm breeze   sometimes I get the aroma of unknown herbs   in an easterly direction smoke waving from the chimneys of houses over the gravel bed   I stop a while   my thoughts run down all the floral species that I know   I think I search my nose's archive to ascertain the fragrance and find the lost aroma is a brown cow on a slope lying up opposite the steppes of an almost horseshoe-shaped arch   with the support of hands on each knee alternately you tug yourself higher and higher up the steep slope and discover a lawn on top where a man lies down and binds himself fast by the arms, hugging himself, but with his feet the man pushes his body away and rolls ledge to ledge and the ocean covers its sexual instinct in its clean image and green grass and the ocean swallowing cherished stones in the cool grass on the flat land perhaps existence itself

I haul a few steps further. Dusk comes rapidly here. Brass braces glow on the edges of the steps. I reach my arms up and by squeezing my belly I pee freely in my pants, unhindered. I have not peed my pants since I was a child and do not remember how it felt, but I have often thought about finding out. I know a man pisses himself in old age before dying. I enjoy but find repulsive the warm urine flowing about my thighs, but it is hardly special to pee my pants in the bank where I work. Out on the street it is still raining, on house roofs and gardens. Glimpses of light flow halfway up the façade, but cannot properly break through the windows. On the upper floor the windows are larger and wider. We could watch the traffic on the street by resting our elbows on the windowsill. We manage to see slanting house roofs, two of copper, many house corners, several gardens. Here we will likely have to remain for two nights. Today constitutes a Saturday, according to the calendar, Títa, and the watchman has locked the building. The only exit route is through his apartment and the concrete courtyard so garbage men can easily drive their cars to the bins. The bins with their hinged lids. One has a gray galvanic and fluted exterior. It is private property and was stolen from the American military. Bjössi was probably the one passing through earlier. His pipe smoke lingers in the air; he had to check the lights, lower the heat. In the hallway it is getting cool and I feel the damp cold steal over me through my pissed pants. You're in my bag, pussy, head out of the hole. Eyes a-twinkle, the teeth on the zipper a garland around your neck. Damp cold steals over me like a terrible childhood memory. Lament nothing, Tómas Jónsson; that memory is written off, too. Memories warm no one up. Their life withers as fire does. You will get warmer by the radiator. Central heating is better than memory. Look, a break in the movie. People stream out to smoke in the cool of the evening. Some eat chocolates on the sidewalk; others look at glass displays. One wanders along the sidewalk in front of this building. Most are dog-tired of the movie and the rest of the screening. Three teenagers look for a chance to sneak in unseen during the break, they want to see how the woman is raped, the bank robbed, the criminals die in the electric chair like an obnoxious moral at the end. Indeed, one couple decides not to return after the break. They go home in a car. It's not unlikely they were fumbling with one another under his coat which they spread on their knees in the seats. It's common at the movies. People watch the car disappear. We should see if the picture improves, they say, loitering in dispersed groups, lacking topics of conversation. While the women talk they pick incessantly and brush lint from each other, but the men stand erect with hands behind backs, lifting up on their toes and heels alternately. They rock during the break. The name promised a lot, if only the performance would live up to it, one says. Now light fades and the myopic doorman, who was once a sailor, comes out of the candy booth and holds the door open. Now everyone finishes up and people pack into the theater. While they are waiting in their rows of seats there are advertisements for their eyes, then the film starts up halfway through and people smack and whisper silence. Yesterday the newspapers published a picture on their covers of a cloud that looked like a claw or streaks on the western horizon, but the storm detoured past town and took the land route over the fjords and attacked the houses on the east side with storm and rain. The wind scrapes the streets. Street lights seem to shake their head from the rain dripping into their eyes, but strictly speaking, their helmets are just vibrating in the wind. People dare not leave their houses. A single taxi splashes about the streets and flings puddles from its wheels. I have to get out. For sure, I could pull together a pile of mats from the corridor as a bed to sleep on. I have to break out. I go to the stairs and creep silently down the steps to the door. The wind beats at the oak door. She will swell with water and get stuck in the frame come Monday. If a door is made from good wood, for example oak, it should not swell. Perhaps this is a door made out of recovered organ pine. No, it cannot be. The door is made of ordinary pine. I almost weep to see a latch inside the door. Where else would the lock be, locks are inside what is locked. A man locks what's inside with a key outside. I just need to turn the knob and the door opens. The wind throws rain onto the floor. I find it difficult to breathe in the heavy columns of wind that rage at the entrance to the corridor and creak inside the building. I look around the streets. Tómas Jónsson runs along the sidewalk by the building wall. Slush spills from the roofs. The wall offers considerable shelter so his coat gets wet mostly on the left shoulder, turned away from him. A car approaches. A police car drives past me and moves slowly along the road. I stand in the puddle, which expands because of the congested downpour. Where are you going, they shout from the car window, grimacing at the torrents. Tómas does not reply. Now he attempts to know how to shut up. To just look at the puddle without having to go wading. I set off. The puddle is deep. If I go any farther water will fill my overshoes. His overcoat absorbs rain and gets heavy. The car drives backward. What route are you taking, they call out. Returning home, I answer. Where do you live. Water ripples as the storm squalls and swells about my overshoes. Where are you going. I do not answer, but try to see if I can avoid the puddle. My right to remain silent is indisputable. A person is free to remain silent in the streets; this is not a visit. I'm in public. Two police officers exit the car. Best to drive him back. I'm not going anywhere with you. I am going my own way. Do not resist. Everyone has some resistance. Do not obstruct. Where do you live. I do not answer. I have not committed a crime and am under no obligation to speak. I'm free to be silent in a free country. Can any lout jostle a citizen, demand his name and address. Come on, buddy, don't be obstructive. It doesn't pay. No, I'm not going anywhere in a car. I will walk. I get carsick. Come on, it's blowing the roofs off houses. I don't care if the roofs blow off. Do you want a roof on your head. I do not want anything. They seize the man. I taste salt in the wind and hear the murmur of the sea, unburdening myself from my wet coat. Come on. I clamber into the back of the car. I sit on the bench. I have a clean reputation. I was returning home. I sit on a hard seat. They sit on foam cushions. You cannot see people's intention. I am oddly calm. The police speak into the radio, give call signs and change directions, satisfied with the transceiver. What is the address. He will not say. He does not give anything up. We will drive him downslope. No, no, he's calm. Where is this bloody downslope, I yell. Do not yell. It does not pay. Everyone yells. You, friend. I do not yell. Things go badly for those who yell. The wind tugs open the door. Outside there are two police officers. It is really windy in the courtyard and they say: Come out, do not yell. You yelled, says the young detective who had sat facing me and looked curiously at me in the car, eager to be of assistance, but never a word past his lips. Now they lead me in and get reinforcements at the door. I do not want to enter, but they swing me over the threshold. I am surprised that the seams in the old coat hold. It has not fused together. As soon as we enter, the night watch flows in from the break room to surround us. The police officers are wearing creased, damp clothes, which smell of their body heat and I recognize a crotch smell. Katrín said policemen always had a crotch smell. They are total crotches. Steam rises from their dark clothing because they have placed them on a glowing electric radiator to dry. The mood is calm yet I say: You have no right. He does not want to say his name. No one cares about my name or where I live. You think, he says and rummages on the shelf and calls a police car. He hands me a booklet about shooting off my mouth from a glass panel. His eyes flicker and he asks, disinterestedly: do you understand. Yes, I reply. What is your name. Tómas. Tómmas, he replies and thuds open a thick book with typewritten names in columns. Is this the population register, I ask. It does not concern you, he says. That fits, he says, Tómmas. The book does not draw my curiosity, but I ask: What did I do. I want a lawyer immediately tomorrow. You head home. Are you going with me. I am farther away now than when they arrested me. No one arrested you. What is it then. A warning. You have a nice stroll and read the article along the way. He looks accusingly at the policemen and they drift into the break room, stretch their legs by the glowing radiator, and take off their jackets. Steam rises off their shoulders like scattering fog. All in black galoshes. No roofs will fly off the houses. Barely fly past your head. I am alone on the floor and when I turn a sleeping drunk rises from the wooden bench and looks at me for a moment. Did you call me. Keep sleeping, they say. The man removes a stretched wet jacket from his head. One eye looks down at me. He sticks his tongue out, and gives a signal that he needs a cigarette. Bring me something to smoke. I yell and the police officers grab me and throw me down the stairs through the back door. I fall in the dark and the door bursts open. I fumble along the ground in the dark and touch pieces of wood and rocks. I get up and check my leg and arm bones are intact. The route, though it is long, has an end. I will get home to the divan in my overcoat and in overshoes, which are soaked through to the wet feet. They puddle with every footstep. As I grope under my coat, the bag with Títa lands in the puddle. She is sealed inside the bag and catches her breath. The rain pounds on the leather. A car turns the corner and a puddle sloshes out from under the wheels. The car approaches the bag. Títa kicks her legs. She doesn't do so much as hiss. She is crushed. Tomorrow someone will find a high-quality leather case with a crushed cat, a letter smeared with fish, and some composition books. Never again will I go to work an unbroken   a sore heavy sound   I wrestled me down onto the divan I shut my head under the covers   I get bonechills, am sick   I am vomiting   I feel the body being crushed   I shiver, dressed warmly in blanket and coat   from this I wake up crying in the middle of the night and hear a rustle in the corridor   Katrín comes home at night having gone out, amused herself   but she never turns back to me

Epilogue (only for Reykjavíkers)

After some effort I have been able to finish typing the few composition books that Tómas Jónsson left in drawers and had been crumpled

there since 1956. At that time I was renting a room in his apartment from people who rented off him, then sublet to me. I was a student; I sometimes played guitar and no doubt often irritated him.

Examining the books, one sees the pages are handwritten; the handwriting is sometimes illegible, the script blurred, the content a babble. Often one does not know where he is going. In terms of meaning and purpose, it should be borne in mind that no one knows with certainty where art is headed, as much in its poetry as its other elements. Usually art is a journey out into the unknown, unless it is for profit, whether in the form of glorious praise, favors, or hard cash. In some places the script used by Tómas is big and clumsy; it seems to have spurted from the fountain of memory in short rough arches. But perhaps it is that way for natural, external reasons; for example, his poor vision. The reason could be that these books were written blind. Blindness and writing often go together. The poet is in some sense blind when writing. One thing that supports this is that the reader quickly becomes aware that he could start reading even in the middle of a sentence, just as a person can get to know another person anywhere in his life span. Still, Tómas did technically organize a lot. To write, he used a homemade card with two holes. In the holes he put two nails and wrapped some sewing thread around their heads and moved the nails in parallel down the page to mark a straight horizontal line. He did not use ruled paper.

Most people know these writings as a kind of anti-platform from a man who was the whole of his life deeply ingrained in being defiant. No one, however, should let his opinions hinder them. Opinions can change daily. There is little to the intellectual character of a man who is unaffected by his experiences during a day's twenty-four cycle.

Some people are the result of thought. Their lives and actions are not spontaneous, but are grown with care, a hotbed of humidity and the release of moisture. Without thinking, their lives would basically amount to misery. Other people live a wild life that requires little thought. Such people grow everywhere soil is found, fertile or infertile. Their life requires no fertilizer, it just is. Tómas Jónsson is in both categories. As one can see, his life was the sand grain that chance placed inside a shell; because of the constant friction and the wave motions in the sea, lime heaped on the sand grain. (Somewhere he says he is a pearl.) In such cases, it might be chance that decides whether the pearl becomes large or small, ordinary or extraordinary, clear or flawed, with a catch that reduces its value on the market—until it becomes clear that most pearls are this way, are like sea urchins inside.

Tómas Jónsson is another kind of reality.
The signature is missing, but it is probably Hermann or Svanur.

(Written on a loose page.)

. . . Shortly after noon, it was decided that the car would come for me. This morning while I was unraveling from my unconsciousness taking in oxygen, I asked Anna to look over the newspapers for me, for they have long been my contact with the real world.

Is there anything in the news, I asked.

No, it's all the same: advertising, political squabbles, obituaries and personal essays.

No new scientific discoveries. No new bombs, I asked.

Are you interested in bombs, Tómas dear, she asked with the simulated joy healthy people use in the presence of the patient, especially if they think he is not long for this world. They long to cheer him up.

I am interested in all forms of progress, I replied.

No one lies to old men who vegetate and slumber away their life experience and wise manner in apathy and futility.

Old men need to choose a place to live with suitable conditions and a proper environment.

Everyone has his trash dump.

My place is an old people's home with sick, invalid people my own age, people who drag themselves onward by means of cough mixtures and oxygen. In my oxygen-high my brain has recovered weeks of itself. I feel the difference. I think I have never been as independent, happy, and outside myself; I now feel that eternity will not get discovered in the near future, probably never. It's probably pointless for me to wait any longer to say farewell to this short life.

Hermann.

. . . now it is indeed evident that man's duty is not to believe in a Tómaslife but to bear a yearning in his heart for his nation   nono   he thought   no no

Then he rose from the divan stiff from dozing and sleeping all day Sunday, hungover, and exhausted with an ache in his arms.

With weak fingers he scraped the composition books off the floor with shaking hands and threw them into a closet along the wall.

He thought: I Tómas

Before he closed the closet door he set the letters between the frame and the door because the latch was broken; he grabbed his overcoat and threw it on the divan. His jacket lay on the floor. He put the jacket on then the overcoat on top and sighed, rubbing sleep from his eyes, wiping the sweat from his forehead, looking at his fingertips, wet and clammy, feeling the air in the room stifling hot, saturated with the scent of liquor. Wine in splotches all over the floor. He tried to rub them away with his toes and he felt about his chest. The pump was running, pumping foul air. And after having discovered where it was, he ambled into the laundry room, let the water run a moment before he bit his teeth over the faucet, turned it on and swallowed icy water that became rocks in his stomach once he raised his wet mouth and tried to urinate. Only a few yellow drops fell from the creased flesh   it will leak out as sweat   he thought   in the hallway he came across a fearful, nervous woman:

Good morning escaped from her.

Good morning, he said, and got out of the way. He lay in his coat on top of the covers. After a moment thoughts whirled in his head. There was something so peculiar about the way he retreated into slumber and dreams. He was going to get up to shake off his somnolence. At once, sour water rose in his throat and flowed unhindered out in spasmodic spurts over the divan and floor.

. . . you go ahead . . .

. . . the man fumbled a few steps along the stairs   the woman pressed a finger to the collar of her nightdress at the chin so her breasts did not flop out the wide neck they flutter after six mouths have sucked milk from them and she had no breasts to drive them from the door that gives life to them in her mind and they have so to speak lived under her feet the whole winter drinking and not drinking   she wakes at times with her palm over her mouth or to her throat and listens sitting halfway up on the pillows and mornings she slips down into the room and gives him this what the young and presumably poor get in books warm milk and aspirin and she says

svanur have a little bit of salt and take a B-vitamin and come bathe in hot water upstairs with us

she bakes pancakes while the one who appointed her to turn on the light at the door goes to work at the butchers   she obeys without a word and turns on the light and looks into the bathroom and looks searchingly at the man pitiful in the dull shine of bulb light as it falls onto his head recently woken from sleep   he is in a quarter-sleeve shirt and messy hair with creased pajamas   in mind the sight is probably more abhorrent to her than him but the half open door if someone should come   he sees a gleam of light from the room beyond the darkness of the hallway which is crosswise along the corridor   her husband is not gone to work he looks along the wall and barely realizes that for the moment he lies asleep in his lukewarm bed with his loose skin clammy on his middle-aged body like a pair of freshly-plucked chickens   he sleeps a captive sleep uneasy dreams in which he stuffs himself with sedative drugs from doctors valium and librium and belladonna against nightmares but suddenly the woman pushes in and says, agonized

    I heard a cry from the cellar

    an awful scream   she added   is svanur committing suicide

    he is probably just writing some nonsense about us

. . . now there is snow on the shoes in the hallway that she has never yet been out in lousy enough to watch from the stairs   she is barefoot in clogs in the middle of the night she thinks about the scream and her uncomfortable breasts contract and grow firm in the cold she feels how they pull together and tickle at low speed up her sides   to gather her thoughts she feels hastily about her nipples with her cold fingers

it would not have occurred to them to rent out the single room in the cellar with a door to some uninvited person had not all the cellar holes in town become jam-packed every damp corner crowded even cellars buried below the sidewalk where no daylight ever shines in except perhaps through rusty grates or window squares on the sidewalk so kids cannot kick stones and gravel at the panes   so kids jump and rail on the rattling frame   she thought and said in the afternoon in the shop

    I rang up I just put an advertisement in *Scene* it doesn't make sense to have a small basement room empty rent it to a single seaman on international voyages who is rarely home

    at this moment she is smoking a cigarette by the telephone her fingers drumming she is hardly a person to engage in a great undertaking   she goes into the kitchen and warms coffee in the same breath a ring she strikes her breast does not know if it is the phone or doorbell

    it's the doorbell I am going   he says

    let me I am more meticulous in handling these things than you he agreed later to her proposal to change the living room to a bedroom because of the noise that echoed in the room with no furniture just a boy with a guitar in the basement full of smoke and sometimes people who had no place to go and sat around the floor Svanur and his colleagues who came one time with a closet and a divan and these furnishings so the white walls bore some sign of human habitation   he was from a family in the same village as she was and she brought the crew coffee and bread sometimes and envied being young like she had been once and longed for something uncertain to become something that was really nothing

there was one more day after this night and it was on the next day after that the night disappeared

the young man lay on the divan and longed to smoke but did not ask for a cigarette   he kept the couple fixed in his mind   she is coming downstairs   the woman opens the door   he holds the paper he has caught her writing on the sheet

"The husband is decently dressed, no different from those newly-married husbands who buy meat at the store and have well-established homes, first in the basement because of the lack of rental properties; they may not have a house, but they have a roof over their heads."

what should I let come next in the story
the woman opened the door and said
yes
what else did she say

. . . in such times as I well knew it was possible for someone to rent a cubbyhole even the potato storage under the stairs   the nation growing rapidly and thank god she is not asexual cultivating mushrooms in the basement and she is profiting you say and in another language   you think there are enough humans in this country and

in the world but fertility does not get viewed as the greatest danger to the world   rather suicide than birth   mankind kills himself with his sexual functions   you should live in China   it is easier for the inhabitants of Hvolsvöllur than Peking   Hvolsvöllur is not Reykjavík there is plenty of rental housing   no one lacks freezer storage or ships   don't people lack things everywhere and you think the problem is overpopulation in the world could we have rented the basement unless people increased in number I wonder and for a woman what is healthier than to carry a child for nine months young women is it not too painful no you got me pregnant six times how could I have gotten pregnant in the basement with no running water   in her husband's mind no arguments arise against her claims he sits belching and shamefaced on the chair feeling heavy after having bread soup for lunch and most of all he wants to crawl into his lair and wait for the clock lie on the divan until bedtime listen to the radio wiggle his toes and have no idea that he is just Tómas Jónsson like other Tómas Jónssons   neither better nor worse a Tómas Jónsson but   perhaps dozing inside him is another person other than oh no he has become and is nothing but Tómas Jónsson   he longs to take a spoonful of fruit salad and fall asleep   now she's come up the stairs after showing the young man the room
      I rented it, she says
      and what now
      now I think we have a house have become homeowners because we can rent to others and charge excessively for the lease the way the man charged us

She, who later became Katrín, led Hermann down the internal staircase and warned him about the matting on the floor under the lowest step, which was too high compared with the others.
      That step is dangerous, she said. I have often tripped on it. All steps should be the same height.

The basement appeared, sound-deadened, doorless, and with wiring poking out visibly from the walls like rusty nails. Seven inner and outer walls divided this sarcophagus into compartments of various sizes. One had a door and she led him to it over the uneven floor. Inside the door there was not too much.

Here is the room, she said. It is spacious and heated with twelve elements, which is plenty. You should be snug. And the central boiler is on the other side of the wall—feel.

They placed their hands on the wall and said simultaneously:

It is hot.

They looked at each other.

The window faces the street. It is a great advantage. We just happened to have carpeted the floor. If a house is new, it is rarely debt-free. Am I being too casual?

No.

You can hire someone to do the housecleaning or clean yourself. It should not be a hassle for you.

This will be great, he said.

You can put pictures on the walls to liven them up. Our daughter is into art and can lend you some. Reproductions irritate her, but they are convenient and cheaper, I think. You can also wash them.

It's fine as it is.

Yes, and here, she said, and led him down the hall to the next compartment, which was tiny. This is the bathroom. You can temporarily hang a carpet over the door so no one can see inside. The girls are here all day playing ball.

Then he said:

It won't be necessary. I never defecate during the day.

She was taken aback and dropped her chin, but bore up and said:

That is damn convenient.

I piss during the day with my back to the door. The lack of a door is not a problem.

She ducked her chin so tightly to her neck she got a double chin and said:

Perhaps you were born to live in unfinished houses. Look, a sink with a cold tap; the hot water supply has not yet reached us. god knows when we will get it.

It's not a problem, he said.

If you need hot water to shave or wash your head on Saturdays, you can get hot water from us. We have a heat can. That does not include access to bathing. There are drafts, of course. That is always so in a basement—it has a new and basic building character throughout.

No problem.

Well. I feel like I'm in a windy hell. But you're young. Are you opposed to cursing?

No, I curse when I need to. I use obscene language, too. Obscenity is in my eyes a spiritual defecation, a cleansing.

Good. I like people who curse. They're cleaning themselves with damn, hell, go stick your head up the devil's asshole. My husband never curses. He says I frightened his curses away with my own. Very strange. The worst thing is that you have no closet. We do not want nails in the walls.

Maybe I can get what's know as a gentleman's closet.

And he thought of Tómas's closet, he had a gentleman's closet.

I am accustomed to cellars—to living under others' feet.

Don't be so agreeable, it's not healthy. A person progresses by complaint and dissatisfaction. That's the root cause of progress. The basement doesn't shock you?

No, no.

Well. You were born in the war, right.

More or less.

Perhaps you're a kanakrakki, a child of circumstances.

I suspect, but I don't know. Maybe I'm just ahead of myself.

I had to settle for the basement. We are now on the second floor. Everyone advances.

She coughed and asked:

Yes, but which of you am I to rent the room to?

Having said this, she turned to me.

Me, he answered.

I was silent. This was his chapter in the book *Tómas Jónsson—Bestseller*.

The man trailed down the stairs and announced himself at the door. He said:

I see you are showing the boys the room.

This is my husband, the gem.

Not in front of others, he said, and extended his fingertips toward us.

What is your name?

Hermann.

You're a soldierly young man.

And you?

Svanur.

Even worse.

Do you drink?

Sometimes.

All young people drink.

The man chirped. Then he coughed. His wife was coughing too.

We are not renting to this one, she said. We are renting it to the other one.

The man chirped and gave a flabby laugh.

She poked him several times with the head of the scrubbing brush, then with the end, prodding him like a dangerous animal, ready to run away at any moment. Hermann twisted from the pillow, and looked at the chart on the wall, and said:

Do you remember any Monroe movies?

No, I forget movies as fast as I see them. It means I can go to the movies and see the same picture over and over again.

She made maps and did not know where she was from, but marked routes to destinations in lipstick. The way I made schedules.

What do you think?

Paris—Moscow; who knows, he said with an ironic expression. Like the great writers of the past marking the end of their publications with: London, Paris, New York, Moscow, Rome, Barcelona . . . now, one only gets to write Sauðárkrókur, 1960-whatever.

Simply yuck, she let out.

Over which are you yucking? What makes you yuck at Moscow and Paris?

She closed her eyes then looked at him and said:

You ought to pay attention to what I am doing. It is not often I give you a good cleaning.

She sat with stretched legs on the rug.

A woman who wasted the best years of her life working to wash fish, ending her worst years over a bucket.

Hermann fumbled obtusely about his forehead and tilted his head.

Did I finish what I was saying? . . . Did I?

He looked at her with his head on the edge of the divan. One arm lay down on the floor.

Have you cleaned many places? he asked. I am not trying to make you into some heroic figure; just asking.

Countless places, she said proudly. I'd be happy with more. No one complains; just the opposite: I'm sought after. Some are difficult—others easy. I am not difficult, just the floors are.

Do you think that the floors in the Kremlin are more difficult than other floors?

Depending on the materials. In my house there are tiles. I will not touch wooden floors.

I assure you that the floors in the Kremlin are made of marble.

They will clean up nicely.

I don't know about that. The streets of Athens are made of the same material.

And you have been there to survey them.

Often, many times. As recently as yesterday.

I saw you on the divan Saturday, no indication you were traveling. No luggage to be seen. Here there's nothing, not even a table, just a divan. You didn't travel to Athens.

The woman looked confusedly around and stroked her finger on her half-parted lips. She smoked intensely and smoke came in columns out her mouth and nose.

Can you smoke through your ears.

Sometimes I stick a cigarette up my nose and smoke like that, she said, and struck the ashes into the sewage pail.

White eyes rolled in his head. He thought:

This old woman is sexy, only missing one tooth, and not her sex appeal

But he said:

One time, I traveled from Ibog to Dal. There are crossroads on the highway.

Didn't you get lost. I can find my way. I would happily get lost. I have night vision. god knows a bus could take me anywhere in the country providing I had a seat and could keep track of where I am. I have a crooked back and cannot bend except at my knees. It's impossible for me to see in a crowd. I need to decide where I will get out. A lot can happen if I am unobstructed in a vehicle for a whole day.

Stop. I know you could be lost a whole day. Stop. I am trying to tell you that at the crossroads there is a road sign with four branches that point in the four cardinal directions. Along the streets so no one gets lost. There is no chance of getting lost. Getting lost is frustrating.

If you can't get lost, roads are boring.

The woman shook her head, rubbed her nose, and asked:

You are smart; is that true.

How can one be smart when he has no money to buy vitamins and so develops abrasions on his body. I need money to be intelligent.

I guess you are really deprived, seeing as you're drunk every day. I'm not looking for payment, just surprised to see a grown man lying carelessly on his divan, sometimes immoderately so, a man who turns everything around him into a pigpen and has walked away from a credible job.

You are a strange hen.

The woman giggled, grimaced, smoothed her hair, and adjusted her braces.

A goose, because no sane man is attracted to hens.

But I am totally prepared to wash shit. I take my scrubbing brush, take some alkali soap to the straw with my fingers, and scrub and work devilishly hard—you never offer me wine.

She sniffed hopelessly and snorted through her nose.

The women who clean hotels and wine shops are lucky. They sip from glasses or collect it in a bottle. By contrast, someone living in a basement where you can party and have fun in peace is lucky; others bring them a liquor stash—is it not true?

True!

He laughed and poked at the old woman on the floor with a ruler.

Don't you have a girlfriend, loser?

Why?

Just to have and to play with.

She sighed, her breasts fell. She hunched over and coughed. The cough flushed her face.

A person will never have anything unless they have something to buy it with. If you own money, you will own money—if you own a girl then you get other girls. If you're in a good position you get offered a better position. And if you have nothing, nothing gets taken from you.

A man always has something. If you say something, you have something.

Stop thinking. Your lips have gone deathly blue from thinking. You are . . . how old are you?

Sixty-three, I say. Sixty-eight, my sister says.

He reached out. He said:

You are a fossil from the Quaternary Period, totally unable to understand your environment, used to keeping mastodons company. I, however, am from the last period of geological history, the Pecuniary Period—do you have some fetching mastodon somewhere?

I have neither a mastodon nor anything, just the clothes I am wearing; however, I had the good fortune to be raped. I clung to my chair during my labor pains and my belly shook. I could hardly think balanced thoughts. There was barely jealousy, I said. The kid is coming early. She came out. I held her head. It was a girl. She died. Nothing else. First: I have no money. In other words, I'm bankrupt. Unemployed. Do not bother to work in a bank. Be wary of becoming a new and endless Tómmas. I.e. nothing. In most ways a rather poor draft of a man. Only doctors, engineers, pilots, and imbeciles get women. This is an enormous change from what once was, when people lived in a fantasy of mastodons with two-meter tusks pushing at your tambourine belly. Now you say: I want you all or you will no longer get to touch my trumps.

What will you do if all hope is lost?

I've done something. Written Tómas Jónsson, Bestseller; I will wait for my returns.

When?

I do not know exactly.

If you knew, you would be able to pay me at some point.

And so the fossil awakes from its hibernation to life in the Pecuniary Period next to a sewage bucket of red plastic.

If you're not going to go out and find a wife, the couple cannot bring you prepared food from the butcher free of charge, and I cannot clean your crap and get paid in bullshit. You make an art of laziness.

Get to the privy, he ordered.

She immediately got up, scrambled to the privy, drew back the curtain, and disappeared in.

I do not bring an old woman to my room for her to use foul language! he cried.

The woman sobbed. The privy was an area in the corner demarcated with a brown carpet. He came to it and lifted the opening. She lay there among the buckets and sobbed.

Keep quiet and lie in your place, he ordered.

Do you think I am some show animal?

The woman had left her clothes in the middle of the floor. He slipped his fingers into his pants opening. He thought:

I hate that voice

When the woman heard the water gurgling she yelled

For shame! For shame!

Shut up, he said. Shut up, he repeated, laughing.

I dozed in a pile on the floor under the radiator. I rolled to my side and pulled my jacket around me.

He went unnoticed along the hall in the basement and up the stairs by the potato storage. He strolled unsteadily down the street. A short time later, he discovered that the sea was not far off, lapping in stacked crests, colorless and spread out before him. From the ocean came a coolness. Hermann looked at the bay and said:

Look, the sea is blue.

And he thought:

the sea is never calm the sea is always in motion streams excite the ocean and winds too

He noticed the salt smell of the ocean. His ears heard the voice of the sea.

He thought:

there are six senses one additional one missing there are six senses nothing exists without them without them the sea is and the sea does not know that it is though the animals know it the animals become frightened

His thinking went no further. He followed the street along the shoreline. The street came to an end. At the end the harbor and in the harbor a ship. He went along the harborside. A considerable way away he saw two men in a hurry and thought he knew both, so he jumped and cursed his feet for doing nothing but slipping off his shoes and socks. The overcoat coiled around him; his overshoes. He stumbled. At the corner of the warehouse, he managed to produce some sounds, but the wind scattered them. He tried again in the shelter of a large D.F.D.S. shipping crate.

Guys!

They looked over their shoulders and strolled to meet him and he saw they were not Svanur (how could it have been me if I lay there on the floor) and Óli Iodine (how could he escape the house unless his old woman lay dead). It was Doddi and Viggó. Still, they greeted him and said:

Where did you saunter over from?

Viggó cracked his knuckles. Both stared at Hermann a long while until Doddi broke the silence:

You look awful. Are you hungover? Seems that way. You're cooked.

Where did you come from?

He did not feel like saying that he had seen them slip by and made a beeline along the harbor. He was silent. They grinned. A car drove past them and they moved over to the crate.

We came from a lair although by boat, said Doddi. That's the ship docked there. You recognize the man on the jetty, Uncle Stein.

The man stood on the jetty with a box in his arms. He set the box down. He stood there straddling the box across his crotch. The man bent his knees at the jetty and supported his right hand on the box. The man appeared to stumble. He disappeared down past the edge.

Now a boy must take his chance. We will not sail with Kristján this time. We were gone just over a week.

They looked at the box on the pier. The man scrambled up to it and brought the box closer to the edge, then he leaned back, jumped down, and disappeared. His hands came up and snatched the box. The box budged. The man jumped back up to the jetty, lifted the box, and looked at the bottom. He set the box down. The box was on the jetty, but the man jumped into the boat. Then another one came out of the boat and lifted the box and staggered with it a few steps up the pier. There he bent his knees and disappeared, but after a little while his torso surfaced, hands snatched the box, and it disappeared along with the man. Then he came up to the jetty, looked around, and disappeared as before.

You are blind drunk; you can hardly stand on your legs.

Hermann felt faint. He stuck out his tongue and shrieked.

My mouth feels like smoked fish, he said.

He added:

Why don't we sit under this crate or lean our shoulders against it.

One might believe you had sea legs, said Kristján.

No, a man shall not deceive himself in vain, said Viggó. Listen, don't you believe it, we were sitting calmly in the car, then Stein came and said to Doddi: Pay attention, do you have any porbeagles; there is money to be made. And we had all our equipment in the car—tape recorder and all—for an article. Everything already in the trunk.

I don't recognize you, Hermann said, and leaned against the box.

They stood in front of him and Kristján said:

One would know you a mile off; we're always hearing stories about you, when people come to town to make something of their lives in books. You are hungover and they see you hungover. Are you done with banking?

Hermann waved that away:

Now I recognize you. What news from home?

From Tanga? asked Kristján.

We were just saying. A man makes a fine fox of a plan, then Stein turns up—boom-boom and drags you porbeagle fishing, as if nothing happened, said Viggó.

Take the next bus, said Kristján impatiently and tore into Viggó. Take the next bus and don't loiter here over a man who is past drunk, as out of shape as a badly made thing.

Yes, replied Viggó.

They walked away, hands in pockets.

You are like newborn surrealists, said Hermann. Let's get coffee.

No, they replied. We should drag ourselves home.

They came back to the D.F.D.S. crate.

People are getting scared, said Viggó. The man has been wandering a week or who knows how long and out to sea. And the sea is large. He has quite a story.

No, I'd rather you tell it, Viggó said. It's impossible for me.

The box offered shelter from only two directions. They set another small box under the D.F.D.S. crate. While they prepared they smoked and beat their heels on the jetty. Hermann thought:

now it would be good to go get a hotdog

A man might talk about things differently if he had the heart, said Kristján. A man allows himself everything. He plans something—all well and good—then someone comes along, he says, come on. And the man takes a different path.

He clicked his fingers.

A man takes a different path—all well and good—then someone comes and says, come on. And the man storms in the opposite direction.

They laughed. Viggó waited for Kristján to get into the storytelling mood, so he could interrupt. Viggó did not know how to pay compliments, but enjoyed interrupting folk. It confused Kristján who would get mixed up.

One starts off stiff, said Kristján.

A large crane swung its arm over their heads. Two workmen came to the box and gestured to the operator to let the hook down. One of the workers stepped up to the D.F.D.S. crate and raised his arm to the hook; the other walked around the box and slipped the sling under him and passed it to the man. He took it without dropping the hook. He folded the loop and drew it over the hook. The box lifted and the man jumped down.

Now they are taking the crate, said Kristján.

They stood up from the little box and turned their heads all around. The large crate swung in the air. The workers stood still and raised their arms against the sky and the crate.

One cannot loiter here indefinitely without shelter, said Kristján.

We were sitting on a small box inside a larger one, and the big crate was ripped away so we're sitting on the smaller, Viggó said.

Let's go then, said Kristján. And do not let Stein talk to you and hypnotize you out to sea with him.

The workers uttered a sharp cry. Too much. The crate seesawed in its sling. They seized some empty cement bags and slung them up to the box. The wind tore at the bags, then stopped and flung cement from them. The bags fell in tatters on the quay. The man came out of the lift cockpit with the bag tatters and aimed at the crate. The workers ran about in tattered windbreakers and collected cement bags and slung them at the crate. Mas. Their eyes could barely see for dust, but when the clouds broke they saw a little rat run out from the crate's edge. Two men attempted to go up in the elevator. The crane operator pushed them away with a foot that dangled from the cockpit threshold. They ran off and grabbed a long pole made of wire and used it to scrape at the crate. The rat jumped from the crate, climbed up the sling, and sat by the hook. The operator kept the bag, but threw things at the rat. The rat turned his head and jumped up on the crane's arm. The workers raised their caps. The crane operator stepped along the arm with the bag and the rat retreated. He swung the bag in a blow toward the rat, which stood there at the tip of the arm. The bag flew near the rat, but she escaped and dropped back to the crate. The operator lay on the arm and looked down at the pier. Two men attempted to climb in the cab.

He won't talk me into anything, said Hermann.

He will nevertheless talk to you, said Kristján, he might latch on to you and talk.

The workers had come out of the cab and formed a chain along the lifting arm. Kristján, Viggó, and Hermann said goodbye. Kristján said:

We were mad not to drink coffee with Hermann who has a bedroom we could drink in; we could have got ourselves a bottle. Everything ends with us getting a bottle.

No, we are going home, said Viggó. I have a car on the jetty, so long as no one stole it.

Kristján pushed open the door. They looked around in the dining room. Hermann came after them.

Now we really need to have a coffee after all that drivel, said Kristján. They poured coffee from the glass bowl into thick clay jars they brought to the empty table. The coffee was too hot to drink. While it was cooling they took turns going to the bathroom.

Have you noticed that when you come in from the cold to the heat your bladder fills? said Kristján. I'll go first.

He went to the bathroom. Everything was all smashed: door handles, mirror, sink and paneling. No light. Hints of light passed through tiny air holes with netting over them. On the floor lay underwear and socks and a toilet brush. Only two steel bases on the toilet bowls were unbroken. A man was standing against the wall and peeing and groaning. Kristján peed in one of the bowls and sent some of the stream into the other, then he went out and said to Viggó:

Now its your turn, spring heels. It's like getting lost in the piss inside an old woman's bladder, the stench is so bad.

Hermann covered his mouth. Acid coffee came up in his throat. He got up and spat just past the door. Viggó went in and peed. The man and he pissed long and spoke about the wet weather. Viggó was cold and peed a lot, and while he was at it he glanced up in the air saturated with yellow drops, and felt sure it was caused by the steam from the bowls, then he looked at the other man's stream, and he looked furtively at his stream. Then they locked eyes in the twilight, saying almost simultaneously:

No, what a coincidence; you are airing your socks here?

Neither responded directly to the exclamation, but the man in the booth reached in his coat pocket, pulled out a bottle, and handed it to Viggó, who drank from the neck.

The man said:

These are the city's best toilets.

And so they drank alternately, one drinking while the other peed.

Viggó was done first and did not like to hang around pretending to pee.

He went, kicked the underwear to the wall and said:

We have met before.

When Viggó came into the refectory, he slapped Kristján on the back.

Who do you think is taking a leak in there?

I am not in the habit of studying people while they pee, said Kristján.

Only Silli, with a full bottle.

I'm leaving, said Hermann. I don't want to get into anything.

Kristján went in and pretended to urinate. Silli pulled out a bottle and they drank and peed for the hell of it and enjoyed it.

I did not recognize you, Kristján said.

If a hundred men were made to piss through holes in a wall, their faces covered, I'd know you by your stream, said Silli.

He backed out of the booth. He brushed the dirt from his shoes with the underwear on the floor and threw them into the booth. They went out, and Hermann was gone. He walked aimlessly out of the harbor and probably thought to himself:

it doesn't matter even if in front of you there's the mug of an old acquaintance

He got there as the ship was docking and heard a shout:

You there!

Stein called out. Hermann continued, turned around, walked to the prow where it touched the pier's deck, and cried:

Hey, you there!

His feet took him toward the twenty-ton ship that rolled on the waves. The box was at the opening to the hold. He asked:

What?

The man told him to move closer. He noted a milk carton afloat in the harbor. Without paying attention to Hermann, he said:

They throw rubbish from the ship even though there's a whale belly for trash hanging outside the hull.

Hermann stood with one foot on the jetty and saw the milk cartons caught in the suction current from the ship's propeller and floating in the harbor, White-brand condoms distended like jellyfish in the calm waves. He crossed the jetty and looked down into the sea on the other side. Then he went back over and looked at the man standing bent over the line in the shadow of the engine housing. He waved back and said:

Are you going fishing?

The man knew he was standing there. His shadow fell on the white engine house. His eyes were fixed on something. His tongue dry in the mouth. After some hesitation he moved closer to the battered boat and saw a bearded head peering out from a window of the engine housing. The eyes looked around and regarded the man.

You coming? We are setting out.

The man's head looked down from the wheelhouse. Hermann did not answer. He thought:

i'd kill for a hot dog

He said:

I'm no sailor.

Oh, it doesn't matter. We're not going out to sea.

His feet took him down the harbor stairs, cautiously along the pier to the boat deck, to stand by the wheelhouse under the men's eyes. The boat moved. He felt a thin, solid layer between himself and the sea. It was different standing with the ocean under your feet instead of firm ground. He said:

I know nothing about boatwork.

Doesn't matter. The fisherman inside you won't be hiding any deeper than two days' seasickness.

He thought:

fishing

He looked over the railing and saw the harbor like a metal sheet. There were clear markings on the color of the sea at the harbor entrance. Small beautiful fishing boats sailed in, but the big ugly ship with its unwieldy bulk sailed out. The boats sailed about the harbor, their movements agile and sharp-hulled, like they were sleek surface fish. The transport ship sailed out like a dead whale.

He said:

I did not bring any clothes.

He grabbed at his pants legs, spreading them, and pulled open his jacket to tug at his dirty shirt. Look.

We'll loan you something from the trunk. Come on down and get out of your coat. We'll try you as chef first.

The feet obeyed and traveled down the stairs. His head disappeared at the same time the man raised the gangplank. He stood on the deck, swinging the ladder over his head and knocked it against the pier with a quick blow and shouted:

Get some coffee. You'll feel better.

The face in the window of the wheelhouse growled with dissatisfaction. A swollen fist stretched from the window and brushed dirt from the solid pane with the flat of its hand. Below, in the hold, his head rolled, too sluggish to resist. The only logic was to throw oneself anywhere and try to sleep. In the narrow cell the unclean environment, bleak and cold, was all too evident: a table on the floor splashed with coffee, dirty jars with a dried coffee crust on the bottom, matches, cigarette butts. His feet dragged him to the table, to the stove, where his hands cleaned the blue coffee pot that came trembling near to his mouth, which opened halfway and sucked the spout then gulped down cold coffee. Movement stirred in the body: a growling stomach and in his head the old woman crouched inside the closet of the basement bedroom, but he did not know why she was there or how she had gotten there and then she broke into pitiful giggling. Drool leaked from her mouth. Slow vibrations tickled the legs and bottoms of the feet.

Feet in heavy clogs hustled down the stairs, heels first, then the man was standing on the floor, rubbing his hands and asking:

Are you hungover?

The shoulders shrugged but the hands did not release their grip on the spout.

Lie down and you will rise again like a newborn foal. I will clean the ashes from the machine in the meantime.

newborn baby

He repeated the sentence several times in his mind. The man grabbed him and threw him to the cot. A hard mattress, a moldy smell. In the bunk lay crumpled newspapers; no blanket, sheet, or pillow, and he mustered the energy to ask:

Do sailors sleep under newspapers like winos and bums?

Hurry out of those overshoes and your canvas overcoat and lay it over yourself.

The man was down on his knees struggling in front of the coal stove, poking in the fire-box, but he noticed immediately that Hermann was finding it hard to take off his coat. His arms got tangled in the sleeves, and finally he gave up and fell groaning on one side on top of the coat. He drew his heavy legs up into the bunk since it was too short for him. At once everything was in motion and things were moving about inside his dark crying brain where thoughts burst out in a colored pile:

if you open the flesh with a knife blade you see momentarily white tendon tissue and nerves that bind the body together but its fluid is brimful and flows over the arm in a struggle a thick stream onto the bedraggled floor mat the flat floor sloping a fearsome cord of blood searching out the doorway you hold your hands away from you the blood searches a central pipeline while you lie and no aid comes you there prone on the floor watching how blood oozes from the wound you see that the flesh is just scratched but they do not know it standing scared on the stairs because they woke up and heard the cry reverberate in the basement they are still on the cool steps listening hearing neither sound nor sigh she says:

you go first

he steps hesitantly down some steps

The limp body asleep lashed in the overcoat. When the eyes woke they opened wide. He realized without moving he lay crushed between clothes and the head of bed and had a poor memory of how he got down here. Light from a bulb shone from the ceiling. Behind him, conversation carried from the table, emerging from a cloud of cigarette and coal smoke:

. . . political guru?

It is self-evident that if absolute constraints prevail in the Soviet Union, no one is free to develop private enterprise so that he can eke out the little he has and cultivate it and move his family to a sunny country.

The man drew up his leaden legs. The sound of clogs kicking table legs that were bolted to the floor. As he listened to the men's discussion he closed his eyes and drew a newspaper over his face. He was breathing heavy under it and the conversation through it was muffled. Then he moved his head on the bed and the paper fell off his mouth and nose.

Do you think people in the Soviet Union are sacred and just and there's no crime?

Not sacred. It's just a new people there—a brand-spanking-new race. A chosen race sprouted from Leninist-Marxism.

Race?

Yes—what's the name of the famous ugly French philosopher with chameleon eyes and a pipe?

. . . why is it not possible to remember . . .

He hears the interlocutor get impatient, a man who does not tolerate forgetfulness. He snaps his fingers and Hermann gets interested in the topic of conversation though he has heard something similar a thousand times.

Silence continues.

Listen! shouts the interlocutor.

The man pushes Hermann's leg firmly, but he does not move. Then he moves up and breathes out in his face. Hermann feels the stench from his mouth and nose, but does not answer.

Do you remember what the famous frenchie with chameleon eyes is called?

No response.

Do not pretend. You are not asleep. Your eyelids are trembling. I can see you are awake and listening.

The man moved back to the table and said to his companion:

It does not matter what his name is, but what he said: In the Soviet Union, a marvel has happened, a new race has come into being, and it can grow potatoes in the snow. A new type of man has come into human history there in the plain and in the potato gardens of Moscow where Napoleon lost and was driven home.

and that's where a dead man is best preserved on the ground in the snow his blood perfect

The eyes woke up completely. The lips smacked. His ears awoke and listened because the curiosity in Hermann had woken, too, as he listened to the men at the table.

As if that helps, protested the other. No one can eat frozen potatoes.

People are taught to raise themselves up.

Who doesn't raise themselves? Don't be absurd.

People do, I know, but not the right way; as the Soviets do.

What's right? What's wrong? Everyone has an example that works for himself.

We are all our own judges. But the Soviets have this spanking-new method of fishing. You bring out to the ocean several thousand suction disks with pumping equipment, head to where the fish are, and pump them directly onto a conveyor, which runs the fish right to the automatic floating factories in the area, staffed by just one woman in a white gown—totally automatic—and the fish get processed into cans or packages straight to the consumer, straight into the pan. Now the idea bulb lights up! The suction disks are at different depths so you get all the fish and you take one bank at a time, empty it, go to the next, and re-cultivate it in the meantime. A fishing system. That's how the Russians do it. Here, we can warm the sea, perhaps all the nation's spas, with water pipes from the hot springs. We could place enormous pressure equipment systems around the country and trigger a new icelandic Gulf

Stream, just for us. It's only water from the tropics and are the tropics out there in the wider world somehow better than our geothermal regions? Listen to this famous French guy. What's his name? You! Then it would become fun to live in iceland; people would stop living a hundred kilometers away from each other, like now, but with less poverty and ignorance. Back then, if someone needed to look you in the eye, he might as well stare up at the clouds in search of an angel.

Hermann rose on his bunk and regarded the men at the table, their suspicious faces and arms stretched from the upper part of their body and cracked index fingers hooked into the ears of the coffee jars and indifferent about the future of socialism in iceland.

Here, you look like some pasty sea lion. Don't dawdle there, not with your crown pointing toward the stove! Point your toes at her, the brain can dry out, but it's healthy to warm your toes. Who is that famous Frenchman with chameleon eyes?

You are mad, the man said. This is all nonsense.

Really, the thing the brightest men in all the world proclaim, mad: Þórbergur, Kiljan, Elizabeth Taylor, this french guy, and Ben Hur and jesus too, if he were alive. Did you see *Ben Hur*?

The older man got off his bunk and drank from the pot with it raised over him like a dead flounder. Then he put his pitcher away and shuffled with open hands to the table and eased himself over to the stairs. He looked stubbornly at Hermann, with his pale face, ruffled hair, and his raggy clothes crumpled from sleep, before disappearing on deck.

You look awful. Hurry up out of bed and get yourself some coffee and salt.

As Hermann dragged himself out of the bunk he noticed a stink emanating from the neck of his shirt; he hauled himself over the bench, feeling like he had not shit in two weeks, everything stuck firm in his guts.

The man gave him coffee in a thick mug. Outside was a pitcher filled with a lubricant and he offered it to him.

Having brought him the pitcher, the man went to the stairs and called up to the opening:

Listen up, troll!

No answer. Then he rushed over to the fire pump, shook it, struggled and rummaged in the cubby by the stairs, moving the life preserver, dirty socks, and rubber lifeboat from the floor. Finally, he found what he was looking for.

Sunday—lemon drops, he said, and emptied the glass into the coffee. Monday—almond drops.

He grabbed the pitcher, held it to his mouth and nose, but did not want to drink the coffee.

Damn cardamom drops every day of the week.

I do not want this piss.

Piss? he asked, surprised. Swig it! Drinking it is like being equipped with an automatic oil-heating device. You get to a certain level, and if you plan to go past that, the device turns your stomach off by closing the opening. Should you try to force down a single drop more, the safety valve automatically opens and you vomit a mashy pulp. If you are on some different drink, the heat supply enters from the top without the valve loosening. See? That's the way alcohol renders men senseless. Everything boils and bubbles; nothing ever gives.

Where are we going? he asked, half-interested. Are we headed to sea?

Hold your nose and take a sip.

He did not delay, but grasped his face with his paw and gulped the drink down. His face fell onto the tabletop.

Feel better? he asked, and laughed vilely.

A bit, he said, trembling.

Yes, where are we going? he asked, and laughed scornfully. Toward the porbeagles.

Did I sleep for long?

Half a day and a whole night. Since yesterday.

Anxiety seized his features and he grimaced with disgust over the drink. Like a fog the harbor ran past and he pressed his fingers to his eyes as he swallowed saliva poisoned with lemon drops.

What are the porbeagles for? he asked.

For profit, came the reply, and he slung himself shakily onto the bench face-first, so hard that his sense organs could taste the cardamom as he thought:

neither Sunday nor Monday, but all the other days.

The man looked at his swollen eyes and said, without pausing:

so everyone can profit, but you intellectuals do not understand, your soul governs you, but a single porbeagle lasts longer than twenty exams, those things you misers collect. Industrial freezing plants cannot sell examinations to Italy; they sell black creatures with rough skin from the sea. The porbeagle basks on its back and lets the waves tickle its belly like a lover. We are prepared to look amid strong currents to find her, though we've found none. When we get her fast, our hooks deep inside her, the freezing plant will buy her and trim her and sell her to Italy and the Italians go crazy for porbeagles; they eat it like tuna. Want a longer lecture?

He shook his head. The man appeared on the stairs and said:

I have lost faith in this venture. We are fishing neither one thing nor another. Those boys you picked up some devilish place have jumped ship; this one does nothing but sleep and vomit. It was enough before, the two of us, and then you wanted to expand, and where is everything? I am leaving. You can keep the ship.

He crawled into the bunk and turned his back.

Why did you head out and let yourself be fooled?

If we hang about down in the ship, we can't catch anything, the man said.

They climbed the stairs and he squeezed out from the bunk and followed them. Hermann went back down. The sunlight had cut into his eyes. The cabin door opened and sun glared on the table.

Come back up when you have recovered.

Hermann heard him mutter:

The sun never shines on the fishhook. There is no hope for the fisheries.

The muttered words reverberated in his dull ears. The eyes looked over the table and discovered three hard pastries in an envelope. He fumbled in it, took his fingers back out, reached over to the stove, lifted the lid from the pan, and wolfed down the remains of roasted meat inside. The pan was on the stove and the meat was warm, dry, and fried; he washed it down with coffee. His stomach grated at the unexpected arrival of guests and threw him in the direction of the door. He vomited coffee and meat over the hotplate. He gagged, paled, and clutched at a brass rod on the machine. He screamed, sweat-covered, and when nothing more came up he pushed the mix together with his toes, crumpled some newspaper around it and put it in the firebox. A concentrated lemon odor erupted from it. The other man came down and said:

What's up, citronman? Did you vomit?

He looked at him there, saliva drooling from his mouth, and shook his head in disgust.

No porbeagles to be had and steam rising off that man. He is howling something about an experiment and railing and demanding damages and saying: the banks must pay the fishing company damages, not me. Let him rail against the birds.

What is this ship called?

Katrín, he said, and stood at the edge of the table. Katrín Jónsdóttir.

He did not stand there for long; he went over, opened the siding, and drew a glass from under the lifeboat.

You're a sight for sore eyes. Nothing is better than to vomit and to shit and to get rid of the pulp inside your body.

The other man came down and asked:

Are you just going to loiter about in here? What is your name?

Tómas, he said. How about you?

Yes. Tómas. I think so. Tómas Jónsson, national bestseller.

My name is Tómas, he said, pointing to his chest.

They were all silent and stared at each other and thought about it:

Three Tómases on board the national ship.

Then one asked:

Can you feel the climate changing? A fog is approaching. Breezes are an omen of fog.

Yes, said Tómas, sluggish. Sea fog is common in Portugal.

They arose simultaneously and surged to the stairs. Out on deck, they laughed. A white haze lay over the ocean; its waves had turned green from their usual blue. They sat morosely on the hold hatch, and Tómas said:

I'll go down and fetch something to cheer us up.

He came up again, pointing out to sea into the fog as he sat down.

There goes the Gullfoss, he said.

Yes, there goes our flagship, the others replied.

The black bow of the ship towered up out of the fog with the sun shining behind it and the wind swirling in transparent wisps. The fog flew forward like a thin, tattered curtain, covering parts of the ship so that it no longer looked like an ordinary ship, jumping out of the water in dolphin leaps, striking under the wave peaks and kicking up spouts and sea-spray. It did not sail in a straight line but instead in an eel-like curve, forming a circle around the Katrín. The ship sailed, turning about itself, and Tómas said:

It seems that we are looking at the icelandic national vessel, going in circles around everything and nothing.

He went into the wheelhouse and pointed a telescope at the ship. He looked long in the telescope.

I don't see a soul on board, he called through the window.

Darkness fell over the ship and the eyes of the men on deck became watery with the spray. The sun shone again and wind scattered the darkness and fog. The Gullfoss sailed constantly around them in a wide or tight circle, but the Tómases were neither afraid nor surprised there by the railing.

Is this flagship only in our eyes? asked Tómas, asking for the telescope so he had something to rely on other than his naked eyes. He pointed the telescope to the ship and said:

It is drunk. A ship won't behave that way unless it's drunk.

He was relieved, glad that his eyes were sober, that they weren't marbles in his head full of blood and wine. He slipped, fell on the deck, and lay senseless for a moment; when he woke up, he was sober. He checked the engine, set it full speed out of the vicious circle to avoid the collision. The Gullfoss was raging, blowing its foghorn, its propeller at an evil speed. Tómas said:

We need to head down and fetch the lifeboat. This ship is berserk.

Together they dragged the inflatable lifeboat on deck, filled it with air; in the same breath, the side of the black ship loomed beside them. They read: GULLFOSS.

This is the flagship, no mistaking it, the font is plenty large, said Tómas.

The ship sailed uncontrollably in large curves, but when it went in a reverse circle Tómas saw that the passengers had arranged themselves along the railing and were staring down into the sea, resistant to cries and calls, only their tongues moving, lolling from their open mouths. Fog covered the surface of the ocean and soon they could see neither the ship nor its errant circle. They no longer knew where they came from or where they were going, but they could feel the ocean under their feet. Tómas came numbly down from the wheelhouse and said:

The best thing we can do is drink and wait for day to come.

Suddenly the fog and first light enveloped the ship. The Gullfoss seemed to be there and sped toward them on its next curve. The passengers were still at the railing, heads drooping with hanging tongues flapping like skin newly slipped off fish. They wondered if they were vomiting or if they were airing their tongues after drinking.

Perhaps they are lookouts for porbeagles, said Tómas.

No, he replied. The bar is open and they are having a session. After a ship leaves port, the passengers no longer know this world or any other; chance decides whether it will dock somewhere. It rushes about the ocean and they're used in Scotland to seeing ships lapwing out on the firth, and if it cannot find the right way, then it cannot find it. But as soon as it appears as a shadow, tugs are sent out to drag it confused to the harbor.

They settled into the lifeboat and could not agree as to whether they had seen the ship or not.

I never saw anything, said Tómas.

Nor I, said Tómas.

Then nor did I, said Tómas.

What's this then?

A jaunt?

Night came and they felt for each other.

We are three, he said.

They found six arms, but just five feet. They searched for the sixth in the dark, but could not find it.

We are three, we all have two feet, there should be six feet, they said, and bent down to check whether they could feel their feet.

It is gloomy here, they said, and we have no maritime navigation devices.

In the cabin, the stench of lemon drops. The counting began. They arranged themselves on the bench and ordered themselves to let their feet dangle down. Tómas stood up and said:

I will count.

He tallied carefully on his fingers, but the result was always the same.

Five, he said.

He had a good mind to give Tómas a slap in the face with a dirty table cloth. He rushed up and attacked him, but it came to light that Tómas had been all the while sitting on one foot and hiding it. Tómas cursed:

How stupid.

What does this mean? he asked.

Blows rained down on him; he noticed a fire extinguisher on the wall, took it, and pointed its trumpet at the limp shapes of people swaying there and making unintelligible sounds. Carbonate sprayed out. The pictures fell and he threw himself over the others like a sprinkle of coal from a pail. The pictures flocked against him. Men and pictures rolling on the floor, finding faces, holding each other fast, kicking their feet.

Eventually he gave up the vision, his head lolling helplessly to one side. He cried and felt a face coming toward him and sticking a slender tongue between his lips.

Stop! he cried. Stop!

He lay on his belly and repeated:

Stop, boy, stop.

The interior was dark and the outside dark and foggy. The old man saw Hermann rolling on the floor covered in ashes and tears.

Tómas, Hermann said, you are my concept.

Tómas Jónsson looked suspiciously at Hermann lying euphoric on the floor and said:

You cannot trick me.

Hermann stood up and flopped over to the bench. He took the old man's shoulders and said:

Say nothing more until you have died and I have finished the work. Then you may go back to this book: Tómas Jónsson, Bestseller.

Sometime during the night, the three drunk and doubting Tómases came on deck and crawled into the lifeboat. The ship adrift on a sea of fog and darkness.

If the ship sinks, he said, and if we are drifting to shore, I know Faroese Óli will come down to the skerry to welcome us.

Do not worry, we will drift to land before shellfish weigh down the boat and sink it.

In an inflatable lifeboat, we're safe.

He managed to think:

i call the northern lights night rainbows

Guðbergur Bergsson (b. 1932) is the author of twenty-one books, including novels, poetry collections, and works of childrens' literature. He is also a translator from the Spanish and is responsible for bringing Gabriel García Marquez into Icelandic. He won the Icelandic Literary Prize twice and, in 2004, received the Sweish Academy Nordic Prize, commonly known as the "Little Nobel." His novel *The Swan* is also available in English translation.

Lytton Smith is a poet, professor, and translator from the Icelandic. His most recent translations include works by Kristin Ómarsdóttir, Jón Gnarr, and Bragi Ólafsson, and his most recent poetry collection is *The All-Purpose Magical Tent*. A graduate of Columbia, he currently teaches at SUNY Geneseo.

**OPEN
LETTER**

**OPEN
LETTER**

WWW.OPENLETTERBOOKS.ORG